Congleholme
A WARTIME ROMANCE

James R Warren

BLOXWICH
2025

Published in the United Kingdom in 2025 by Midland Tutorial Productions

First Edition 1 April 2025

File Prefix Code: CONG

ISBN 978 1 915750 11 2

Email: MTP1586@gmail.com

CONGLEHOLME
A WARTIME ROMANCE

James R Warren

MIDLAND TUTORIAL PRODUCTIONS
BLOXWICH

Other Books By James R Warren

Boscawen-Ûn
Beyond Tourist Britain
Gleanings as I Pass
Exordium
Meditations
Gamma Solution
Moddeshall Hydropower
Unreasonable Mathematics
Mathematical Explorations
Researches: Volume One
Researches: Volume Two
Researches: Volume Three
Researches: Volume Four
Pi and Phi
Four Famous Numbers
Progress in Iron Smelting

AUTHORIAL STATEMENT

"Congleholme: A Wartime Romance" is a religious, anti-war novel.

It is however a departure from usual MTP offerings.

This book explores man and woman, predicament and destiny, service and humility, under extreme stress.

It includes love, compassion and gentle humour.

It also presents:-
HORROR
EXPLICIT SEX
DISCRIMINATORY LANGUAGE
OBSCENE DIALOGUE
throughout

PLEASE DO NOT GIFT THIS BOOK TO A CHILD OR TO ANYONE WHO MAY BE DISTURBED OR OFFENDED BY THE TEXT

Controversial religious, political and scientific concepts are discussed frankly.

All scenes are fictional.

Names were created intentionally to be unusual but credible. The identity or similarity of names to living persons is fortuitous.

Thank you for your purchase.
Enjoy your read and whatever your beliefs
take your time to think or to pray.
May God Bless You.

JR Warren

With Great Love for and Respect to My Wife

Myung-Ja

TABLE OF CONTENTS

PROLOGUE

It reminded me of the evening of Wednesday 18th September 2024 and my first attempt to generate an image from text. I entered the prompt "A muddy Roman road with elms and oaks on its left and a hedge on its right."

I suppose I had in mind terrain similar to the Peckforton Hills or some other elevated position before Chester.

The results were strange.

Winsome, yes, but not really what I had in mind.

The muddy straight lane vanished into the distance sure enough, but the scene included only sparse verging poplars and pollarded willows, and a hedge, if any, was on the left.

I amended "a moonlit muddy..."

Now I had an enormous full moon presiding over a bleak vignette of the poplars and withies.

I added "a man and woman walking." The first-generation image showed realistic silhouettes with their backs to the viewer; the second etiolated wraiths of the kind favored by architects.

Then I added "A dilapidated public house is beside the road."

Strange pantiled and stuccoed apparitions entered shyly hiding behind walls.

How odd, I thought. Was the generative system programmed by Italians?

The scene was now very suggestive of the ancient sites I had walked as a young man, an amateur Romanist, in Suburban Lazio, maybe Veii, maybe Palestrina.

I added "An old gibbet stands on the left beside the road." Now the mechanics of the system had real issues. A giant silver picture frame stood hard by on the right, much out of the image. Or else a broken down wooden structure not unlike the support of a windlass or a fire precautions broom-stand appeared to left.

Every educated Englishman of my generation and older knows what a gibbet is. I sometimes passed them in my boyhood. Most had been untouched since they were erected two hundred or three hundred years before. It was illegal to tamper with them in any way, even for road-widening. They were in various states of decay. Often they were no more than marked by a steel post stuck in the ground, or a stone, or an inscribed plinth: Essentially twentieth-century triangulation bases set down at a lonely place in recognition of if not salute to the unshriven dead.

I powered down the machine.

At maybe three o'clock the next morning the resolution hit me.

I had specified a *Roman* road and the machinery took it literally.

As myself a computer programmer of fifty years' experience I should have known better.

I had been using a first-class Generative AI tool suite mediated by my superb hardware system. After all the artificial intelligence PR hype, a young man would have been bitterly disappointed and probably broadcast an angry Tweet without further ado. I am an old man. Old men are never disappointed. Old men never twitter, except in the final extremity of decrepitude. Old men resign.

You see it is like this. All machines are not men: No man is a machine. But men and machines have this in common: They are all the same, and differ so very much.

An algorithm is a narrative but it is not a story. A story is a narrative. Algorithms and their compositions are instantly recognisable. As recognisable as student reports pieced together from Internet pages. You will recognise my narrative as the work of a human. All Jim Warren's books are the same at least in tone: This book is so very different.

You see, if you want to be a writer you will weep lakes of tears. Most of your readers will think you are mad, bad or worse: In it for the cash. There are many fallow years, many months of bleak obscurity.

Robots cannot cry.

It takes a human to tell a story.

CHAPTER ONE
BARDO

The rain started again. I was grateful for my full breathable waterproof suit and my motorcycle helmet as I had been on many occasions of my youth. Beneath the thorny bush the cobwebs sparkled in the fleeting moonlight as the saturated foliage afforded scant shelter.

Some creature, possibly a mouse or weasel panicked in the undergrowth.

A half-torpid French Widow, black and bulbous in perpetual mourning, carefully tried her gossamer cables in the hedge above me.

Cities were nearby. Their orange glows suffused the Northern sky and the white noise harl of wet motorways carried through the steeping air, even at this unholy hour. But here on the hills, above it all, the muddy, die-straight road, the Portway, lay silent and unlit as it had for two millennia.

I edged out of the rain, cooling despite my waterproofs, and tried to resume my fitful slumber.

I heard chains rattle.

My blood ran cold.

Surely, no farmer was using the lane at this hour? Surely he was not using horses to drag a harrow along an already damaged road, a Scheduled ancient monument? Why could I not hear a tractor. Why had no lights shone through the hedge? Ah, the binding chain of a field gate was rattling loosely in the wind, that would be it!

Why the primordial chill of chains? Was it some atavistic intimation of renewed captivity, as bounty-hunters detected one's lair. After all, the Saxons would not build within four furlongs of a Roman road for fear of ghosts patrolling, or perhaps a natural fear of more temporal evildoers?

Chains do not exist in the natural world. They are the primordial artifact of the Civilisation that superseded the Ages of Stone. Every link follows its identical precursor. Every link is the same, but the chain is so very different. I am a Black Country man. Black Country men know about chains. If you are old enough you may have watched as a chain was wrought. The chains the *Titanic* took with her were made in the Black Country, as were her anchors on this most inland of inland coalfields. The chains and anchors were tested for strength before they left Netherton. Neither could save the ship they graced.

You may have forged links yourself. Not of course for the great ships: You are too young. But maybe links in the chain of the Story of England, even if you are not English. There are large links forged by men in long chains to bind ships, and short chains forged with small links by women to bind slaves. The spirit of the chain is constraint and limitation, strong only in tension. The Chain is itself the slave of bondage, the secret indenture that binds Mankind and Satan.

All this talk of chains. Its reminds me of the ancient fable of the good philosopher Athenodorus, teacher of Octavian. He rented a house where he could live cheaply and work undisturbed. Athenodorus wrestled in the toils of Stoic doctrine that bind tighter than any chain could.

On the first night he sat at his desk working and writing long into the small hours. His servants had placed before him his bread on a silver platter and a dish of oil and thyme to lubricate his morsels and lend his bread a piquancy. They gave him a fresh fig in a basket and most important of all, a golden goblet of wine circled with a frieze of purple amethysts lest the wine should inebriate and spoil his labours. And of course his desk was graced with a tall bronze oil lamp to light the sunless hours.

The good master sat and worked and worried. The bread was untouched. The fig was unmolested. And of course the wine was foresworn. In the small hours a shining wraith of an splendid old man with a long wise beard in a shimmering shroud appeared to Athenodorus. The ghost was bound with chains and rattled them at Athenodorus. The ghost beckoned.

"Go away", said the Stoic, "I am busy."

The spectre faded.

On the second night Athenodorus continued at his desk. A mouse appeared and ate the innards of the loaf to satisfy her hunger, and make a nest for her pinkies. The kindly philosopher did not evict her. A wasp alighted on the fig and drank some juice. The kindly philosopher did not swat it. The wine remained undrunk.

The ghost returned. The ghost glowed and rattled his chains. The ghost beckoned Athenodorus.

"Depart, vain fancy", shouted Athenodorus, "I am a man of reason. Go and dismay some young boy or old woman."

The ghost faded.

The Stoic worked on. He was now two days unfed and unwatered. His servants worried. His wife worried. His daughters worried. But none dare interrupt.

Athenodorus lit his lamp for a third night of labour.

The mouse slept. The wasp slept. None of Creation touched the golden goblet or its pregnant content.

Midnight came and so did the old man. The ghost glowed with a stronger white light that made the lamp redundant. He rattled his chains and approached Athenodorus importunately close. The ghost addressed Athenodorus and said:-

"Come with me"

Athenodorus rose stiffly and followed the ghost to the centre of the courtyard where the spectre promptly vanished.

Athenodorus woke his servants and ordered them to lift the stones and dig the spot by torchlight as he watched.

The workers uncovered a skeleton bound with chains. Athenodorus stepped forward and struck the chains off the old bones. Athenodorus ordered the servants reverently to lift the remains and he and they conveyed them to the sacred place appointed the dead, and reinterred the skeleton with holy rites.

The ghost never returned to Athenodorus or his house.

An autumn beech leaf spiralled groundward in the breeze and hitting my visor startled me.

Was I the victim of some hypnagogic fallacy?

"Hang there, you dog-fucking old caitiff!" half-screamed, half coughed a course old female voice.

Was it addressing me? If so, why?

"Sod off, you evil old witch" responded Simon Peter the Stockwright, an equally rasping, equally inarticulate male, croaking barely audibly above the breeze and the susurration of the desiccating leaves, as if, despite the rain, communing in the final stages of thirst.

And chains rattled again.

"I hate this. It is so cold and spooky. Let's stride on, Mistress Maisie. We can make Congleholme ere the dawn", whined a third voice, with spirit. It seemed to be a boy, maybe twelve or thirteen.

"Shut up, you little fucker", counselled the course woman.

I was by now terrified.

Gingerly I removed my helmet, and slowly peered through the hedge.

The rain had stopped again, and been succeeded by a freezing Autumnal breeze. As the sky cleared, the moonlight discovered a gibbet cage swinging suspended beneath an oaken bough on the opposite verge.

Inside the horrific contraption a man stood, or you might say slouched, against the iron bars, fully clothed and saturated, freezing as he dried.

Below and before him, the crone and the boy stood with their backs to me. I ducked into better cover of the hedge, and knelt alert in silence.

Presently, the lad sloshed into the cattle-carved slough at the open field gate and furtively scanned around. I surmised that he was too shy to piss in the presence of the harridan and conned the privacy of the hedge. He may have glimpsed me, and quickly retired unrelieved.

"Mistress, there is a man behind the hedge", I heard him state when he returned to the road.

This intelligence was rewarded with a brutal clip round the ear.

"I felt that", I silently reflected.

"You rat-faced little liar!", informed the crone, "You are too old to see things that aren't there. What do you mean 'spooky'? What are we, Dutchmen!?"

There was a benighted ignorance in her voice, unapprehended and unregarded, for sure, but informed with a callous contempt beyond mere crudity: Perhaps the latent hate of a repressed jealousy beyond my knowledge?

At any event it was something diabolical, not human, a contempt beyond disgust or of outrage or of anger or of distain or of any human emotion, a contempt for Creation itself.

But I noted with a gratified astonishment that throughout this obscene altercation there was no breach of the third of the Ten Commandments: "Thou shalt not take the name of the LORD thy God in vain; for the LORD will not hold him guiltless that taketh his name in vain." Not even the "witch" had blasphemed. Could I claim as much? Could you? Whatever of God's Commandments the three had broken (if any) it was not that.

I tried to place the costume of these protagonists in the chronology of demotic fashion. It seemed to me that their dress was circa 1650 but before the age of mass-production peasant garb changed slowly and they could have been of almost any era until about 1800. The "witch" was gowned to the shoes, but displayed the upper surfaces of both ample breasts, as I noted when she suddenly turned and I ducked.

The last Englishman reliably attested to have been gibbeted alive or "hung in chains" died in 1683. How come I was witnessing this process in 2036?

An old pedant like me reminds you that a man killed through suspension by the neck is "hanged." A "hung" man is something quite different, unless he is "hung in chains"!

A petty traitor is a woman who murders her husband or father, or else counterfeits the king's coin. The English penalty for petty traitors was burning but by the seventeenth century such women were invariably strangled to death before ignition.

The last Englishwoman intentionally burnt alive was Elizabeth Gaunt in 1685 on a charge of high treason in the aftermath of The Rye House Plot.

There were, however, as with other methods several horrific mistakes born of cowardice or incompetence on the part of executioners.

The last woman burnt alive in England was Catherine Hayes at Tyburn in 1726 for killing her husband. The executioner had rigged a hempen strangulation loop about her neck to be tensioned after he had lit the faggots. He intended to hold the free end at a safe distance and kill her remotely before the flames touched her. The faggots flared suddenly and burnt through the rope, which may have been cheaply-purchased tarred ships' rigging.

The Murder Act 1752 explicitly forbade *live* gibbeting or *live* burning in line with the new Enlightenment concepts of more humane governance, but on the other hand it *mandated* either scientific dissection or alternatively gibbeting for the corpses of murderers, or petty traitors otherwise than burnt. Women not burnt were invariably sold to medical schools. Moreover, The Murder Act formalised and standardised judicial procedure across England and Wales, specifying *inter alia* that those who murdered must be killed and those that were killed for whatever reason must "hang by the neck until dead."

Illegal burnings of women, who were usually strangled before ignition, continued for at least five years. Local magistrates often behaved at whim, regardless of the King's Writ.

After about 1600 witches were never burnt in England: They were hanged. The last English heretic, a male, was burnt in 1612. The executioner attempted to shoot his brains out before the faggots caught flame: Sadly he failed. Special provisions remained for petty traitors: Adulteresses, counterfeiters and murderesses of husbands were burnt until the Treason Act 1790 specified hanging.

The thing that put an end to the gibbet was the turnpike trust. The very last thing turnpike shareholders wanted were scenes of horror garnishing the routes of their gentle paying passengers. The Turnpike Act 1706 permitted capitalists to combine to lay smooth and well-maintained roads, the first trust paving the old Roman Watling Street between London and Chester, a road that passed within sight of several gibbets. And with better and swifter carriage came swifter notice of the will of the King in Parliament and less latitude for the cruelty of the petty provincial potentate.

I could not imagine that this present execution was the work of Magonians. Like any occupying forces they were capable of casual atrocity if provoked but on the whole they were good masters, humane and tolerant of English ways and failings. I am as patriotic as the next Englishman, but by and large I was grateful for good order and good governance after a hundred years of corruption and ineptitude under our own leaders.

Was this an illegal execution? After all informal lynchings of various kinds long post-dated the official abolitions of the respective methods. Where these spectres of some kind, revenants re-performing to perpetuity the evils of their lives?

I did not know what to think.

Presently the old woman said softly but in my hearing, as if speaking to the boy, "Look Thomas, the poor man shivers. It is a sair cold night as you justly observed. Gather some sticks and light a fire beneath him."

"No!" shouted the lad emphatically.

I recollected that it was in olden days itself a capital offence to interfere with a gibbeted man in any way, either to protract or to curtail his torments.

An impious thought clouded my thinking, as ineluctable as a flake of iron drawn to a magnet by some invisible imperative. I thought of the Mockery of another hanging Man pinned by iron many years ago, and of his friend Simon Peter inverted on a cross in the Vatican Circus a few years later. For it seems to me there are two species of Evil: Inversion and Perversion. For example, mockery partakes of both contempt and cowardice, aimed at the integrity of Creation, and is a purely Satanic quality that seeks to invert the good carefully avoiding any benefit to mortals, as Nero inverted the fisherman literally. On the other hand, a crime of perversion like murder or theft distorts love of the self or love of something else to issue damage: Patriots beware.

These are old but still incondite ideas and you can improve them. But you will need to believe that Evil exists, or is capable of existing, outwith the human mind.

I do not know what next happened.

When I was next sentient I stood at a crossroads, about a mile further on, where Pilgrims' Lane intersects the Portway at right angles as the lane passes along the bluff.

I paused to admire the darkling vista of the blue and pink and yellow stars of city lights, glimmering in the rising heat, as the old colony nestled in serene but busy slumber within the great embrace of its mighty incised meander.

One of the many foreign innovations of the Magonian Federation was 24-hour working, not invariably a contribution to productivity. The wide River Brider shone a pale barely differential navy blue under a starry cyan sky, twinkling as in sympathy with its ancient counterpoint.

Congleholme was an affluent and compact city of around one hundred and twenty thousand souls, formerly a great center of the lead and silver industries but its cupolas, shot towers and assay office had long given ground to shops, hotels, commuter villas and Victorian canal and railway suburbs. It has a new university and an old abbey, but today the tourist industry is dominant, if we discount public administration. It had taken a "pasting" in blitzes of the Second World War but it was untouched by the current hostilities. As you may imagine, the wide and shining curving waterway was an absolute gift to the enemy fliers of World War Two. I cannot remember what the Romans called their foundation, this that they made a seaport, but the modern Saxo-Norse appellation paid homage to the great crook of the river and the erstwhile "island" at its core.

The city's limit was a good thirteen miles from my vantage, and I thought my entry to the city impossible before the dawn.

I had fleetingly visited Congleholme on three previous occasions: First with friends from my undergraduate hostel at Manchester; secondly whilst researching a novel, set during a reconnaissance by the Roman Navy; and thirdly I drove through after my Wife and I had a brief holiday in North Wales.

I heard a bus labouring up the scarp to my right. It was a kind of archaic sound, redolent of the weak petrol coaches of my toddlerhood, spluttering and grinding up some hidden acclivity. The gears ground as the box changed down and whined. No synchromesh, of course. Presently, it rounded a fold in the hill and emerged into sight.

The interior glowed yellow in the feeble light of twelve-volt Swan lamps. It was a red or maybe maroon old Albion single-deck bus of circa 1935 vintage. There seemed to be no passengers aboard. Well, it was three o'clock in the morning in rural Cheshire! But what was infinitely more remarkable was that there was no driver either.

I stood stupidly in the intersection. The bus turned onto the level of Pilgrim's Lane and accelerated towards me. The last I saw was the blue and white Scottish sunburst of the Albion marque plate hurtling toward my face. I made no attempt to evade it. It later occurred to me that I must have been a suicide, conveniently appointing myself the crossroads.

I next found myself at the Eastern gate of Congleholme. I was trying to doss down on the tourist bench in the reconstructed barbican. Suddenly I was aware of the presence of a Roman soldier in full marching kit, smoking a cigarette, and watching the cars driving up and down the decumanus below. I was trying not to notice his extremely short skirt and bare legs on this freezing October night.

"Good morning, mate", I said trying to be cheery but not familiar. I was curious: Curious to know whether he was a tourist guide, or an actor in tourist tableaus, maybe a re-enactor. God forbid that he was another bloody ghost I thought profanely. If any but the latter why was he abroad at this hour? This was after all, so they say, the most haunted perch of land in this most haunted city of God's Earth.

Briefly, and for the first time in my inane mind, the thought brushed across my conscience.

Was I in Hell?

My thoughts drifted back to the days of the Seventies when I lived in a Glasgow hostel and read the Sayer's translation of *The Divine Comedy* in English. Specifically, the verses set above the Ditch of the Thieves, where Virgil and Dante view the Seventh Circle of Perdition, where all personal identity is lost as men transform to serpents, to ash, and back again. For to be damned is to aspire, to strive, and to be brought to naught again like a spider attempting to escape an empty bath.

"Excuse me mate, I hope you don't mind me asking", I started tentatively, "but don't you feel cold in that gear? I am bloody freezing even with all this hiking clobber on."

The "soldier" chuckled, I thought a little self-consciously. "I don't mind, mister. This might sound daft but I am very proud of this get-up, and of the opportunity to wear it. In fact, I insist upon several changes so that I can wear the ancient uniform all the time."

Well this I thought eccentric. The faux Roman, if that was what he was, seemed a little hesitant further to confide. He took another long drag as he leaned across the parapet, contemplating the busy decumanus, called in this district, rather pleonastically, Hodgate Street. Ahead of him, picked out with sodium lamps, were the remaining standing and decumbent columns of the monument known as the Grave of Graccus, ostensible site of the resting place of the legendary Roman sailor who founded this city during the time of Caligula and now little more than a glorified traffic island.

"This is how it is, mate", continued my interlocutor.

"Sorry to interrupt", I said. "But we must stop calling each other 'mate'", I objected rather snobbishly, masking vice as the false virtue of bonhomie.

"I am 'Chuck': What is your name?"

"Ennias Mickawber, but my friends call me 'Mick'."

Understandable, I thought, in my captious schoolboy manner.

"Mick, I know this is a cheek. I am pleased to have met you, but I am afraid you might take this amiss."

The man visibly steeled himself for what he thought might be a very unpleasant invitation.

"Are we in Hell?"

Mick burst into laughter, beyond the pretence of the Lupercalian, and into the sincere and spontaneous emotion of relief.

Mick pulled himself together.

"No, Chuck"

"This is how it is, mate", my new friend resumed.

"I had a had a bad patch in Loughborough, you know... with drugs. I lost my woman and I was thrown out of uni..."

"What were you reading?", I interrupted.

"I was doing a Masters in Generative AI as applied to graphic design in publishing."

This man is clearly no fool, I thought fatuously.

"Anyway I was arrested by the local Superintendent of Order."

He was referencing a small-time Magonian magistrate with limited summary powers over British citizens. Some of my countrymen referred to them, out of earshot of course, as gauleiters.

"Anyway, to cut a long story short he said he would send me for six months in the mines, or if I agreed he would arrange for my employment as a street actor for tourists for a minimum of three years all found with training and a thousand crowns pocket money a month, as long as I named my dealers and kept clean myself. I lept at it."

"I don't blame you Mick", I acknowledged. It was again my turn to show diffidence. Summoning all my courage I essayed:-

"Mick, I had a very strange experience early this morning."

"I was trying to kip under a hedge on the hill beside the Portway and I could swear that I saw a man gibbeted alive being taunted by an old witch. What do you make of it?"

"What was this old witch called?" queried Mick with a rather sceptical air.

"Mistress Maisie", I replied.

The man blanched.

After a moment Mick said:-

"The world plays strange tricks upon men who are tired and hungry." My Wife had explained hauntings in such terms many years earlier.

My mind instinctively considered how Simon Peter the Stockwright must have been feeling, and whether his sentiment somehow informed my perception, a sentiment transmitted through space and time, by means inscrutable. I wondered if the stockwright shared his Primate's certainty in The Redemption of Christ and whether that consoled him through his torment.

"Or you may have been having a schizophrenic attack"

"Nothing to be ashamed of or worried about", Mick quickly qualified.

"I had them often when I was younger, but they are now well-controlled."

"But with respect you are a bit old for those, at least if you have never had such before", Mick continued.

So little time so many questions.

I was no wiser than before, though I had shared ten minutes with a likely genius.

The apparent Roman and I exchanged further pleasantries, but I cannot at this remove remember what they were for even then I was eighty-four.

I descended the Wall, gingerly picking my way in the gloom, balancing with my stick and backpack, down the sandstone steps to the gaslit, cobbled street below. The mist was coming in from the river like a silver wraith: Not the car, like a white shroud. Even then gaslight was unusual in Congleholme, the town used LEDs or sodiums like everywhere else, but gas was thought locally to preserve an olde worlde allure for nocturnal tourists. Rainwater, or maybe dew, glistened a ghostly green on the stones and was starting to turn to ice. I walked carefully.

I found myself in a Victorian Conservation Area of red-brick terraced houses, prim and gentrified. On a corner, in Albion Street, gayly lit and vocal, stood the Albion Hotel.

Pressing the brass latch of an etched glass door I diffidently entered the dim and fuggy saloon. This room was lit by fishtail burners lambating fitfully behind white-etched glass diffusers. The feeble yellow glow I found unwelcoming, if only that it was difficult to distinguish the detail of the fitments and the customers. Contrastingly, there was a strong daylight white of an obsolete fluorescent strip visible through a doorway behind the bar. It was that I found comforting, phasmofugal.

On the left, beneath a mahogany-framed window leaned a uniformed and discretely armed Magonian, nursing a pint in his right hand. I am not an expert on military uniforms or any other sartorial refinements, and as I said the light was bad, but he seemed to have the cut and bearing of some sort of young officer. Most of the rest of the clientele were seated in threes around those fretwork cast iron tables they used to have in pubs: Not in 2036, more like in 1972 where I last encountered such delights at the long gone Whitworth Hotel in Manchester, a very rough establishment.

Slowly my eyes acclimatised and I noticed that at the Albion old men seemed to preponderate. But it was wartime and England was under foreign occupation.

The Albion was larger than a simple nineteenth-century tavern, but smaller than a modern hotel. It advertised a two-star rating, but of which validator I was unaware.

I was determined urgently to ask a very stupid question. I approached the bar. I asked a young woman serving there:-

"Can I have a room with a shower?"

I desperately needed the latter.

"Most certainly, Sir. That would be twelve-hundred crowns per night. Would you like a drink whilst the room is prepared?"

I fought shy of asking for a discount given it was four in the morning and the dawn was in barely two hours. Presumably I could spend a day asleep if I could book a further night.

I ordered a pint of local IPA. Taking my glass and turning I was impeded by the young Magonian.

"Good morning, Sir. Thank you for visiting Zone A6. May I see your identity please?" said the tall foreigner in a clipped but faultless diction.

"Yes, good morning officer", I replied, proffering my Registration Card.

The official scanned the card's QR code and offered the document back to me with an unsmiling but cordial formality.

"Welcome, Dr Charles Charmliss. Enjoy your stay"

"Thank you", I replied.

I appreciated the fact that Magonians of most of the nations in their extensive Federation venerated the old. Unlike in former days we enjoyed a certain solicitude beyond courtesy, not to say toleration.

I found a spare table near the wall on this, Eastern, side of the bar and sat down with my pint, which was actually 500 millilitres. Sorry to break your concentration. I tried to make sense of the day and to take stock. I basically did not know why I was here.

"Would you like a meal, Dr Charmliss?" the barmaid shouted above the hub-bub. "We only do chicken or burger and chips until the delivery."

"No thank you", I shouted back.

Curiously, I did not feel as tired as I was. Even more remarkably, though a diabetic myasthenial with a dislocated right shoulder I felt no pain, not even the natural pains and cramps of old walking legs. In fact I felt like a twenty-year old. I had had no insulin since, oh, I don't know: That place outside Stoke, Audley was it? I don't know. I was not thinking like a twenty-year-old.

Presently, the young officer finished his drink and, striking his cane ostentatiously on a radiator valence, strode off into the early morning mist.

"Right lads", said an overweight tough-looking individual rising from a table on the other side of the room. About four or six other men and a young woman rose from adjacent tables.

The party strode purposefully towards may table.

Another man, say 72, silly moustache and a cloth cap parked himself behind my right shoulder. I think he was standing against the wall. I did not check. A man around his early forties with a well-groomed blond KG5 beard and a polo-necked woolly abruptly commandeered the iron seat to my right, and turning it, sat down leaning on the back, at my table. He looked like a refugee from a

Sixties sea-shanty ensemble. Or maybe a profile from some Renoir oil of happy young diners beside the Seine. Two or three lads in their late twenties and a girl of twenty or twenty-two, perhaps older, stood looking at me across the table on my left. They seem purposively to have left the third chair vacant. All were white. None were uniformed, but all were dressed fashionably and were clean if a trifle shabby. But of course this was Britain in wartime.

There was the proverbial pregnant pause. The beard took out a mobile and placed it on the table before him for some reason. I later surmised it a voice recorder.

"Look, you can have my cash and I will buy you a round and a square meal apiece but that is the length of it, and if you threaten me I shall call the police", I said by way of introduction.

There was another tense pause. In my imagination, maybe, there was less noise and chatter and suddenly a lot of people seemed to be wishing the staff good-bye and leaving. Perhaps they were merely heading to work. Some of the younger toughs seemed to be offended by my offer and scowled down at me.

I noticed that the barmaid herself was taking an interest in my table from her position behind the pumps, and was leaning her wrist absent-mindedly, or perhaps very alertly, upon the finial of one.

"Are you a spy?" asked the beard almost uninterestedly speaking over the table without looking at me.

"Most certainly not"

The girl was dressed in dungarees, but she was unmistakably not a garage mechanic, though garage mechanics are often very intellectual, especially today. She asked quietly:-

"Why are you here?"

I sat back and gazed at her in open mouthed astonishment.

Then I said:-

"I do not know"

"I left Nuneaton four weeks ago. I wanted to walk. I wanted to clear my mind. I wanted inspiration for a new book. I wanted... I do not know what I wanted. When I was younger, when I was angry or perplexed I walked."

The young woman persisted:-

"Did you feel that you were on pilgrimage to somewhere?"

"Now that is also a very intelligent question", I said condescendingly, switching to my old lecturer mode, where I could command ground more confidently.

"Do you know that I do not know, and cannot surely tell you?"

"When I was 38 and had been denied a promotion I was so angry I just walked. I walked along the Shropshire Union canal from Featherstone to Brewood and Brewood to Wheaton Aston, a round trip of 22 miles that took me three hours."

"Are you angry now, Sir?"

"No, I am not"

"Are your family still alive, Dr Charmliss?"

She had obviously been paying attention.

"My wife is still alive. She is 101"

At that point someone behind the bar, or someone else staffing the hotel turned off the gaslamps without turning on the LED house lights, but it was dawning anyway, and there were big Victorian etched-glass windows facing South and East, and we could see well enough for these proceedings, such as they were.

The tough, overweight character with a limp who had said "right lads" now arrived with a very different neurasthenic type who took off his brass-rimmed glasses and wiped them. Both men grabbed chairs from other tables and settled on them at the table opposite me, leaving one seat spare which the girl squirmed into awkwardly. Presumably both men had adjourned to the gents to have a piss and discuss pre-fight strategy. The nerdy type who reminded me as it were of a seventy-year-old Alec Guinness in character as George Smiley continued to fiddle with his specs, taking them off, peering at the windows with them at arm's length, and putting them in and taking them out of a case, that he placed on the table, to keep company with the beard's cellphone.

Overweight spread his fat arms over his half of the table. He was wearing a tee-shirt but there were no tattoos except a very professionally drawn fouled anchor.

Overweight asked:-

"So, you're a doctor. We need a doctor"

"I am sorry. I might disappoint. I am a doctor of soil science."

"Well, we have to make do with what we can get these days", conceded overweight weakly.

I was not sure I was flattered, or appreciated.

I was getting the impression that these were middle-class, or even upper-class people, university types, professional proletarians, or artisanal designers displaced by the Magonians.

Overweight resumed with a scowl:-

"Are you an Old Etonian?"

"No", I replied with a tone of query. "Why have you asked that?"

"You are wearing an Eton tie, and the accent"

Englishmen notice these things.

And I noticed that a lean rat-faced individual with a shock of ginger hair had joined the back of the crowd. He had the fixed smirk of a schoolyard bully or a used car salesman, and could have been 40 or 45.

He interjected:-

"You know what they say about Clarendon boys: Wykehamists are naive; Harrovians are merely arrogant; and Etonians are both naive and arrogant!"

He chuckled a little at his own drollery and quickly scanned the crowd for approval, but finding only bemusement left to get himself a drink. I wondered what his assessment of Rugby or Merchant Taylors would have been. I once knew an Old Pauline at my Manchester hostel. One dark and rainy, very well-remembered night, five or six of us piled into a mini and drove to Macclesfield to view a motorcycle the Pauline was interested in buying. It is the only occasion I have ever visited that Cheshire town. We were all thoroughly inebriated of course. Our Old Pauline friend did not purchase the machine but we all returned to the big city thoroughly entertained. A little later the hostel's dour but foul-mouthed Australian Head Man reprimanded the Pauline for discharging a pistol in the Hall precincts.

Oh, this must be at least sixty-four years ago. Different days, different ways. It could have been in a different universe.

I glanced down at the dark blue and light blue banded tie I had worn at school and now used to tie my storm hood to my anorak.

"I am wearing a Potter's Bar Secondary Modern tie and I do not know about my accent."

"Who trained you to present as you do?", entered the specs man, without eye-contact but continuing to play with his glasses.

Who trained me to present as I do? What sort of a question was that? I was not satisfied that I was leading this interrogation in the way that I wanted to lead it. But equally I was beginning to lose my temper.

I replied:-

"I am going to lend you a shovel so that you can dig up Julian Retravas and fucking ask him!"

Specs man received the offer with equanimity but did not take it up.

A lad at the back asked, "Who was Retravas?"

"He was my headmaster at Potter's Bar Secondary Modern School", I replied dismissively.

Cloth cap behind me softly placed his hand on my right shoulder and said "Please do not be offended, Brother. Can we confine ourselves to pertinent questions, lady and gents?"

I glanced round. I felt like saying "I am not your Brother and this is an insolent imposition on a lawful traveller." Instead I scowled and kept silence.

A tall young man with a sensitive and thoughtful face had arrived at the back. He asked me:-

"Can you handle a rifle?"

"Well I considered myself a good shot as a young man, but I haven't held a weapon in decades, or kept one. I am a Quaker. I think that guns tend to create more problems than they solve."

"What I mean is, would you be willing to train us?" continued the clever newcomer.

The barmaid Maggi Landheart interrupted us, pointing her finger over the pump finial.

"You are a strange Quaker, sinking pints in pubs and swearing in front of a lady." I took it she was excluding herself, but did not then realise that she spoke of another, and literally.

"Yes I'm a bloody strange man and a very wicked Quaker!" I shouted bad-temperedly. The woman ducked abashed and pretended to fiddle with her cloths and drip trays. I had noticed of late that my stammer was starting to come back under stress along with my Wolverhampton accent.

Cloth cap touched me again and said "Friend, please don't be angry. You are with brothers and sisters and there is no need to swear. Maggy, a round on the house, if you please."

"Are you payin'", retorted the barmaid.

"No", retorted Cloth Cap.

"Then the answer is no. It is beyond closing anyway", shouted the barmaid back.

I especially resented the use of "Friend" in this context.

I was getting hot now and Commissar Cloth Cap had, it appeared, allowed a much-needed cold pint to slip through my fingers.

Specs man waved his hand limp-wristedly as if groping for the right words from out of a conjurer's black plush bag.

"What I want to ask, is well...you know...are you, ... you know...conservative. What I mean is...you know...immigrants...the Occupation. I suppose what I am trying to ask..."

And abruptly he leaned forward across the table and spat or shouted "...are you an Englishman!?"

"You have no right to ask that question", I replied.

"*You* have no rights", said the beard. "None of us have."

If this was the "English Resistance" I thought "there is no hope for England." Then I said:-

"Look, lady and gentlemen. I am not political. This is how it is. Britain is an island. Britain has fifteen warships or twenty-five if you include submarines good only for sinking Argy cruisers or removing whole cities at a time. The Magonian Federation has 1213 ships of war of all kinds. You have good leaders now, whatever their races or religions, or lack of the same: Don't piss them off. Because you won't pay: It's the poor bloody plebs who will pay in blood..."

I stood up to leave.

I cannot remember anything further.

CHAPTER TWO
ARNOLDINA FENG

I awoke in broad daylight. I was supine in a soft but comfy bed in a slightly Spartan room that needed redecorating badly. No: It was already that. It badly needed redecorating. Beside me, in a chair with thin varnished wooden arms sat what appeared to be a Chinawoman wearing a Magonian uniform of tight-fitting black jacket with plenty of buttoned pockets and one of those stupid little bonnets worn by policewomen everywhere. I hope you will forgive my non-PC ways of putting things. I try not to offend but I also attempt not to be mis-understood.

"Are you a police officer?" I greeted in my usual daft manner.

"Yes, Sir" it replied whilst remaining stock-still.

I had risen and was making my way to the en-suite bathroom. The facility was clean enough but suddenly I stopped and wondered why I was there. I did not feel like urinating or defecating. I rubbed my left palm under my right armpit and sniffed it. Most odd. I had obviously been bathed whilst sleeping.

I returned to the bed and lay on the duvet. I was in pyjamas. I had not packed any in my sack on leaving Nuneaton, and had not purchased any on the way.

After a couple of minutes the apparent policewoman stated apropos nothing:-

"I am Colour Major Arnoldina Feng, Senior Deputy Assistant Commissioner for Senior Welfare in the Sector B77bCHE Command of the Auxiliary Nursing (Aliens) Corps. Welcome to Area A6. I am a fully-qualified doctor of medicine and a Registered nurse. I am a Christian."

Oh God, I thought, in my very unchristian habit, not another of those ghastly pseudo-Japanese performing bots that they used to show at exhibitions before the war.

It seemed that the Magonians were also becoming infected with local politically-correct bullshit in which even the humblest operative was never a junior trainee toe-rag or tea-maker allowed to take pride in his work however basic.

For my part, apart from casual blasphemy, I was sinking to other petty vices of my Late Father. One of his favourite phrases was "Before the War." He meant of course the Second World War. For example, around December 1975 I brought a scientific pocket calculator home from Glasgow. It was hand-sized and seemed to be made of a pressed thermoplastic, probably polystyrene. Father turned the gadget over in his hand and remarked: "Before the War, assuming they had such things, it would have been made of metal." I did not dare explain that the case was of a dielectric material essential to the reliable operation of the device. Father was no moron, but I cannot remember him approving anything or anyone unless it was a firearm or something or someone in a cowboy film, or was one.

"I need to get out of here. I have only 3000 crowns", I told the auxiliary nurse. I did not know what I expected her or it to do about the problem. Presumably say "I will fetch your check" or something.

A fully qualified doctor is of course useful, especially if you are an eighty-four-year-old diabetic with heart trouble and even if you have to pay her. On the other hand I did not understand the relevancy of her final statement. Of course, Christians are rare but present in the Orient, but though one's Faith must readily be Confessed at all times, it is hardly the "done thing" to tell perfect strangers one is Christian. It is just not "British", and there is the ever-present danger that one will be mistaken for a proselyte, disastrous if you are trying to pass muster as a Quaker.

I had no idea what a Colour Major was, and had even less interest.

I had noted from the outset that the thing, whatever it was, had unnatural neuromotor tendances. It moved its head in a jerky, arthritic and Cartesian manner, if you ascertain my meaning. It moved its lips without moving other face muscles, and batted its gorgeous eyelids seemingly at random.

I realised I was dealing not merely with an autistic, but either with a badly-damaged human being or a robot.

I was of course aware of the Turing Test, and knew that at a certain level of development it would be impossible to distinguish man and machine.

I was now on my way back to the lavatory. I did not want to use it as such but I had felt something warm trickle down my face. I looked in the mirror. I did not recognise myself. Bright red arterial blood was oozing from my scalp and slowly but perceptibly moving south.

I returned to the bedroom and said:-

"You need to dress my scalp. It has started to bleed"

Feng replied:-

"I am not authorised to escort you beyond the limits of Sector B77bCHE"

"You are not permitted to wear a helmet or a hat unless you can prove Magonian citizenship. The privilege of citizenship is unlikely to be granted unless you have been microchipped and found reliable."

Escort? Reliable? Microchipped!!?

I returned to the bathroom, and tearing sheets of lavatory paper from the roll fitted them to my scalp. These staunched the flow quite efficiently.

"Only animals are microchipped", I advised Feng.

"Darling Charles, you *are* an animal!" it replied.

Robots are said to be constitutionally incapable of irony, humour or sarcasm, much less flirtation.

I was potentially in a very dangerous situation. A much more serious bodily peril than, say, an encounter with ghosts in a country lane.

I needed urgently to establish whether this was, you know, an *actual* woman woman complete with pimples and a temper or just a damned bot. If the latter I was going summarily to "kill" it and escape before either the Magonians or the rebels killed me.

I flounced back to the bed, and sat on the edge. I took care spitefully to knock its bonnet off as I passed.

"Don't be childish, Dr Charmliss" reproved the Colour Major, making no attempt to retrieve its headpiece.

I was alone with an apparition. It was *something*. It might have been a woman or a very effeminate man. It might have been a holographic simulacrum projected by technologically-advanced aliens using a method unknown to humans. But it was *something* and it was a proximate and present danger.

But even I sometimes have ideas, and I now had one that might save my life.

"Colour Major Feng, can I ask a favour?"

"You may call me 'Dina' or if you insist 'Arnoldina'. Never 'Arnie' and never use my rank. I shall call you Charles."

"I would prefer 'Chuck' never 'Chas' and 'never that man over there'. And by the way, I am never 'Doctor' anything unless you want a fist."

"I do not know what a fist is or what I would do with it. I am here to serve. I am here to serve Charles Charmliss and his needs but mostly I serve The Magonian Federation, and principally of all I serve The Lord God, the only true lord and king, the source of all Creation."

I felt chastened.

I also felt vulnerable.

"Arnoldina is such a beautiful name. Please let me call you Arnoldina."

"You may but I shall call you 'Charles'. We are equals."

"Thank you, Arnoldina" I replied.

I was grateful to be with a plain-speaker, but I doubted our equality.

I would have to prove that if I could.

"I had a bit of a working-over last night, didn't I?"

"Working-over?"

"Yes, those rough people in the bar around four or five in the morning. They struck me and hit my head with a blunt instrument. I lost consciousness."

"You did lose consciousness, Charles, but no-one attacked you. You stood up suddenly, slipped and hit your head on a table."

Ah, the official version is known, I accepted, cynically.

"What was that favour you wanted to ask, Charles?"

I rose from the edge of the bed, and pulled the top sheet clear.

"I want you to go into the bathroom and to change out of your uniform and into this bed sheet and only this bed sheet and to return here in the character of Minerva the Roman goddess of wisdom."

"I know who Minerva was", replied the thing in a slightly shirty tone (no pun intended and I trust none taken).

"Minerva wore a brazen cuirass over a red tunic", Arnoldina objected.

"Sadly, Arnoldina, I do not have those properties to hand at this time", I replied without, I hoped, the appearance of sarcasm. "Please use the bed sheet."

Arnoldina took the sheet from my hand and adjourned to the bathroom. She or it returned a couple of minutes later wearing the bed sheet. Whatever it was, it was unspeakably gorgeous, with its kind if impassive face framed by straight lank raven hair which extended to its sacrum. It resumed its seat.

"I can do nothing which subverts the people or government of the Magonian Federation or which brings the Federation into disrepute. We are alone. What I can do is entertain an old man who wants to play charades."

"Arnoldina, I respect your virtue and your patriotism. I also value your candour and your piety. I know you are not a Roman goddess or any profane thing. If you maintain your solicitudes I guarantee such shall profit your country and mine saving many lives in the outcome."

"You are a Quaker, and you have a Quaker's idealisms."

"No, Arnoldina, I am a Christian, I hope and pray, but I am a man of experience and a pragmatist. You are right that I am old, but I have seen a lot, most of it unpleasant."

"Arnoldina, do you mind if I ask you some very personal questions?"

"I cannot stop you, but I am here to serve your needs, not your cupidities."

"Firstly, Arnoldina, how old are you? I would have said around twenty-seven perhaps a little younger."

The Colour Major paused. I found it difficult to say whether from female reticence or consternation, or because she or it was performing elaborate calculations.

"Sorry about the delay. I was trying to relate my native tides and measures to terms intelligible to an Englishman of the twenty-first Christ century. I may be out by a few years but I estimate 976 years give or take."

"Arnoldina, are you a demoness?"

"I am not a demoness", replied Arnoldina carefully and with a hint of repressed resentment. "If you are asking in my theatrical character as Minerva the answer is obviously 'yes'."

"Are you a witch?"

"I am not going to dignify that with an answer. I thought you were a clever man and a kindly one."

"I am very sorry, Arnoldina. Please forgive me."

"Arnoldina, do you have a boyfriend?"

"I have a husband and a young child"

"How old is your child?"

There was another pause, as a look of intense concentration clouded the hitherto impassive visage.

"I don't know. He could be 435 or 436. I am not sure."

"Arnoldina, I wish to ask another hard question, but it may cause you real anger or distress. Do I have your permission?" A long silence.

"Are we in Hell?"

"We are not in Hell, Charles", responded Arnoldina calmly, but possibly with repressed anger. I had to judge, but judgment is dangerous as well as blasphemous, but greater outrages were at risk.

"Charles, you are a mathematician", alleged the Colour Major.

"How do you know"

"You must just accept that I know"

"Very well"

"I will try to bring it down to your level", said Arnoldina.

"Oh, thank you kindly!" I thought.

"You learned, I suppose in high school, of the Dimensions of State that define the physical parameters of a given force field, for example that in some conventions electrical voltage is $ML^2T^{-3}I^{-1}$, where M is Mass, L is Length, T is Time and I is Current?"

"Yes, I often used that concept in my professional career."

"Now imagine that there is some universe in which $ML^2T^{-3}I^{-1}Đ^{-7}Ⱶ^4$ is Energy where additionally to your electro-mechanical forces Unstanchehood Đ and Stork Ⱶ forces are also at play and have to be allowed for in viable models of reality."

"If you are worried about the idea of more than one universe remember the brilliant work of George Cantor in the 1870s. Not only did the German genius prove that infinity existed in real life, not just as a convenient mathematical figment for solving calculus problems, but also that there were at least two sorts of infinity, and then went forward to prove that there were an infinity of different flavours of infinity. The logical corollary is that everything is possible, because all infinities are the same but they are all so very different."

Yes I remembered. They put the poor man in a lunatic asylum.

My mind wondered back to another hostel man who had befriended me. One evening we stood outside my room and I said to him "Nothing is impossible." Pointing at the door he replied "crawl through that keyhole." One learns so much when one is twenty.

"Yes, yes. I think I have followed your drift so far!" I interjected.

"Now I invite you to consider one of the infinitely many universes in which Time T drops out of the dimensional equations of parameter definition. Time still exists at some philosophical level but it is irrelevant to the physics of this world in question. Neither your old universe nor this is such a kind."

"Yes, I think I see what you mean" I agreed.

"Congleholme exists in such a world. English is a common language in the Federation, though most of us struggle with it. In English we call this infinitely-extensive universe containing Congleholme FUGON 78V. The Chester you knew and vaguely liked was in FUGON 80V, a closely-similar universe. Of course, your watch still works, and the planets still turn giving night and day, but there are subtle variations due to modified physics. For example, in some geographical sense, Chester is Congleholme, but so are Regfeld, Valchester and a place called Ƀ⸮⸮ were the people walk through walls at will and things fall upward, if they have sufficient Atomic Weight: All of these places simultaneously exist and are co-located in the geographical, or rather cosmographical, sense. They are also contemporaneous with slight technical variations. In some of these worlds the Brider does not meander at all because the hydrodynamics is not suited to that. Populations of people and animals adapt to the various environments and *when they die they seamlessly transit to another universe* whilst their biological remains, if any, do just that: They remain. In Chester the river is shallower and not as loopy as in Congleholme so that ocean-going ships could dock until 1300AD but as late as 1850AD in Congleholme, and in Ƀ⸮⸮ the River Brider is just a narrow ditch accommodating a rivulet of gallium: All of these cities are the same 'thing' but are so very different and many were founded by Romans and all exist in *North-West Cheshire, England*. All five of the cities I have named have an Albion Hotel or Albion Inn in the shadow of the city wall, but there are plenty of Chesters that do not, and some are without surviving walls."

"Because the humans in Ƀ⸮⸮ can walk through rock they sometimes have serious inconvenience and often 'trespass' in parts of both Congleholme and Chester", continued Arnoldina, "The people of Ƀⱸ as they insist upon calling their universe have had serious problems developing nuclear power because throughout Ƀⱸ pitchblende falls upwards under gravity so they cannot store it in bouse teems or any open heap and U^{235} can *only* be separated from U^{238} using a centrifuge. Meanwhile, visually impaired people and animals, and people with learning difficulties often get lost in rock strata and can only be rescued with extreme difficulty and expense. Is that Hell, Charles?"

"I do not know", I admitted.

"It is not about Hell or Purgatory. God exists and creates *ab initio*, but he is not interested in punishments or persecutions. It is about the Laws of Continuity"

"God is a res, and an extant Superagent which creates energy and its expressive universes by thinking about them counter-entropically, actions which are reacted to by the internal thermodynamic deterioration of the universes concerned. I oversimplify, Charles, and of course all universes are 'concerned'. FUGON series universes are so called because they fly from a locus, reach a stationary point of dilation and cycle back to self-annihilate at the point of origin, and repeat. The summated entropy is zero. This makes time dimensionally an indispensable ingredient of energy in such a universe." Arnoldina dilated and superadded, "It is literally the case that everything is possible for God because his thought is limitless and he cannot die, because the sum of the sums of cosmic entropies that include Him ubiquitously is itself zero. This also explains why he can read your mind."

"Satan is not a res, but an epiphenomenon of the summative interplay of all the evil in the human psyche. Evil is intrinsic to the human brain which accounts for its simian cunning. Evil is therefore a localised electrochemical phenomenon. Accordingly Satan is a truly supernatural Agent whereas God is a natural agent." Arnoldina continued.

"Where do Christ and the Holy Ghost fit in?" I queried.

"We don't know, Charles"

"Heaven and Hell are what you make them", continued this auxiliary nurse, policewoman and cosmological philosopher or maybe physicist. "Obviously, some universes are 'nicer' than others. FUGON 80V seems hellish to me: God took thought and watched 80V reify. Then he thought 'Well I really fucked that one. I'll try again', but we are blessed with a world in which pain is often absent or dull, because the thermodynamics of alkaline reactions is unsuitable to pain transmission, except at a very basic level. Nevertheless, some people or other animals feel the cold and many do not. This is why I am relaxed about your head injury, knowing that you are not really in pain, and that it will pass. You are still old and very ill, but you feel rejuvenated", explained the lovely presence. "By the way, there is no evidence that either God or His Enemy intentionally assign animals to any particular universe when said creatures die. They, too, are victims, and beneficiaries, of Free Will."

"Much of this is a simple corollary of the imperatives of quantum dynamics."

"It may be simple for you, Madam", I thought. "But I am much less intelligent and it boggles my mind." I also remembered that if she had spoken like this five hundred years ago she would have been burnt to death.

To my poor mind much of this doctrine appeared to be atheism, I supposed they would once have called it heresy, or perhaps some Oriental philosophy of re-incarnation. But then I remembered that Christ has promised us Resurrection of the Flesh, so in humility under God I accepted that this woman was as Christian as she professed.

The Colour Major continued.

"Now I know you are worried about the Turing Criterion, Charles, and I agree to co-operate with your further examinations if those are what may help you."

"Thank you, Arnoldina. You have been more than helpful already, but I wish to continue if I may."

"No problem. I am here to help."

"Arnoldina, here in England, we do not say 'No Problem' or 'You're Welcome'. That is American. We say 'It is a, or it is, my pleasure', or in the case of an unpleasant duty discharged 'It is an honour'" I remarked.

"Don't be silly, Charles."

The Colour Major walked over to her or its bag that she or it had left by the door. The bag was an old fashioned doctor's Gladstone bag with compartments and a hinged lid, capacious but potentially heavy for an old woman but not necessarily for a robot.

She retrieved a small brass gadget and what appeared to be a fly-fisher's lead sinker at the end of a foot of string.

The Colour Major returned to the bed where I continued to sit and ordered softly:-

"Hold out your right hand"

She fitted the brass gadget over my thumb, over the basal carpo metacarpal. She then slowly tightened a brass screw. I felt a slight pressure.

"Doe's it hurt?" the Major queried, as she or it gazed concernedly into my eyes.

"No?" I replied.

"In FUGON 80V you would be screaming by now and be begging for mercy. I won't go any further else I would smash the joint."

The Colour Major operated a quick release and removed the thumbscrew.

My skin crept cold as I wondered what she would do with the string and sinker.

She held up the line by the free end and moved the sinker aside as if to form a pendulum. She then released it. Obviously,

I expected a series of Galilean oscillations damped by air drag for as long as the demonstrator could hold the simple device aloft.

What I saw was this:-

The sinker described a thin ellipse not unlike a Foucault Pendulum. The next cycle was a wider ellipse and so for several cycles until a perfect circle formed. The pendulum sinker then spun two cycles clockwise, four anti-clockwise, then eight clockwise, then sixteen anti-clockwise, as the circles gradually diminished due to air drag. At that point Arnoldina threw the very simple contraption on my bed.

"Physics and Chemistry are different in FUGON 78V", remarked my nurse.

CHAPTER THREE
GALATEA UNDRAPED

"Arnoldina, would Minerva have known any of these wonderful things that you have briefed me about", I asked the Colour Major.

"Charles, you are not a boy. You must know that Minerva never existed, not even in Classical times, and not even in 80V."

"You are right, Arnoldina, I am not a boy and I must put aside boys' things. But Galatea did exist, at least in the minds of Greeks, and for any god to think is to create. Now I am no Pygmalion, but even I, an animal as you say, know that Roman gods and goddesses were always draped and Greek ones always nude."

"Rise, and stand before me", I ordered.

The nurse did as she was told.

"Remove your gown", I ordered even more peremptorily.

Arnoldina complied, neither with haste nor reluctance. I was surprised to see her stand wearing a prim cotton vest with a little sky-blue bow at the neck and the unmistakeable contours of a brassiere beneath. To complete this very Mais and Spender under-outfit she wore a frumpish pair of underpants almost like cream-coloured men's boxers.

Perhaps she truthfully was an old woman.

Her dress was of course in contravention of my explicit instruction at the outset of this examination. But from a scientific point of view (you understand) pudicity is a very good indicator of animality: Robots are never ashamed. Neither, however, are they shamed, and this creature did not seem abashed or discomfited.

"Remove the rest of your clothing", I demanded.

Again without eagerness or reluctance Arnoldina removed first her vest and then her brassiere and lastly pulled down her pants and threw them aside. These clothes were perfectly clean. Perhaps cleaner than a living creature could keep them.

Now I have always taken a vain pride in my powers of description. But I am neither a poet nor a pornographer and I shall struggle to convey the sheer and transcendental beauty of what stood before me.

The head was so finely modelled with its doe-black eyes and little pert nose shading her little mouth with its bud-like lips. From her scalp cascaded raven-black, blonde-fine perfectly straight, never dyed and, so it seemed, never cut hair. The expression of her face was serene but not sombre.

There was no trace of the down, the half-visible moustache or of the vestigial axial or pubic hispidities that so often adorn or disfigure the woman who has passed child-bearing age or of any hair other than that of her scalp.

It was a vision of loveliness that I am not worthy, let alone able to describe. I could not imagine that this was the outcome of some Palo Alto progress meeting of yesteryear in which the board had concurred that the product should frame a kind firm face in a pentagon of a perfect golden-yellow hide, and agreed such flawless skin should bound her faultless body.

It was a god, and only a god, that could imagine this and grant it the powers of profane replication and freedom of will.

She had a delicate and distinct umbilicus, perfunctorily tied in some unique convention of a human midwife, a feature alike redundant on gods and robots. Onward I shall say 'she' without demurral or qualification.

Her breasts were perfectly alike, perfectly spheric drops of flesh neither gross nor small, with pink, smooth aureoles, neither too broad or too brief, with pert pink nipples, with stars of crevasse at their ends as if waiting to squirt and nurture. There were few Montgomery glands.

I seized her breasts, massaged and palpated. The creature, hitherto casting her eyes downward, suddenly tossed her head and hair rearward as if in shock or outrage. Otherwise she did and said nothing except stand.

I felt the nipples stiffen beneath my palms.

I removed my hands.

Disturbingly, I felt myself begin to erect. I had not suffered, and I mean suffered, such a condition for thirty years.

"Please excuse my tumidity, Arnoldina", I pleaded.

"You are a man and you have a man's instincts and desires", replied the Colour Major.

I resumed my seat on the edge of the bed to examine the portal of life. As I have remarked there was no stubble or pimpling or any trace of unsightly or unhygienic hair. If there was cosmetic practice then I lacked the skills to detect it. Unless of course the design decision had been made not to feature it.

I opened her vulva as gently as I was able. There were perfectly symmetrical occluded labia and an intact clitoris. There was a little oozing of a clear, odourless fluid.

I removed my hands and stood up.

"Turn around", I ordered.

That long hair was something else, as they say, ceasing only at the gluteal cleft, and in the ancient Western vision of the Chinawoman, or indeed her male counterpart. Each buttock was perfectly hemi-ellipsoidal and perfectly alike without any trace of cellulitic degeneracy. The skin was not coarse through too much sitting. It differed from the rest of her perfect integument only in this: There was a delicate roseate hue.

I gave her right buttock a hefty slap. The body recoiled in an slight backward arc before regaining its erect stance.

"Do you need to punish me, Charles?"

"I have never met a creature less deserving of correction", I answered.

"Then do not hit my bottom. It is an insult."

"I am dreadfully sorry, Arnoldina."

"You are forgiven. In any case, the gesture was nearly painless."

"Please turn round and hold out your hands", I requested.

Arnoldina did so.

I could distinguish no dermatoglyphic ridges on either the fingers or the palms. I gently rubbed their surfaces and detected what I thought might be corrugations.

"Excuse me", I said, "I shall have to get my reading glasses."

I walked to my sack and retrieved them.

I examined the skin closely and distinguished friction ridges with whorls and arches. There may have been sweat pores, but my eyesight is too poor to be sure at low magnitudes.

"Please sit", I said, "I need to examine the soles of your feet."

"There are no stigmata", remarked the Colour Major startlingly. I felt this was not an occasion for jest, especially such a profane joke.

"Now it is my turn to admonish you!", I said with a smile. Arnoldina remained solemn. Perhaps she was getting impatient.

But Arnoldina did as she was told.

Sometimes, cybernetic designers include friction surfaces or treatments on hand palms. Attempts to simulate the human skin structure beneath the foot are very rare.

The dermatoglyphy of Arnoldina's soles was consistent with human development.

There were no facilities for testing DNA of course.

Please excuse my clinicisms, and my use of the passive voice.

"Are we quite done?", said Arnoldina with the sweetest closed-lipped smile, a smile like an angel in heaven. It was the first time I had seen anyone smile since leaving Stoke.

"We are done", I confirmed.

Arnoldina stood and walked again to her doctor's bag.

Her perfect breasts swung playfully, first in one orbit, and then the other. Her receding buttocks alternately reciprocated like the connecting rods of an old Hathorn-Davy waterworks engine.

She came back with a plastic clip folder, roughly A4 size.

"I brought x-rays because I thought you would ask for them."

She sat beside me on the edge of the bed and opened the folder. Her skeleton looked vaguely like a woman's though bits were obviously modified. With regard to soft tissues, some vital organs were absent and appeared to be replaced by geometric, obviously manufactured, configurations. Most strikingly, the heart had been replaced by what I guessed to be some sort of electrical peristaltic pump wired to I suppose a pacemaker where her thymus should have been. Only a little less remarkable something had supplanted the auditory cortex.

"I lost my pancreas when I was 109. It was replaced by an artificial insulin-generator which so far has given excellent service. It is a De Hont which I had installed privately."

"Can I have one?" I asked half jestingly.

"We are not sure you can benefit. I think you will have only three or four years with us", added Arnoldina matter-of-factly. "If it happens that you still need insulin we can tide you over with it."

"I am unable to pay for medical help, or indeed hotel fees", I complained.

"Don't worry about any of that. Your fees and expenses, and indeed my pay, are all being found by the Magonian Federation, and we will invoice the British Government accordingly at the peace conference. If you become a Magonian citizen costs will be written off, and you will of course enjoy Magonian retirement and health provisions, as indeed shall I. If you become a national of a third power, we shall invoice you personally. This is not malice or persecution: It is merely business."

"You and I have work to do, and I have been ordered to see that you are able and willing to do it. Notwithstanding what we know about Universal Continuity, lives are at stake and they are not to be squandered", concluded Arnoldina.

"Yes, thank you, I quite understand" I agreed.

I now knew that I was talking to, and tampering with, an actual woman, born of man through woman, a bionic woman as forecast by the fantasy of my old world.

I knew something else.

I was either dead or mad.

CHAPTER FOUR
COMMUNION

Arnoldina rose and and leaving her folder and negatives on the bed returned to her own chair, still naked.

"Remove your clothes", she commanded. "We are equals", she reminded me, "and we must be naked under God."

I was sure this had not been the custom at any Quaker Meeting for Worship, or any of the Anglican or Catholic Masses I had attended.

I complied.

I still sported what remained of an old man's tumescence.

Arnoldina stood portentously and stated in an authoritative tone:-

"Your death released you from your vows but I am a married woman, a happily married woman, and I yet live with a husband alive in 78V. Do you understand my meaning?"

"I do Madam", I affirmed solemnly.

"And don't call me 'madam'. It has a most unfortunate resonance, especially in the light of events, and in a cheap hotel. And more especially during Holy Communion."

"Yes, I am most dreadfully sorry, Albertina", I squirmed.

"Since when have I been Albertina?"

"I mean I am very sorry, Arnoldina. I will try to remember myself."

"Do"

The Colour Major walked slowly back to her bag. I had wondered why she did not bring it to her chair.

"About the thumbscrew, Arnoldina. Why do you carry one?"

"I had it made specially for you", she replied.

I was not sure if she was being sarcastic.

"Torture is illegal in the Magonian Federation, and perfectly useless anywhere in universe 78V", Arnoldina confirmed.

"Please have it destroyed, Arnoldina", I begged.

"I shall", promised my lovely nurse and wardress.

From her all-comprehending doctor's bag she retrieved a thick black book bound in what seemed to be imitation leather. She took it back to her seat and flicked through the pages. I saw on the front of the tome what I surmised to be Mandarin characters embossed in gold leaf.

One of the characters was 經 (yyng) which I knew to indicate "sutra" or "sacred text."

From my position I could study little more except the lady's delectable form, as delectable as Bunyan's Delectable Mountains as distant but as accessible.

"I am a vegan", Arnoldina seemed to explain, as if in some kind of self-conscious justification. In the idle and captious spirit for which I was elsewhere notorious I wondered whether her scruple extended to the gesso with which the gold adhered.

Her deep and liquid eyes looked up for an instant.

"It is acrylic, Charles"

I shivered. My blood ran cold. Could this thing read my mind?

Arnoldina commenced to read from her book:-

In the mystic wastes of far Tachin, long ago, a poor leper had an old donkey whom he loved. The old donkey loved the leper, whom all shunned, not for his putrid sores, that the dogs sucked, but because he was poor. The donkey was old and lonely, and her hair fell out, and she was shunned by the asses of her tribe. The donkey loved her leper.

Each morning, in the cool of sunrise, the leper and his donkey would slowly walk, painfully walk, to the olive groves to glean kindling. One morning the donkey stumbled, for she was old and lame. "Do not fret, my love, my donkey, do not die", begged the leper, and lifted from her a faggot and added it to his own heavy burden. The donkey rose and walked.

They arrived at a twinkling rivulet of the coolest freshest water called by the local people Kidron. The leper and the ass he loved stooped to drink and they were slaked.

Presently, a proud warlord galloped up on his own fine horse with its tinkling lorinery and its golden caparisons.

The two equines reached their heads across the Kidron and kissed. Then they held their heads together in love, in the way that creatures of their kind do.

The yapping curs who had followed both men at some distance approached the fine horse and bit his legs. The horse kicked and reared and jilted the lord and his golden cup. The lord broke both legs as he fell to the ground. His wine spilled.

The lord seized his cup and threw it to the leper, across the rivulet, commanding "Fill this cup with Kidron, fetid peasant, and bring it hither."

"Excellency, I cannot", said the leper, "It is forbidden me. I cannot cross the bourne. You must thirst for evermore."

Arnoldina placed the book on a small table with some reverence and crossed herself in the Eastern manner.

No man knows what thirst is unless he is diabetic, or suicidal.

"Luke 16:18 to 16:31" she said.

"Yes, I recognised it: The Narrative of Dives and Lazarus, a Parable of Christ unto the pharisees. Do you rate me a pharisee, Arnoldina?"

"I do not"

"I prefer the King James Version: It is briefer and it makes the point that both men have died, and that one is in Hell and the other in Heaven. Equines are not mentioned."

"Furthermore", I continued, "Every clause of your Version is ambiguous."

"Life is ambiguous, Charles, and The Words of Jesus bear an infinity of implications."

"Do you not know how it is, my good Friend? All such stories are the same, but they are all so, so very so, different."

"And another thing", Arnoldina persisted in her womanly way, "It is a heresy and a blasphemy to criticise Holy Writ, whether it is written in Mandarin, Hindi, English or Aramaic, carved in hieroglyphics or beaten into a copper scroll."

"There is such a thing as higher criticism", I objected.

"Yes, but you are not learned", Arnoldina advised a man with four science degrees, "and you must school."

"Why do you think I know grand things, Dr Charmliss? Do you think it is because I am intelligent?"

"Yes, I rather do", I thought unvoiced.

"A woman learns things in nigh on a thousand years that are not possible for a man of eighty-four", said my fair advisor.

I, Charles Edward Charmliss, was born in the corner of a farmer's field reclaimed from a marsh in the far North of England. My Father was an ordinary seaman in the Royal Navy, and my Mother a technical Petty Officer, recently deserted. My Father was my Mother's student. My Father persuaded my Mother to abjure her Faith. Both were atheists. I was raised an atheist. At the age of forty-five I endured a specific experience that I am not ready to discuss. I turned to Christ. The alternative was suicide. I am not by nature a gloomy man, or a depressive. I have never contemplated self-murder before or since.

But a large part of my Faith is the issue of intellectual conviction, since as a scientist I had known for some years that oblivion was mathematically impossible and that infinities were ubiquitous though I was yet to encounter a personal Christ.

Arnoldina rose and returned her Chinese, or perhaps Mongolian, Bible to her case. From this seeming well of plenty she retrieved what was obviously a Mais and Spender 330ml plastic bottle of red wine and a crusty bread roll.

Returning she visited the bathroom and liberated two polystyrene disposable cups, presumably placed there by a maid or male cleaner for the convenience of guests.

"Come and sit with me at the table", offered Arnoldina.

I did as bidden and we both sat on the only two chairs available there. Always fastidious about such things, I wondered what subsequent guests would think or do if they realised we had parked our naked anuses upon these plush supports.

"During the Eucharist you must rest in silence at all times. You must pray inwardly if you will or can. I shall voice a brief prayer and a simple observance. I shall break the bread and serve the wine. I shall tell you when it is over and you may speak."

"Thank you, holy woman. I *will*"

Arnoldina smiled her solemn but stately smile a second time. We were strangers and political enemies sitting naked in a slightly dowdy wartime hotel somewhere in Europe, somewhere in time.

But I was content and the Immanence of the Sacrament was overpowering.

Arnoldina continued to smile. I was not sure whether it was because I had called her "woman" or because I had called her "holy", or both or neither.

"Oh Lord of Hosts, I do not know the words, and I do not wish to offend my patient, a devout man, please forgive and Lord of Hosts bless this our Host", Arnoldina commenced with unspeakable reverence and the deepest of ambiguity.

The Chinawoman clapped her hands once. The gesture startled me.

Arnoldina opened the bottle and raising it poured the wine. She then break the bread. Handing me a morsel she said "Eat." I did. Then she said "Drink." I did. She partook.

Then Arnoldina said:-

Please, Jesus,
strengthen and sustain your servant Charles in the inhuman and enormous work that he must do for the survival of the People to whom you promised Eternal Life in the Commitment of Men. Give him the Reward of continued improvement in all things Holy in the Knowledge never complete of all Progress, and defend him from the wiles of Evil that always skulks in the cloak of benefit. Defend and protect his good Wife benighted in age and desert in a cruel World that only death can remit.
So help him, God"

"**Amen**" I voiced automatically and unintended. Arnoldina did not reprove the coda.

Arnoldina sat in silence.

Presumably she prayed for her family, for peace, for the concord of our diverse peoples.

As I sat I also prayed, but in silence:-

Jesus Christ, only righteous lord and king,
I turn to you again. Console now and hereafter my suffering faithful Wife whom I have deserted five times: Once in the body, once in the life and thrice in the spirit. I do not know where I am or when, or worst of all, why. Guide me. Protect also this good woman. I doubted her, even unto her very humanity. Forgive me. Protect her from pain and find her ever Worlds without suffering, without discord, without prejudice, without dogma. She forgave me my Trespasses in Imitation of your Holy Spirit. Make her forgive herself. Lend me your strength. My Late Mother was an instructress, I was an instructor. This woman instructs me today and does it diligently. I need her. Maintain her. My Lord of Wonders, my thanks You sense in my Spirit.

"You may speak, Charles"

"Thank you, Arnoldina" I replied.

And seeking succour and finality in the support of formal Friendhood I added:-

"Thank you for your Reading, and for your Ministry."

CHAPTER FIVE
WE HAVE DINNER

I visited the lavatory. I was beginning to show success in that department, the first real excretions since my death. I opened the window and had a shower. The air-conditioning kicked in.

Arnoldina abluted after me.

I did not have any clothes suitable for dinner in a British hotel, not even a two-star hotel, not even in the public bar. I had a clean change of temperate woodland camo trousers and a clean dark green Navy pullover that I had impregnated with waterproofing, and it still stank. I also of course had a capacious camo anorak and marching pouches. I had only my hiking boots and breathable waterproof socks for footwear. Unsurprisingly, I decided to leave the anorak and the pouches in the bedroom.

"I shall have your kit cleaned and new underwear requisitioned for you", said Arnoldina as she dried her gorgeous body with a hotel towel.

"Thank you, Arnoldina" I replied.

"This is a war and we get what we are given", she added.

"I quite understand. You are a very great help to mc", I replied.

"I know", said the Colour Major.

"Completely bullshit free, this woman", I thought.

Arnoldina of course replaced her undies and her uniform. She retrieved her hat and fitted it carefully in the vanity mirror.

We squeezed into the old-fashioned elevator on the landing. One of those with a steel concertina lattice that you slam shut with a brass handle.

As we arrived in the bar room we observed that some familiar faces were already seated and people were chatting amongst themselves. A man showed us to our table.

"Good Evening, Major Feng: Dr Charmliss, I am Jason Warble, owner and manager of The Albion Hotel. Here are your menus for this evening. May I get you some drinks whilst you decide?"

"I will have a large IPA and the Major will have..."

I gestured to Arnoldina

"A Bloody Mary and hold the Worcestershire Sauce"

"Yes Colour Major Feng"

Mr Warble brought the very welcome drinks, and a clean pair of menus in their well-wiped cushioned folders.

As I studied the menu I presently became aware of a presence in front of me. It was Cloth Cap looking very sheepish.

Without seating he said:-

"Dr Charmliss, I really am most sorry for what happened the other night. The young people concerned will come and apologise later. I am Bollington Shrigley. Inevitably everyone calls me 'Pott'", qualified Cloth Cap, as without sitting he proffered his hand across the table.

Shrigley ignored Arnoldina, which I thought most rude, politics notwithstanding.

I rose and grasped his hand firmly.

"I am Chuck Charmliss. I am pleased to see you again." and I sat down.

Shrigley returned to his table some way across the room.

"You want to watch him. He's a bad-un. A communist", Arnoldina advised quietly in a perfect Black Country-ese which startled me.

"I would not trust him with a dead toad", I observed.

I did not give a rat about Shrigley's politics, left, right or centre, but I have an innate suspicion of men who speak for others, especially if I sniff the stink of an agenda.

"What shall I order, Arnoldina?"

"I hope in due course you will become a vegan if you are not already. Even anchovies have a Right to Life", Arnoldina asserted, doubtless alluding to the Worcestershire Sauce not to pollute the Bloody Mary at all costs. "I want Frankies in Tomato Soup"

"I shall order Roast Beef"

Mr Warble returned and took our orders.

Maggi Landheart, the barmaid during the 'incident' brought our food. She smiled at us and said:-

"I am glad to see you here again, Dr Charmliss. You look so much better. I am sorry about the accident. I was not paying attention." The plot thickened like cold tomato soup, I thought.

As she left Arnoldina remarked, "Is it all you English do, apologise? You must be a very naughty people!"

I turned to her and smiled.

As we began our meals gaggles of apparent tourists, mostly middle aged, gradually came through the doors and chatted volubly and happily in little knots. Some ordered drinks that they brought from the bar, but few sat. They were of all races and styles of casual dress. I thought I detected American accents among some.

"We do not arrest visitors from hostile powers unless they prove a problem", explained Arnoldina, somewhat *post facto* I suppose in my case.

Presently who should march through the glass door from the street but Ennias Mickawber. He was still in full uniform as a Roman centurion.

"Good Evening, Mick!" I shouted.

"Hello, Chas" Mick shouted back as he approached the bar and waved. I did not resent the diminutive. After all we had only conversed for ten minutes, and that in the dark above a busy street, and there was no particular reason why he should even remember me.

Anyway, he seemed preoccupied and engaged the woman behind the bar in earnest conversation.

Mick turned his back to the bar and in a fine stentorian bellow declaimed:-

"Ladies and Gentlemen, welcome to Congleholme, and a special welcome in the days leading to All Saints, and you know what that means?!"

General laughter, not only amongst the tourists. Then the bar room simmered down, perhaps out of respect for Mick, perhaps to hear what he might say.

"Ladies and Gentlemen, boys and girls, I have got to ask you to take special care tonight. Sleet is falling outside and the stones are becoming very slippery, and remember there is only the green glow of the Welsbach mantles anywhere in St Olave, so please be very careful where you step and enjoy yourselves at all times. The roads have been closed to ordinary traffic, but emergency services still patrol by vehicle so watch out. And remember, Congleholme is a town at war. In the unlikely event of an air raid, I shall escort customers of any company to the nearest shelter. Do *not*, that was negative *not*, take alcohol out of the building!"

"Ghost Tours (2011) Limited customers are fully insured at all times, but can I respectfully request Halloween A6 and St Olave Travel customers *not*, I repeat *not*, to follow me from the building. Your own guides will turn up shortly."

"Now, Ladies and Gentlemen, forget Poveglia Island, forget Amityville, forget the Tower of London. This hotel is the most haunted hotel, in the most haunted street, in the most haunted city in the most ghost-ridden country of God's Good Earth. Nay, of the whole universe!" claimed Mick with a smile to a titter of appreciation.

Suddenly, a leaping, jumping ape-like apparition burst through the street door in the sort of black and red witches rag weeds and pointy black hat you sometimes see on children's television or at pantomimes.

"Orl...Ar...My little treasures. Come to me", she or it cackled.

Some of the tourists giggled politely but I thought it was a meretricious choreography, vulgarly presented, unsuited to the apparent age and quality of the clientele.

"She is Bernice 'Bunny' Balfour. She is a pain. In other seasons she often comes in to solicit men, or even women, who pay. She really makes life difficult for the staff and for Eugen", said Arnoldina disapprovingly.

"I suppose we should take pity upon her, as Our Holy Saviour did upon the Magdeline", I ventured.

"Charles always kind. Always thinking the best of folk", responded my nurse.

"Don't worry about Mistress Masie. She is with St Olave!" shouted Mick to the room.

One and all burst into unaffected laughter and there was a ripple of applause as Mick led his party into the wet Autumn dusk.

But my own blood chilled again.

I turned to Arnoldina. "Who was Mistress Masie?" I asked the thousand-year-old polymath.

"She was a Tattenhall witch, Margaret Hogg, who was burned to death in Congleholme Ladyfair under Mary the First", Arnoldina explained.

I felt that the performance brought little honour to either Margaret Hogg or to the prancing dancer. Margaret Hogg was someone's daughter, someone's wife, someone's mother. They had to watch as her fibular arteries burst and committed her life's-blood to the steaming embers. Her kinsfolk had to watch in the greasy smoke of roasting flesh and to hear her scream and howl to the living sky and sever her tongue in the final rictus of agony. They had to listen as a smirking fellow-auditor turned to his drunken companion and remarked: "Hogg by name, and hog by nature."

There was no photography in the reign of Mary Tudor, daughter of a tyrant who authored an empire and his devout Spanish wife. Antonis Mor well captured with his brush Mary's cruel thin lips, her drawn visage, her spiteful eyes in her gloomy setting. The face of a doctrinaire, a fanatic, a face that claimed to speak for God, but spoke for Satan. Not the face of a woman. The face of a hell-bound demoness.

"These frankies are really yummy. You must try some tomorrow. We will have them together and then I shall gradually introduce you to other fair fare."

"You are an absolute angel!" I told the Major. Arnoldina looked up with a shy, but almost coquettish smile, like a Leonardo matron or Madonna.

Was I not in Hell but in Heaven?, and was this or was this not an Angel of God? But I remembered the woman telling me that Hell was what you made it, and Heaven also.

As I bent over my food, trying not to spill gravy down my napkin, I sensed someone before our table.

I looked up to see two lads, late teens or early twenties. I am very bad with ages: Maybe a little older? I recognised the one on the left as the lad who a couple of nights ago, after I had just arrived, asked about rifles. His companion I did not recognise.

They both bowed to Arnoldina and the taller, rifle young man said:-

"Excuse me, Sir. I am very sorry to interrupt your meal and I earnestly apologise for jostling you on Monday morning. It is not an excuse I know, but I was very drunk. I am Joseph Hotcarp. My friends call me 'Fishy'. I am a paralegal in town. I am doing Law at Hatton."

I rose to shake his hand. He took mine in a gentle but firm grip.

"Fishy is trying to take the blame, Sir. It was really me. I pushed him when he asked about your rifle-training us. He lost his balance and fell over as you tried to leave your table. I am Duncan Heldrew. I am a tenant farmer on the Chamberfield estate. I am sorry."

As we stood Heldrew and I also shook hands. What absolutely splendid young men I thought. They were the type of men we lost in the First War and never recovered, I added to my mental narrative.

"Draw up an extra chair, and I will order you drinks. What would you like?"

"It is very kind of you, Dr Charmliss, but we must not waste your money or your time with the gallant lady", offered Fishy with unintended but very slanderous ambiguity.

"Nonsense! What would you like" I said.

The men drew chairs and sat.

Warble appeared as if by telepathy.

"Gentlemen?" said the manager.

"Is it okay if I have a Stella?" said Hotcarp, looking towards Heldrew.

"I will have a pint of dry cider, please, Mr Warble"

Warble fetched the lads' drinks.

"I will put it on the Account, if that is appropriate, Colour Major Feng?" asked Warble. Arnoldina nodded.

Both men seemed a little embarrassed. Maybe they thought they were obtruding a tryst?

"We will have no more rough house, and definitely no more talk of rifles or training. We have all got to pull together. We will hang together, or we shall hang separately, boys", advised them Arnoldina.

"First of all, Colour Major Feng, we are men, not boys. And secondly we abhor violence, but we are Britons and we must look to the health and safety of our people. You are very welcome as Arnoldina Feng but not as a foreign occupier", confided Fishy.

Arnoldina sat impassive.

Heldrew shifted uneasily in his seat, and grated his throat.

"Tell me, Dr Charmliss. Do you fish or shoot?" invited Heldrew.

"They are both fine sports", I lied, "but I am a pathetic angler and I am not nearly as practiced a shot as you think I am. However, I think we should change the subject. The Colour Major is a vegan."

"We are most dreadfully sorry", said Heldrew, turning to Arnoldina. It was difficult to know whether he was sympathising with the foreign officer for her scruple or apologising for raising the subject of blood sports.

I stated "I am helping to organise a dormouse survey in Denbighshire with Bangor University. If you two are interested I will try to organise your joining the party. We will be able to discuss science, the law and other issues of mutual interest in a sympathetic setting."

I was trying to think on my feet. We were at some sort of impasse and I could see that things could get very nasty, especially for Arnoldina.

"We would be absolutely delighted!" averred Fishy, quickly, and with a an unaffected boyish smile. "Count me in!" agreed his friend.

"Very good, Gentlemen. We shall speak shortly. In the meantime I ask you to finish your drinks and return to your men. I must entertain the Major."

The lads enthusiastically did as bidden.

For our part, Arnoldina and I finished our meal and retired to my bedroom.

Arnoldina shut the door carefully and quietly. She closed the bathroom window and briefly checked the mattress and the furniture for any obvious devices. She settled back in her armchair and said:-

"There is no Bangor University in 78V, Charles. Bangor, Gwynedd itself does not exist. The rebels think you are a spy or saboteur inserted by British Special Forces."

"On the other hand I am equally eager to join your dormouse survey. They are such cute little creatures!"

"Do *you* think I am a spy or saboteur inserted by British Special Forces, Arnoldina?"

"Don't be ridiculous, Charles"

"Now I know you feel strong and youthful, but you are still a very sick man, Charles, and you need your sleep. If you wish I shall have a camp bed brought in and sleep in your room with you. I am after all a hired nurse, but you are not in imminent clinical danger. You are not a baby, and you are not afraid of ghosts, are you?"

"Of course not", I lied again.

"Very well. I will leave this gadget on your beside table with this flashlight. If you need me press the red button, or if you are able, walk to Room 2.13 and knock."

I was surprised that a 976-year-old (or was she 978?) would speak to an eighty-four-year- old professional man in such a condescending manner, but women are women the world over.

"I shall return at 0700 and we shall descend for breakfast. Good night, Charles"

"Good night, Arnoldina"

Arnoldina closed the door and locked it from the outside, I was not sure whether to keep me in or to keep others out.

CHAPTER SIX
BREAKFAST FOR DUCKS

There was a rap on the door at 0700 sharp.

Automatically and without thinking I turned the internal brass latch knob and opened the door, in my pyjamas.

Arnoldina stood outwith.

"Why did you lock me in?" I snapped at Arnoldina, abruptly and without greeting.

"I did no such thing. I locked intruders out, but you always had the internal brass knob to unlatch the door and escape. It is required by British fire regulations."

"Oh, yeah", I agreed stupidly.

"I am sorry, Arnoldina"

"I hope you are not this daft if you are interrogated by American intelligence", added the Major.

"Come in Arnoldina. I am just getting up. I overslept."

I stripped and showered as the Major sat flicking through a copy of Country Life that she had found somewhere.

"Before I forget, my eminently fuckable young man, there is no such thing as Denbighshire. The Welsh have not spoken Welsh for eight hundred years. The whole of North Wales constitutes the Semi-Palatinate of Angarn."

"Angarn? Isn't that in Russia", I asked.

"No, Sweden", answered Arnoldina, and continued:-.

"It says here that dormice start hibernation in mid-October and sleep for seven months. It is October 14th. The rebels think they 'know' that you are giving them some kind of coded signal and that they just have not received the right pad. They will check their DLBs pronto. I only hope there are none where we are going, and the SIS will think it is a primitive watchword being passed orally on account of the exigencies of the situation. The current predicament, Situation Raysboro, is highly unstable and the enemy will be using AI swiftly to determine the implications of the dormouse invitation."

"We are both in imminent danger of being arrested by Emfis [MFIS], and they are complete bastards, I guarantee it Charles."

"Who are Emfis?"

"The Magonian Federal Information Service, our equivalent of the CIA or SIS with a dash of the Gestapo."

"I have really fucked up, haven't I", I observed rather redundantly.

"Today, Charles, you need to get some fresh air and exercise. We are going to Belsize Park to feed the ducks, like the harmless old couple that we are."

"What, you mean London?" I asked quite seriously.

"This is the wrong time for drollery, Charles"

"You will never pass for old, Arnoldina"

"Oh, we really are the roué today, aren't we", commented Arnoldina with a nasty switch-on switch-off smirk. It was the first time I had seen a trace of malice in Arnoldina.

But she was right. My sheer incompetence would likely kill us both.

"What about breakfast?" I pleaded.

"Fuck breakfast. I'll give you a Venus Bar and a bottle of water, Charles. Put your togs on including your anorak and sack. Put your pouches in the sack. We may have to escape by road or rail. I will carry my doctor's bag, in case you need emergency medication, of course."

"You are talking to me as if I am an idiot", I griped.

"Charles, you're brilliant!"

"Our cover, for as long as it sustains, is that you are a semi-senile old man who rabbits on about dormice, even when they are unavailable, a former environmental scientist who says Bangor when he means Belfast."

"Which is all basically true, isn't it?" added Arnoldina wickedly.

"There are no dormice in Ireland, Arnoldina"

"I have no idea if that's true but its fucking irrelevant if it is. Anyway, there are sod all in Angarn. If we survive the day I will have a chat with Shrigley. He worked as a gerontologist, and we are both worried about your health. Which is also basically true, isn't it, Dear?"

"If you say so, Dina"

"I do say so"

"In the annals of war this is not even a footnote", I resumed. "You are panicking, and panic is the mother of defeat, whilst planning is the father of victory. Did they not teach you that in spy school?"

"I never went to spy school, Charles."

"No, and it shows", I answered, "anyway, Bangor and Belfast are easily confused: They are at opposite ends of the same railway."

"Yes, they are in Down, not in Angarn. Your luck won't last for ever, Charles. There is only so long we can keep pretending. See me outside the door to the rear car park at 0740 exactly. If anyone asks we are going shopping."

With which Arnoldina stormed out.

I did as bidden.

As if to add to the stress of this early morning rush sans breakfast Shrigley came out brandishing his mobile:-

"Hello, Chuck", he said cheerily. "Going hiking? Want a lift?"

He shone the gadget at his car. The car squeaked, flashed, and unlocked its doors.

"No, thanks, Pott. I'm waiting for my lady. We are going shopping."

"You don't waste time, you don't", chuckled Shrigley as he jauntily departed.

Arnoldina turned up on the dot.

We ambled into a pretty Victorian backstreet. There was a large chapel immediately on the right. It was garnished with notices and notice boards relating to its rôle as a community centre-cum-occasional place of worship. It was clear that the little estate had been developed as a unit by the same landlord. We were within metres of the river, and the riverbank may have accommodated a lead refinery, removed of course by Nazi airmen. The Magonians achieved what the Nazis and many others yearned for, the conquest of England, but fortunately the Magonians were not racist or extremists.

Soon we arrived at the splendid wrought iron gates of a compact but diverse Victorian municipal park. There was an ornate white-painted cast-iron canopied bandstand in the middle of a lawn, mature trees and fringing, unkept, rhododendron bushes, and not far beyond the bandstand was a lake with ducks. There was also a flock of Canada geese near the water, feral of course. We were within half a mile of both the Albion to the East and the main Hodgate shopping street to the North. Busy traffic was audible but the park seemed deserted.

As we were passing an especially sprawling and dense rhododendron bush on the left Arnoldina suddenly said:-

"Follow behind this bush, Charles. I want to show you a flower."

We went behind the bush. I could not see any flowers. After all, it was Autumn and rhododendrons bloom in May. Suddenly, Arnoldina turned and seized me, expertly operating the catch-release on the sack she let the load fall. She powerfully embraced me and pressed her lips to mine, dry and with no penetrative attempt. We squirmed together where we stood fully clothed. I suppose it was not the most romantic of clinches. She had pressed my head to hers, with her right hand powerfully applied to the back of my cranium.

She released her grip and our heads parted.

"Oh, Charles. I loved you from the minute I saw you lying there snoring with your head covered in blood. You are such a brave, kind man", Arnoldina gasped.

For my part I had loved Arnoldina from the moment she first had said "We are equals." No robot would have dared, whatever the intent of its programmers, and this was a very alluring living woman, alluring indeed.

I fumbled for the clasp of her police skirt. I could not operate it. I pulled the drape firmly downwards, and it followed with those ghastly underpants.

We feverishly stripped naked, and grasping Arnoldina I wrestled us to the ground and assumed mastery. Arnoldina was now flushed and panting as she gazed lovingly into my eyes from her supine position. Neurotically, I noted that there were none of the discarded syringes, needles, or soggy strands of used lavatory paper that I should have expected to find in such a place.

But I was happy beyond description. I felt myself engorge. I intromitted as gently as I was able. Arnoldina assisted me. I felt my glans pass the threshold. Arnoldina's pulsating muscles grasped it. I pumped and thrusted like an animal. I squirted the Seed of Life in such copious gouts that it drained from her vulva and inseminated the grass.

We embraced again and Arnoldina screamed and groaned ecstatically.

Presently I heard a rustle of leaves.

One of those old-fashioned English policemen stood above us, complete with silver numbers on his immaculate blue serge uniform, a holstered truncheon and a ridiculous domed helmet with a silver spike on top, the sort that drunken debutants used to knock off and steal.

"Is this man bothering you, Miss?" softly questioned this new apparition.

"No, it's okay, Officer. He's a patient. We will dress and move on."

"That is for me to decide, Miss", replied the policeman. "May I see your papers, please?"

I fumbled for the Registration Card in my anorak and from her uniform jacket Arnoldina retrieved I presume her Warrant Card.

We stood up naked, and handed the documents to the police officer.

He read them and handed them back.

"In future keep your clothes on in Belsize Park", remarked the officer.

"Yes, we shall, Sir. I am most dreadfully sorry", I grovelled.

"How old are you, Sir?" the officer asked me.

"I am eighty-four, Sir, and the lady is 976"

"You are not in the first flush of irrepressible youth, are you Sir?"

"No, I am not, Sir, and I shall be more responsible in future."

Arnoldina and I put our clothes back on and the policeman walked away.

When we reckoned him out of earshot we sniggered quietly like naughty teenagers. We joined hands and walked out of the bushes and onto the tarmacadamed path.

"Let's go and feed the ducks", invited Arnoldina with girlish charm.

"Sounds good to me", I replied.

After a couple of hundred metres of slow dally we arrived at an ornate iron bench by the ornamental lake. A platoon of ducks left the water and waddled up to us. They were of differential appearance and presumably were a mixture of males and females. But the presumable males had light mauve heads, not bottle green, and the feet of both sexes were black not orange in colour.

Arnoldina smiled as she gleefully distributed bread crumbs. To my great surprise a rat with sky-blue fur suddenly emerged from a drain at the lake's edge and made a bee-line for Arnoldina. The rat stood up and begged, his intense black eyes gazing unflinchingly into Arnoldina's as his long black whiskers twitched with comic anticipation. The ducks dressed back. Arnoldina took a small chocolate wafer from the doctor's bag on the bench beside her. She broke the chocolate biscuit and fed it to the rodent piecemeal. He had obviously been expecting her. It put me in mind of the Holy Eucharist that Arnoldina had officiated in my bedroom.

Unbidden I began silently to pray. "**My Holy Saviour**", I commenced:-

Defend and protect this good woman and her friend the rat and her avine congregants. Give them succour and delight in this World and the next. In this time of war, hazard and confusion, school us to help the weak, regardless of race or species and defend us from bigotry, especially the evil that issues from our own hearts and brains. Do this, only Lord and King, I beg you.

At length Arnoldina exhausted her supplies.

The ducks left for their lake. The rat ambled away, sniffing this and that invisible to human sense, and eventually found home.

"What about my Venus Bar?" I asked Arnoldina.

"Oh, Charles, my love. I forgot it. And your water. In the excitement of the morning I remembered the ducks and the rat but I forgot my Love. Charles, you may punish me."

"It is enough that you remembered your friends. Very often, I have not."

"Arnoldina, as I waited in the car park this morning Shrigley appeared and asked if I was going hiking and whether he could give me a lift. I replied that I was going shopping. Am I a liar, Arnoldina?"

"Oh, Charles, darling. You could never lie. I told you to say that. I am the liar!"

I stood and shouldered my sack.

"Pick up your bag and come with me", I ordered.

I led her out of the park onto the busy lunchtime shopping street, the Hodgate. There was the usual Mais and Spender and even a branch of James Mathews: Yes, even here in 78V. The street had shops, and some obviously expensive ones, sort of on flanking raised pedestrian platforms. I could not remember seeing the like elsewhere.

It put me in mind of a day trip I had taken to see an industrial monument at a place called Styal, just south of Manchester. It was 27 October 2017 and I was retired but not yet dead. I was in 80V. As I left I took a bus to, I think Alderley Edge to catch a train home. We passed slowly through Wilmslow, only a provincial small town and I was astonished to note that the High Street was lined with Continental jewellery dealers and other very expensive international luxury shops. Then I remembered that this was Premier League footballer country, and the heart of the Manchester stockbroker belt.

Arnoldina and I mounted a flight of steps from the sidewalk and strolled along the gallery. Then I found what I sought. It was an expensive jewellery store called White's with the legend "Est. 1787" engraved on an oak lintel above the door.

We entered.

A short, balding, Jewish-looking fellow stood alone behind the counter. If there was any security it must have been very discrete indeed, but I had got the impression there was very little crime or anti-social behavior in Congleholme.

"Do you have anything bearing the Congleholme mark?" I enquired.

"Sadly not, Sir. The Congleholme assay closed in 1967 and we only sell the very finest newly-made goods exclusively sourced from Great Britain or the Magonian Federation states. May I assist in another manner, Sir, Madam?"

"Yes, I would like to see a selection of two-carat diamond 22-carat gold engagement rings, please."

Arnoldina suddenly started to take interest in our little diversion.

"Yes, Sir"

The man took three out of his cabinet, opened the case lids and placed the rings on the glass display counter.

"I especially like the style of this one, but I wish to leave and discuss the rings with my intended", stated Arnoldina firmly but without fuss.

"Most certainly, Madam. I note from your uniform that you are a Magonian police officer. Would you like to take the rings to your quarters and examine them at leisure?"

"No, that would not be necessary, Sir. But I thank you for your offer and for the compliment of your confidence, Sir", Arnoldina replied to the shopkeeper.

"Thank you, Madam"

We walked out.

"We will walk along a little further and see if we can find a nice tea room or a bank", Arnoldina clarified.

I did not understand the relevancy of the latter. Surely Arnoldina did not intend to pay for the ring from her own funds?

Presently we found a magnificent Edwardian-style branch of the Hatton and Congleholme Banking Corporation Limited, and entered. The public hall echoed to many voices. The walls were of pink, white and gray Serendip marble shot through with gold. I had seen this wonder in the Geological Galleries of the London Natural History museum when I was a boy, but by the time I grew to manhood, in 80V of course, it had been quietly spirited to "a secret location." The tellers' positions were framed in mahogany. There was no visible security and I saw people leave bank notes loose on tables as they ducked out to answer queries elsewhere. A strange white mist hung around the ceiling. Previously I had only seen this effect in the Pantheon, St Peter's, and other large Italian buildings. Here it was doubtless something to do with the air-conditioning.

As we entered a slender young man in a frock coat and an opera hat said:-

"How can I assist today, Major and Sir?" and bowed at me.

"Can I have a private office for one hour only, and coffee and biscuits for two?" asked Arnoldina.

"Most certainly, Madam. May I add it to your account?"

Arnoldina nodded discretely.

The young man (remember: He may have been 206-years-old) snapped his fingers and a shorter older-looking fellow in a green uniform escorted us to a vacant office overlooking a car-park. This room was air-conditioned and had three clean leather or artificial leather cushioned business armchairs around a desk topped with safety glass over a figured-oak platen. There was a telephone and a laptop computer.

Arnoldina and I sat.

"Look, Charles. You must not do these things. I know you always mean well. It is not about the money. I can pay without hardship until you are able to reimburse me. I can even offer the ring to Treagh and his staff for requisition by the Magonian forces and compensation for me personally."

"I am a Nestorian Christian and there is no divorce in my community, though divorce is legal in China and in the Federation generally. Most importantly of all I am happily married to a kind and gentle husband who has loved and cared for me for more than seven hundred years, paying not for diamond rings but for much of the surgery that has kept me alive."

I began to weep, whether out of self-pity or out of shame or out of sympathy for the predicament of this selfless woman you must judge.

"Look, Charles, it is like this"

"I was a postulant in a nunnery, a convent, somewhere on the remote steppe. One windy afternoon, a dusty army of a thousand men shambled in behind their lord, a great fat man on a mighty white horse."

"When was this?" I interrupted.

Arnoldina paused her narrative for a few moments.

"Around 1140AD. Stephen and Matilda. The Anarchy. Is that right?"

"I don't know"

"He ordered us taken into the storm beyond the wall, and we were stripped. Unspeakable things were done to the Abbess. You can work out how old I was."

"About a hundred", I guessed.

"They examined us to see which of us were virgins. They took us back into the compound. They kept our clothes and tossed them onto a mule cart. The rest they left to the wind and the wolves. The men raided the kitchens and the cellars looking for drink, and they drained the well with their thirsts. Then they auctioned each of us in turn to the highest bidder. The lord seized and redistributed the payments. I was purchased by a soldier. He proved a good husband, kind and generous, my husband forever. He had then and subsequently no other woman."

I did not for one moment doubt the truthful intent of Arnoldina but amid the more trifling ambiguities of this bleak narrative I was finding it difficult to reconcile the chronology with the surgery, and the technical advancements which permitted the latter. I realised that Arnoldina would have been conscious throughout most or all of these procedures, probably assisted the surgeons with fine-tuning, and may even have learned a few of her own skills from these experiences.

"Arnoldina, I am truly, desperately sorry for the things I have done", I snivelled.

"And if your husband ever flies in I shall go down on my knees before him and beg his forgiveness."

"Don't you dare", said Arnoldina with angry severity.

Then someone knocked at the door.

It was the little green man with the coffee.

CHAPTER SEVEN
THE KOREAN CHARGÉ-D'AFFAIRES

Arnoldina and I slept in the double bed in my room that night.

We did not bother with night-clothes.

I hated the uniform she wore. Not for any political or military reason, but because it was so very unflattering and was meant to be.

I longed to go out and buy her a tweed suit and a nice floral cotton dress and a string of matronly pearls to set it all off. But one had to be careful with vegans. She would say even oysters have a Right to Life, and she would of course be correct.

But I had no access to my independent funds here in 78V. My Wife would have had the lioness' share of my estate, quite rightly, and Manchester University would have an endowment to support a postgraduate degree and build a new block, the Charmliss Block, at my old hostel. My agent would get five thousand sterling in recognition and he would administer rights on behalf of my Wife.

I could not of course access my pensions from here and I needed some sort of job and an account separate from anything to do with the Occupier. In any case my pensions, state and private, would have been voided, except in so far as my Widow retained rights.

I was always a morning man.

I rolled over and kissed the ineffable loveliness awake.

"Arnoldina, will you bear my son or daughter?" I asked tenderly.

"I am here to serve", replied Arnoldina.

I parted her legs. I plunged deeply. I knelt and held her ankles and plunged. I donated the Seed of Life as all men should, delivered to its rightful place. Arnoldina moaned and flushed. It was done.

We showered and dressed and went down to breakfast. It was a buffet today and we helped ourselves. I was looking forward to the Full English course but at the start we began with cereal, myself with shredded wheat and muesli soaked in full-fat milk. Well why not? What was the use in thinking of my heart and arteries here? Arnoldina had rice crispies and honey with a little sugar-free oat milk.

"Isn't honey an animal product", I teased.

"We feed sugar to the bees so that they produce excess honey. They are happy to work and we encourage them, but too much honey would cause fungus and the bees would suffer", Arnoldina explained po-facedly.

It was at that juncture that the young man I had seen in Magonian uniform nursing his pint and whacking his cane on the radiator valance materialised in front of us and gave the Colour Major a desultory salute.

"I am Commander First Class Eugen Ionescu of the Magonian Navy, seconded to Tourist Services. I am glad you have decided to stay in Area A6 as long as you will, Dr Charmliss, and I am dreadfully sorry to interrupt your breakfast with Colour Major Feng. This is incredibly unfortunate and if you permit I will personally reward you and the Major with a private champagne hot breakfast later today. I have orders to ask you if you will to escort me to an audience with High Suzerain His Excellency Major-General Lord Manville Treagh at the Presidium. Lord Treagh is a very sympathetic man and won't detain you longer than is strictly necessary. I have a statocar hovering outside and the journey is fully air-conditioned and won't take more than ten minutes. Lord Treagh has expressly ordered that I convey his apologies."

As I have previously stated, I am not and never was, a military man despite my brief RN commission back in 80V, but I think that a Colour Major and a Commander are of approximately equal rank.

"May I bring the British chargé-d'affaire?" I answered.

"Sadly not, Dr Charmliss. There isn't time to summon him."

I rose and escorted Ionescu to the car. I had noticed two or three of these things when I was speaking with Mick on the barbican. They kind of hovered ten inches above the road and seemed to be very manoeuvrable at speed. I did not understand the technology involved but recollected that back in 80V the Nazis had experimented with 'flying saucers' that locally cancelled gravity using some kind of gyroscopic principle. Clearly, the technology did not exist to make such transport practicable at that time.

For all the world the contraption looked like an old DeLorean without wheels. It emitted a quiet but irritating high-pitched hum. A gull-wing door opened. There was a driver. I stepped in and the thing bounced unctuously. Ionescu followed and the same sickening motion ensued.

"Sedately please, Igor" Ionescu told the driver.

Igor flicked a switch and put his hands in his pockets.

The vehicle whined and took off down the street turning into the Hodgate traffic without pause or further human action, and it continued until we arrived at the old Assize Court buildings, an imposing Gothic complex, where it stopped before the porte-cochère, turned off its motor to settle on the tarmac, and opened all four gull-wing doors. If I recollect correctly, the Assize was a squat, red sandstone, Neo-Classical structure in the Chester of 80V.

The three of us climbed out. At no time were seat belts offered or requested.

We entered the echoing antechamber and marched through to the Presence Room. This was a vast unsupported and very bare oak-panelled room a bit like the St Pancras Hotel is imagined to consist of. I recollected the Enormous Room of the eponymous E E Cummings [Dreyer insists] Great War memoir.

There was an enormous teak desk with a bronze-fastened glass top in turn fitted with one of those thin leather surfaces that the Victorians designed to spread steel nibs without encouraging them to score the paper.

On the left was a large teak humidor, and on the right, from the viewpoint of the Suzerain, was a brass pen holder accommodating no pens but mounting what appeared to be a Somali horse-warrior complete with keffiyeh and holding a lance erect. "That thing could take your eye out if you stumbled", I surmised gloomily.

Behind the desk sat a consonantly enormous black man, tall and broad with a very black, somewhat chubby face. He could have been Ghanaian or more likely Nigerian. He looked very like the late Idi Amin, the self-anointed "King of Scotland." This man however evidently worked out, for beneath his sub-cutaneous fat his tight black cotton uniform betrayed a powerful musculature. He would make an excellent Othello in any production, I thought, and cause a sensation naked with blonde Desdemona in the death scene.

Ionescu parked himself behind the black about two metres diagonally to the Suzerain's right shoulder.

Beneath a window maybe ten metres to my right a third man, perhaps an NCO, beavered away at paperwork. I could detect a telephone or a computer nowhere.

Three chairs had been placed at random positions in front of the Suzerain's desk.

The black rose slowly. I guessed he was 57, but he could have been older: This was 78V and that could have been *much* older.

Proffering his right hand he said:-

"Good morning, Dr Charmliss. I am war-substantive Major-General Manville Treagh, High Suzerain of the Magonian Federation for West England and Wales and Director Emeritus of the Occidental Study Institute."

He seemed to pronounce his name "tree."

"I am desperately sorry to have interrupted your breakfast and more especially your convalescence."

"I am in a pickle and I should be grateful if you can help."

"I am told that you are the only man in the sector who can speak Korean. Is that right?"

There was a distinct West Indian twang.

"I do not know, Excellency. I speak Korean fluently. My Wife in the old world was Korean. I also speak a smattering of Japanese and Spanish."

"Yes, fascinating. Quantum theory and all that. We will have a proper talk about that later, perhaps in the gunroom over a straight malt. But if you will pardon me I do not want to seem rude, but we have to press on. The Korean chargé-d'affaire is coming at 1000 hours. He will only speak in Korean, I don't know if he is scared he will say the wrong thing, or as I suspect it is a *ruse diplomatique.* But there you have it Charmliss. Will you interpret for us?"

"I would be honoured to, Sir. What is the topic?"

"We do not know. I was only told at 0545 hours. The Anglo-Americans are big on the Shetlands right now. We don't know why though there a plenty of theories. But I can't do anything about it. They are in the Scottish sector under Von Karper."

I checked my watch. It was 0943. Treagh turned his attention to a sheaf of about six A4 sheets held together with a corner staple. He did not seem to be able to concentrate. He now ignored me. He took an oversized Sauloff havana from his humidor.

"I will offer you one later, Charmliss. I cannot actually light up. My doctor's would bollock me beyond the sunset."

Treagh seemed nervous. His hands trembled as he turned the leaves though he tried to conceal it. I marvelled that a Major-General with unchallengeable authority would be nervous. I could not imagine that MacArthur was like this with the Japanese.

He cut the mouth end and sucked his dummy and fanned it up and down in his fingers, replaced it between his teeth and resumed the up and down arcing risibly like a latter-day Groucho Marx. The action could have been interpreted as suggestive or insulting in polite circles. I could not envision MacArthur doing similar with his corn-cob pipe. Treagh started to bite the the nail of his right pinkie but quickly checked himself.

Shortly there was subdued shouting and shuffling near the grand door, and the chargé-d'affaire strode in with two aides.

Treagh turned awkwardly to Ionescu and said:-

"Eugen, can you get another chair?"

Eugen stood to attention with his hands behind his back not shifting and looking straight ahead. "Eugene Ionescu", I thought idly, "Military interviews are not so much Theatre of the Absurd as theatre of the fucking ridiculous." But in my experience that is true for any convocation involving senior executives.

"Edmonson, get another chair!", Ionescu bawled in his perfect Naval manner.

Park Baek Hyeon, the Korean chargé-d'affaires was ushered in with two younger aides. Park was a slight man with a scraggy moustache. The three men shook hands and bowed to Treagh, as he stood and bowed back. The three Koreans were wearing Naval camouflage uniforms with a lapel-less collar and those stupid chin-strapped hats which look like frogmen's helmets with swept-up peaks in the style that was favoured by some Nazis and all Latin American dictatorships of the Twentieth-Century.

The men sat with me to the side.

Diplomatic introductions followed with me translating Korean-English-Korean for each party.

Ionescu was also introduced and he went round shaking hands from a standing position. At that juncture I stood and bowed to the Koreans.

Park Baek Hyeon opened:-

"I appear with plenipotentiary powers in regard to Great Britain and Ireland on behalf of the Ithaca Coalition. I have the honour to assist Your Excellency."

Park then stepped forward and handed a folder of papers, perhaps Credentials, to Treagh.

Treagh handed them back to Ionescu unopened.

"Thank you, Major-General Park. How may I assist you?"

"Grant to the Ithaca Coalition a 48-month sovereign lease of The Shetland Islands effective 1 November 2036 at 0000 hours."

"What is the consideration, Major-General Park."

"The Government of the Republic of Korea grants a 36-month sovereign lease of the Cypriot and British parts of Cyprus plus Lebanon to the Magonian Federation."

"Why do you not apply to Major-General Von Karper?" responded Treagh.

A slight hesitation.

"Major-General Von Karper is on leave", answered Park, "and you are the senior of the three." I interpolated that I assumed Park meant of the three Great Britain High Suzerains.

Treagh sat back in his chair.

"I shall refer your proposals to my seniors by diplomatic telegraph", stated Treagh for the Koreans, "in the meantime, gentlemen, [and he meant only the Korean delegation] would you like to dine with me in the gunroom here at 1830 today?"

"We should be most honoured, Excellency" replied Park as the men stood.

They shook hands with the High Suzerain and turned to leave. I walked to leave behind them.

"Dr Charmliss!", bawled Treagh, "please resume your seat."

CHAPTER EIGHT
THREE INTERVIEWS

"I most sincerely thank you for your timely services, Dr Charmliss", said the High Suzerain with unexpected humility.

"It was a great honour, Your Excellency."

"Yes: you are correct to address me as 'Sir' or 'Excellency'. I much prefer those styles to 'Major-General Treagh' or 'High Suzerain' or whatever."

"Secondly, Dr Charmliss..."

"Please call me Chuck", I interrupted.

"No, it will be 'Dr Charmliss' or simply 'Charmliss':- I am obliged by Magonian legislation to say these things and I apologise for any offence in advance."

"I have war-substantive summary sovereign powers in all dealings with non-Magonians within the West England and Wales sector. The Magonian Federation is signatory to no UN or Geneva protocol but it endeavours to exceed the standards of those treaties at all times..."

Treagh paused, not I thought for effect, but to gather breath.

"In theory, I could have you hung in irons or drawn and quartered, French or English style, if I thought it would assist war aims or bring the Federation into better repute. On the other hand, if you refuse any request of mine, no matter how insolently, you walk out of here a free man, and without prejudice. Do you understand what I have said, Dr Charmliss?"

"Thoroughly, Your Excellency"

"Good!"

"Are you willing to undertake further work should such arise?" added the Suzerain.

"I am most eager, Sir"

"Good!"

"Do you have any questions before we compile your package, Dr Charmliss?"

"I have a request if I may"

"I am obliged and delighted to be of service", announced the Suzerain, opening his humidor and throwing a Sauloff and a plastic lighter across the desk to me. I pocketed the Sauloff. I stopped smoking many years ago, but I would show the souvenir to Arnoldina.

"I wish you to grant Colour Major Feng immediate retirement on full pension, with leave to enter into a Civil Partnership with me."

The suzerain fell back in his chair with open-mouthed astonishment and stared at me. Ionescu stared straight ahead expressionless Navy-style, hands linked behind back. Edmonson continued with paperwork.

Treagh slowly turned awkwardly in his non-swivel chair, halfway to face Ionescu.

"Do you have any observations, Commander First-Class Eugene Ionescu?"

"None, Sir!" shouted Eugen staring fixedly ahead.

Treagh turned back to face me.

"Dr Charmliss, your remarkable and impertinent request is determinately refused. I should tell you in fairness that your liaison with the Colour Major is the subject of extensive adverse comment in civil and military circles, though you have only been present a matter of days. Colour Major Feng is a serving Magonian officer in wartime and a married woman."

"It is for the latter reason and the lady's scruples that I sought a Civil Partnership, Sir."

"I shall terminate this matter by affirming that the officer in question shall not be approached or disciplined in regard to this matter. This matter is closed."

"Did you get all that, Chief Petty Officer Edmonson?"

"Yes, Sir"

"Enter it in the log"

"Yes, Sir"

Treagh retrieved his lighter and lit up.

I rose to leave.

"Sit down!" ordered Treagh.

Treagh sat regarding me and drawing on his fine smoke. I was desperate for a pee. The perfumed miasma brought back my longing for nicotine, though any alkaloid, including strychnine, would have been most welcome.

This charade continued for what seemed an hour, though it was probably less than sixty seconds.

At length Treagh asked:-

"How old are you, Dr Charmliss?"

"Eighty-Four, Sir"

Treagh placed his smoke delicately in the brass trough of his pen holder.

He again turned awkwardly, and I thought now arthritically to Ionescu:-

"Commander First-Class, how old are you?" asked the Suzerain.

"Ninety-Seven, Sir"

The heavy black slowly resumed his pose facing me.

"Very cleaver man, Ionescu", Treagh confided, "He speaks eleven languages, you know."

Turning again to Ionescu, Treagh shouted:-

"You are a very clever man, aren't you, Ionescu?"

"I couldn't say, Sir"

"Tell Dr Charmliss what your job was before the War"

"I was Emeritus Professor of Comparative Semiotic at the University of Hârsova, Sir."

Treagh slowly, it seemed painfully, turned once again to face me.

"Let me show you something, Charmliss"

Treagh rose and facing me he started to fumble with the buckle clasp of his belt. I wondered what I was about to behold.

Treagh removed his uniform jacket and put it on the desk in front of me. He then started to undo the bottom buttons of his shirt, and once completing the whole row removed his shirt and placed it on top of the jacket, carelessly but not roughly.

He was indeed a fine man, muscled with a cover of subcutaneous fat that did nothing to diminish his statuesque appearance.

Treagh turned and sat on the edge of his desk with his back to me.

"Tell me, Dr Charmliss, what do you see?"

There were high and puckered, but long healed, welts and ridges disfiguring the back's whole surface and anastomosing like perhaps a siphonodendron colony fresh-hacked of the living limestone, or maybe a tassel of cotton cord dishevelled upon a counter.

"It looks almost as if you have been flogged", I remarked.

"'almost'...English..."almost'", Treagh spat with a sotto voce contempt.

"I was born in 1768 on Barbados. My Mother was a slave. I do not know who my father was. I was a slave son of a slave. My owners were Cornish Muggletonians. By the lights of the time they were good masters. Were your folk good masters, Charmliss?"

"I do not know, Sir, but I am today a Quaker, and the Quakers freed their slaves in 1734."

"By the age of 24 I had risen to be the chargehand of other cane slaves. One day the plot overseer, a free white, came to me and said 'cut the plot fresh, Mr Treagh's customers demand the finest white sugar, not burnt sugar, muscovado or caramel'."

"'Master,'" I replied, "'Let me burn the brash. The plot is infested with snakes and spiders and men will die in agony'."

"'I shall fetch Mr Treagh', promised the overseer. He returned later with the owner. The under-niggers were ordered to seize me, the very men I sought to protect, and they did. Mr Barratt, the plot overseer gave me 72 lashes of a loaded cat-o'-nine-tails."

"I am unspeakably, abjectly sorry, High Suzerain Manville Treagh", I said, "corporal punishment is a great obscenity. I have thought so since boyhood."

"Why are you sorry, Quaker, did you sanction my flogging?", Treagh asked, I thought with intentional ambiguity.

Treagh replaced his jacket but not his shirt. Where is the soldier or sailor who will tell an absolute suzerain that he is in a state of undress?

"Chief Petty Officer Edmonson, is the corpus available yet?" shouted Treagh.

"Yes, Sir"

"Bring it here"

Edmonson brought one of those A4 size padded plastic boxes of the type they sold as music-cassette magazines so many years ago. Snugly fitted was a charger lead for a mobile; the modern smartphone itself; a full transcript of proceedings from when the Koreans entered until "Did you get all that..."; a mysterious sealed brown envelope of approximately A4 size; an unsealed white envelope of A5 size; my UK Passport and a Magonian 'Licence'.

Ionescu came round to help Edmonson check for completeness as they unloaded each document and loaded them back again, leaving the Licence on the desk in front of Treagh.

As the sealed A4 envelope was unloaded and reloaded, Edmonson shouted theatrically "Sealed Envelope: Unknown Content; - Sir!" presumably at Ionescu.

Treagh studied the Licence. Ionescu had returned to his station.

Presently, Treagh motioned back with his right arm and said:-

"Commander First-Class, your pen if you please."

Ionescu took what looked like a 22-carat gold Hockley fountain pen from an inside uniform jacket pocket and handed it to Treagh.

I could make out that Treagh wrote something on the Licence and then signed it at the bottom. He replaced the cap on the gold pen and placed the instrument on the desk surface, not the penholder. I presume Ionescu retrieved it later.

Treagh called Edmonson and gave him the Licence. Edmonson folded the document in half. Edmonson put it in the white envelope, sealed the same and put the envelope in the case. The CPO then latched the case lid and stepped away.

Treagh pushed the case toward me with the remark:-

"That will be all today, Dr Charmliss. Please be discrete. The Commander will escort you to your billet."

Ionescu stepped forward smartly. I lifted the black cushioned document case. I followed Ionescu from the premises and we returned to the Albion Hotel.

We arrived and Ionescu escorted me to my room where I placed the case on a table and Ionescu took me to a private function room.

Arnoldina was already seated at a table for two with flowers.

"I am sorry, your honours, but it is a little late for breakfast. I have arranged for you to have a four-course dinner with the complements of the Presidium. I will purchase the champaign breakfast at some near date."

"Thank you, Commander Ionescu", I said.

"I tried to get you retirement on full pension", I remarked to Arnoldina

"You are a cunt", replied Arnoldina with seeming uninterest.

I was astonished beyond all confusion. Had I heard right?

Anger welled within me.

"Do not ever do that again. Never insult me in front of an officer or anyone else. Never use that word. It is still illegal."

Ionescu seemed wholly discombobulated.

He left quickly and shut the door completely but quietly.

We completed the meal briskly and in silence. Arnoldina avoided my gaze and appeared to be sulking. She rose and flounced out, slamming the door behind her.

By the time I got to my room Arnoldina was sitting up in my bed, naked and reading the Country Life again. I climbed in beside her, still wearing my street dress of pseudo-combat camouflage strip.

I knelt on the bed beside her.

I took each of her nipples between thumb and forefinger and gently pulled. She did not tumate.

"These shall nurture and nutrify our darling child", I forecast.

I released her teats and her lovely dugs fell with a bounce.

"Womanhood has its peculiar function and estate", spoke Arnoldina.

"The work of a man differs. A man must probe, explore, improve and correct. Ask any explorer, or engineer, male or female. Even any common driver or pilot. You must have known these things from your days in science and technical education", Arnoldina added and continued:-

"How can you grow your son to manhood in firm and kindly love, caress his soul and furnish his mind, if you cannot even control your woman?"

"It is not about control or coercion", I replied.

"Go to the bathroom. Have a good piss and defecate if you are able. Briefly shower and dry yourself", I commanded.

Arnoldina obeyed closing the door.

I rang Warble and asked him to bring me extra towels. He did so immediately.

I sat on the edge of the bed, still in my fatigues.

Arnoldina emerged naked from her ablutions and stood before me.

"Do you intend to punish me, Charles?" the loveliness queried with a severe quizzicality.

"I do not. But I may correct you if it is to your benefit or mine."

"Are you going to use your belt or some other instrument?"

"Arnoldina, I would never whip any man or woman, or even an animal."

I placed one of Warble's bath towels over my lap.

"Come and lie tummy downwards across my knees, Arnoldina. Make yourself as comfy as you can."

Arnoldina complied.

My left hand gathered her wrists to her sacrum, where I took care to set a finger gently against her right-hand ulnar artery.

"I love you, Arnoldina. I love you indescribably. I love you more than I have ever loved before. Open your legs just a little."

She had just showered of course but I could see that the whole of her body was flushing. Her pulse beat very rapidly according to the ulnar artery. For a moment I thought the machinery might give out.

"I love you too, Charles", Arnoldina squeaked, beginning to cry a little.

I inserted the index and middle fingers of my right hand, parting the labia and causing Arnoldina's clitoris to move proud of its hood. The thumb I placed upon her anus as delicately as such a proceeding would allow.

I squeezed a little.

"Oh, don't, Charles, please", Arnoldina gasped.

My Holy Saviour, give this woman a clean mouth, a clean mind and a clean soul, purged of all sin, obedient and serene in the care of this man who loves her and wishes, if he can under God, to beget her second child in Your Holy Image, a child who shall live straighter, better and more healthily than his father. For this means I hold her Holy Portal of Life in trust for You. Let my correction of her will and spirit, if any should be necessary, be complete, condign and not excessive.

I softly said.

"Arnoldina, when you think back over the last few days, do you think that you could have done anything better?" I asked.

Arnoldina was sighing and moaning so I paused the massage.

"I think I could have been more tactful to those young men. I do not resile but I think I should have been more considerate of their feelings."

"We men have fragile egos, Arnoldina. If you are to lead, you must deploy your powerful charm, not exhort or debate."

"Is there anything else?" I asked.

"That policeman who reproved us behind the rhododendron bush. I wondered if he would fuck better than you."

"Dear Arnoldina, do not compare men. They are all the same, I know, but they differ widely, and they are individuals with their own attributes, strengths and weaknesses, some are good some are evil, some are clement and some are cruel, most mix all these qualities and more."

On that note I gently retrieved my right hand. My right shoulder is dislocated and was weak and painful in 80V, especially as I lifted my sack. Notwithstanding, I had had no trouble with it since my death.

I brought down twenty-four rapid blows with the flat of my right hand, twelve for each buttock and then I stopped.

I noticed that Arnoldina's "heart" rate fell precipitately after the first blow.

My hand was hot, and Arnoldina's yellow bottom was flushed red. She wept abandonedly. I doubted that she felt the physical pain that would have afflicted anyone in 80V, but her turmoil of mind and spirit would have been mighty.

I took her in my arms. She composed herself a little. She embraced me strongly wrapping her arms around my shoulders. I felt her teats harden, even though I was wearing a cotton combat blouse.

"Thank you, Charles", she said delightfully.

"I feel purged of my arrogance, lust and malice"

"That is all I wanted for you, and I salute your courage, your love and your trust. I shall never betray you, Arnoldina. If I hurt you I had too. We shall never do this again, unless you need it and want it. Confession is for the Lord."

"Do you mean Lord Belsize or Lord Nugent?" Arnoldina said wickedly. I laughed and redoubled the strength of my cuddle, moving her to and fro like a favorite teddy toy. We kissed. To my astonishment my right arm and shoulder started hurting again. They had not since well before the incident at the gibbet.

We were soaked through with sweat and bodily fluids. Warble's towels were soaked. I wondered what the chambermaid would think. I wondered what she would tell her employer.

We showered together. We kissed beneath the warm clean stream. We had Sacred Union.

CHAPTER NINE
A BOX OF POWERS

I had never begat a child in 80V. Before diabetes set in, I could do the deed well enough, but I only ever inseminated the one woman, my Wife. My Wife for her part, had suffered a hysterectomy before we met.

I was greatly looking forward to my child, and my consummation as a man.

But my testicles had never descended properly and I doubted my fertility. It was also the case that my girlfriend, though very willing, was nearly a thousand years old and had the one child born in the days of Elizabeth the First.

Arnoldina had retired to her room the previous night. I do not think she was still sulking. I just think she needed some uninterrupted sleep.

I had spent much of the night digesting the contents of Treagh's "diplomatic case."

I gave priority to reading the "Licence." The document, an ordinary laser-printed sheet of A4 was headed "LICENCE OF SUPERINTENDENCE" and stated *inter alia* "The bearer, if CHARLES EDWARD CHARMLISS, has full plenipotentiary powers to remove, confine or dispose any non-Magonian good or person within Sector B77bCHE of the West England and Wales Area of Great Britain, subject to the Control and Authority of MANVILLE DENZIL WILSON TREAGH, High Suzerain of the said Command or his lawful successors or surrogates until 1 January 2040." The Date was interpolated in Treagh's handwriting and Treagh had signed the document at the bottom. Incorporated on the face of the document, which was on high-quality, water-resistant paper was an unflattering photograph of myself, my right thumbprint, a QR code, and a microchip. I did not know the content of the chip, but I suspected DNA profiles. There were printed contact details for the Presidium at Congleholme.

This was power indeed and had to be used with discretion. I would have to create a high-definition computer scan and print copies if I could obtain the requisite resources. I wondered how many others had these devolved powers, and in particular how many British.

I next wished to satisfy my curiosity about the big sealed envelope. Using a steak knife out of my sack I eased the sticky seal apart, a trick I had learnt in the old days when the practice of the IRA was to send letter bombs to suspected Government spies.

I poured the contents onto the table. I counted one thousand one-thousand-crown bills. I estimated that all of this was around £100000 sterling in old money. I stuffed it back in the envelope and shoved the envelope under the mattress.

I noted also that there was a Hatton and Congleholme Visa debit card concealed in the mobile case. It had not been adverted to in Treagh's office, and I did not know how much was in the account, if anything.

I checked the list of numbers on the mobile. They meant little to me, but I recognised the telephone number of the Suzerain's office. I could not make sense of the apps, and gave up. I plugged the charger into a wall socket, and connected the mobile to it.

I wondered what to do with the case itself. I decided to place it in the left bottom draw of the wardrobe, under spare blankets, until I could think of something better. The Licence I zipped into an inside pocket of my camo anorak, with the debit card.

Around 0700 I heard a knock at the door. I thought it was Arnoldina, or conceivably Ionescu. I bawled "Come In!" The knocker tried the door handle and I realised Arnoldina had locked me in for my safety. I turned the internal brass knob.

Surprisingly, it was Shrigley, who stood outwith.

"Come in Shrigley. How can I help?"

"Professor Terring is giving a digital slide slow about voting reform in the Library at 1900 tonight."

I had no idea who Terring was, I hated politics and had no intention of wasting good fucking time.

"I am sorry, Pott, I know nothing about it, and have other plans for the evening."

"I think you rather ought attend", said Shrigley, in an unpleasant polite tone of the minatory that I had last heard in the St Ermin's Hotel in the bad old days of the early Eighties.

"Very well, Pott. I have no idea where the Library is. Can you give me a lift?"

"See me in the car park at 1830", demanded Shrigley with no "please" or "thank you, Dr Charmliss" or "sorry to spoil your evening" or even anything ruder.

"How about removing your cap in the presence of a gentleman?" I responded testily.

Shrigley was already leaving and pretended not to hear.

I put the anorak on and went next door, Room 2.14, Arnoldina's room, and knocked. Arnoldina answered in a very fetching powder blue silk nighty with a big light pink pussy cat bow about the neck, some little better than the ghastly policewoman's outfit. She threw her arms around me and kissed deeply.

She stood back with a broad smile and said:-

"How is my brave, kind, delicious Charles this fine morning, Big Ears Bunny Rabbit!" a little over the top you may think. And she a vegan.

I quickly relieved her of the nightdress and resumed our close embrace, she holding me gently about the neck as she stood on tiptoe: Me with my left hand on her smooth left buttock.

After a good snog I patted her bottom, and stood back.

"There is your 'insult' for today!" I jested.

"Oh, Charles. I got what I needed and I shall put it to good use. I also promise that we shall do it again whenever the medicine is called for!"

As she turned to dress I noted that both buttocks were a deeply livid purple.

"After we have had our breakfast, Arnoldina, we will walk round to Eugen's billet and you can apologise to him for your disgraceful behavior yesterday."

I had looked it up on the mobile: 4 Albion Place.

"That is a good idea, Darling, but we will probably see him in the bar at breakfast."

We descended in the lift.

As we arrived in the bar many of the regulars were also having breakfast, as were some new guests we had not seen before.

Warble showed us to our table.

Presently, Ionescu sauntered up with his standard Tourist Service grin.

"Everything in order, Charmliss?"

"Everything, thank you, Commander and Good Morning. By the way, thank you for helping me out yesterday."

"It is nothing, Sir, I am pleased I could assist."

Ionescu turned slightly to face Arnoldina. He bowed slightly in the Eastern European way.

"May I say you look more radiant than ever, Colour Major Feng!"

"Thank you, Eugen, and I want to apologise for my foul language and attitude yesterday. I should know better at my age!"

Ionescu said nothing. He stood and smirked. He briefly covered his eyes, then his ears in simulation of a wise monkey, and walked on. Had the ears of the thin hotel walls heard the blows?

"I want to try whatever you have this morning, Arnoldina", I declared.

"I am going to have black coffee without sugar; shredded wheat and muesli with unsugared oat drink; and then croissants made with sesame oil filled with orange and lemon marmalade."

"Sounds great!" I lied.

"Arnoldina, I am going out on business this evening and possibly won't return until the small hours."

"Charles, take extreme care. I wish you carried a pistol. Come back to me my Darling."

"I will do my best Arnoldina, Angel"

Arnoldina ordered for us both. It was not a buffet day. We ate and drank, left together and returned to our separate but adjacent rooms.

I rang the number for Treagh using the mobile, which now reported 100% charge.

"MacKinnon", answered the voice at the other end.

"Good Morning, I am Charles Charmliss. Please assign me an office near to the High Suzerain with a microcomputer and a laser printer as soon as practicable."

"Good Morning, Dr Charmliss. We were expecting you to ring. I am Seargent Major Edward MacKinnon of Presidium Logistics. We have got B45.8 which is a couple of corridors from Lord Treagh's office on the same floor and which has the outfit you specify, but we would need to move you within three months, and the office won't be available until 1600 hours today."

"That is excellent", I responded, "I will arrive after 1600 but possibly not until the small hours tomorrow."

"That's fine, Dr Charmliss. The night staff will sign you in, and take care of your needs."

"Thank you, Seargent Major MacKinnon", I responded, and rang off.

I took twenty thousand-crown bills from the envelope and stuffed them into a tit-pocket of my anorak. I went window shopping. I went into the bank Arnoldina and I had had the coffee in was it yesterday? Was it a couple of days ago? It was all becoming a blur, if you will forgive the cliché.

I inserted the card in an ATM and discovered a credit of exactly 100000 crowns. I withdraw the card and replaced it in my secure pocket.

It was time to try a little experiment. I would return to my billet, remove the money envelope from under the bed along with my British passport and take them to the bank to deposit the cash in a new account.

Within 45 minutes I was back on the threshold of the bank. I approached the fellow in the opera hat and tails.

"May I see the manager, please", I asked him.

"I am very sorry, Sir, but you will need to ask a teller to arrange an appointment with one of the executive staff. They will action your requirements, or refer the matter to the Manager for further management."

It was reassuring to know that the British bullshit mechanism was fully alive and operational at least within these hallowed halls, and at least to the detriment of British citizens.

"Situation Raysboro", I said.

"What?" queried the doorman.

"Situation Raysboro", I repeated with emphasis.

"Oh...Yes Sir." The doorman called over his deputy and he himself rang someone with his mobile.

Presently, a security man complete with walky-talky and peaked cap turned up.

"Can we go to your office?" I asked this security man.

"Follow me, Sir"

His office proved to be little more than a cubby-hole. Sheets of A4 and holiday photos covered the wall. The atmosphere was vaguely fuggy, but smelt mostly of fart and instant coffee.

I removed both the passport and the Licence and placed them on his desk. The security man studied both documents with a quizzical frown. I was becoming unsure of his literacy. Presently, he rang someone on the internal landline, and I took care immediately to seize back the documents.

The man rang off and said:-

"Follow me, Sir"

We entered an elevator and rose at high speed to a sickening jolt on some upper floor.

"Follow me, Sir"

The security man entered a plush office with a view of the Hodgate without knocking.

"Situation Raysboro", announced the security man and promptly left without other ado.

The Branch Manager sat back in his black leather swivel chair behind a huge polished mahogany desk. Somehow the room smelt of cigarette smoke and I noticed a little gray ash on the carpet. He studied me quizzically. I use that word too much in this report, but no other seems adequately to fit the behaviour of many of the perplexed denizens of my new world. I was not invited to sit.

"How can I help you?" said the manager after some delay.

"Is the Hatton and Congleholme still under British management?" I enquired.

"It most certainly is, Sir", the 'manager' announced proudly but I thought with a trace of the defensive.

"I wish to deposit 980,000 crowns cash in your preferential 4.5% instant access card and cheque account please. I shall need to open such an account now."

"I am very sorry, Sir, but British money-laundering regulations still in force limit such deposits to 18000 crowns. And in any case we need 72 hours' notice to open an account."

I kept a tight hold on the brown envelope, but took out my British passport and handed it to him.

"I do not need to read this, because the regulations apply to British citizens", stated the 'manager'. I did not feel either the urge or the necessity to discover his name.

I retrieved the passport from his hand.

I took out the white envelope.

I removed the License and handed it to him.

The 'manager' read the document.

He handed it back, and I tucked it safely away.

"I am a British patriot", the 'manager' puffed, "This is not germane to us."

"There has been illegal smoking in this office or nearby. It has caused a fire which shall shortly engulf the entire premises including the paper assets vaults. I shall have the Fire Department discover it and report. They will find that a cigarette or cigar carelessly discarded in the Manager's Office led to the conflagration. In the meantime I suggest you activate the fire alarm", I advised.

"I shall have security manage the outbreak. In the meantime may I personally action your valued deposit, Dr Charmliss?"

"That would be nice", I responded with a sneer.

I took very great care with the receipt and the account details. They went to keep my License and my passport company.

There was still time to spare, or you possibly think, to waste. I went into an expensive-looking Italian restaurant and ordered a 12-inch thin crust pizza con funghi with a large Frascati, a delight of my demi-vegetarian, semi-alcoholic youth. I took a table near the busy street and planned my next move.

I waited for the pizza to arrive. I had watched it being made fresh in a stone oven in the shop. I took one look at the food and called "Waiter!"

"Yes, Sir"

"Can I see the manager, please."

"Yes, Sir"

The pizzeria manager arrived, a fat, balding, very Italian little fellow trying to suppress a defensive scowl.

"Can you print out a local street map showing the location of the Library and then explain how to get there from here, per favore signore?"

"è un grande piacere, signore. I go now", answered the manager, relieved to apprehend that there was no culinary complaint, no unpleasant and unprofitable TripAdvisor post.

I took a deep draught of the wine, and flattered myself that I had earned it. I ordered another.

The manager arrived with a computer street map which marked street names in the immediate vicinity. The Library proved to be in the old cardo, a street called Old Hiding, very near to the abbey cathedral. The manager helpfully explained how to get there on foot.

After a leisurely half-hour I finished my meal. "Right, I thought to myself." I called the waiter. "Can I have the check, please?" The bill was about 15000 crowns plus a 15% service charge. I did not leave a tip.

When the debit card was returned I thought "Now to pin down this Professor Terring bugger", and started to rise from my seat.

As I did so a blinding flash of white light seemed to suffuse the street outside followed by an ear-splitting detonation. The safety glass of the restaurant window crazed in large shards which did not fall. Commercial burglar alarms and car alarms seemed to be ringing or perping all around. Within a couple of seconds a small white van, perhaps a Berlingo, fell from the sky in a burning condition. It had "Batesons" painted on the side in red and it landed on the port side and skidded along the road camber towards me. The curb arrested it. It began to burn more thoroughly and I felt the heat. Someone shouted "What the fuck was that." A distant male voice shouted back "They've taken out the Hatton."

I was in a state of shock but knew I had to pull myself together and quickly. Was it meant for me, and if so by which enemy?

A rain of human body parts and general debris was now falling.

Down the road a gas main had burst and was flaring, whilst a neighboring water main, not to be outdone, was offering a beautiful fountain.

As I watched in frozen horror little rectangles of coloured paper began delicately to float down from the sky with a graceful rocking, fluttering motion, almost like dainty birds or big butterflies. Then suddenly a crowd of people materialised before the window and frenetically danced around, slipping on human parts, dead rats and other debris as they tried frantically to grasp the little papers. Suddenly I realised the little paper falling things were currency bills. A woman in high heels mis-stepped on a slick cast iron manhole cover and appeared to injure her ankle. A man with an opera hat, perhaps a doorman, was running hither and thither like a demented contestant in some ghastly game show trying to gather the notes as they fell.

It was a Dance of Death. It was a scene that could only happen in war. It was like men dancing on hot coulters, a diabolical choreography.

I recollected my Late Father, a Navy man, telling me when I was a boy about the Japanese dollars floating in the gutters and clogging drains as the Allies re-occupied Singapore. These falling dollars were very wanted indeed.

In the restaurant everyone else seemed to have disappeared. I walked behind the bar in the general direction of the kitchen.

"c'è una via d'uscita da qui?" I said as I saw a cook.

The man showed me the rear trade entrance and I took to back streets. It was already obvious that I could not get to the Library: I could see from the window that Police and Army cordons were already starting to crystallise.

If the Presidium was where I thought it was then it was no more than two hundred metres from where I was standing.

Within ten minutes I was at the porte-cochère where I showed the guards my Licence. I was escorted to Seargent Major

Edward MacKinnon's office. There seemed to be a lot of panic, soldiers toing and froing, coming and going.

"You must be Seargent Major MacKinnon", I observed, preferring my hand.

"I know I'm a bit early but..."

"Sorry I can't deal with it, Charmliss. There is a bit of a panic on at the moment. Sit over there."

MacKinnon pointed to a chair in a corner.

Five minutes later a very fresh young Caucasian, also in Magonian uniform walked in. He did not appear to see me.

"Is there a Charmliss around somewhere? The chief wants to see him."

"I'm Charmliss", I stated.

"Follow me", said the young man. We almost immediately arrived at Treagh's grand audience chamber, the one where I translated for the Koreans.

Treagh was standing behind his desk giving orders and gesticulating at people.

"Ah, Charmliss, the man of the moment...Edmonson!, I am not to be disturbed for 45 minutes!", Treagh shouted.

"No, Sir", Edmonson agreed.

"Have a seat"

"The Shits have bombed the Hatton Bank. Do you know anything about it, Charmliss?"

"No, Sir"

"Charmliss, you really must take charge of the fuckwit element. That is after all why you are here. If you spent less time fucking my officers and more apprehending Shits I would be well pleased."

Taking the cue I replied:-

"I have a meeting with Shits starting at 1830. I have booked an office here to compile the report."

"Bravo! This is more like the Charmliss I was told about! Make sure you are not late for them."

"Where have you put the cash?" asked Treagh.

"I deposited it in the Hatton and Congleholme Bank in the Hodgate just before it went up, Sir."

Treagh sat back in his chair. It tilted under his weight and he gazed ceiling-wards.

"Fucking...", he exhaled under his breath and then had a fit of coughing, an inveterate smoker's cough.

"Don't worry, Sir, I've got a receipt", I jauntily reassured.

"Fucking glad to hear it, Charmless", the High Suzerain replied.

"Now, Charmliss I have read about Quantum Entanglement and the Continuity of the Plenum and all that, and I am genuinely a great believer in science and progress and the possible light that science can throw upon the paranormal. But I suppose I am just a simple soldier at heart, and to me the simplest explanation is the most likely explanation", opened Treagh, cosmographically.

"So this is how I see it: You were hiking along the Portway, a secluded lane over the hills and dales, in full yomping strip but naturally unarmed, making for Congleholme and possibly for secret munitions works around the Brider Estuary. You are no chicken, and somewhere near the Menlow scarp you had some kind of heart attack, or more likely a stroke or breakdown. You somehow got up and made your way to Burwardsley where you collapsed or kipped in the village public telephone box. A woman walking her dog rang for an ambulance and Colour Major Feng, on light duties in view of her age, turned up with colleagues in an ambulance. Somehow you escaped and shortly emerged actually in Congleholme, in a place called Albion Street. Is that a credible account, Dr Charmliss?"

"It is a credible account, Sir, but unfortunately that is not how I remember it."

"Then how do you remember it, Dr Charmliss?"

"Somewhere along the Portway, probably on the Menlow Rise, I was trying to sleep under a hedge when I heard obscene shouting. I peered through the hedge and saw a witch taunting a man hanging in chains. I next found myself at a crossroads where I was knocked down by an Albion bus. The next I knew I was chatting to a tourist guide in the East barbican."

"You are clearly psychotic, Charmliss, but you are a Brit with several science degrees and even more languages. This is a major war, nutcases are everywhere, many of them in uniform, we have occupied one of the strongest of the third-rate powers, and we have to work with what we have got..."

If he was thinking aloud he now fell silent.

Treagh took out one of his havanas and started playing with it. He sat back in his chair leaning to the right, cocking his head to one side, and pretending to draw on his unlit smoke.

"I have real doubts about what I am about to do..." observed the Suzerain, before falling into another trance.

Treagh took out a lighter and lit up. Then he studied me again for some minutes, after which I was thoroughly shaken.

"Are you a British agent?"

"I am not, Sir"

"Are you any kind of Ithaca Coalition operative?"

"I am not, Sir. I do not seek a restoration of the old regime. Quite the opposite, Major General Treagh."

Abruptly, Treagh sat forward and removed a pistol from one of his desk draws. He threw the weapon to me across the table. I picked it up. It appeared to be a Wrortlemonger and Bierce 9mm semi-automatic, a good make. I say 'appeared' because Far Eastern counterfeits are numerous. I withdrew the magazine. There was a full rack of fifteen shells. I pushed the magazine back to engagement.

I put the pistol down on the desk.

"I am not going to carry a weapon, Sir. I am a pacifist and have abjured firearms."

"You are going to carry it, Charmliss."

"No, Sir. With respect, Sir."

"You are going to pick up the weapon, put in your pocket, and take it to your meeting, Charmliss."

"No, Sir"

"If you do not uplift the weapon and sign for it, I am going to have you placed naked in an unlit cell with no window or lavatory and leave you there until you take the pistol and sign for it, Shit meeting or no."

I picked up the pistol and put it in my pocket.

Someone threw a fitting shoulder holster on the desk. I looked round. Edmonson was standing behind me with a clipboard.

"Sign here, Dr Charmliss."

I walked the few hundred metres back to Albany Street.

CHAPTER TEN
DISQUIETUDE

Arnoldina and I were both quite naked below my duvet. We were having a quiet time, she resting beside me, me teasing and tenderly pulling her nipples and massaging her delightful breasts. I longed for the days when these lovely paps would nurture and nutrify our child. Her nipples, through this exercise I thought were burgeoning and lengthening, and if only in my imagination her breasts grew bigger.

Something was troubling Arnoldina. I could tell.

"Arnoldina, don't you trust me?" I said.

"Oh, Charles, why do you ask? I trust you with my whole being."

I cast back the duvet and sat on the edge of the bed.

"Come and assume the position", I ordered.

Arnoldina complied.

I placed my right hand softly over her gluteal cleft at about the height she had requested.

"Say what you wish to tell me", I asked softly.

"Charles, I had a debate, more an argument really, with my Commanding Officer about the appropriate nursing strategy for fracture patients. No conclusions were drawn of course but the discord upset me."

"Is any disciplinary action to be taken against you at work?"

"I don't know but it is unlikely. There is a shortage of senior nurses because of the War; especially in the Europe theatre."

"Arnoldina you must obey your Commanding Officer promptly and wholly without answering back. He has..."

"It is a 'she'", Arnoldina interrupted.

"Do not interrupt, my Delight", I countered, "his sex is immaterial. Listen to Charles who has your charge, and your interest at heart."

"Your Commanding Officer has a very difficult job to do: Do not make it worse. She respected you and thought she could rely upon you. You have hurt her feelings and raised doubt in her mind. Arnoldina, you are an intelligent and educated woman, which incidentally makes your transgression the more reprehensible, but though you are probably right at the technical level, you are very wrong morally. We are human. Sometimes the cleverest of us are wrong."

Arnoldina was now weeping steadily. I had not landed a blow. I had not fondled Arnoldina's private parts.

I paused for her to collect her thoughts, and myself to formulate mine.

"Arnoldina, what sin have you committed?" I asked.

"I have committed the sin of Pride, My Love, which causes debate without product when we think we know best and have ascendency over our protagonist", responded my nurse and mentor.

"Arnoldina, this is what we will do. After we have had breakfast you will check that your uniform is perfect and you will walk to the Nurses' Institute and ask to see your Commanding Officer. You will tell her you were in the wrong and that you apologise and beg for her forgiveness, because you respect her and value her authority. You will do this without any affectation or suggestion of sycophancy."

"Oh, Charles", she wept, "You are so wise, and kind, and just, and merciful."

Arnoldina propped herself upon her elbows and beamed through her tears.

"I did not tell you to move", I observed in as soft and cheerful a tone as I could manage.

I moved my left hand to the back of her gorgeous head and slowly pressed her prone.

"Arnoldina, every 'Please', every 'Thank You', every 'I am sorry' every little act of submission that you freely make burgeons and strengthens my manhood, physically and spiritually. Most of all I glory in your courage and your faith as you grace my lap, not knowing what will succeed, or its degree. Arnoldina, I had lost my ability to be a man and you gave it back to me."

Arnoldina said nothing. She just cried and cried into the pillow I had positioned for her head.

Arnoldina had a pronounced full body flush and was starting to gasp through her sobs.

I gently lifted her and turned her onto her back. I smiled to her and gave her lips a dry, chaste kiss. She showed more agitation. In this position, her portal of life was raised and proud (I refuse to call it a pudendum because it is not shameful).

"Don't move, Arnoldina, just part your legs a little."

Arnoldina complied.

I inserted my two big fingers into Arnoldina's vaginal vestibule to check that she was moist enough for Sacred Union. She was.

"Thank you for your counsel, and I am sorry I have caused you this trouble", sobbed Arnoldina.

"Arnoldina, I accept your thanks and your apology with awed humility. Thank you, *too*, Arnoldina. Know that every moment I spend in your love is an ecstasy that I have never earned or deserved. It is a free gift of yourself and Another."

As I rose I lifted her supine onto the bed and grasping each ankle raised her legs into the diaper position.

I thrust in and probed strongly, completely, fast and relentless. Arnoldina gasped and screamed. I ejaculated the Holy Seed of Life copiously. We climaxed together and fell to sleep in each other's arms.

We rose and had breakfast as usual, Arnoldina in full uniform, including that stupid and I thought, demeaning, hat.

Arnoldina went to the Institute and I waited in bed with trepidation. Eventually cleaners came, and I dressed and went for a walk.

I had time to kill. I visited the ladies' lingerie department of a store and purchased a powder blue diaphanous night dress of about Arnoldina's size with a fetching white pussycat bow and a frilly hem.

I returned to my room. I stripped, showered, dressed and sat to read and consider my next moves, whatever the contingency.

It turned 1500 hours. Arnoldina had spent most of the day at the Institute or somewhere.

At about 1530 there was a diffident knock at the door. There was Arnoldina, still in uniform, beaming ear to ear.

"Come in and tell me all about it", I said.

"Colonel Vanini was very gracious and cheerful as soon as she saw me. She accepted my apology and remarked that she had been taking an interest in my work for some weeks. She said she valued my maturity and reliability. She then said that she had been considering applying to the Board of Control to give me promotion to Lieutenant Colonel and would now do so instantly. She briefed me over lunch and until past three. Then she ordered me to return to my patient. I saluted and said 'Thank you very much, Madam'"

By now it was my turn to weep and I did so with smiles of joy. When we are kind and forgiving all profit.

"Take off your uniform and hang it carefully. Have a shower and put on this nightdress. I have plans for it."

Arnoldina complied.

As she stood before her loving master and surrogate husband I said:-

"Congratulations, Arnoldina. You are a woman."

I embraced and kissed her passionately.

I took the nighty by the shoulder straps and removed it briskly.

"Arnoldina, I love you and you are lovelier than lovely itself", I remarked inanely but with feeling.

I had a strong erection, but I was still fully clothed.

I soon rectified the latter.

If you are a man with a woman who has the expressed or inferred will to bear your children, then it is your right and duty steadily to magnify her in all good things, to build her self-confidence and her will to correct and improve her world. This is why I did not spank Arnoldina on this occasion: Arnoldina had corrected herself.

This is the true meaning of emancipation and empowerment.

CHAPTER ELEVEN
A TUTORIAL

I was a few minutes early and took a walk on the wall to waste time with the minimum of ostentation. I stood watching the last stragglers in the Roman Gardens before the gates closed at sunset. It was indeed an atmospheric place in an autumn twilight, but despite the gaslamps there was plenty of ambient light from the city center shops and the traffic and I idly surmised that those who wished to capture a ghost with a camera had their work cut out.

My watch turned 1828 and I descended the steps and entered the Albion Street car park. I was about to start loitering at the rear entrance of the hotel when someone parked flashed his lights and blew his horn at me.

I recognised Shrigley's car and went and sat in the passenger seat. I noticed in the semi-darkness that a well-endowed female was seated behind the aging gerontologist.

"Who is the lady?" I asked Shrigley.

"It is Arabella Queenborough, The Baroness Sperstow"

The Baroness proffered her hand forward and I grasped it gently and it proved cold and sweaty.

"Delighted to meet you again, Dr Charmliss", she said in a well-bred accent and I recognised the dungarees girl with the probing questions during my first night at the Albion Hotel. As my eyes acclimatised I realised that she was wearing a light-coloured evening dress with a much darker jacket and a four-lap pearl neckless. I thought it odd that such a young woman would wear pearls until I realised that the whole ensemble set off her breasts nicely. In fact the dungarees had suited her because she was a rather plump and comely young woman without being obese. It was too dark to say anything sensible about her eyes or hair colours.

"I am honoured, Madam", I replied.

"We are a very broad church in The Albion Club", stated Shrigley tritely. "It is fair to say that the majority of us are nationalists, but I am a former trades-unionist and Arabella is a monarchist. We are multi-racial and ecumenical. The only membership we discourage are the old-fashioned communists of the agitprop persuasion, BBC types if you will."

"How many members do you have, Pott?"

"Around 250 paid-up but they are not all regular attenders of course. Maybe one tenth of that number turn-up religiously. The hotel could not accommodate all of our membership."

"Do you use the Albion often?" I asked.

"We use the bar a lot and I have a pair of rooms on long-term rental, but otherwise we fit in where we can. Arabella and others have country houses where large gatherings could be accommodated."

"How do I join?"

"You have to attend a six-month probationary period when you may assess your interest in the Club's affairs and promotions without commitment. If you are then proposed by two members, the Board votes on your candidature. If you are successful the annual subscription is 10000 crowns, plus costs of any literature or services required. In return you get one vote per event to use for motions or candidates, free admissions and the right to propose."

This I thought steep. They obviously intended to keep out those they regarded as riff-raff.

The evening rush-hour was starting to subside and it took Shrigley only ten minutes to get to the library. Surprisingly, at least to me, there was an adjacent municipal car-park where Shrigley easily found space.

As we walked to the Library door I saw two men smoking outside and chatting to each other. I immediately recognised Specs, aka Nikolous Terring, and Overweight, sometime Church of England vicar, otherwise known as John Grassfold. "In wartime, dogs return to their vomit", remarked Shrigley.

I was startled by the Biblical allusion from this reputed 'communist' and almost more so by the fact that we were in earshot.

Only later did it occur to me that he referred to their smoking. I suppose he meant that in peacetime they had given up the habit, and possibly in the last century.

"Good evening, Gentlemen", greeted Shrigley as we passed. The two were deep in themselves and Shrigley and I were ignored.

Shrigley and I entered a gloomy conference hall, not a big one, and I was invited to sit at a top table on a low dais. There were five hard wooden chairs behind the table and behind Shrigley and I, was a high projection screen of the old-fashioned analogue type. In the body of the hall a bright light betrayed a digital projector. The light and its fan hum were uncomfortable and it made it difficult to see the size of the hall or the audience, but auditors were obviously present according to the low murmur of voices. The hollow screech of swing doors occasionally punctuated our little vigil as new audience drifted in.

After a few minutes of this Terring and Grassfold entered and sat on the other side of Shrigley. The house lights were dimmed and thankfully someone turned off the projector meantime. There was that musty smell of damp panelling and human sweat and castoreum.

Shrigley slowly rose to stand.

"Thank you for coming, Ladies and Gentlemen, Comrades, for this important briefing, and despite the dire forecast", opened Shrigley to a titter of laughter.

"First of all, it would be impolite not to introduce Dr Charles Charmliss, a highly important figure in the diplomatic world, and a true English patriot, who has expressed an interest in Membership if you choose so to honour him."

This was answered with a storm of applause from the floor.

I rose, bowed and grinned self-consciously to the mass barely visible beyond.

More applause.

I bowed again, smirked into space and sat.

Shrigley was still standing.

Then he continued:-

"Dr Charmliss, he prefers to be known simply as 'Chuck'..."

A ripple of clapping.

"... is a Liaison Officer meantime attached to Magonian High Command."

A low murmur of surprise and confusion from the floor.

"He is an important link smoothing our transition to representative government after the War, moderating the Occupation, and countering the Fascist terror elements. Chuck is opposed to the King and the Ithaca puppet regime."

A ripple of dubious applause.

"But you have not come tonight to hear me rabbit on. Professor Terring and Dr Grassfold have a package of important proposals about Voting Reform for you to consider and debate."

"Professor Terring!"

Shrigley sat down. As he did so I tapped him on his arm and whispered that I wanted to see him in private after the lecture. I gleefully allowed the cloth-capped Machiavelli to spend the next couple of hours thinking I was going to bollock him for his lies and mis-representations.

Terring stood.

Someone switched the projector back on. Terring was holding a WiFi gizmo that changed the digital slides projected. All equitable voting systems are extremely complicated from the mathematical and statistical viewpoints and much of Terring's presentation zoomed straight over my head, but the essential gist of his system if I understood it right was that at the age of twelve months a boy or girl would get his first vote and on each subsequent birthday an additional vote. Three bonus votes would be given for each complete year of training as defined by qualifying degrees and apprenticeships. Also each year of military service would contribute four bonus points and service in front-line combat, one extra point for each 28 days under fire.

Because the voting strength of any particular population cohort was thus a function of age, education and experience the entire electorate formed a non-Gaussian grouped frequency on the age axis whose Grouped Frequency Mean was a calculable average age which Terring designated "Electorate Maturity".

He used slides of such distributions to show that the Electorate Maturity of his proposed system was about twice as old as the "One Man, One Vote" of pre-War polling, given the British demographic pyramid.

In Terring's opinion this would give the educated classes and people who had served the country a greater say than irresponsible elements of the nation.

This was an intelligent and well-meaning idea but I could see immediate and dangerous drawbacks.

The 1944 England and Wales Education Act had sought to improve access to good secondary education for the lower classes.

State Elementary schools such as my Late Father attended were abolished. A so-called Eleven Plus examination of arithmetic, English and IQ was instituted for ten-year-olds. If the Child failed this examination he was consigned to a Secondary Modern day school for a minimum of four years. If he passed he was sent to a Technical School or a Grammer School.

The Secondary Modern was essentially custodial, though the upper forms were taught history and geography, with simple English and mathematics, but mostly Anglican religion and sport.

The Technical Schools were intended to focus upon engineering and industrial arts, but withered to a mere handful within ten years.

The Grammer Schools focused upon Latin and a few Ancient Greek. Romance languages, Science and English literature were also taught. The number of children entering Grammar Schools varied between zero and eighty percent depending upon local physical availability of school desks. In England, Wales and Northern Ireland some 85% of all children attended Secondary Modern schools. I did. The system in Scotland was and is different.

My Late Mother was the daughter of a heavy electrical fitter and his assembly worker wife. My Mother attended a Grammer School before the 1944 Act, probably because her manifest genius indicated that Elementary secondary education was wasteful. Working class girls, whatever their abilities, if any, were essentially precluded by the 1944 Act.

The net upshot of this "reform" was that within thirty years national adult literacy declined from about 95% to 70%, and the 70% who could read and write were largely incapable of organising or operating a modern industrial economy, irrespective of their social background. Forty to fifty years later Britain rapidly de-industrialised and became incapable of self-defense.

Another strange and unlooked-for consequence was that the day Grammer Schools produced an entitled but rather characterless two generations of old boys and old girls, whilst the private boarding schools and the Secondary Moderns taken together output cohorts of vigorous but chippy old boys, capable of leadership, who disproportionately dominated the fields of organised crime, the print and broadcast media, gambling and the Armed Forces.

As my Late Mother often reminded me: "The road to Hell is paved with good intentions." And she was an atheist.

The reason I am telling you all this is that good men like Shrigley and Terring who wish to incept a shining New Republic must tread very carefully and think very deeply if they wish to avoid a New Directory and its New Terror.

Also, the foregoing bears directly upon Grassfold's contribution to follow.

Grassfold worried that the British population was inadequately trained for responsibility. His proposals were essentially complementary to Terring's.

Grassfold wanted secondary education to cease altogether at fourteen years of age, and to that extent was superficially regressive. But Grassfold proposed two years of compulsory National Service in which children would learn to drive, swim, type and become grounded in such very basic skills. They would also be trained in how to care for the elderly and the vulnerable, including babies, and also including conducting wildlife surveys, improving the safety of roads and waterways, etcetera. National Service children would live in camps or bivouac in a different nation of the current UK territory and be paid a small salary 75% of which would be invested for them. They would not be eligible for military conscription but interested lads and lasses would be taught basic yomping, sailorship and how to shoot straight.

At sixteen NS children would leave to go to college or an apprenticeship or could apply for a further two years of leadership training, with commanders' approval. During this period time would be allowed for university preparations or developed apprenticeship.

A tiny elite could continue for a fifth and sixth year of military training with a view to graduate officer service.

I thought this another patriotic and altruistic piece of original thought like Terring's and I wanted to stand and applaud, as some on the floor did. But Terring (Specs) was a retired particle physicist and Grassfold (Overweight) a Church of England vicar. I thought they had not perhaps thought through the literal long-range consequences of their programmes. They were highly intelligent and caring men. I was neither but I knew that people were individuals, that there was infinite scope for abuse and corruption, and that the lower orders in particular would need extensive accommodations.

Shrigley stood to request questions from the floor.

As he sat I tapped his upper arm and sternly ordered: "Follow me."

Poor Shrigley must now have wondered whether I was going to bollock him for lies and inconfidence, ring the MFIS, criticise the presentations or possibly all three.

We walked down a ghostly corridor lit only by the red glow of the fire precautions pilot and I found a room in darkness and switched on the lights.

Shrigley followed me in.

We stood by a mass-produced library table.

"Look, Shrigley, I have evidence that atrocities are being committed on the Menlow Rise."

Shrigley gazed into my face with slack-jawed surprise.

When he collected his thoughts he breathlessly exclaimed:-

"Who by?"

"I do not know but I intend to find out"

"What atrocities?"

"And least one man is being gibbeted alive and if we don't pull our fingers out the frost will kill him tonight."

"I have got to tell the speakers", said Shrigley and rushed out.

They must have have concluded the lecture meeting pretty pronto because within five minutes Shrigley was back with Terring, Grassfold and Earnest Pratley (Beard).

Barely had they arrived and I had briefed them in outline but a fifth man presented at the door.

He wore a beige cotton overall with buttons very like an old-fashioned grocer's coat. If you remember the late Mr Ronnie Barker in *Open All Hours* then it was very similar and so was its inhabitant similar to Arkwright.

"You should not be here", shouted the janitor figure, "haven't you buggers got no home to go to? It is fucking eleven-thirty. Get out now!"

"Come here my good man!", I shouted back in my best fake Worth accent.

The man approached me.

I took out my License and my UK Passport and offered them. The janitor read both as we all stood in silence. He handed them back without comment.

I resumed with:-

"What is your name?"

"Jack Stroller, Sir"

"Well Mr Jack Stroller, I am going to arrest you and take you to see the High Suzerain. I assure you he is still at his desk. Unless you do something for me."

"I am sorry about my language, Sir. What can I do, Sir?"

"Get all the OS maps in the library that show the Menlow area and bring them here."

"Yes, Sir"

Stroller returned five minutes later with an armful of tattered maps.

He dumped them on the table and stood gazing at them disconsolately.

I glared at him.

"That will be all, Mr Stroller"

"Yes Sir", and with that Jack Stroller gladly departed.

Terring took most of the maps to an adjacent table and picking one brought it back to our table and opened it.

It proved to be of Menlow Rise at about 25000 scale.

"I cannot see any linear tracks or any feature called The Portway", Terring complained.

"No, it won't be easy. This is not 80V and the road may never have been laid, but there is somewhere beside a track in the Hills where a man is being tortured to death."

"I need the four of you to come by car with me this minute to look for atrocities in execution."

"You better not come, Charmliss, because if you encounter your corpse there will be an existential contradiction. The antimatter of 78V and the matter from 80V will mutually annihilate taking this solar system with it", advised Terring.

To me this showed a fundamental misunderstanding of the mechanics of universe intertransitions on the part of this particle physicist.

My mortal remains remained in 80V by definition. But that of course did not explain how my clothed person and my rucksack materialised at the Barbican!

"I am coming anyway", I averred.

"If you say so, Chuck", contributed Shrigley, "You, Erny and I will go in my car; and Nick and John will go in Nick's"

"No, that is just too inefficient in unlit countryside, and far too conspicuous. Do you or anyone you trust have a Land Rover, people carrier or similar?"

"Yes, I have an old long wheelbase Land Rover with seats", volunteered the Beard, Earnest Pratley.

"Perfect!" I said.

"Have any of you got firearms?" I asked.

"Yes, I have a double-barreled shotgun", said Pratley.

"I have a Magonian pistol", I stated.

"Yes, we noted", confirmed Shrigley with an at least equal lack of security.

Unlike Maggi Landheart would have, none seemed eager to query why a Quaker was packing heat, or how he had acquired it.

Terring stole the OS map and we left the rest to Stroller.

Fortunately, Pratley had actually come in his ancient Land Rover and parked it next to the Library. I later discovered that he lived outside Alpraham which in 78V was called most suggestively Stretton Kinglake.

We all piled in.

We pretty well combed the Hills by car and where drivable roads were absent by footpath. We dared not use flashlights but carried them in case. The Hills turned out to have numerous well-metalled bridleways and I neurotically picked my way with care in the light reflected from the cloudbase. I wanted to avoid soiling myself with dog and horse excrement. I was wearing town shoes. I had many arguments with polluted puddles and always lost them but took for consolation a pair of squelching, freezing foot covers. It quickly became apparent that the footpaths were favourite resorts of dog walkers and the Palatine horsey set.

We found nothing.

About 0500, as the first glimmers of dawn lit the eastern sky, we very tiredly ambled back to the Land Rover and immediately perceived that a police car had double-parked it on the narrow lane.

As we approached two officers of the civil Palatine Police stepped toward us.

"Good Morning, Gentlemen", said the elder, heavier, man.

"Good Morning, Officers", I returned greeting.

Turning to Pratley the younger officer said:-

"Why are you carrying a gun, Sir?"

"We are searching for evidence of terrorist atrocities, Officer, and my friend is carrying for our common defence", I stated.

"Excuse me, Sir, but I was speaking to the bearded gentleman", replied the young policeman, then turning back to Pratley.

Pratley followed my lead.

Then the older man said:-

"We are arresting all of you under the Game, Wildlife and Countryside Order of 2026. You are severally advised that you are not obliged to say anything but anything you do say will be taken down and used in evidence. Give me your gun."

They thought we were common poachers!

Pratley handed over his shotgun meekly.

"I shall reach into an inside pocket, Gentlemen, and take out my Diplomatic Immunity credentials", I warned.

Before I had finished the sentence both officers had whipped out their pistols and pointed them in my face.

The younger stepped forward and reaching into my blouse quickly pocketed Treagh's Wrortlemonger and Bierce and took out my Licence and UK Passport, passing them to the senior and holding a flashlight whilst the latter read.

The older policeman handed the credentials back to me without comment, and said to Pratley:-

"Report to Nantwich police station at 1000 to sign for your shotgun."

"Yes, Sir", answered Pratley.

"Return my pistol and credentials", I demanded.

The younger man did so with I thought an air of contempt.

The two officers got into their car and drove away.

We got back into Pratley's Land Rover and Pratley gave us all a lift to Congleholme and then drove home himself.

CHAPTER TWELVE
THE BRITISH FLAG OFFICER

By 0700 I was back in my room at the Albion.

Arnoldina was waiting for me, already in full uniform for breakfast. Not that her uniform was breakfast, if you ascertain my meaning.

I stripped and showered, and changed into my clean hiking boots and a clean pair of fatigues.

"If I had returned from some stupid adventure so dirty you would have spanked me severely", observed the eminently spankable loveliness.

"I think I will spank you anyway!" I bantered.

"Charles do not joke about your Sacred Rights or your Sacred Trust", replied Arnoldina, with a forensic frown of disapproval.

"Sorry, My Love", I meekly replied.

We caught the lift and went down to breakfast.

"What shall we order today?" I asked the mistress of vegan compliance.

"Today, Charles, we will each have four slices of toast with sunflower oil spread and black coffee. If you wish you may have a little damson jam on two of the slices", defined Arnoldina with authority. "Don't worry about the jam", Arnoldina reassured me, "It is pectin only: I have checked."

"I shall lose weight rapidly under this regime" I thought gloomily. But I had still not injected myself for days, in fact since I had died, and wondered if the insulin in my sack was beginning to get stale in the ambient heat.

"Great!" is what I actually said.

We were finishing these short commons when another apparition strode into the Public Bar in this city of apparitions.

He was wearing full British Army regalia and one of those stupid new helmets that look like neoprene frogmen's helmets with thick chinstraps, set off by a risible swept-up plastic peak. On the apex of the peak two toothpicks of little flag posts formed a V-shape: On one fluttered the Union Flag and on the other Old Glory. I say "fluttered" but they only flew limply in draughts from air-conditioning or when someone opened a door. He was not armed. But he was a little corpulent and obviously beyond normal retirement age.

The other officer was in Royal Navy uniform, and was visibly younger, fitter and more credible, even though he was wearing shades and did not see his way to remove them in the gloom of the room.

The flag officer and his aide strode up to the bar self-importantly, but then the flag officer turned to the clientele and bellowed:-

"Is there a Charles Charmliss here?"

I rose instinctively and bellowed back:-

"I am Charmliss..."

I was universally ignored.

Landheart came out of her kitchen and said to the flag:-

"You cannot barge in here like that. I have got a business to run. You are frightening my guests. Dr Charmliss is very ill and being nursed."

"Don't you recognise me, woman. I am a local man. I am Flag Officer Commanding Europe Theatre Field Marshall Sir Alan Arthers-Nugent."

"Yes, I know, Sir. My late husband used to work in your factory", replied the barmaid. "May I get you breakfast, or perhaps something to drink?"

"Don't be so bloody silly. Where's Charmliss?"

Ionescu had been slowly striding his way to the British officers. As he converged at the bar he said:-

"I am Eugen Ionescu. May I assist, Gentlemen?"

By way of reply Arthers-Nugent said:-

"You are trespassing in the United Kingdom, and you are armed contrary to the Firearms Act 1921."

I was not sure whether he meant that Act or that date, but never mind.

Ionescu slowly took out his pistol and placed it on the bar outwith his easy reach. Landheart quickly took it and placed it below the bar.

"I am going to report your abduction of a British citizen to High Command", added the flag officer.

Shades remained mute and inscrutable.

Arnoldina rose and paced over to the party.

"Good Morning, Gentlemen", my Delight greeted professionally and with courtesy. In fact she curtseyed at them.

"I am Colour Major Arnoldina Feng of the Auxiliary Nursing (Aliens) Corps. Dr Charmliss is very ill and cannot be removed from St Olave without the written authority of the High Suzerain. I shall apply to my Commanding Officer for permission for you to interview him here but I emphasise that Dr Charmliss must not be stressed or alarmed in any way. Dr Charmless has not been abducted and he has not been arrested."

"Liar!" shouted Arthers-Nugent in her face, his own reddening by the minute like a turkey-cock's, "He was seen not four hours ago in Menlow."

"Please do not traduce my honour, Field Marshall Arthers-Nugent. Dr Charm..."

She was interrupted by a very irate Charles Charmliss who accosted Arthers-Nugent and said with feeling:-

"Fatface, I don't know who the fuck you are, but you cannot insult the lady with impunity. I have a pistol and you can borrow Ionescu's and we will go into the street and try conclusions like men of honour... "

"No, Charles!", Arnoldina shouted or rather screamed almost hysterically.

Fatface just glowered at me.

The RN officer took off his sunglasses and turning to me said:-

"Look here, Charmliss, I am Gerald Mowle of the British Legation, and I grovelingly apologise for the offence we have given ever since we arrived, but our country is in a most parlous state. The Koreans want extensive concessions and you are the only trustworthy Korean-speaker in theatre. Please translate for us."

"I will consider your request, Mowle. But first your commanding officer must take off his hat, go down on his knees before Major Feng, withdraw his aspersion upon her honour, and apologise. Do you agree?"

Mowle turned to Arthers-Nugent.

Arthers-Nugent removed his hat. He slowly and arthritically descended using an iron table for support. He put his hands together and looked up to Arnoldina:-

"I wholly withdraw my accusation of dishonesty that I made, Major Feng, and I apologise for my conduct and offence. Please forgive me."

"I forgive you, Mr Arthers-Nugent", replied Arnoldina pointedly.

The cock's crest fell and he blanched.

Mowle and Ionescu helped the oaf back to his feet.

I turned to Mowle:-

"When do we start?"

"The flag officer and I have a 1400 appointment with the Koreans."

"I will be there. You will provide a car at 1330 hours", I promised and demanded.

"Yes, Dr Charmliss"

The two British representatives returned to their car in silence.

Whatever happened next, I knew that Arthers-Nugent's war was over.

Arnoldina and I lept up the stairs giggling like teenagers.

We bounded into my room, stripped simultaneously and showered together.

As we bathed Arnoldina said:-

"I am sorry I was so sanctimonious earlier, Charles."

"No, you were completely in order, and your Love and your Trust under God are admired beyond my ability to express in any language."

We kissed.

Arnoldina grabbed my arms as the warm water rained down unregarded. She beamed into my eyes and exclaimed:-

"Charles, you were magnificent!"

And paused a while.

Then she said:-

"I still have not Corrected you for ruining a fine pair of new shoes."

And I replied:-

"And I must Correct you for calling a Knight of the Realm mere 'Mister'."

Arnoldina screamed with laughter.

We ran from the bathroom and hurriedly dried each other.

Arnoldina sat on the bed edge.

I settled across her knees.

I received three surprisingly robust slaps on each of my damp nates. It hurt more than I thought possible in 78V.

Then we changed places and Arnoldina received the same.

We leapt onto the bed.

The sex was fantastic.

I felt a brisk shaking.

Arnoldina still had her tender, slender arms around my naked shoulders.

"Charles, Charles, it's 1315!" said the urgent loveliness.

"Damn!" I thought and jumped from my bed.

I had the most perfunctory of showers and put on a clean suit of hiking fatigues. Arnoldina and I embraced, kissed with passion, and I hurried down the stairs to meet the British.

Without anything to eat since breakfast and still sans insulin I found Arthers-Nugent and Mowle nursing halves in the Public Bar.

"Good Afternoon, Gentlemen", I said. The two men exchanged the greeting addressing me as "Dr Charmliss" and we rose to enter the sunlit street and the car they had hired with a civilian driver. They did not appear to be armed. I was, but I thought discreetly. I was of course carrying my British Passport and my Licence.

As the doors closed I stated "My rate is 20000 crowns an hour and I require treasury bills up front for the first hour."

"What?!", exclaimed Arthers-Nugent in his fat faced blimpish way. "What about our country!"

"What about it?", I responded, "Your class betrayed it"

Mowle opened his case and said "This is 10000 US dollars on account, Charmliss", handing me a banker's paper foreign currency wallet.

"It is all we can can give you today, and you should canvass the Koreans for the rest", he added.

I pocketed the payment.

Arthers-Nugent was sitting beside me still wearing that bloody ridiculous hat, complete with the little flags of the Ithaca allies.

Without a by-your-leave I undid his chinstrap and removed the hat, carefully placing it in his footwell.

"To avoid unpleasant embarrassments, Sir" I remarked.

Hardly had this second farce played out than the car drew to a stop outside the Hodgate entrance of The Belsize Hotel, the swankiest in the swanky little city.

"Is this where you have agreed to convene, Gentlemen?" I asked pointlessly.

The driver opened our doors and we climbed out, Mowle leading the way past the hat-tipping doorman to the elevator. For his part Arthers-Nugent had already replaced his hat and looked perfectly undignified.

Mowle had hired a conference room on the second floor. An aside to my American readers, the third floor. There was a large polished table and the three Koreans were already seated along one side in silence, but had brought numerous cases and papers which they now studied minutely.

As we entered the Koreans rose and shook hands across the table.

They were the same Koreans we had negotiated with in Treagh's office.

I opened in Korean with:-

"I am sorry we are late, Gentlemen. This is the British chargé-d'affaire Field Marshall Sir Alan Arthers-Nugent, Flag Officer Commanding of Ithaca Coalition Forces Europe, and this is Mr Gerald Mowle, Military Attache at the UK Swiss Embassy at present attached to the British Legation to the United Nations."

My long hours of day and night study of Treagh's confidential papers at the Presidium were starting to pay off.

I then introduced Park Baek Hyeon, the Korean chargé-d'affaires, and his two aides.

As interpreter I took the chair at the head of the table nearest to Park and Arthers-Nugent.

It suddenly dawned on my slow mind that I was *de facto* Chairman and referee of this obscure little meeting and that I was tampering in the foothills of a global Armistice:- Or possibly the hotting of a so far desultory global war.

"Order some refreshments", I said abruptly to Arthers-Nugent in English.

Mowle had already opened his case and took out his mobile. He rang for refreshments unspecifically.

Without further ado Park said, seemingly to anyone who would listen:-

"I need Cornwall, Devon and Portland (Dorset)."

I turned to Park and remarked in Korean:-

"I need 10000 US dollars for the first hour."

One of his aids took what appeared to be an old-fashioned cheque book out of his inner jacket pocket and scribbled something on it and passed it to me. It proved to be a promise in $15000 drawable on the Japanese firm Kaorutomo Bank.

I turned to Arthers-Nugent and said, in English of course:-

"His Excellency respectfully demands the Assignment of Cornwall, Devon and Portland to the sovereignty of his principals."

I realised I had flummoxed this one and turning back to Park I asked:-

"When you say need, do you mean on behalf of the Ithaca Coalition or do you mean the Republic of Korea."

"I mean the Republic of Korea", clarified the Korean chargé.

I translated at Arthers-Nugent. The flag officer coloured but said nothing. Mowle was inscrutable but appeared to be feverishly scribbling shorthand. He had already deployed a recording machine.

Just then there was jangled confusion at the door and a uniformed porter entered stooping over a polished chrome tea trolly. It is fair to say it was creaking beneath the weight of individual pork pies and cheese portions and bread rolls with sliced ham inside and chocolate biscuits of various brands. For liquid refreshment there was tea, coffee, hot water, chilled fizzy water, full fat and oat milk, plus a litre bottle of Islay malt and a litre bottle of premium brandy. I noted that ladies were ill provided for, but then again the management would have realised no ladies were present. There was no beer. Perhaps the management thought that diplomats would turn their noses up and complain.

The porter carefully served all six of us, myself translating where necessary as we went along.

Arthers-Nugent turned to me and remarked:-

"I need a stiff brandy"

"Yes, Sir" I replied.

I rose and walked to the trolley. There I identified a 330ml mass-produced (i.e. non-24% lead) whisky tumbler. I broke the seal on the brandy bottle and filled the glass. I also lifted a small fizzy water bottle and took the pair to Arthers-Nugent.

As we ate the atmosphere relaxed and mellowed, at any event for the diabetics present.

Having drunk half his glass neat Arthers-Nugent unexpectedly turned to me and said:-

"Look here, Charmliss. Thank you for your service so far. I am most dreadfully sorry I insulted your wife this morning. I have no excuse."

You cannot know how my heart thrilled at the word "wife." It was like the occasion some forty years ago when, back in 80V, my Korean Wife and I took my Korean nephew-by-marriage to a diner outside Cannock and the waitress came to our table and asked "What would your son like to eat?" It is trifling, but unforgettable to a childless man. I did not of course disabuse her. My nephew must be nearly sixty now. I wonder if he too remembers, and remembers my non-response with pride or loathing.

"Mrs Charmliss has forgiven you", I stated, "and for my part I wish to apologise for my rudeness in the car."

"That's okay, Charmliss:- You were right" said Arthers-Nugent.

"Sir Alan" I responded, "I do not wish to be impertinent, but is it acceptable if I continue the dialogue with the Korean gentlemen on behalf of the British Legation?"

"Go ahead, Charmliss!"

Turning to the Korean delegation I said in the Korean language:-

"Gentlemen please finish your meal without any sense of urgency. Sir Alan Arthers-Nugent has instructed me to advise that none of the territories that His Excellency specified nor any part of the former United Kingdom will be ceded. This is because the English successor state shall build a thousand-ship navy and needs to accommodate it. Port Hamilton is yours forever, Gentlemen, not because it is little but because it is a corner of a foreign field that has ever cherished six Englishmen."

Then in conscious imitation of Douglas MacArther as he concluded the Second World War I said:-

"These proceedings are closed."

The Koreans rose as a man. One of the aides, who clearly spoke fluent English said:-

"This is most irregular. I shall report this matter to my superiors and to the UN Committee on De-Colonisation. I bitterly resent your insulting coda."

And pointing at my face he added:-

"...and you are in breach of contract."

"Sue me", I responded in Korean with contempt.

I was driven back to the Albion.

Arnoldina was anxiously waiting in my room, not naked but in her floral dressing gown. I breathlessly related the history of my conference.

I showed her the $10000 from the British and the Koreans' Kaorutomo cheque.

"We will have to bank these instantly", I said handing my new Wife the cash and the cheque.

"Charles, you are the man of honour *Sans Pareil*", said Arnoldina.

"You cannot bank the Kaorutomo cheque. They thought they had bought you, and you did not deliver up the country they wanted. If you leave it with me I shall tear it up and put it in the discard."

I snatched back the promise.

"Arthers-Nugent was wrong: You are no wife of mine", I said with unforgivable spite.

Arnoldina burst into tears.

"Charles, I was purchased at a slave auction. My marriage was never celebrated in a church or a court of law. I was Blessed with a kind, generous, merciful, forgiving husband by the Will of God in Person. I am neither an adulteress nor a bigamist, and neither are you because you are dead in the universe you deserted. I love Mr Feng and I love you, Charles. I am entitled to take the seed of any man and in return I pledge my faith and obedience in all conducive things. Take me or leave me, Charles."

"If it helps with your fear or guilt or avarice, Charles, I shall Correct you reverently under the Gaze of Christ. You have won a country. I have only won you, Charles."

Now I burst into tears.

I handed the cheque back to Arnoldina.

She tore the cheque to sixteen pieces and let them flutter to the floor.

"Charles, you are pure as well as kind. You are purer than any man, bar one."

"Mr Feng?" I queried.

"Don't blaspheme, Charles"

I took her.

CHAPTER THIRTEEN
BUNNY TEACHES ME A LESSON

It was a Sunday and Shrigley had promised me a walk in the hills, possibly the Cadair Cymru. I loathe politics and dreaded nine hours of conversation with a man, who whatever his several merits, could think of little else. It was a fine day but cold as I loitered in the car park, beside the back door.

Bunny Balfour sidled in and parking her backside on the boot of Shrigley's yet unattended car, she stared at me speculatively for two or three minutes, smoking a cigarette.

Presently she cast the butt to the ground and shouted across the tarmac:-

"Fancy a good time, love?"

"I was having a good time studying the arse of Shrigley's car until you supplanted it with your own", I shouted back.

"I have something to show you that you would like to see", replied Bunny with ersatz sensuality.

It was not that I hated whores, more that I hated the trade. Personal solicitation had only happened thrice, but on the first occasion I was well into middle age when in my ancestral city of Wolverhampton, then a mere town, I walked round a corner from the loading bay of the local hardware store of all places, and on the opposite corner, quite literally under a lamppost, but in broad daylight, stood a woman in her early thirties. She had risibly cast herself as the cliché prostitute of lore and legend complete with excessive and garish make-up and cheap clothing. She eyed me. She shouted over the narrow street "Got the time, love?". I checked my watch and shouted back "One-thirty-seven." She flicked back her head and rolled her eyes as much as to say "What an idiot!". I just walked on but I was beside myself with anger. Women don't always understand that there is a hidden, and very offensive, implication.

The second incident was also in Wolverhampton, but I cannot recollect the details. The third and last solicitation was on the Everton Road in Liverpool. An aged and obviously very poor Irishwoman walking in the opposite direction greeted me with "Have you got the time, love?". I checked my watch and stated "Eight Minutes past Twelve". She said "Bless You" and moved on. Rightly or wrongly, I did not resent this encounter. My feeling was more of pity for a toothless, ragged old girl. We were both around my own age, which was sixty-three at the time.

For my part I have visited two and maybe a third brothel on as many occasions. On the first occasion I was very green, indeed I was still a virgin. I studied the classified ads in *Time Out* under "Secretarial Services". I needed three pages in IBM Diplomat, as demanded by my doctoral referee, to complete my PhD thesis for award. I visited a girl in Conduit Street who seemed annoyed at my request, but referred me to an establishment in Shepherd Market, Mayfair. Fresh from wild Ross-shire I had no idea where or what Shepherd Market was. I turned up at the said establishment and was greeted by six cheerful, well-spoken girls who were indeed equipped with IBM golfball typewriters. They seemed amazed at the character both of my enquiry and my highly mathematical manuscript. The charge would be £35 per page which was two weeks wages for many men in 1980. I left the script with them and they promised to have the work ready in three days. When I returned I beheld three immaculate pages of advanced mathematical typescript, faultless and much better than that of either of the professorial scientific typists who had typed-up the original thesis. The cost was of course £105. At the time, I was paid £6,550 per annum as a civil engineering computer programmer, about three times the average male salary. In those days, a premises with more than one woman for hire was a Disorderly House and the owner and the girls were subject to lengthy custodial sentences if arrested.

The second occasion nearly fifty years later was wholly different though the girls involved were equally cheerful, professional and helpful. I found myself in Birkenhead, Merseyside researching another of my light theological essays of the Liverpool suite. It was only the second time I had visited the town and I got lost. But I found the main street and walked down it. I went into a brothel and asked the girls at the desk where the bus station was. They kindly directed me, standing in the street to point out the correct turning. There was no charge.

Bunny continued to drill my eyes with her own gaze. She folded her arms, but if it was such it was the only token of impatience.

At length Bunny said:-

"We can't talk here. We will go onto the Hodgate and hail a taxi."

"I am not interested"

"I think you may profit from the experience", replied the whore.

Then it occurred to me that I could lose little and may gain something, I was not sure what.

I hitched my sack further onto my bad shoulder and said:-

"Let's go!"

As you now know, the Hodgate was a busy throughfare only metres from the Albion.

Bunny hailed one of the many cabs and we climbed in. Bunny was at least superficially clean and healthy, but smelt of male cologne. I hoped that Arnoldina would not detect the same when I arrived back home.

After ten minutes of largely silent and uneventful riding, if you will forgive the vulgar but quite unintended pun, we arrived in a dowdy street of prewar council housing in the north of Congleholme.

Bunny paid and tipped the driver without comment and certainly without expectation. She used her front door key to enter a brick two-bed terraced house, either social housing or former social housing.

In the front room a man in a cotton vest sat watching the wrestling with a pack of lager on an occasional table beside his sagged and soiled sofa. Sorry I again mis-speak: He was watching two men wrestling in the television image whilst the beer-pack remained on the table beside him. The man noted but neither greeted nor commented upon my appearance. The entrance to his room smelt of beer and sweat.

"Have you got my fags", he shouted, probably at Bunny Balfour. Another aside to American readers: In Britain 'fags' are cigarettes. I have not smoked for decades, but Bunny threw what may have been a packet of twenty No.7 on his table. I am old and doubtless out-of-date but I am sure you get the picture.

"Come upstairs", Bunny commanded me.

We arrived in a clean and surprisingly tidy small room delicately furnished with a low bed covered with a clean, tasteful duvet. On the wall above the bed was a large crucifix and displayed floral fans.

Bunny took out her mobile and started tediously to scroll it as we sat together on the edge of the bed.

"Have you seen this woman?", asked Bunny as she handed me the cellphone.

There was a cellphone photograph of a brunette possibly thirty or a little younger, head and shoulders with a serious but not sullen expression, a very ordinary face that could be any North European, I thought.

"She is the North-West Palatinate ringleader of the English National Liberation Army. She lives next door but one. Are you going to arrest her?" said Bunny.

"I don't know yet", I responded.

I laid the gizmo on the duvet and said to Bunny:-

"Bunny, how much did you pay and tip the driver?"

"Oh, don't worry about that, Dr Charmliss. It is my treat."

"Well at least let me pay for your husband's cigarettes."

"They cost me 250 crowns, Sir"

"Just call me Chuck", I asked.

I ferreted in my pockets for enough of the new low-value plastic and aluminium coins to make up 250 crowns. They still bore British Wildlife on the reverse but the King's head was omitted from the obverse and replaced by the Magonian phi symbol and other tom-foolery, on some coins by overstrike. At last I gave up and taking a 500 crown note from my wallet I said:-

"Get him another packet tomorrow", as I handed it to Bunny.

"Thank you, Sir", persisted Bunny.

Then I said:-

"If we were having sex, Bunny, how much would you charge?"

"It would depend, Sir. Straight sex would be 100 crowns for each fifteen minutes or 1000 for the whole night if you were an approved regular. We would both shower and clean before the act for which there is no charge. I work naked. Discipline given or received is 75% extra if it is just hand on bottom. Instruments are on a case by case basis, but would be very expensive. Refreshments and contraceptives are at cost."

"What is the name of the woman in the mobile picture?" I asked.

"Felicity Goodleague"

"And her address?"

"43 Manningfield Crescent"

"Now, Mrs Balfour, I have wasted enough of your time. I offer two thousand crowns for our hour's work, as long as you pay for our taxi back to the Albion, at least for me. Is it a deal?"

Bunny quickly proffered her hand to shake in accession. I shook.

I took two 1000 crown notes from my wallet and set them on her dressing table. She observed them with a slightly avaricious smile of satisfaction. She then rang for a taxi.

The taxi driver arrived and parped his horn at the roadside.

As I stood to leave, Bunny gave me a brief hug and a pecked kiss.

"We'll meet again", she said.

It seemed more like a threat than a valediction.

When I got to my room I quickly showered and put the strip in the laundry shoot incase Arnoldina smelt the cologne.

CHAPTER FOURTEEN
NURSE KNOWS BEST

We returned from dinner and Dina sat in uniform in the chair I which I first saw her.

"Arnoldina, do you mind if I ask you a very personal question?"

"This from the man who had his thumb on my anus and two fingers trapping my clitoris! How more personal could it become!" replied my nurse and mentor with a cheeky smile.

"Did your husband ever fellate you?"

"Fellate me? What does it mean?"

"Did her ever insert his erect penis into your mouth and emit?"

"I am surprised you ask me this, Charles. He never did that. My Husband is a man of devotion and of honour, a true Christian man."

"I am sure he is all of those things, Arnoldina. I am sorry I have offended you and traduced your good Husband."

"Charles, would God look down upon a man created in his own Image and think to Himself: 'I see my Image at work placing his Holy Seed of propagation in a place where it cannot be employed to make a baby in my Image' and be content."

"No he would not", I replied.

"You have answered your own question, Charles."

"Arnoldina, I am very sorry if you find this further question offensive, but do you still have your periods?"

"Periods, Charles, what do you mean?"

"Well, women of childbearing age expel the lining of the uterus every lunar month. When this ceases, so does their ability to bear."

"I see, Charles. Are you fitter to beget a child than I to bear one?"

"I can see that I have angered you more, my Love. I am sorry. I suspect that I am infertile." I replied.

Arnoldina lifted her Bible from the table beside her.

She flicked through to find the page.

In the sacred wastes of far Tachin where the Sun lies down to sleep and the dead rise up to live there was an aged goatherd. His wife baked bread in their tabernacle as her centenarian husband worked outside. One fine day God come to the goatherd in the avatar of three men. Their foreman spake; "Goatherd, we are men of a wicked city, and we return thence. We thirst and hunger. Please victual us." The goatherd realised he was speaking to God Incarnate. The goatherd dined and watered the men generously. The foreman said "Your wife shall bear a son. He will be very important." The goatherd was called Abram and his wife was called Sari. But when this ninety-year-old wife overheard this speaker she scorned him and laughed within her heart. The foreman told the goatherd: "Your wife laughs at me. Henceforth her name is laughter." But God privily knew the woman would delight in her son, and laugh again, not with mockery but with delight.

"Genesis 17:16-19:8", said Arnoldina laying her Bible aside.

"That was lovelier than loveliness. Thank you for the Reading of your divine sutra, and your Ministry, My Love", I replied.

"I am here to Minister to your needs Charles, knowing that you are fragile but useful.", replied the Colour Major, or, who yet knew?, maybe Lieutenant Colonel.

Arnoldina continued:-

"Do you *really* believe in God?" asked the near-perfect Imitation of Christ.

"Of course I do. I am a Christian", I snapped defensively.

"Are you, Charles? Do you, Charles? Do you believe in the Will of God unreservedly? Do you believe in *Almighty* God?

"I do not know, Arnoldina. I struggle"

"All men struggle", counselled Arnoldina.

As Arnoldina took the Bible from her lap she crossed her legs. From my low vantage sitting on the bedside I could see that she was wearing those ghastly cream knickers and furthermore a brassier was obvious beneath her police blouse.

"Arnoldina, when you wear your uniform or anything else, please do not wear that ghastly underwear, or indeed any underwear."

"I shall wear underwear, and from an Army point of view I am improperly dressed without it."

"Arnoldina, it would help me to be a man, and perform the rightful office of a man under God."

"You are a man anyway"

"Please don't answer back, Arnoldina. Just remove your bra and your knickers."

"I am an Army nurse with the additional war-substantive rôle as a policewoman. I thought that I had explained at the outset that I am here to serve your needs and not your cupidities."

"I shall be obeyed by any woman who takes my seed", I insisted.

"Strip and shower", I ordered.

"Charles, I shall return to my room, strip, shower and return here in my dressing gown, with my room keys. You may do as you will."

Arnoldina, returned some ten minutes later the picture of loveliness in her cuddly, fluffy dressing gown with its hazel bushes and playing squirrels.

I rose and removed the gown, folding it into a cushion for Arnoldina's pelvis.

I sat down again and placed the folded dressing gown on my lap.

"Assume the position", I ordered.

Arnoldina gracefully climbed prone. I said:-

"Dear Arnoldina I love you. I love you more than life itself. You admonished me to control my woman. I honour your advice and execute your will. You have a right to speak and record your thoughts as you will, a right that God vouchsafed to you and all your kind, and to fight for those rights for all men, which you are doing. This is not about dominance, feminism, chauvinism or any other political or conventional thing. This is about man and woman, Creation and pro-creation in the Sight of God by the method he ordained. We honour God and we do his Will as He wishes it."

"You are a Christian, a vegan and a democratic liberal. Such are rights inalienable to any man or woman", I continued.

"But in little things, helping your man to expand and beget, you have every right and duty to vary your habits."

"Please obey your man, Arnoldina."

Arnoldina kept silence. She lay passively across my lap. I could see my object clearly and I wished, no yearned, to enter the portal of life. I paused a while more in silence.

"Please do not defy me, Arnoldina", I begged.

Silence.

I spanked her fast and hard, on each alternate buttock, as before. Arnoldina began to whimper, then to weep fluidly. I do not know how many blows I landed, I wasn't counting. At length Arnoldina began to scream and I stopped.

I picked Arnoldina up in my arms and cuddled her as we sat together on the edge of the bed. She embraced me and we kissed tenderly.

Then Arnoldina said:-

"Thank you for your Correction, Charles. You are firm and manly. I delight in you, and the correction is very welcome and useful to me. It literally and metaphorically draws a line under things, and it is exciting and stimulating for me."

"I have two observations to make if I may speak, my Darling Lover?"

"Arnoldina, you are a free woman, and you fight beside your comrades to remain one. Notwithstanding, My Love, I want and need to hear your every lovely word, for you are a good woman, sage and kind as befits your age and experience."

"Charles, you are a treasure", replied the Loveliness and continued:-

"This first part is a *statement* not a *request*. I *must* wear my Service uniform complete and spick whenever I appear in public, even at hotel meals. What I propose when we are alone, Charles, is that I wear nothing, or if I am cold my dressing gown perhaps with a jacket. If we go to some remote place, perhaps hiking, I will wear appropriate civilian attire, or walk naked if no-one is around. Is any of this acceptable to you, Charles?"

"It is all acceptable to me, My Love. I am delighted. You are a real woman, and I am very grateful for your insight and advice."

"Good!"

"My second point is this", continued my nurse.

"I am an old woman. My bones are brittle, and there is a serious risk of damage to the pelvis if you continue to strike as you do. Please aim to strike softer and with fewer blows. Can I recommend that you aim for the lower, fattier part around the gluteal folds, perhaps with a couple of little pinches to finish?"

"Arnoldina, I must follow your medical advice at all times, I hardly need to say. And if I act dangerously, tell me to stop. I shall follow each particular."

"Good!" exclaimed Arnoldina. "Now give me your sacred seed in the name of Jesus Christ! I am ready to bear your child, if God wills."

CHAPTER FIFTEEN
THE ATTEMPT

We rose and breakfasted.

Arnoldina walked to the Nurses' Institute, possibly to be assigned an office and to receive further briefing in line with the promotion resting with the Board of Control.

I sat on the edge of the bed, in my usual street garb of camouflage hiking fatigues. I was breaking-in a new pair of street shoes. My eyes have always been weak. They were in 80V. Both corneas had been replaced with plastic ones set to infinite focus, but I had bought a pair of reactant anti-UV sunglasses and wore them habitually, removing them whenever I thought the respondent found them rude or intimidating. As we noted before, I had separate reading glasses.

I picked up the mobile Treagh had given me and rang his number at the Presidium.

"MacKinnon", answered the voice at the other end, abruptly.

"Seargent Major MacKinnon, it's Charmliss. I have new intelligence and I wish to see the High Suzerain around 1030 if he is available."

"I shall send a car immediately, Dr Charmliss, but you may have to wait a little at this end. In any case, I can detail a man to type your report to dictation, and print it ready for your presentation. I am afraid it may be early afternoon before Major-General Treagh is available."

"That is excellent, Seargent Major MacKinnon. I shall see you shortly."

I went downstairs to the main entrance, the one with the brass latch and the etched glass window.

I stood on the pavement but had hardly done so when I saw a statocar draw round the corner and hover at the entrance. Igor was at "the wheel".

I climbed abord and Igor took off.

"Do you mind if I smoke, Dr Charmless?" Igor asked as he flicked a switch and fumbled in the glove box on the passenger side.

"Not at all"

Igor turned to face me as I was in the back seat, and proffered a packet of Bonanzas. For some reason, maybe a subconscious premonition, I had fitted the seat belt.

"No thanks, Igor, I gave up before the War."

The car had swooped its unctuous way onto the Hodgate and was gathering speed, weaving through traffic without active supervision.

We were nearing the western end of the shopping street when there was a blinding white flash and an earsplitting concussion. The car's mechanism somehow unbalanced and the thing described an upward swoop along I suppose a segment of a spiral. The vehicle lodged halfway through the plate glass window on the fourth floor of a furniture store, with the front half precariously suspended over the pavement. The car started to rock on what appeared to be a rebar beam. The glass and brick facade had blown out and the building's skeleton was exposed. The car's windows had automatically opened upon impact, whether by design I did not know. The chill Autumn breeze fitfully gusted about us.

"Do not move, Igor, or else we fall", I counselled. "Wait for the Fire Officers."

But Igor was slammed head first into his dashboard and did not reply.

I had always a horror of heights, from toddlerhood at least, and when the car tipped forward I could see how far above the Hodgate we were.

There was something eerie about this. The place was perfectly silent except for the clangor of far and near fire alarms. The store's alarm was vibrating against its half-rotten plywood base and the muffled echo of the deafening bell grated upon the teeth like cardboard. As the car swung forward I glimpsed the street covered in rubble. Curiously there was no-one. No traffic. Silence beyond the bells.

The contents of some jeweller's shop window was spilt across the rubble. No-one had rushed forward to steal the gold, the diamonds or the watches. This was diametrically different to the scene that ensued the bombing of the Hatton Bank.

This reminded me of similar events in the Lebanon and Iraq.

I leant back instinctually. The car tilted to slam down on the concrete floor and I looked round to see that the floor was largely intact behind with beds and sofas surreally undamaged.

The nearest stores' alarms had one by one ceased and a chilled silence descended. I dared not try to open the door.

Then I heard the light careful footfall of a something on the concrete steps of the store's now-open fire stairs. It was either a ghost or a woman, I thought. There was no scape of claws, so it could not be dog or demon.

The woman emerged behind me, perhaps twenty metres, and walked slowly pointing a sub-machinegun from navel height. She fired once, perhaps to test for living resistance. The thing was obviously set to single-shot. I drew the Wrortlemonger and fired in her direction more or less at random. The woman fell against a sofa with blood falling from her right knee. I turned forward and noticed that Igor had lost half his head, and blood and brains covered the front passenger seat. But there was no arterial spurting so he had obviously been dead already.

A squall played about the empty facade. The car started to rock up and down. I felt it tip forward. I was still in the inertial harness, but instinctively covered my head with my hands and cowered in the footwell behind Igor's seat.

I woke in an iron institutional bed in a busy ward with military nurses darting to and fro. The Loveliness was sitting beside me gently smiling her dignified, devout, closed-lipped smile, so reassuring, so accessible, so knowing in unknowable intimacy. She was in the full uniform of a Magonian lieutenant-colonel, minus the stupid bonnet. Tenderly holding my other hand much to my surprise was a burly black, also in full uniform, smiling kindly. It was Manville Treagh. This was Magonian territory. This was Magonian territory in wartime. All wars are the same, but this was so very different. It was 78V. It was so verily, very much 78V.

"Congratulations, my Dearest Arnoldina", I whispered through a dust-parched throat.

"Congratulations to you, Charles, my last and nearest love. You are still with me in 78V."

Treagh gently squeezed my hand and left.

Arnoldina did not use the regulation bedside water carafe. Instead she took a bottle of chilled fizzy water from her bag and held it as I drank.

"Arnoldina, what happened?"

"The ENLA blew up your car as it passed over a manhole cover. Igor died instantly. The woman who pressed the detonator climbed the stairs of the store where your car came to rest. She tried to finish the job. You shot her."

"The car fell out of the shop window. Edmonson calculated it would have been travelling at 38.7 miles per hour when it hit the street. It is a good job you wore your seat belt. The statocar crumpled. You were sawn out by fire officers."

"Where am I?"

"In the Presidium sick bay"

"Did I kill her?"

"No, Charles. Be at peace. You shot her right knee cap. She is in agony. I gave her diamorphine. I stripped and bathed her and dressed her leg. She is going nowhere. She is in one of the old Assize Court cells under the Presidium."

"Arnoldina, you are an actual Saint sent to suffering men by Christ. I would have dismembered her alive."

"Charles, wrath profits no woman. I am a nurse and a physician. I have taken the oath. My knives are for saving life. My pistol is for my honour."

I quickly threw aside the blanket and made to leave. Arnoldina gently but firmly placed a hand upon my sternum.

"Neither shall you leave, Charles. You must rest"

"I must interview her. I have important intelligence for Treagh."

"Denzil already knows about Goodleague and her collaborators. Balfour's cellphone was traced and invigilated. The dialogue in her brothel was monitored. The Suzerain is very pleased with your work. It was Felicity Goodleague who blew up your car and Goodleague whom you shot and who now lives in an Assize cell."

"I have got to interrogate her"

"Today you rest, Charles"

"Is Balfour also a fascist?"

"We don't know, Charles. We think not. But she evidently hates Goodleague. Now rest."

CHAPTER SIXTEEN
THE COMMISSION

When I awoke Arnoldina was absent. I suppose she had gone to prosecute other duties. I called a nurse and asked her to help me rise and find my clothes. She said my clothes were in my bed chest, but that she would have to have the Matron's permission for me to leave.

The Matron presently appeared and stated that I could go and perform light work in an office, but the instant I felt unwell I must ring her, and on no account must I leave the Presidium, because I was in a state of psychological shock and might experience PTSD for many months.

I took her card as she gave me my clothes. I took off the hospital pyjamas and slowly proceeded to dress. From earliest infancy my parents had schooled me to be naked without shame in public places with witnesses. Such was illegal anywhere in England, even on beaches, and sometimes severely punished, but it was an impudicity that had stood me in good stead, at school, at university and in naval life, Quaker or not a Quaker.

My clothes had evidently been cleaned overnight and seemed to smell of carbon tetrachloride. I was surprised it was still legal in 78V.

I left to find my office. I was surprised to see MacKinnon in my seat.

"Hello, Dr Charmliss", he greeted, "I will type your report personally. Major-General Treagh will see you here at 0830 hours."

I checked my watch. It was 0623.

"In the meantime, Chuck, can I get you a coffee and a sandwich, or perhaps a little snifter to greet the dawn."

"I would be very grateful for food and maybe mineral water or coke. If you permit me I will treat you to a drink in the CPOs' mess at lunchtime?"

MacKinnon rang someone and said something I did not quite catch. I was pre-occupied.

Shortly, an able arrived with a trolley. He wore a steward's badge. There was a selection of fresh sandwiches, some toast and marmalade, fresh coffee black but with attendant milk, and both a fizzy water 500ml bottle and a zero cola.

I rose and offered to serve MacKinnon some coffee.

"No, Chuck, I've already breakfasted. Is it okay if I type whilst you eat?"

"By all means"

I recited the events of the last couple of days from Bunny entering the car park until I woke up in the care of Arnoldina and her nurses. MacKinnon dutifully typed it up on his microcomputer and emailed the report to Edmonson. He also printed a copy and gave it to me.

There was still a good hour and a half to kill.

"Is it all right if we watch the cricket?" I asked.

"Sure", replied MacKinnon.

He called up the relevant app on his computer and we sat and watched.

I have always hated all sports, and cricket in particular was like watching paint dry.

After five minutes of this torture I said to Mackinnon:-

"Seargent Major MacKinnon..."

"Teddy, please"

"I am sorry if you are enjoying the game, but do you mind if we turn it off and talk. I want to be political, if that is acceptable?"

"Anything is acceptable for you Chuck", said Teddy, switching off the app and going back to a blue and silent Desktop.

"Forgive me if I err, Teddy, but I think from your accent that you are an Ulsterman?"

"Portadown born and bred, Chuck"

"Tell me, Teddy, why do excellent servicemen and women who are of European race and bred in the Occident join the forces of the Magonian Federation?"

"With respect, Chuck, it is much like your own motivation. None of us are venal traitors or collaborators. We want our countries to be true democracies where everyone has a say and can speak without fear, and print and publish what they think, and only what *they* think, will serve the common weal. The pay is poor but the comradeship faultless, the leadership modest and self-sacrificing, and the people we guide and cherish happy."

"Dr Charmliss, I respect your country and I also value and respect America. I am an Irishman. But I want the people of Ulster to decide for themselves, independently of Britain or the Republic." [He meant the Irish Republic: The Thirty-Two Counties.]

"Whatever they, and *only* they decide, I shall live with, if it means I suffer the everlasting contempt and contumely of my countrymen, or even if they take my life forfeit."

"Seargent Major MacKinnon, I honour you and I agree with you", I replied.

Teddies eyes watered with tears. He looked to his keyboard.

Sadly, not everyone he guided and cherished were happy.

At 0830 on the dot Treagh entered my office. He was accompanied by Edmonson and a Magonian naval officer: Not Ionescu, someone I did not recognise. MacKinnon stayed, after liberating extra chairs from surrounding offices.

"Dr Charmliss, this is Marine Pro-Admiral Michael Slummers, or as he was in the RN, Admiral Sir Michael Slummers", said Treagh.

Slummers and I rose and shook hands.

"Good to meet you at last", I commented at Slummers.

Slummers kept silence.

We resumed our seats.

"Firstly, Charmliss, I find it difficult to express how grateful I am for your courage, loyalty and initiative. We now have in custody I think the entirety of the ENLA Northwest-Palatinate command. The people of Congleholme can now walk without fear."

"Secondly, when we are in private, for example the present company or with your good Wife, I want you to call me 'Denzil'. In other circumstances, 'Sir' or 'Excellency'. I will call you 'Chuck' in private, and 'Charmliss' or 'Dr Charmliss' in public."

Denzil paused. He rapped his fingers on the table. He took out a cheap ballpen and played with it. I felt very sorry for him. I felt like saying "What do you want to say, Denzil? We are your friends." I kept silence.

"Charmliss, promise me you will not be angry or bawl me out in front of junior officers", said Treagh, surprisingly.

"I know you are a very loyal Briton, and you have every right to be. You are a born Englishman and your country has gifted so very much to the world."

"Chuck, I am your friend and I want to offer you Magonian citizenship."

"You can call it Anglo-Magonian citizenship and I will try to have it recorded as such. All entitlements.", said Treagh.

I kept silence and tried to look dignified.

"Lastly, if you permit, I wish to request Admiral Slummers to offer you the war-substantive commission of Commodore First-Class in the Magonian Navy (Atlantic Approaches)", Treagh added.

Slummers looked at me and said:-

"Yes, he means Rear Admiral"

"Do you accept any of this, Dr Charmliss?" resumed the High Suzerain.

"My friend, High Suzerain, I accept all of it with indescribable thanks and pride."

"Good! You will be under the command of Slummers. But we still have work for you, and if you and Admiral Slummers agree, I shall retain your services meantime."

"I look forward to working with Charmliss, but if it assists our aims, Major-General Treagh, Commodore Charmliss will be based at Congleholme until further notice, and I delegate command to you", asserted Slummers.

Treagh looked at Edmonson. Slummers had a voice recorder running on the table beside him. Treagh said to Edmonson, who was of course recording separately:-

"Did you get all of that, Edmonson?"

"I got all of it, Sir"

"Good!"

Treagh stood with a flourish of triumph and the others marched from my office.

"Stay, Seargent Major MacKinnon, please."

MacKinnon returned to my chair as commanded.

I waited until the others were well out of earshot.

"Right. Let's repair to the Wardroom. I owe you a drink. Where is it?"

"Follow me, Sir"

It would have been about 1700 when MacKinnon ordered me a car. Within ten minutes I was back at the Albion. Arnoldina was sitting up in my bed wearing a dressing gown and watching some Australian soap opera. She was far above that sort of thing of course but we are all entitled to a little rest and recouperation, even saints like Arnoldina.

I stripped, showered and climbed in on the other side of the Loveliness.

"Charles!", Arnoldina exclaimed with a shocked expression, "You're drunk!"

"I am not drunk. I just had a couple of bourbons with MacKinnon to celebrate."

"Celebrate what?"

"Arnoldina, I have just been granted Magonian citizenship and commissioned as a Rear-Admiral in the Navy", I said matter-of-factly.

"You're joking!" said Arnoldina her eyes wide and their pupils dilating.

"Ring Treagh or Slummers and ask them", I replied.

"Now that does deserve a hiding, drunk or sober!" claimed the Colonel.

I rose from the bed seriously, and lifted the slim beauty to a standing position. I reverently removed the dressing-gown. I commanded:-

"Sit on the edge of the bed"

Arnoldina complied.

I awkwardly assumed the position.

Arnoldina placed my pillow under my head.

"Christ Jesus" she commenced

"Forever keep this good man humble, sedulous to tread in your footprints across the chill waters and the burning sands. Let him always reprove the proud, but chastely, gently and with love. Let him console the weak, the destitute, the defeated, be they of the nation he loves and serves in his own fashion, or the creatures of time and your eternal Ministry. So help him I beg, you God and you Best of Men."

"Christ, my only Lord and King" I responded

"I have pledged faith to others today, not in treachery or abandonment, but better to serve your sacred and inscrutable intent. Teach me. Keep me straight. Make me a better Husband, a good Leader, a Man your Imitation. Please help me."

"You are indeed a man", commented Arnoldina, "so I ask you this: Are you ready."

"I am ready"

Arnoldina delivered the blows of her life. I did not count. I just wept. At last she lifted me from her lap and embraced me like a stern Madonna. There were tears in her eyes also. You may ask what sin I had committed, aside perhaps from Gluttony. I do not know. But this was maybe her painful admonition that drew a line under things and beat the bounds, say to say, warning me never to transgress or fall into the corruptions of pride.

We showered and dressed. We showered in silence. We did not cuddle or have sex.

We dried ourselves.

"Would you like an analgesic balm, Charles?" Arnoldina asked.

"No thank you. I wish to smart and remember."

"You shall remember, but not always smart, Charles. Today you fulfilled your half of our contract, a contract the more binding for being tacit, unspoken and unwritten."

We returned to bed and slept in each other's arms.

CHAPTER SEVENTEEN
THE ASSASSIN

"Charles, when you Attended did you ever succor those who fell?"

I did not quite know what she meant by 'fell'. Was this a theological question, or was it literal? Perhaps both? How did she know I was an Attender and not a Member?

We had both skipped dinner. It was now 0800 and I was ravenous. I leapt out and showered.

"It is a little early for the profound, Arnoldina"

"It is never too early. It is never too late"

Arnoldina went to her doctor's bag. As she bent over I beheld the sacred portal that would convey my only child to the world, God willing. I had to look away, as if I had gazed into the glory hole of an arc furnace.

Arnoldina took out a chocolate wafer and gave it to me:-

"Eat this. I had meant it for Mr Rat but I can buy him another."

I ate it.

I checked my pistol. Four shells were left, so I must have fired eleven at Goodleague.

We then dressed and went to breakfast.

Barely had we sat, my thighs stiff and my backside sore on the hard bar chair, than Ionescu walked up beaming:-

"Welcome aboard, Commodore!" he said as I rose and we shook hands.

He took a bosun's whistle from his pocket and blew it comically.

The room quietened and then laughed. Some applauded in a desultory way, including the gaggles of night tourists beginning to saunter in from the street.

I had noticed that some of the latter were studying each other's mobile phones or checking out camera screens. Occasionally they giggled or shifted whilst others looked on with concerned or bemused frowns. I asked Ionescu:-

"What is happening over there?"

"Oh, they are just comparing 'ghosts'", he remarked dismissively and sauntered away to get his own breakfast.

I decided to walk over and investigate. An American proudly showed me his cellphone screen. It depicted what appeared to be a vaguely anthropomorphic green smudge, diaphanous against the red sandstone Roman wall outside. I formed the opinion it was some artifact of the Welsbach light playing amid the coated internal elements of the lens optics, but then wondered if mobiles employed geometric optics. I lost interest and returned to Arnoldina.

"I need a shot of insulin", I confided to my nurse.

"No Charles, what you need is to eat properly, give up drinking, and get more exercise."

"You sound like my Wife of the Old World. I will have to spank you!" I jested.

"You can do that Charles, but you promised to obey me in all matters medical."

"I did and I shall. Sorry, Arnoldina"

"Good! This morning we are having Staffordshire oak cakes cooked in sesame oil with black coffee!"

"Thank you, dear. That sounds just right!" I lied.

When I arrived in my office at the Presidium I could not collect my thoughts. I checked my watch. It was 0817. I tidied my desk. Either Edmonson or MacKinnon had placed the typescript of my report about the late events on the surface of the desk. I filed it in a near-empty cabinet. I checked that I could boot my computer, and then powered down.

After a few minutes of this nervous fidgeting I walked along to MacKinnon's office.

"Good morning, Sergeant-Major MacKinnon" I greeted "Is Denzil in?"

"The Magor-General has been at his desk all night, Commadore Charmliss. I will take you right in."

We marched out and had soon joined Treagh, dozing behind his enormous desk in his enormous room.

He was otherwise alone.

He stirred dozily. He had removed his jacket and was lounging in shirt sleeves.

"Thanks for coming, Chuck. I have read your report. My gamble paid off."

Treagh did not elaborate or explain.

"Sir", I commenced, "Please tell me if my Licence of Superintendence is still valid?"

"I don't know, Commadore. Hand it over and I will read it."

Treagh seemed befuddled like a man who had just woken and not yet showered or eaten.

"This just gives you summary powers over all non-Magonians on the patch. It still applies", Treagh said, handing it back.

"As a Commadore, do I have powers of command over *all* Magonian personnel of lower rank?"

"Chuck, you have never had a complex or problems about leadership that I know of. You can safely command most of my men without future reference to me, unless you sense there is something special about the situation, when I must intervene. If you get the wrong call, you call it wrong. Now I have to be careful not to offend Slummers or the rest of the Navy, and you too should take care, but until further notice you may command any more junior man or woman in my Area. Ionescu will call at your billet with a tailor this afternoon and measure you for a set of Commadore's uniforms. This uniform, when delivered, you shall wear at all those times when Naval brass may reasonably be expected, except when you are on leave or I give you permission to vary."

"Oh, and I almost forgot..."

Treagh opened one of his left desk draws, and removing some heavy object threw it on his desk toward me.

It was a full fifteen-shell clip for my pistol.

"Thank you for your advice, Sir, and thank you for the ammunition."

"It is an honour, Charmliss. Now is there anything else?"

"I do not wish to impose, Sir, but may I be excused caps. They irritate and aggravate my psoriasis."

"You must wear a cap in front of Slummers or other admirals. Otherwise I gladly excuse you."

"Now I don't want to be rude, Chuck, but I really must get on."

"Please forgive me, Major-General Treagh, but I must interview the prisoners. Please may I have CPO Edmonson with audio-visual recorders for the rest of the day. Also a nurse good with dressings together with MacKinnon and the Chief of Guards?"

"Chief Petty Officer Edmonson is yours to command, Charmliss. You may command Sergent-Major MacKinnon and Lieutenant Slenderman for the duration."

"Thank you, Sir"

I rose at attention and saluted Treagh with the old RN salute that I knew because my Father had taught it to me. Treagh rose slowly and saluted back.

I went back to my office.

Edmonson knocked tentatively at the open door. I beckoned him in. "CPO Edmonson, get your video and recording tackle. I am going to interview prisoners." Edmonson left smartly as the telephone rang.

"Charmliss", I answered.

"Commadore Charmliss, I am Lieutenant Patrick Slenderman, Chief of Guards, I understand you wished to speak to me?"

"Yes, Lieutenant, please come to my office now and bring any work you have regarding the prisoners taken after yesterday's Hodgate bombing incident."

"Yes Sir"

Presently, Edmonson returned hefting two large crash cases I presumed of camera and recording kit. He had also fitted a bodycam to his chest.

Slenderman shortly strode in with a sheaf of papers and arrogated a seat.

"Right, Sir, we have seven from yesterday's assault including the ringleader, one Felicity Goodleague, a motor restorer by profession. James Mann, an unemployed shipwright, is said to be her boyfriend. The five others are Tracey Bulloch, who is male; Harold Makepiece; Ernest Parker; Victor Mature and George Webb."

"Is Victor Mature a nom-de-guerre?"

"We do not know, Commadore Charmliss. It appears on his current British passport."

"Goodleague and Mann are known neo-Nazis. Goodleague is intelligent and a manipulative writer. She is also a good markswoman."

Slenderman did not see fit to compliment me on my marksmanship. Then I remembered that Arnoldina had admonished me to walk with humility, placing my feet in the steps of Another.

"Thank you, Slenderman", I said.

"My friends call me 'Slim'" confided the lieutenant with ultimate predictability.

"Lieutenant Slenderman", I resumed, "what are the ages of these people."

"Goodleague is thirty-three, Sir, and Mann thirty-four. The rest are mostly in their twenties."

"Casualties?"

"Egor, your driver, Sir, and two Palatine policemen shot dead. Three on their side dead, Commadore Charmliss"

"What about bystanders?"

"Seven dead and twenty-one critically injured, Sir"

Just then a nurse appeared with a case. She was in a white and blue uniform which nicely-complimented her dark South Asian complexion.

She got no time to rest.

"Right, Lady and Gentlemen, let's go!" I commanded.

We rose as a man and Slenderman led the way.

Slenderman found an elevator and we squeezed inside. The conveyance stalled as it reached the ground floor. Slenderman inserted a key into the console and the machine edged down two further, "secret", stories. As it stopped at the lower of the two basements we emerged to find a Palatine custody sergeant at his brightly-illuminated desk.

"Who would you like to see first, Gentlemen?" he asked.

"Goodleague" I said.

Another guard said "Follow me, Gentlemen" and we were led to a stone cell with a cream painted interior. It was an unfurnished but claustrophobic room of I estimated five by three metres. It would of course have been drawn in Imperial days using feet and inches but that was my guess. Someone had installed a shower and lavatory combo in a corner. The whole place stank of Lysol. It felt cramped with seven people plus Edmonson's tripod and other kit.

In an opposite corner, sitting with her knees drawn to her chest, and on a thin blue washable palliasse was a naked white woman with long chestnut hair and a bloody white bandage around her right knee and the adjacent leg parts.

Even more disturbingly, someone had recently fitted a steel plate to the wall and a new galvanised chain extended towards a manacle round her left wrist.

She glowered a look of pure malice at me. She obviously knew who I was, and from her viewpoint had narrowly failed to destroy an implacable enemy.

She attempted to stand, and uttered a brief shriek of agony before cowering in the corner.

"Good Morning, Miss Goodleague", I commenced "have you had something to eat and drink this morning?"

"I don't talk to traitors"

"They are not traitors, Felicity, they are all brave British patriots. I picked them personally so as not to offend you", I softly lied. "And if you mean specifically myself, I am an old Briton who is doing the best for his old country in the very difficult circumstances in which he finds himself. Is that what you do, Felicity?"

"What about the wog?"

"There are no wogs here, Felicity. The nurse is a brave, patriotic Englishwoman like you. She has come to give you a shower, change your dressing, and if you want it give you an analgesic injection."

Goodleague was trying to suppress shivering.

I turned to the guard who had opened the door and said:-

"Get her a duvet and some breakfast."

"Yes Sir"

A few minutes later the guard returned with a wrapped sandwich and a polystyrene cup of black coffee. He had around his shoulders a disposable bedcover. He gave these things to Goodleague and she ate ravenously.

"Now give her a bottle of water", I commanded

The beverage was duly found and given.

All the time I remembered Arnoldina's saintly words that she had impressed upon me.

"Now, Felicity, I shall unlock the chain at your wrist and carry you to the lavatory as gently as I can. There you may defecate if you are able and the nurse will shower you and change your dressing. Are you ready?"

The woman nodded disconsolately with a downcast gaze.

I motioned to the guard.

He unlocked the chain.

I carried Goodleague to the steel pan and she sat. She did not fart or defecate, only urinated. The nurse showered her, dried her and changed the dressing.

Goodleague whimpered and thanked the nurse.

A very meek Nazi, I thought idly.

"You will not need the chain just yet. We will see how you go. You will be able to visit the lavatory freely, and we will bring you some food and water later in the day. At 2000 hours we will switch the light off and you will be able to sleep. We have important questions to ask you but you have had enough for now. By the way, the cold water in the wash basin is potable. You can fill your water bottle and have as much as you need."

"Thank you, Dr Charmliss. I thought you were going to rape me."

"Felicity, you are a murderess. You killed my driver Igor and you tried to kill me. You are a woman who brings death not life. No man will entrust his Sacred Seed of Life to you. What would you do with an inconvenient baby, his child? Would you strangle it at birth and hide it in a sewer?"

Goodleague burst into tears.

The nurse, MacKinnon and Edmonson returned to their duties. I had asked Edmonson to compile a coherent forensic video and a textual report of dialogue.

I commanded Slenderman to accompany me to my office.

"What are your observations, Lieutenant Slenderman?" I opened after we had taken our seats.

"About the background, Sir, or today specifically?"

"Both"

"Well I think you are too clement, Sir, or perhaps reckless. This is a very dangerous woman, Sir, and should be chained at all times. If she shits where she sits so be it. We can hose her down later."

"First of all, Slenderman, none of your commanding officers are ever reckless. Is that understood?"

"Yes Sir. Sorry Commadore Charmliss."

"Very well. Now, Slenderman, you have some very good men under your command. Do you think any of them would be so careless as to let a prisoner escape the custody suite? Or do you think a naked woman would pass unnoticed in the shopping streets of Congleholme?"

"Thank you for your words about my men. They are indeed excellent and that is why I am sedulous to protect them. As to your remarks about escape, they are sensible, Sir."

"Your response is first-class, Slenderman. You will bag the prisoners' clothes and shoes separately for forensic analysis. They will remain naked until the day after tomorrow when they will be issued with orange prisoner jump suits after medical examination and photography. No-one is to be manacled or chained. This lunch-time today all will have a hot meal in their cells, a clean towel and a disposable duvet. They will each have a light cold snack at 1900. At

1930 wounds will be dressed and lights out is 2000 as I remarked. These orders are effective at 1300 today. If any want a Bible or other Scripture you shall provide it. Do you have any questions, Lieutenant Slenderman?"

"None, Sir"

"Now you will be very busy, Slenderman. I shall return to the custody suite at 1000 hours tomorrow and you shall accompany me on inspections. Forgive me, Slenderman, but I must now leave for an appointment at my billet."

Slenderman rose from his chair and saluted briskly.

"Yes Sir, Thank you, Sir"

"You are dismissed"

Slenderman marched out.

I ordered a car and was driven back to the Albion without incident. As I entered the Public Bar I saw that Ionescu was seated with a rating in Magonian uniform.

"Chuck!" Ionescu alerted as I entered.

I sat on the third seat at their table.

"What are you drinking?" he asked.

"I would like a pint of IPA please, Eugen"

"Maggi", shouted Ionescu to the barmaid. "A pint of IPA and a ham sandwich for the Commadore, please."

"Yes, Eugen. Coming up."

We were essentially alone that lunchtime except for a couple of old boys shooting the breeze in the corner.

"This is CPO Midas Montgomery, our Navy tailor. He will take your measurements and have two pairs of dress and undress commadore's uniforms made for you. We will do it in your room, but there is no need to rush."

Montgomery, a trim mixed-race man, rose to salute. I rose, saluted, proffered my hand and said "Pleased to meet you." Montgomery answered in a South London accent "I am pleased to meet you too, Sir." We resumed our seats and Maggi brought my food and drink.

Maggi proffered her slender hand, and said:-

"Congratulations, Commadore Dr Charmliss. Welcome aboard."

I think the coda was quite unaffected. It is a British colloquialism though of Naval origin of course.

I rose and gently shook her hand as she beamed.

We finished our drinks, and went upstairs where I was measured and calibrated photographs taken of me in my underwear. Ionescu and Montgomery left after twenty minutes or less, and I sat on a chair to think. It was very quiet, still only about 1400.

Clearly I needed to know about the local ENLAs source of firearms and explosives. There was very little aviation these days, largely because anything which appeared in the sky was automatically shot down by defensive missiles even if it was a meteorite. Indeed large birds had been known to suffer this reaction of the artificial "intelligence" systems.

My instinct, or rather prejudice, was that the materiel was landed clandestinely by small cargo ship very locally, perhaps in the chemical industry complexes around Queen's Quay.

I surmised that the firearms might have been imported separately. In a war small arms are everywhere, and road commerce from the London underworld could not be ruled out.

I needed to know more about ENLA comings and goings. I rang Bunny.

"'Ullo", bellowed a drunken male voice, bullock-like from the other end.

"Hello", I responded, "Is Bunny in?"

"She is with a customer. Is that you, Charmliss?"

"Yes"

"She will be down the Albion after she has finished the trick. About three-o'clock, mate."

"Thank you, that is very helpful"

We exchanged pleasantries, as some say, and rang off.

I loitered over a pint in the Public Bar. About 1500 early commuters began to drift in and at 1505 dead Bunny Balfour flounced through the door.

"Bunny, I am over here", I shouted.

Bunny turned to my voice as Maggi shouted "Out!" from behind the bar.

"It's okay, Maggi", I shouted, "I will take her elsewhere"

Bunny and I walked onto the Hodgate and found a tavern called the Wheatsheaf in an alley way off the main street. I went in and asked to hire a private room for an hour which was granted.

The prostitute and I went into the room and were asked to order drinks, which we did.

We sat and I asked:-

"Are there any suspicious comings-and-goings in Manningfield Crescent on a regular basis?"

"Ah, plenty. If you mean in relation to Goodleague there is often a small white Transit-type van that parks on the grass near her house every Thursday afternoon and stays for around thirty to forty-five minutes. It has "Bellingham, Queen's Key" in purple lettering on each side. Usually a large parcel is transferred to her house. The driver has short ginger hair."

"Bunny, why do you do this? Why do you take the risk?"

A pause.

"I do it for England"

Another pause.

"And another thing", Bunny resumed in her womanly way, "The ENLA are very bad for trade. The Pakis and the blacks will not come onto the estate in case they are beaten-up or worse by the Nazis."

"Splendid, Bunny", I answered, "You and I have done an ace five-minutes work. Here's three thousand crowns for your trouble. Next time you see the van, photograph it or take its number, preferably both."

I placed the notes on the table and marched out. We did not exchange valedictions.

I entered the Presidium, a mere ten minutes brisk walk from the Wheatsheaf, even for an eighty-four year old.

I marched into MacKinnon's office unannounced and said:-

"Find out where the firm 'Bellingham' is in Queen's Key. It may even be on Internet maps. Also, check the times of high tide on Wednesday and Thursday."

"At Queen's Quay, Sir?"

"Yes, then order a car"

We drove to Bellingham's at Queen's Quay no more than fifteen miles away. They were importers of gravel and road stone, with a side-line in concrete paving slabs. There we saw six Transit-type vans parked in the yard, which I surreptitiously photographed. Over a gravel service road in front of the yard was a tidal flat. The tide was out. A small steel barge was moored at the quay. It was the only vessel visible, and its hold seemed to contain silt, whether the remains of a cargo or natural wash from the sea I could not tell.

But another small vessel, a keeled vessel, sometimes rested immediately North of the barge: Fortunately the tide was out and I could tell from the keel's imprint upon the estuarine silt that it was a coaster-type vessel of maybe 750 tonnes gross register.

"At high tide some sort of coaster docks here and unloads parcels", I confided to MacKinnon, "when is the next high tide on a Wednesday or Thursday?"

"1806 on Wednesday, 0645 and 1818 on Thursday, Commadore."

"We will invigilate all three. I need four armed MPs, and ten Palatine police for chase and arrest duties. Also an infra-red photography expert like Edmonson and a sledge hammer", I commanded.

"A sledge hammer, Sir?"

"A sledge hammer"

We were in position at 1806 on the Wednesday. Nothing happened.

We drove back to the office. Rather than waste time I asked Edmonson to escort me down to the cells to have another interview with Goodleague.

I rang Slenderman to tell him to escort us but he was apparently at his billet sleeping or at least his phone was diverted to the duty Custody Seargent who agreed to have us escorted from my office.

The lights were switched on.

Goodleague had wrapped herself in her duvet. She seemed surprised to see us and rather alarmed.

"Why did you do this?" I asked.

"Because you are an important traitor", Goodleague replied.

"I am not a traitor. What I meant was why are you a Nazi", I said.

"I am not a Nazi. Do you want England to be overrun by Muslims and kikes who have hatred for us and defile our country? Is that what you are fighting for, Dr Charmliss? We will round them up and throw them in to the sea", Goodleague replied.

"We need to stop any more immigration from any land, but the immigrants we have we must assimilate. We must school them to be good Britons, ready to help build our country in peace. Cruelty is not the answer, Felicity. Love and respect will restore our country", I lectured.

"Do you have any information that will help us restore our country that we so love?" I asked.

Goodleague was silent.

"Would you like some cocoa and biscuits before we leave you to sleep?"

"Yes please, Dr Charmliss. You are a much kinder man than I thought. Thank you."

Her cocoa and biscuits were duly prepared and given to her where she sat on her pallet.

We left and I told the guard "Turn her light out in fifteen minutes."

"Yes Sir"

By 0600 we were back at the wharf in Queen's Quay. As the darkness resolved to a damp dawn the yellow sodiums cast pools of sunny yellow in the cold morning mist. We sat in our cars waiting. I did not commandeer the Bellingham offices which had a second storey vantage for fear of alerting whoever or whatever might appear.

For the present the wharf was deserted. In the twilight the dripping trees formed a still tableau of Autumn grace. Squirrels gathered acorns of the mature oaks and chased each other around the trunks as male pursues female through the eons. A very occasional fit of breeze would rustle the high twigs and precipitate a rain of golden beech and birch leaves.

It occurred to me that with my field glasses and camo fatigues I might pass muster as a matutinal bird-watcher and so I quietly left the unmarked car with Edmonson's tackle in it, and slowly walked to the edge of the quay.

The tide was of course almost at the peak and the seawater lapped against the sheet-piles and had floated the derelict barge with the silt in it. This vessel itself banged against the piling with a gentle metallic rhythm. Hempen ropes tensed and relaxed with a low creaking.

I did not know if Bellingham's had security surveillance and I did not invite attention by searching for any, but the place appeared barred and shuttered.

A low and ominous mist hung over the estuary but it was not deep and I suspected a temperature inversion.

At one distant spot a black pall of smoke seemed to be spreading over the mist.

I consulted my glasses. A black dot appeared to be under the smoke suspended at or just above the visible horizon.

Less than five minutes later I could hear the definite thump-thump-thump of an old fashioned oil engine. Using the binoculars again I could see that it was a coasting vessel of obsolete pattern and maybe as much as a thousand gross tons.

I did not of course know if the master was using glasses or modern inshore radar. So I returned to Edmonson's car to await future developments as my sailor Father used pleonastically to say.

I had briefed Treagh's men to park an Army car two hundred metres up the access road and block all incoming or outgoing traffic. This spot was chosen to be just out of sight of the wharf. I would wait until the first van set off from the premises and then fire an exploding white very flare. I some ways 78V technology was fifty years ahead of 80V: In other respects fifty behind. I did not know for certain how much briefing had filtered through to the Palatine boys.

Slowly the small ship dilated and resolved. It was a bit of an environmental nightmare. Black partially-combusted paraffin billowed from the single stack.

Within fifty metres of the wharf the engine was stilled and the boat allowed to drift under its momentum to the mooring-place.

Suddenly four men appeared from the Bellingham compound and four from the little ship, two at each end. So there were at minimum five aboard the coaster whose name I could now descry as MV *Conwell*. She flew an Irish flag at the stern. A small Magonian military ensign flew as courtesy from the single crossyard.

Hawsers were exchanged and the the ship hauled snug, before a single gangway was swung ashore. Several men issued carrying ordinary cardboard parcels 60 by 60 by 60 cms.

I counted 64 parcels as the vans were loaded. Then the first van left the gates.

I walked to the edge of the car park and fired the white very skyward. At a hundred feet it detonated. All hell broke loose. Some ran aboard the ship. Someone fired at me from the Bellingham compound. A Palatine policeman with a sub-machine gun ran towards me and also MacKinnon armed with his sledge hammer. I took out my pistol with the full magazine and ran aboard the MV *Conwell*, closely followed by MacKinnon and the Palatine.

Those aboard quickly surrendered and were made to lie prone on the weather deck by three more Palatine Police with machineguns. The motor was still running and the master tried to reverse the ship from the quayside but of course that was hopeless. He soon gave up and presented with his hands on his head.

"Let's go below", I said to MacKinnon. I drew my pistol and descended the companionway. MacKinnon followed closely with the hammer. We entered the engine room and the engineer-com-stoker put his hands up. I motioned to him to run up to the weather deck.

I took the sledge from MacKinnon and brought it down as fast as I might upon the cast iron inlet main for the cooling system. The pipe smashed and the sea entered volcanically. The engine raced. Shouting was impossible to be heard, so I indicated to MacKinnon to leave with all speed.

As we regained the quayside the little ship was slightly listing to port away from the moorings. It was important to get away before the hawsers parted, if they would part, and everyone ran for the car park. Palatine black marias were already waiting and everyone we could not account for bundled in.

I waited half an hour with Edmonson. At 0708 the hawsers gave way and the vessel settled on the silt with its starboard hull above the sea.

After the Palatine Police had taken stock of the parcels, 48 were found to contain cannabis, 14 cocaine or fentanyl, and two Semtex.

CHAPTER EIGHTEEN
RUCTIONS

I do not know what it was about that morning. We had awoken under a black cloud below the setting of a malign star. Arnoldina seemed sullen and taciturn. Very unlike my Arnoldina.

Maybe she was having a period, or whatever it was here in 78V. Maybe it was just her age and the unaccustomed sex, or the peculiarities of her semi-artificial physiology.

I do not know. I wish never to learn. I wish to remember a woman mistress of her own destiny.

We went silently to breakfast. Arnoldina in full lieutenant-colonel's uniform complete with bonnet, shoulder-holster and underwear. The holster and its pistol added an extra dimension of hideousness. It made her splendid breasts appear large and lumpy.

It was a buffet day, but as usual on such days the table places were set with a fork, two knives and a large China plate, besides cup and saucer.

There was also on each table a clear glass vase with artificial flowers.

There was also a carafe of tap water.

We sat at our usual table. For some minutes neither of us approached the buffet. At length, I went to the counter and helped myself to a full English which I took to the neighboring table, and started to consume with porcine rigour.

Arnoldina sat mutely and glowered at me in pure anger.

"So you want to clog your arteries, Charles, and leave for another universe?"

"What arteries. I am dead. Remember?"

"Your victims have already departed. Enjoy biting creatures who cannot bite back. But turn your gaze to them. It is their turn next."

I was aware that an uneasy quasi-silence had fallen and patrons were attempting to pretend nothing was unusual.

"You should follow your man", I added.

I was aware that we had raised our voices.

I felt our argument childish and vulgar.

"And another thing, if you think I am coming with you to visit whores, especially Goodleague, you are sadly deluded."

There was an intermission of repressed hostility.

"Think of your duty as a Christian", I responded unwisely.

Suddenly, Arnoldina rose from her seat and threw her heavy stainless steel dining knife onto her plate with force. The crockery shattered and shards flew everywhere, some onto other tables as guests breakfasted.

"By Christ, Charles, you sanctimonious little fucker. You are an arsehole. You are too stupid to lead a troupe of apes through Hell!" Arnoldina shouted.

With that the gentle woman I thought of as my Wife stormed back to her suite.

I made to follow to mine but Warble shouted:-

"Commodore, in my office now!"

I followed the owner and Head Waiter into a small paper-strewn room with a small paper-strewn desk. An old Osram, or even maybe a Thorn, strip lamp hummed brightly overhead. Maggi followed silently with an extra chair for me and promptly departed.

"Commadore Charmliss, I have to ask you and Mrs Feng to collect your belongings and leave by 1400 hours. I am sending an email to Major-General Treagh to request that you and she be re-billeted elsewhere, and that memorandum will be followed by a couriered letter from my solicitors."

"I am very sorry, Mr Warble. Please let me pay for the breakages and the solicitor's letter", I said as I reached for my credit card.

"Do not insult me, Charmliss", Warble voiced with cold spite, "for two weeks I have had to field numerous complaints verbal and written about noisy sex and other very inappropriate behaviour. I have had letters from tour operators and Mr Ionescu has with manifest regret forwarded my complaints to his own superiors without result. Reviews have even surfaced on TripAdvisor and my bookings have slumped. I employ four in a Depressed Area in wartime.

Charmliss, 'Commadore', [Warble added with a sneer] you are a disgrace to your suffering country and to the uniform you have sought to adopt.

Good bye."

I packed my bags and called MacKinnon for a car. It arrived promptly and I was in MacKinnon's logistics office within ten minutes. MacKinnon escorted me to one of the old Assize Justice's Lodgings behind the building. It was spacious but archaic, luxurious and musty. It had a single bedroom, a large lounge where the judge would have convened with barristers, a small kitchen, a bathroom with a bath and shower, and a separate lavatory and washbasin. From a physical point of view, it was better than my room and en-suite at the Albion.

You may or may not be gratified to learn that Warble later sent me a letter of apology for his complaints and his gratuitous remarks about me. For my part I understand his anger and think his complaints were justified, but I think his interpretation of my motivations misunderstanding. I did not reply. I did not appreciate his implication about Arnoldina.

CHAPTER NINETEEN
RESTORATION

That evening I sat disconsolately in the Judges' Lodging reading *The Times* and trying to forget the recent unhappy events. In the morning of the day before yesterday I had put on my No.1s and I had visited the Nurse's Institute again to ask where I could find Arnoldina. I had simply been told that they could not discuss the movements of Magonian officers, and that as one myself I would surely understand.

When I returned to my billet I began to cry and wept bitterly and cursed my selfishness and ineptitude. As in days long gone and irrecoverable I thought that I must walk. Any walk, anywhere, for as long as it took. I hoped that in the Autumnal gloom no-one would notice that an old man was weeping. The rain started again. I changed into my hiking fatigues and had just taken out my hiking boots when I thought I heard a woman weeping behind the heavy oaken door of the old Assize lodging.

The hair on the back of my neck bristled in horror.

Then there was a diffident feminine knock.

Summoning all my superstitious courage I opened the door and beheld Arnoldina. As she saw me she dissolved into a paroxysm of weeping and threw her arms about me. I likewise wept uncontrollably and took her in my arms.

As we stood upon the threshold Arnoldina gasped through her tears:-

"Oh, Charles, Mr Feng has died. I must return to bury him. Will you honour my Husband? Will you be at the graveside with me?"

"Arnoldina, I have always honoured your Husband, and I shall be with you. Come in Arnoldina."

I closed the heavy wooden door behind us.

I embraced Arnoldina again and in conscious quotation of Our Holy Saviour I softly said:-

"𝕿ake no thought for the morrow, for the morrow will take care of itself. 𝕴 am with you always."

Arnoldina was wearing a thick tweed skirt suit over a white linen blouse. Around her neck were not four courses of pearls but a crucifix on a silver chain. She would have passed muster as a Quakeress or even a Mennonite. As it was she was the perfect picture of an English country gentlewoman.

"Arnoldina, why are you not in uniform?"

"I was dishonorably dismissed the Magonian Army and my Commission revoked. My Police warrant card and my pistol have also been confiscated. But do not worry Charles. I have a full officer's pension and benefits, and a cash gratuity, and we will survive."

"Why?" I asked in astonishment.

"The official charge was 'Bringing Dishonor upon the Uniform'. So now, Charles, I have no uniform. I am wearing the type of outfit I thought would please you."

"I pleases me vastly, Arnoldina. Would you like a drink and perhaps something to eat? I have bread and wine and other vegan food."

"No, Charles. Thank you"

Arnoldina walked slowly to one of the old leather armchairs. She began to remove her clothing. As she did so I noticed that she had sensible country shoes and no underwear to remove.

She stood before me sobbing, folded her hands as if in prayer and bowed her head. I thought that indeed she might be praying and I was reluctant to speak or move. At length she raised her head and placed her hands by her side. Then she folded her hands again and bowed deeply in the Oriental manner. Then she clapped once. She seemed to have calmed a little. The general atmosphere of the room seemed somehow suffused with a holy serenity, like many country churches. The abiding aroma of old leather, mahogany, sandalwood and oak intensified the effect.

"Arnoldina, why have you undressed?" I asked with my usual stupidity.

"Firstly, Charles, I know you like a woman's nakedness and think it her fit state in the privacy of the home. Secondly, and more importantly, I need Holy Correction. You are my Husband now and I have the Right to demand it."

"Arnoldina, I am most honoured and delighted that you are here with me, and I humbly accept your love and your trust as my Darling Wife. You have no need to demand anything, because what you want or need is yours for the taking. I cannot express how much I love you, and your every godly wish I cheerfully supply where I am able."

"Thank you, Charles. I love you. There are no words to measure the extent of it. I am yours. I surrender body and soul knowing I shall not be betrayed. I ask only that you commit my mortal remains to the earth in the sure and certain knowledge that Christ shall billet my Immortal Soul Elsewhere."

"I intend to be an undemanding Wife, but I do not like that long leather sofa. I do not expect to find a comfy double bed in a Georgian Assize lodging. But this is war, and we are content with what we find, content to be alive. Take me in hand, Charles, and lead."

I tenderly removed her neck chain and placed the crucifix in her right hand.

I gently took hold of her cold and slender left hand and led her to the bedroom. The room was small and the bed barely adequate for one portly justice, but we made do.

Arnoldina assumed the position.

"Arnoldina I abhor lectures and recriminations, but I need to formulate my thoughts, and perhaps guide yours too. Do you mind if I explain what I am about to do and why?"

"You are master", Arnoldina responded, I thought abruptly, but foreign conceptions of politeness differ. I should have been grateful that this fine woman, or indeed any woman, would consecrate me with a child of our separate and equal patrimonies.

"Firstly, I award five blows to each cheek for your breach of the Tenth Commandment of God. You have no cause to be jealous of a poor woman languishing naked in a cold cell below us, not knowing whether her next visitor is a torturer or someone to take her out and burn her."

"Secondly, five for succumbing to wrath."

"Thirdly, ten for insulting your man in public."

"And fourthly, and most importantly of all, breaching the Third Commandment, fifteen."

"You would get many more for the first and second except that I doubt your physical endurance. My arithmetic says that is sixty spanks. Is that correct?"

"No, Charles, it is seventy", Arnoldina corrected. "You already know my opinion of Goodleague. She tried to kill my Husband. But you are right. As a Christian woman I owe a duty of care to the incarcerated. I shall ask to visit Goodleague and ascertain her needs and whether I can ease her sufferings. If she voluntarily apologises I shall forgive her. That is my Duty, a privilege of my Free Will vouchsafed of God."

"Charles, I do so hope that lectures and rationalisations will not become a feature of married life."

"Arnoldina, please do not answer me back. But I will not lecture you again. This is of course *your* Correction and you get only sufficient to your needs. I love you, Arnoldina"

"Are you cold, Arnoldina?"

"It is a little chilly. Please may I have the duvet across my shoulders?"

I grabbed the duvet from behind me and laid it over her torso and shoulders. Her lovely bottom was still naked.

"Now, Charles, we are profaning a Holy Sacrament. Please say your prayers aloud for my instruction, and then I shall say mine. 𝔖ufficient unto t𝔥e 𝔡a𝔶 i𝔰 t𝔥e e𝔳il t𝔥ereof"

"Thank you, Arnoldina. I shall: And it is:-"

My Holy Saviour
Award your daughter Arnoldina fortitude
The courage to endure and the strength to pray
Let her pain be light and the
chastening of her spirit complete
Take her sin and set it at naught
Restore to her the Innocency
that her trespasses adulterated
Forgive her now and forever
And prompt the forgiveness of those she wronged

Please help her God

Please help me God responded Arnoldina

Then Arnoldina voiced the traditional Prayer of Contrition:-

My Dear God, I am sorry for my sins with all my heart.
In choosing to do wrong and failing to do good,
I have sinned against You whom I should love above all
things.
I hate my sins and I reject them with loathing.
I firmly intend, with Your help, to use the pain of penance
To sin no more, and to avoid whatever leads me to sin.
Your Son, Jesus Christ, suffered and died for us.
In His name, my God, have mercy. Amen

"*Amen*" I responded.

Then the Loveliness continued:-

Darling Lord Jesus, please support this
good, kind, forgiving man
My Master and my loving Husband. He is not experienced.

Stifle the whisperings of Satan in his tender ears.
Make me the Wife he always wanted,
the mother of the child he sought in vain.
Make me respectful, helpful, obedient and loving,
the woman You always wanted me to be.
Make his sanctified castigations condign, cleansing,
adequate and firm and his mercy as a
shower of cooling rain in the
arid wastes of our condition.

"*Amen*" we chorused.
My eyes teared and I started to whimper.
I asked:-
"Are you comfortable My Love?"
No answer.
I delivered thirty light smacks. She had stopped crying as our prayers began and a supernatural calm seemed to fall about us.
It seemed to me that contrition had well antedated Correction, even pre-dated our reunion.
"For your offences to me I forgive you utterly and remit castigation. The thirty smacks were for breaking the Third Commandment. Call Christ only in prayer", I counselled.
I turned her onto her back, tenderly kissed her lips and prayed:-

My Holy Saviour
Accept I beg you
The pain of your daughter Arnoldina as
Reparation for her Sin
Remove all distress from her mind and spirit
Prepare her to amend and recompense her evil
And please exact no further penalty on Earth
Or in The Life to Come

Amen, *Amen*

Our Holy Saviour, who walked from the
Garden to Golgotha
Forgive this good woman her evils
The sins confessed and those known to her spirit
but not her mind
But guide her to find and confess

her further acts of wickedness
And renounce further sin
Listen to her prayers always and make her keep them holy
Exacting of her no perpetual forfeit
Accept her Sacrifice of pain as Imitation of Christ
Strengthen and Console her
In your Holy Name I commend Arnoldina to you,
my only Lord

Amen, *Amen*

I Crossed her body and lowered my head to her Holy Portal of Life.

"Oh no, Charles, don't!" Arnoldina begged with a little whimper. I kissed her clitoris within its hood.

Arnoldina came to a dramatic climax, the most volcanic of our short relationship.

I gently lifted Arnoldina to sit beside me.

"Charles, thank you for your Ministry, for your Prayers, your Correction, and your Mercy. I am sorry for my disgusting conduct and for wasting your time."

"Time with Arnoldina is never wasted", I responded.

"And the Army has already punished your conduct which they should not have for punishment is sinful. Only love and restoration are righteous."

"Now say this with me:-"

Our Father, which art in heaven,
hallowed be thy name;
thy kingdom come;
thy will be done,
in earth as it is in heaven.
Give us this day our daily bread.
And forgive us our trespasses,
as we forgive them that trespass against us.
And lead us not into temptation;
but deliver us from evil.
For thine is the kingdom,
the power, and the glory,
For ever and ever.
Amen.

Arnoldina echoed each Sacred line.

"Thank you, Charles, Dearest Husband"

"Thank *you*, Arnoldina, Dearest Wife"

"Arnoldina, would you like a massage or an analgesic rub?"

"No, My Love"

"Do you want to shower and dress"

"No, Charles. The duvet will do until they put the heating back on."

"Arnoldina, obey me. Go to the fridge in the kitchenette and bring the small plastic bottle of red wine and the bread rolls in the plastic wrapper."

"Yes, Sir", Arnoldina replied softly, respectfully and without sarcasm.

She left the duvet on our bed. Her receding bottom was a cheery red and the rest of her a tender flush.

She returned with the said Desiderata.

"Arnoldina", I continued, "in the Quaker religion there is no Eucharist but women are priests and may Celebrate every other Sacrament including Marriage."

"We are already Married in the Sight of God. I ask of you this: Get a couple of plastic cups, put in some wine and hand one cup to me. Break the bread, keep most for yourself and give me a morsel."

"Yes, Holy Husband"

Arnoldina handed me a cup containing a few centilitres of the wine:-

"Drink", she commanded.

She brake the bread and handed me a portion:-

"Eat", she ordered.

It was done.

We sat contented and serene for about an hour. There was silence.

We went to bed naked and in each other's arms. I had the privilege of warming my Wife's chill body.

I am an old man and I was tired. I softly intromitted and dribbled my Seed, I trust to her cervix. Arnoldina whimpered and moaned a little. She cast her beautiful head from side to side in a brief spasm of pleasure.

We slept the sleep of the just, as they say, or the just after, as I say in my vulgar way.

The dawn came. There was a wet overcast. This was England as winter was coming. But some small birds still gave an occasional song.

Arnoldina stirred. I rose and brought a chocolate wafer and a bottle of sparkling water from the fridge.

"Drink the water, and eat the chocolate wafer", I ordered, "It will tide you over."

"The chocolate wafer contains cow's milk, Charles"

"Arnoldina, I shall always respect your veganism in future. For now please eat the chocolate wafer. Your Husband is asking."

Arnoldina ate the chocolate wafer and drank the water.

"Charles, you cannot go without breakfast. I will test your blood sugar. At least have a little bread."

I have a blood sugar testing machine by my bedside, but I seldom use it. I had lost count but I think this was my eighteenth day in 78V. I felt a great deal had happened in eighteen days. Men always remember their first days of National Service or boarding at college. I had had no insulin since my last days in 80V.

The blood sugar proved normal.

"I will buy another chocolate wafer and you can give it to Mr Rat", I promised.

Arnoldina smiled at the prospect.

"This morning, Arnoldina, we shower and then I dress in my No.1s and you wear your stunning outfit with your crucifix and we take a refreshing stroll to The Albion. We pay for our breakfasts like the ordinary paying customers that we are and take our usual table or one nearby if it is already taken. Before the meal arrives you stand up and in your fine contralto address whoever is there. I expect most of the Club crew and Eugen at that hour. You say:-

'Thank you everyone for making me feel at home when I was billeted among you. Thank you also for your Love and your Trust. I did not betray that Trust. I love you all and I am very sorry for my disgusting words, tone and behaviour and for spoiling your breakfasts the other morning'."

"Yes, Sir", Arnoldina answered meekly. She threw her arms around me in our naked state, stood on tip-toe and kissed me.

"What Courage. What Trust. What Love", I thought in wonder.

We entered the Albion Hotel and took our table as normal. It was crowded but a universal silence descended.

Warble approached in full Head Waiter rig complete with white towel.

"What would you like to order Commadore Charmliss, Mrs Feng?"

"Could we each have black coffee with butter-free croissants and also a bowl of muesli with oat milk, please Mr Warble?"

"Yes, Sir"

Warble left for the kitchen.

Ionescu arrived and very correctly briskly bowed to Arnoldina and clicked his heals in the Germanic way.

"I am very sorry for the recent unpleasantness, Commadore Charmliss, and for my regrettable rôle in the debacle."

"Do not be dismayed, Ionescu", I replied, "you did what you thought was best at the time. That is all that can be expected of any of us."

Ionescu seemed relieved there was no bollocking or worse.

"Thank you, Sir", he replied. He clicked his heels, briskly saluted and went back to his breakfast.

Arnoldina stood.

A silence descended as if by the magic of her short but commanding stature.

As I said Arnoldina had a fine voice and there was no hint of shrillness. It was slow and stately, inspired by Authority:-

"Thank you everyone for making me feel at home when I was billeted among you. Thank you also for your Love and your Trust. I did not betray that Trust. I love you all and I am very sorry for my disgusting words, tone and behaviour and for spoiling your breakfasts the other morning."

Verbatim.

I have never experienced such loud acclamation, even at a football match. There was a storm of applause in which even the tourists entered into the spirit of the moment. Some young men whistled and others lifted their tables coffee and all and rhythmically beat the floor. Men perched at the bar counter spanked it.

Arnoldina resumed her seat.

Shrigley emerged from somewhere with tears in his eyes and said:-

"Commadore, do you wish to add anything to that?"

"No, Pott: This is my Wife's moment and I wish her to bask in it."

Shrigley bowed to Arnoldina and retired.

Somehow Maggi had received the prompt.

She brought our breakfasts with a broad grin and proffered her well-kept slender hand to Arnoldina. The women held their right hands with firm delicacy as Maggi kissed my Wife's cheek in the manner of well-brought-up working-class Mercian women.

"Mrs Charmliss, I love you too. Welcome back", Maggi greeted.

I smiled to Maggi and said "It is *Doctor* Charmliss, you know!"

"Of course it is, Charles, and she is a *proper* doctor too", Maggi giggled in happy embarrassment.

The barmaid and waitress strode off with a wriggle of delight.

We had more visitors expressing admiration or welcome.

As we were about to pay and leave, Duncan Heldrew, tenant farmer and the Viscount Heronbridge arrived at our table with Arabella Queenborough, Baroness Sperstow, the same as asked me pointed questions on the initial night in The Albion. The woman placed her plump right arm inside Heldrew's left, and contentedly rested her head on his shoulder.

"Commadore, and Dr Charmliss. Would you like to come to my father's terrace party at Challenor's Aske house on Thursday?"

"We would be highly delighted, Mr Heldrew. I do not know where it is. Will you send a car, please?"

"No, I will drive it myself. Are you still at the old Judge's Lodgings?"

"Yes"

Heldrew did not betray any emotion at hearing the honorific. He was of course a gentleman.

Queenborough kept smiling like a girl and gently rocking forward and back on her fiancé's arm.

"Yes, we are getting married in the spring and we want to know how to be happy", said the already happily enchanted young lady.

"Oh dear" I thought but I was secretly elated, and I knew Arnoldina would be righteously proud of the young couple and her high privilege.

"Congratulations!" we chorused.

They left as Warble returned with the bill on a stainless steel platter.

"Thank you, Mr Warble. I will pay by card", I advised as I retrieved my wallet.

Warble lifted the check and theatrically tore it to little pieces as he gazed into my eyes.

CHAPTER TWENTY
CLAMOUR

"Today, Dearest, muesli with ethical chocolate sauce and fairtrade hot chocolate. The nuts will help with protein."

"Yes, My Love. That sounds great", I said unconvincingly, or maybe it was just fatigue?

We adjourned to the canteen.

As my guest Arnoldina was unchallenged.

"Charles, you must stop working so hard. How will we cope without your brave investigations?" said Arnoldina with perhaps a hint of paradox?

Arnoldina had hired a studio flat and returned there.

I went to the office and almost immediately the telephone rang.

A peremptory male voice at the other end asked:-

"Commadore Charmliss?"

"Yes?"

"I am Rosebury Michaelson, Consulting Explosives Executive Officer at the Palatine Police Laboratory, Frodsham."

"Yes?"

"We have checked your prisoners' clothing and found Semtex traces on the jacket and trousers of Harold Makepiece."

"What about Goodleague?" I asked

"Negative; traces of cordite... hang on...Mann, Bulloch, Mature, Parker, Webb: All negative Semtex. Bulloch triple base."

"Thank you, Mr Michaelson. Can you put that in an email please? My address is CEC157@WEW.mil.mf"

"Will do"

"Thank you, Sir", I replied.

It was actually *Dr* Michaelson but he did not correct me so he was likely a real man.

As I awaited Michaelson's email I rang Slenderman:-

"Hello, Lieutenant Slenderman. I need to see the prisoners now."

It was 0851.

"They are having breakfast"

"Now please, Slenderman"

"Yes Sir"

Slenderman was in my office in two minutes dead and escorted me in person to the Custody Suite.

"I want to see Mann first", I said to Slenderman.

"Yes Sir, but you won't get any sense out of him"

We entered Mann's cell with an armed guard.

A chair was brought in and I sat on it.

Mann was in an opposite corner, naked on his pallet.

"Good Morning, Mr Mann", I commenced with a hint of the risible.

"No comment", Mann replied.

I thought profanely "It is going to be one of those fucking days." Mann was an overweight but healthy young man with a death's head tattooed across his hairy chest, a scroll with "Mother" on his upper right arm, and a large arrow tilted at thirty degrees to his medial line and pointing to the root of his penis.

He was clearly "challenged" and did not have either the courage or the IQ to formulate a self-consistent web of lies, even with 72 hours' notice.

"I want a solicitor", he added.

"You can have one, but you do not need one yet", I counselled, probably illegally.

"Are you a lover or life's partner of Felicity Goodleague", I enquired with my usual tact.

"No Comment"

"We will return to the custody desk", I advised the guard.

When we were out of earshot of the prisoners I rang Arnoldina.

"You are at 147B Pencordan Way, aren't you Loveliness?"

"Yes, Darling Charles. How can I assist my splendid Husband today?"

"Please come to the Custody Suite immediately. I am sending a car. Come wearing only old pyjamas, disposable slippers and a padded anorak as it is cold."

"Yes, Master", replied my Wife with a sexy little giggle.

I rung off and turned to the Custody Seargent saying:-

"Send a marked car to 147B Pencordan Way to press for Dr Arnoldina Charmliss and then ring Lieutenant Slenderman and tell him to come here."

"Yes Sir"

"When you have finished those tasks, ring Edmonson and tell him to come here wearing his bodycam and carrying an additional high-quality audio recorder."

"Yes Sir"

Both Edmonson and Slenderman were with me within five minutes and I said to Slenderman:-

"Take me to the main entrance at the porte-cochèr, alight my Wife and bring her here. I shall accompany you."

"Yes, Commadore"

Another five minutes and all four of us were assembled at the Custody Desk with an armed key guard.

"Leave your anorak with the Custody Seargent, Dina", I said.

"Yes Sir"

"Check your tackle is recording, CPO Edmonson", I ordered.

It was done.

"Now follow me", I ordered to all.

We opened Mann's cell. The orange jump suits were not yet issued and Mann was still naked.

"Have you eaten and watered today, Mann", I asked.

"No Comment"

"Take us with Mann to Goodleague's cell", I ordered the key guard. The guard left Mann's unoccupied cell open and escorted us to Goodleague's cell which he opened and the five of us entered.

Goodleague leapt from her pallet casting aside her cover and ran to Mann. She embraced him abandonedly and said "Oh, Jimmy, my love. I thought they had killed you. Have me my darling." Mann stood silent with his hands by his side and his head cast back. He exhibited not the merest signal of tumescence. Goodleague stood back in bewilderment and said "What is wrong, Jimmy?"

Jimmy turned to me and said "I have never before seen this woman. You are trying to fit me up for rape, you bastard."

"Take him back to his cell", I ordered the guard.

"But what about your wife, Sir"

"I shall protect my wife. Secure Mann in his cell and return here immediately."

"Yes, Sir"

Goodleague returned to her "bed" in the corner. She was crying distractedly cowering with her legs to her shoulders and her face in her hands.

"Now Miss Goodleague, have you had food and water today?"

"Yes, Commadore Charmliss"

"Have you been well-treated?"

"Yes, Sir"

"Did my Wife treat you well when you were injured?"

Goodleague paused her sobbing in astonishment. I found it difficult to decide whether it was affected or genuine.

"Commadore, she is an angel of mercy."

Then Goodleague came and knelt before my Wife and clasped her hands together. Gazing into Arnoldina's eyes she sniffled:-

"Oh, Mrs Charmliss..."

"*Dr* Charmliss", I corrected.

"Doctor Charmliss, please I beg you spare my men. Poor Jimmy is frightened and confused. Please intercede with Commadore Charmliss. Flog me but please forgive my cowardly assault upon your husband."

I suppose Arnoldina noted that the woman asked for forgiveness but did not apologise for her offence. Perhaps Arnoldina's assessment was that Goodleague's was a contrition of convenience.

I noted that Goodleague did not say "I hate my crimes and I reject them with loathing" to Jesus Christ or indeed anyone else. That Prayer is a standard expression of spiritual regret and is tantamount to apology.

I noted that Goodleague did not say "I have learnt that my ways were of evil error and I turn my back on Satan forever."

I noted that Goodleague did not say "I am evil and I want you to take me in hand, to teach me ways of righteousness, and lead me to Salvation in the bosom of our Holy Saviour."

I noted that Goodleague did not say, as many young atheist women do, "Just because other people do nasty things, it does not mean I have to."

You possibly object that all these formulations are mere patterns of words, hot air that any cynic could voice. I agree. But in a sincere person they may herald and earnest Contrition. There is still a lot to prove, obviously.

Arnoldina responded:-

"Goodleague, you are a grown woman and you must answer for your actions as I answer for mine. You are the killer of several and forgiveness is neither mine to withhold or bestow. You are indeed a manipulative coward but my Husband is more than a man and he leads real men. If a man rejects your command, as one just did, then it is because he knows you are the way of death. Perhaps a fascist approves flogging. I do not know and it is not mine to know. But none shall be tortured here."

Suddenly Goodleague's eyes set in a mask of diabolical hate:-

"I am not a fascist. I am a British patriot", answered Goodleague with venom and an insolent pride.

"Then if you are a patriot put your pride in your pocket and assuage the sufferings of your people", responded Arnoldina.

"Lock her in and take us back to the Custody Suite", I ordered the guard.

"Yes Sir"

"Here's your jacket, Dr Charmliss", said the Custody Seargent, proffering the garment to Arnoldina.

"No, Seargent, have it cleaned and sent to my billet", I interjected.

"My Wife shall collect it later. I suspect she wishes to return home, shower and change. Order her a car."

"Yes, Sir. I understand her feelings entirely."

"Thank you, Seargent", I concluded.

I returned to my office. There was lots of bumf on my desk that I needed to answer or file, but importantly forensic evidence was accumulating steadily, as was character testimony or the defect thereof.

Suddenly, I was surprised by a call from Treagh:-

"Chuck,...., I mean Commadore Charmliss,...., is it okay if I come to your billet at 1800 today. I need an informal report and to discuss the current civil issues in review."

Treagh sounded very tired or maybe drugged or perhaps both.

"Major-General Treagh. I am delighted. Please come. Shall I get anything in for you?"

"Yes, a large bottle of bourbon, Chuck"

"Will do Sir"

I rang Arnoldina on her mobile.

"Dearest, you were magnificent. Denzil has just rung me. He sounds ill. Can I ask you not to call this evening until I ring you back?"

"Thank you, Charles. I might go to a concert with a nursing friend, but I will carry my mobile."

"Thank you, Loveliness. I love you always."

"I love you too, Water Vole"

It was the first time Arnoldina had used this particular endearment.

I rang the Stewards (Navy) and discovered that they did not stock litre bottles of premium bourbon so I ordered two 0.7 litre bottles and a two-litre bottle of cold fizzy water for my quarters to arrive at 1745.

It was only 1200 but I locked the office and went to my quarters. I changed into a particularly disreputable suit of camo cotton and my hiking boots. I decided to lunch in the nearest 'Spoons. I ordered a grill and chips and a pint of strong IPA and took a seat at a table where two young men were trying to snaffle big burgers without getting the sauce down their jackets.

"What do you think of this latest trouble in the Hodgate?" I ventured.

"What, mate?"

"This terror bombing:- Ten dead"

"Fuckin' string them up I say", said one young professional.

His mate agreed:-

"Yeah, string 'em up, I say."

A lightly dressed young woman on a stool nearby overheard us:-

"It's that fuckin' witch Goodyear or whatever she's called. I'd give her fuckin' Goodyear. I'd fuckin' necklace the cow and set her alight. That poor driver half his head blown off."

It was clear this was not a statistically-representative sample of sober humanity but it was more anecdotal evidence of an ugly and unstable mood developing amongst the more labile minority.

"That bloke with the gelly, Makepeace, that is an irony if you like. I'd cut his bollocks off. Unfit to breed", contributed an older man in a cloth cap from an adjacent table.

All very interesting but not definitive of the settled view, even of the lower orders.

I returned to my office and decided to consult the websites of the local rags including the Congleholme Advertiser and the Palatine Star.

There was the usual journalistic outrage proposing the return of hanging or lashes for terror crimes whether there were fatalities or not, something that would have been considered outrageous in the 80V of the time of my death, a mere twenty days ago, hard to believe. But war is outrageous and in war lashings of fear abound. Perhaps more disturbing from a liberal viewpoint were letters advocating prison camps, the gibbet and the perch. I had a brief look at social media from the convenience of my office computer. This was even more apoplectic. Whatever the true temperature of the mobile element it was clear that our fascists would not survive long if they were released, and of course civilised justice required that they be tried by jury and serve custodial sentences in humane conditions.

Treagh and I shared a common perspective. You may call it a common prejudice if you wish. We both abhorred violence and wanted a domain without bloodshed. Okay, so I have some sadistic instincts as I admit elsewhere but spanking is not serious violence, unless applied to children. No adult is physically marked for life, and as long as it is managed correctly no-one is psychologically traumatised either. In fact, many volunteers know how to ride the rollercoaster and emerge spiritually refreshed. God can help us if we accept his willing Tutelage and allow his Mercy to subvert our pride and wrath. If you are an evil person like me it is your Responsibility, no one else's, to re-invert the state the Enemy disordered and do good with it. You cannot blame your parents, your wife, your genes, the system or anything else. Without trying to be too metaphysical about it this was the Responsibility that Goodleague and her crew were dodging.

Treagh was a truly kind and generous man who had suffered mightily but sought to be restrained and Christian in his approach to absolute power. Treagh was a good man and suffered good men's qualms.

Somehow a formula had to be found, but of course war is chaotic and the best laid plans to save lives can achieve the very opposite when the enemy, or I should say Enemy, strikes in a covert and cunning way.

I did not know whether Treagh was vegetarian or not. I thought I would order two commercial twelve-inch pizzas: One Pizza con Funghi and one Pizza Pepperoni to be delivered at 1815, and let Denzil choose the one he liked. It is not much of a meal for a man, but it is a start.

Time had ticked on with all this talk of Responsibility and stuff and before I knew how to schedule work I discovered that it was 1735 and I needed to get to the billet.

As I arrived I coincided with the steward who had the water and the whisky. Both were nice and cold. Sorry. I mis-speak again. Both the water and the whisky were cold.

I stripped and went for a shower.

When I came out I thought that at least I could put on a pair of clean underpants for the High Suzerain but I could not find any so I put my hiking trousers back on instead and took a hard seat by the table to await developments.

Something, or Someone, told me not to attack the bourbon.

Treagh turned up at 1800 on the dot.

He was conspicuously alone, though of course Palatines and MFIS ("emfis" as in "Memphis") would have discretely been lurking around.

Treagh did seem on edge.

"Chuck, can I use your shower?"

"Go ahead, Sir"

Treagh entered the bathroom in uniform. Five minutes later he emerged naked, sat back in his chair by the table and threw the damp towel over his crotch with a strange pudicity.

He reached for one of the glasses.

"Please do not drink alcohol until the important part of this interview has been heard. Have some cold, sparkling water instead, Sir, if I can say without impertinence."

"Chuck Charmliss, you are never impertinent, but you are often as wise as a man can be in the foothills of a major war."

"Thank you, Sir. I have ascertained that there is major unrest in public opinion which has crystallised around ENLA terrorists and their atrocities. I fear mob violence, atrocity and further bloodshed. I have gathered evidence and I have given thought to the situational volatility. I think I have identified an old method that may appease public opinion long enough for us to organise viable trials of these people and their subsequent humane punishment, in order to control this difficulty without further bloodshed."

"This is very interesting, Charmliss, and I wish to read your formal proposals at 1300 tomorrow. It is late and..."

There was a loud and peremptory knock on the door. I answered and it was the pizza delivery man accompanied by a Palatine constable. I do not know, or wish to know, what the two men thought. I think they mistook us for a pair of abominables, me in fatigues and naked from the waist up, a negro naked but for his loincloth.

At any event, I tipped the pizza man and the pair departed quickly and without thanks or other comment.

"Which would you like, Sir, the fungi or the pepperoni?"

"I will have the pepperoni, please Chuck."

I served him with a china plate and a sharp knife from the kitchenette.

We made a start on our pizzas with water.

Treagh focused on his food with a frown of concentration. He then surprised me again.

"Commadore Dr Charmliss..."

Treagh paused to chew his food and lick his fingers:-

"Chuck...Did you follow the campaigns of Sir Charles Napier in Baluchistan?"

"Napier...good man...A little before my time", I answered captiously.

"Do you possibly recollect his telegraph to The War Office?"

"I do, Major-General Treagh. I am very highly honoured. No one would ever doubt your courage but without Faith and Trust courage would be impossible. I salute your Act of Trust in humility. When you have finished your food and water I shall go and sit on the edge of the bed. Please cross my lap with your body."

Treagh took his time as was his right and his privilege.

"Do you require me to remove my trousers, Sir?", I asked.

"No, we can dispense with that, Chuck"

Treagh was of course a large man and myself a short and weak one. I was under some stress and the bed some strain. I endeavored to prop my sitting position with my left arm. Restraint of my awkward burden would have in any case been impossible.

Treagh drew several breaths with a sobbing action at the ultimate capacity. I suspected angina but if the Penitent died in his own ecstasy it would be down to me and I should have to deal with it.

I did not expect a 300-year-old Major-General to weep under my hand. For one thing I lacked skill and practice. But stranger things have happened and I very much hoped Denzil got full value for the risks he ran.

"What would you like to tell me this evening, Sir?"

"Call me Denzil: I will call you Chuck"

"Denzil you are not obliged to make any comment or request during your Holy Correction: But I shall make an effort to call you 'Denzil' if I can remember. Please wait until your final Blessing to make any recommendations or complaints that you may have. You are a lovely man and I wish I had half the courage and the Faith with which Jesus Christ entrusted you."

I had gently rested my right hand on Treagh's right buttock.

Denzil's body shook a little, and I could tell that this brief induction, for what it was worth, had effect.

"Ionescu is a pain in the arse. He is such an old woman. He is a jobsworth and a sycophant", said the Penitent.

"Firstly, Denzil please do not use coarse words in your Holy Confession: It is *your* Confession and you live with it.

More importantly, Eugen is a man, an excellent man, not a female of any sort. He is very diligent but, and I can testify, no jobsworth. The very last thing Eugen is is a sycophant."

"Denzil I want you to say a little Prayer after me:-

Holy Father who walked on water
    Holy Father who walked on water
Holy Son who stilled the storm
    Holy Son who stilled the storm
We thank you for the gift of
Your faithful subject Eugen Ionescu
    We thank you for the gift of
    your faithful subject Eugen Ionescu
We thank you for the the support of a man
    who could have walked-away
    We thank you for the the support of a man
    who could have walked-away
We thank you for his skill and his tact.
    We thank you for his skill and his tact.
We thank you for a retired professor of semiotic
    We thank you for a
    retired professor of semiotic
Happy to serve as a glorified tour guide
    Happy to serve as a glorified tour guide
Most of all, Holy Father,
we thank you for Eugen's Cheer
    Most of all, Holy Father,
    we thank you for Eugen's Cheer
His grace under pressure, his humility
    His grace under pressure, his humility
Please make us like Eugen, Holy Father
    Please make us like Eugen, Holy Father"

The ambiguity of the last line was intentional.

To my astonishment the 302-year-old male heavyweight began shyly and self-consciously but quite fluidly to cry.

I knew that Treagh had not come to talk about Ionescu and I was concerned about whether he would settle sufficiently to address his main theme.

"Denzil, does it feel good to set your anger aside, and look to the future?"

"Yes, Sir"

"Yes, *Chuck*"

"Sorry, Chuck. Yes Chuck"

"Now, Denzil. You don't have to say anything. You can take a few minutes to say your prayers, perhaps for your men and for their safety, perhaps for the happy retirement of our enemies. It is *your* Confession and it is up to *you*. We do not want a triumph: We will settle for an Honorable Peace. Just relax, Denzil, and take what you are given. You are the most patient and the least selfish man I have ever known."

I wanted the man to calm down a bit. For the next few minutes I gently stroked his ample backside and gave it a few friendly pats. This was not "warming-up" and it most certainly was not foreplay. It was more in the nature of a dry massage. On occasions I gently stroked the reachable small of Treagh's back and those obscene welts. But I did not want to irritate and I certainly did not want to revive painful memories.

After a few minutes of this, Treagh said:-

"Charmliss, you are a saint"

"No, Denzil, I am a very evil man. But all men are evil. We have to work to be good."

I rested him a bit longer, perhaps for as many minutes as preceded the late announcements.

Then I said:-

"Denzil, is there anything else you would like the share this evening?"

Treagh began hesitantly.

"I do not know if you know this, Charles. Some of the planters used to impale slaves with great hooks right through their bodies and gibbet them alive to squirm like mealworms on a fishing hook until they died. I can testify as eye witness, Chuck."

"I did know, and I know you can testify", I replied.

"Well what I want to say is this: For days I have had phantasies about impaling the Shits that way. I have the power. God knows, I know it is evil. I don't mean *your* Shits, Shrigley and that crew, I mean the Shits who tried to kill you", said Treagh.

"Firstly, Denzil, I do not mean to be priggish or punctilious but please do not call people 'Shits' during your Holy Confession. I do not mind but whilst you are on my lap I have to have regard to your welfare and I want you forever to cherish the memory of your Holy Confession. These people are human beings like us: They may be Monarchists, socialists or even fascists, but they try to be good people, however silly or misguided. Forgive, Denzil, and open your heart to love. You are the winner, your patience and your restraint have already proven your maturity and your genius for leadership."

"Thank you, Holy Confessor"

"You are most welcome. Now what I want you to do, Denzil, if you agree, is to say your Prayers in silence for a few moments and then say to me 'I am ready'. Then I will hit you very hard for a few minutes, probably much less. I know that in 78V the physical pain will be dull, but the psychic pain will be nearly unbearable. Now I shall be silent."

Denzil prayed for about forty-five seconds and then said "I am ready."

I struck hard and fast in my usual way.

I made no concession to his age, his seniority, or his already brutal life's experience. After all, the slight and delicate Arnoldina is nearly three times older, though as we have seen medical concessions are needful.

Denzil wept fluidly but with a certain restraint.

I paused:-

"Denzil, have a very good cry. I know you are a man, you need to prove nothing. Wring the anger and the spite out of your soul and leave it here on my pillow. We are almost there, Denzil."

I resumed with all the strength I have, but for seconds.

The man wept without restraint.

I had contrition.

I stopped and turned Denzil supine. He had to help me move him of course.

I said:-

"Denzil, will you say this Prayer after me?"

There was no answer.

My Dear God, I am sorry for my sins with all my heart.
My Dear God, I am sorry for my sins with all my heart.

In choosing to do wrong and failing to do good,
  In choosing to do wrong and failing to do good,
I have sinned against You whom I should
   love above all things.
  I have sinned against You whom I should
  love above all things.
I hate my sin and I reject it with loathing.
  I hate my sin and I reject it with loathing.
I firmly intend, with Your help, to use the pain of penance
  I firmly intend, with Your help,
  to use the pain of penance
To sin no more, and to avoid whatever leads me to sin.
  To sin no more, and to avoid whatever
  leads me to sin.
Your Son, Jesus Christ, suffered and died for us.
  Your Son, Jesus Christ, suffered and died for us.
In His name, my God, have mercy. Amen
  In His name, my God, have mercy. Amen

   I then leant awkwardly and kissed Treagh on the forehead, and sat back.

   "If you don't mind, Denzil, I will not kiss your scrotum", I said.

   "That's okay, Chuck. Just blow a kiss to your fingers and put them on my penis for a couple of seconds. I will take it as your Blessing and hope it brings me a woman and our child."

   "Denzil, I am going to do as you suggest, *and* I am going to kiss your scrotum in Blessing as I pray for your issue."

   These acts were done.

   I Crossed the torso.

   "Come and cuddle me, Denzil"

   He considerately left my lap and sat on the side of the bed beside me.

   "Chuck, I want to thank you but I do not know the right words."

   "None of us know, Denzil, but I have felt the gratitude in your soul so just 'Thank you' will do."

   Say this little Prayer with me, I continued:-

Dear Lord Jesus, my Holy Saviour
  Dear Lord Jesus my Holy Saviour
Thank you for bringing me safely through

Thank you for bringing me safely through
The pains of Holy Correction
The pains of Holy Correction
And for purging my spirit of sin
And for purging my spirit of sin

"Thank you, Chuck"
"I love you, Denzil"
"I love you too, Chuck"

For the avoidance of doubt, Reader, this was not, I repeat, not a homosexual or bisexual encounter. Both Treagh and I were one-hundred-percent heterosexual Christian men.

If you want to think of it this way it was a sexless act of friendship between two chaste friends like Holmes and Watson, the two detectives from the Victorian pages of Arthur Conon-Doyle, who lived together without interference and were assumed heterosexual. Of course, in the setting of the Conon-Doyle stories, homosexuality was a capital offence, no publisher would dare to broadcast such an imputation, and the mere suggestion would end on the field of honour. Either way the result was death.

Sadly, we live in a cynical age. We no longer accept that two men can share the same house as normal, procreative friends, or that spinsters can cohabit in chastity.

CHAPTER TWENTY-ONE
CHERISHMENT

Thursday came.

I had a hangover.

I could not face breakfast.

Certainly not a cooked one.

I drank the rest of the fizzy water and felt better.

I had a shower, and that revived me also.

I put on my No.2s sans hat.

I went to the kitchenette tap and poured a pint of cold tap water, and drank that.

To begin the business of the day I rang Slenderman and asked to interrogate Goodleague. Slenderman came and collected me. It was 0735 by the time we were in the Custody Suite.

The prison uniforms had now been issued and Goodleague had been given a collapsible bed and a mattress. She sat on the edge of this bed in her orange jumpsuit.

"Have you been well-treated, Miss Goodleague."

"Yes, Commadore Charmliss. Thank you."

"Have you fed and drank?"

"I had a cup of water overnight, Sir, and I expect my breakfast soon. A bread roll with coffee and marmalade."

"Excellent. Has anyone since you have been in custody assaulted you sexually, or been in any way brutal?"

"No, Sir"

"Do you have something to read?"

"A kind guard gave me a Bible, Sir, and I read the Gospels until I fell asleep. Jesus said we should turn the other cheek, Sir. I am thinking about it."

She showed me a small book in a plastic cover, the kind of Bible you sometimes find in the bedside draws in hotels.

"Don't think about, do it. Christ was not like other men. He was not self-interested. Any advice he offers; you can take it for granted that it is sound. Take not thought for the morrow."

"But it is the morrow that I wish to discuss with you this morning, Felicity."

"Felicity", I mused, "It is a most unfortunate name for such an unhappy woman."

"Sorry, Felicity. It is a most happy name. And I must not mock you. Mockery is itself very evil."

"Commander, sorry, Commadore, I accept your apology. I am very proud of my name."

"Take no pride, Felicity. Your name was given by another, and is forever is hers."

Just then the door opened abruptly and a burly man wearing a Palatine uniform with Seargent's stripes strode in carrying a bread roll and a short plastic knife and a hotel-type capsule of marmalade, which he put on the bed beside Goodleague. He was armed, as indeed was I, but he briefly left with the door open and his keys in the mechanism. He returned in seconds with a commercially-packaged cappuccino with a cup lid.

For some time, Goodleague had presented a downcast gaze, and had now started to whimper.

The guard wore a name-badge with HARPER, NJ printed on it.

"Please may I have permission to speak, Commadore Charmliss?", asked NJ Harper.

"Yes, Palatine Seargent Harper, what is it?"

"Please do not be too hard on her, Sir. She is trying to find her Way."

"Thank you for that, Harper. I will have a strong, black coffee with dry digestive biscuits, please."

Harper returned within seconds, perhaps from a trolley, and I had the black coffee, packaged as Goodleague's and a railway-style cellophane wrapped bunch of four digestive biscuits.

These were placed on the table beside my seat.

"Harper, before you go, can you give Miss Goodleague a shower, please?"

"What you mean, me bathe her?"

"Yes, Palatine Seargent Harper. I have Licence in force signed by Major-General Treagh and Miss Goodleague is a British citizen. Tell her to strip and shower her. She considers herself defiled by my presence, and she can have another after I leave."

"It will have to be entered in the Punishment Log, Sir."

"When you leave, enter it in germane records, please, Palatine Seargent Harper."

"Please undress, Miss Goodleague", softly ordered the Seargent.

Goodleague burst into tears.

"Oh please, Commadore. You have never defiled me. I admire you and I want to be like you", she sniveled.

"Then in that case remove your clothes and allow Mr Harper to bathe you."

She sat there with her roll and marmalade untouched, and wept.

I turned to Harper.

"Undress her, Harper", I ordered.

Harper made to walk to the prisoner. Goodleague abruptly stood and removed both garments.

"Now go with Mr Harper and have your shower", I said.

This time Goodleague did as she was told.

I did not turn round to look into the shower-cum-lavatory cubical. Instead I drank my coffee and ate my biscuits. But by the sound of things Harper was making a thorough job of it.

The two emerged soaking and Goodleague dried herself with a towel.

"Thank you, Seargent Harper. Now go to the mess and shower yourself. Put on a pusser's gown and take the rest of your shift off. Requisition a new uniform on my account and have it brought to you. I shall brief Lieutenant Slenderman."

"Yes Sir"

Harper left.

Goodleague dried herself and made to dress.

"I did not tell you to dress"

Goodleague sat on the edge of the bed naked.

"I was told you are a sadist. I suppose you are going to spank me."

"Felicity, spanking is for good men and women who have matured sufficiently to recognise their guilt and who wish to purge it. With regard to the other thing, it is not yours to know my private delights, nor mine to explain them to you."

"You, Felicity, are an evil person and I have other plans, for you. You will leave here carrying a lit votive candle weighing one kilo and cross the Ladyfair, and walk along the Northern arm of the old cardo, the street the Saxons called Old Hiding, until you reach the abbey altar. There you will place the still-lit candle on the altar in front of Major-General Treagh who will represent your King. Unfortunately the King is not able to attend at this time. You will kneel before the altar, *apologise for your crimes*, and then you shall fold your hands and beg forgiveness of God, your King, and the relatives of the men, women and children you murdered in that order."

"I am not going to kneel before a foreign nigger, or any nigger."

"He is not yours to choose, Felicity. I shall not explain the character or antecedencies of Manville Treagh to you, because you are unworthy to know."

"I suppose you want me to do this nude for extra titivation?"

"I am not a classicist or an art historian so I am not qualified to discuss the nude. You, Felicity are very far from being a goddess or any ideal of perfection. It will be cold, and this being Britain as Winter arrives it will likely be rainy and windy. You will wear two sets of orange prison jumpsuits and over that a fireproof white linen smock. I shall escort you holding a rope with a slip-knot noose around your neck. This is one of those things that sounds soft or even childish but is actually a severe corporal punishment and has all the obscenity of one. The heavy candle that you hold at arm's length is a firework. The wick is impregnated with saltpeter so that it does not blow out even in heavy rain or strong wind. This is not done to torture, but it is very bright, and the candle spits and sputters and burning wax and potassium nitrate spatter everywhere. You will wear safety glasses. In the olden days, the prisoner, usually female, never had goggles and sometimes no clothes. At the end of the ceremony the candle will need to be extinguished by professional pyrotechnicians."

"At the conclusion of the punishment, assuming that Major-General Treagh forgives you; you are a free woman. But I recommend that you accompany your accomplices at least as far as their remote prison for your own safety. If you fall or fail at any juncture the candle is taken from you and you are tried as an ordinary terrorist murderess, inevitably with ten Whole Life sentences handed down. Your accomplices will be charged with Assisting a Terrorist Outrage, and in at least two cases Unlawful Possession of Explosives with Intent to Endanger Life. They can reasonably expect Life Sentences and with good behavior will be out in eight to twelve years, but on perpetual probation, and any small misdemeanor will see them back in prison without trial. That is ordinary English Criminal Law."

"No-one will be allowed to stand by and mock, jeer or throw things. There will be journalists and television crews from all over the world. This punishment has never been executed anywhere since the 1830s, or in France since the Revolution. It has never been witnessed in an English-speaking country. I have absolute powers in West England and Wales and I intend to use those powers to certify that bloodshed ceases and never returns to our streets."

"This essentially French conception is called an *amende honourable*, or in English an Atonement of Honour."

"Do you have any questions, Felicity?"

"I have several. What if I do not agree?"

"That is the easiest of your possible questions. I shall tell the wire services that you will be released from custody in the Presidium in Congleholme at 1000 hours on a day I shall specify. There will be a Government announcement that you are free of all sanction in England, but equally that you do not have the protection of law. Your clothes will be retained for forensic and evidential reasons and your accounts will be credited with compensation. Meanwhile, all Government loans shall be reclaimed, including the clothes on your backs. You will be released from the main portico. Believe me, Felicity I do not deceive. None of your men, neither yourself, shall reach the far side of the square alive, and many will die horribly."

"Now, put on your jump suit. I shall have a guard lock you in. Think about what I have said and whether you wish to participate."

I went to my office.

I summoned CPO Edmonson and told him to enter my report into the word processor to dictation.

I told him that I had re-interviewed the main prisoner and that I had invited her to consider performing an *amende honourable* in order to appease public opinion and pre-empt civil disorder. I had not told her of motivations but had spelt out the nature and consequences, both of performance, partial performance and refusal.

For Treagh's benefit, I rehearsed what it was and how it elaborated, and his potential part in proceedings.

Edmonson produced a typescript from the document file, and I told him to take the typescript report to Treagh at his desk. It was nearly 1100 and I went for an early lunch.

It turned 1300. Thankfully, I was now clear headed, even without a hair of the dog.

Treagh was at his desk and I made the long, almost Russian, trek hence.

I saluted smartly. Treagh rose arthritically and saluted me.

He sat and resumed thumbing the report with a concerned or bemused frown, I could not decide which.

"Thank you, Commodore Charmliss."

There was no hint of personal friendship on either side, and definitely no matiness, no "Denzil" and "Chuck". We were fulfilling our public functions and junior officers were present.

I noticed that Denzil was not playing with his pens or cigars. He was not threatening to bite his finger nails. He was fully sober. I flattered myself that I detected a new self-confidence and authority.

"Your report is most interesting. I had never heard of this."

"No, Sir. Most have not, even in France. I have had a life-long interest in capital and corporal punishment among my other, more congenial, interests. I am also interested in the general question of how to turn evil to good effect. We need to bring peace to war."

"Quite so, Dr Charmliss. The North Atlantic campaign has never been subject to audit. I shall have a fireproof, long-sleeved smock made to Goodleague's measurements in case we decide to deploy this measure and also fireproof impact goggles. I shall also order the gadget boys to produce a one kilo votive candle with a saltpeter wick and stand-by a man to extinguish it. I am happy to play my part. I shall leave publicity to you. That is all for now, Commadore Charles Charmless."

I stood as smartly and formally as I was able and saluted.

As you know, I am diabetic. I had not suffered the effects since my death in 80V but it would be foolish to fast further, especially since I had had a stressful day so far and expected even more excitement to come.

Heldrew rang to say he would come at 1800 and park on the apron behind my lodging's, as opposed to attempting entry via the Ladyfair.

I went to the canteen and had an early high tea. Heldrew had not mentioned a meal but I assumed there would be drinks, possibly too many. By 1715 I was back in my Lodgings and was surprised to see Arnoldina. She was wearing a stunning off-the-shoulder black evening dress she had just bought, not too tight around the hem, which sat below the knees, and set off nicely for a good puritan woman by her silver crucifix. The woman was in mourning, and of course grieving, but she smiled like an angel. I cheekily lifted the hem: Sure enough, no knickers.

We embraced and kissed.

"How is my water vole today?", she teased, "Busy as ever?"

"It has been hectic, Loveliness"

"Have you eaten", I enquired.

"Yes, Charles. I had some bread and soup in my flat."

I stripped for a shower and so did Arnoldina. She undid her belt, imitation leather of course, and lifted off her dress as a unit. She cast off her black shoes and we showered together. I dressed in my No.1s without my awful cap. I hoped Arnoldina would elect to go to the party as she was, but I realised it would cause a stir and we were already in enough trouble.

Heldrew arrived on the dot. He smiled and shook my hand at the threshold. I invited him in.

"Dr Charmliss, you look absolutely stunning!" Heldrew said addressing Arnoldina, with I think genuine surprise.

"Doesn't she just", I agreed.

"Dina, please, Lord Heronbridge"

"Friends call me 'Dunny'. It sounds disgusting if you are Australian, but fortunately for me I am not, and it doesn't", chuckled Heldrew with a trace of nervous embarrassment.

"Well, Dunny, we're ready. Lead the way!"

I left the lodgings unlocked. There were few valuables within. I was carrying my pistol, and in any case the whole building was guarded like Fort Knox.

Heldrew opened the nearside rear door of his old Bentley for Arnoldina and I let myself in to the other. This of course meant that two men were on the offside, but the heavy, strong car did not notice.

The wartime roads were nearly deserted once we left the city and the damp, dank undulations of the Cheshire Plain sped by. It was already well dark. Heldrew's lights not so much lit the way as reflected from the shifting wraiths of mist where we hoped a road might be. Heldrew's car was almost silent and Heldrew a good, steady driver. He knew his route well and after what seemed only a few minutes but must have been a good half hour we arrived at some tall wrought iron gates, open to the road and giving access to a narrow tarmacadamed private drive.

After a few hundred metres we drew up at a fine hexastyle Roman portico and Heldrew stopped his car and turned off the ignition.

We entered the brightly-illuminated entrance and soon found ourselves in a fine library with leather sofas and armchairs.

"Meet my Father!" commanded Heldrew delightedly.

Heldrew's father turned and proved to be an old man with longish grey hair that he seemed to have blackened in strips like a badger. He had been speaking with three friends and nursing a balloon of brandy. The friends walked to other guests and the earl placed his glass on a table.

The old man slowly proffered his hand to Arnoldina:-

"Commadore Dr Charles Charmliss and Dr Mrs Arnoldina Charmliss", said Duncan.

"I am Medrington Heroncourt. Everyone calls me 'Jimmy' because James is my middle name. I have heard so much of you, Dina. All of it good!" chuckled Jimmy.

Lady Sperstow had appeared from nowhere.

"He is the third Earl of Chamberfield really", she interjected.

"Don't be silly Bella. All that is finished with", reproved Jimmy.

Jimmy released Arnoldina and grasped my hand firmly, looking me with serious eyes.

"Charmliss, I hear you have appeared from nowhere to bring back England. Is that true?"

"I certainly hope so, Sir"

"Good man. There is a war on, and I have only one son. Take care. Now look here, Charmless, is it all right if I call you Charles?"

"I prefer Chuck, Sir"

"Now look here, Chuck. We are farming folk but we are not animals and we want to behave properly. Chuck, you are intelligent and your wife more so", said Jimmy with a disarming candour.

"My son is a homely lad and has little experience. I have tried to persuade him to try the mount before he buys, if you ascertain my meaning."

"Jimmy, don't be so crude!" exclaimed Arabella with faux outrage.

"Now take Bella in hand and show my beloved and only issue how to treat a lady, for that is what Bella is in all senses of the word 'lady'. She consents and she is Harper Adams trained so you will have few problems and I am glad you have such a sober and expert wife. That is why you are here. Good luck and thank you. Now take them somewhere quiet, Duncan."

Arabella was wearing not dungarees but a beguiling orange coloured dress, fully covering the breasts and shoulders. She had two strings of short but not choking pearls and orange slippers (it appeared to me) with sequins. Now my observations about pearls on women still apply and Bella seemed too young, but this was 78V and she may have been much older than she looked. Taking the couple at face value I would say they were in their mid to late twenties, older looking than in the flattering flames of fishtail gaslights.

She was her usual ebullient self and her wavy coiffured hair was a shiny blonde, whether natural or dyed I could not tell. Obviously, Arnoldina would know.

There did not appear to be an elevator and Duncan led us through several wide corridors lined with prints and paintings. At length we entered what appeared to be an artist's atelier near the attic which seemed damp and was definitely cold. There was a low dais against the Southern wall on which was a large damp-looking double bed which may have accommodated artist's models.

Duncan turned on fluorescent strip lamps which gave that annoying fifty-hertz hum.

I said to Duncan "Do you have standard or table lamps with decent LED bulbs?"

"Yes, switch them on and I will turn off the ceiling lights."

I did as asked and the room was just as well illuminated and a lot quieter.

There was a small refrigerator which seemed to be operational and there was a small kettle and microwave on the top. There was a small sink with dirty china cups which Arnoldina took it upon herself to wash.

After she had completed this chore, she filled the kettle and switched it on. She found some instant coffee, tea bags and whitener.

Turning to Duncan she wickedly said:-

"Would you like coffee, tea or me"

"I would much prefer you, Arnoldina, but I will settle for black coffee no sugar please!"

Both Bella and I roared with laughter. Sometimes the old ones really are the best ones.

There was a small table covered in Formica and adventitiously there were four hard armchairs ranged around the four sides.

As we sat in self-conscious silence with our coffee and biscuits a sharp sleet shower played against the northlights. It seemed both delicate and ghostly, at home where it fell.

"Love and Trust under God are the keys to a successful marriage", I opened.

"Duncan, you may or may not have sworn to love and protect your lady but these are words and no priest or pastor can reify them for you. Your moving Spirit and its actions must make love and guardianship a reality. I do not mean guardianship in the sense that you attorney a child or an invalid. Your wife is entitled to continue and develop her outside interests as an adult: Her activities with her friends in charity and in the arts and sciences, and in her separate business interests and finance, and her separate political and religious activities. You tacitly accept these things, and no written agreement can enforce or preclude these Rights.", I continued.

"Firstly, Duncan, I want you to tell me if you accept my counsel as premise, and secondly please tell me if I am too patronising or talk nonsense", I added.

"Charles, your every utterance is golden to me, and you may be as patronising as you like, because I need guidance.", Duncan replied.

With that I knew that Duncan was a real man (though I had not doubted) and that he would live and learn, and his marriage to Bella would likely be long or life-long.

The two women were very quiet.

I turned to Arnoldina.

"Arnoldina, please remove your clothes."

Arnoldina stood and complied.

"Have you noticed something, other than my Wife's extreme physical beauty, Duncan?"

"Yes, she complied"

"She did, and without question. She did not say 'Charles, it is cold in here' which it is. She did not say 'We hardly know these people. They may be offended'. She did not say 'There is another man present and he may attack me'. Arnoldina trusts her husband, she loves him and she *knows* he would never stand her into danger."

"Please dress, Arnoldina", I said.

She complied in silence and resumed her seat.

I turned to Bella.

"Bella, do you have any observations?"

She seemed very serious.

"I think you are both marvelous, but I find the asymmetry of your relationship disturbing."

"Charles, strip", ordered Arnoldina.

I stood and complied.

"Now turn so that Bella can see your genitals in the light."

I did.

"Now show Bella your hind quarters."

I did.

"Dress Charles"

I did.

I sat and turning to Bella I said:-

"This may be necessary in your real life marriage, Bella. I know that Duncan would never betray you with another woman or with prostitutes, but men are men and he may void his Sacred Seed through masturbation or viewing pornography. I sometimes have. That Seed is yours by right because you need it to conceive and bear your children. You think he would never do such a vulgar thing because he is a gentleman. You are right about the latter but a gentleman is a man.

You must defend your man and your marriage, Bella. Reverently, Respectfully, Lovingly you must Correct your man. I say Correct not Punish. Punishment is futile, alienating and destructive. You must Correct your man with prayers, castigations, kisses, cuddles, whatever works. But you must never nag, recriminate, preach or lecture. You must never confront the second woman. All these make matters worse."

"What do you think of that, Bella"

"I would divorce him"

"*Really* Bella? He is the father of your children. What about them?"

"I am wealthy. I can support my own."

"Oh, Bella, Bella. You cannot really mean that!"

Bella began to cry.

"These are hard lessons, Chuck", Duncan intervened. "I will drive you and Mrs Charmliss back to Congleholme and take Bella home. We can meet again at your place tomorrow evening or whenever Bella is ready."

"I am sorry Arabella", I said, "if it is any consolation both Arnoldina and I shed many tears both before and during our marriage, as did my Wife and I during my first marriage, which lasted unto death."

Both of the women's four hands were on the table. Arnoldina grasped Bella's right hand and looking her in the eyes said:-

"It is worth it"

Bella suddenly exclaimed.

"I want to go on! Tonight!"

"I know!", I said, "let's take a break! Let's speak of jollier things! Politics!"

The mood suddenly lightened amid universal laughter and an ebbtide of groans.

"Well I am a Liberal Democrat!" announced Duncan proudly.

"My Dear Fellow, I do sympathise", I responded ambiguously and to laughter.

"I am a Tory!" contributed Bella.

"We will soon cure that!" I remarked to further jollity.

"Charles, you are not Labour, are you?!" Bella asked with ebullient incredulity.

I gave her a look.

The company laughed hysterically.

With her usual sombre cheer my Arnoldina contributed:-

"I am not a political animal, but like many of the foreign adherents of the Magonian Federation I am worried about Freedom of Speech on our planet, a Right purchased in pain and blood. Not only the people and writers but the highest magistrates of every land abuse this inalienable Right and leave it maculate. It is no light matter of words that die on the wind. Speech is the very vehicle of change for good and for evil. Therefore closely guard your counsel, make every word count, and make each vote for peace. I was very recently a soldier of mercy and I know of what I speak."

Remember this is the same woman who had a few days earlier and in public spoken of her husband as a "fucking little arsehole" which is a phrase you may wish to savour and assess whether or not maculate.

But the important point was made and all became silent and salutary.

Arnoldina turned to Arabella and said:-

"Dear Bella, you wish to marry this good man but what sort of a marriage do you want? To answer the question for yourself as in so many plans and sciences you must work backwards. Do you want children who are well-adjusted, obedient and self-confident or do you want your children to be neurotic, defiant and fearful, and possibly remain so unto death of old age?"

"I desire the former: Children who are well-adjusted, obedient and self-confident", replied Bella.

"Then in regard to their mother, should she be courageous, compassionate and cheerful or should she be furtive, unfeeling and surly."

"Mother should be courageous, compassionate and cheerful", responded Bella.

"And what of the father she supports with her love, trust and attendance? Should he be courageous, considerate and clement or should he be cowardly, selfish and cruel?"

"Father should be courageous, considerate and clement to raise a successful family, Arnoldina", said Bella.

"Then Bella, whether or not you Believe, you must honour and obey your husband because you are the mistress of hearth and home. It is a grand paradox is it not?"

"It is a grand paradox, Madam, and a Mystery", agreed Bella.

"Arnoldina I Believe", Bella added in a solemn tone but with no trace of defence.

"You will find ways to serve duty as Mother and Mistress and your Husband shall help you", replied Arnoldina, and continued:-

"Arabella, my Husband came to me a broken man. I nursed him. Now my Husband is powerful and wealthy a mere few days after. You ascribe this to the exigencies of world war and the substantive rôles extemporised, I have no doubt."

"No, Arnoldina, your husband is a very talented man and I celebrate his skill and discretion."

"Bella, please hear me out."

"Sorry, Arnoldina"

"My husband has a thankless and very dangerous job which he performs with great courage. He is a pacifist compelled to fight, not out of cowardice or compromise, but because he wishes to minimise bloodshed. Every hour that he is out of my sight I pine for him. I pray to Christ to keep him safe and that no evil may befall his body or his everlasting spirit.

I long and hunger for his safe homing, Bella. I long and thirst for his tender touch, for his love, for his trust, for his mighty reinforcements. I long and I languish, Bella. I long for his every loving cuddle and caress, for his building spanks and entrusting thrusts that he knows will only be returned with gratitude and, a very remote possibility, the child he always wanted and failed to engender. Above all these sensuous things, Bella, I want his Prayers, and his spoken Prayer, that I may be comforted, strengthened and learn. I want, I desperately yearn, to be his humble Christian wife, following the spirit if not the letter of the Book. Am I wasting my efforts, Bella?"

"You have chosen a long and painful path, Arnoldina, that I in turn must walk for my man."

Throughout this stately oration I had been weeping unashamedly. Duncan had placed a hand on my forearm to comfort. He too had tears.

"Bella, am I a sap and a doormat, a disgrace to womanhood?" concluded Arnoldina, driving the last nail.

Now Bella burst into tears. She did not reply.

CHAPTER TWENTY-TWO
FARMING LIFE

By the time we suspended these preliminaries I suppose it was nearly 2100. It was obvious that things would take much longer than I thought and that we would have to locate a lavatory and a shower, and arrange such mundanities as meals and servants. But first I had to ring Treagh and ask if I could have a day's leave, the Friday before the weekend, and if so that I could be contacted via Medrington Heroncourt at Challenor's Aske House.

I rang MacKinnon.

A standard "The number you dialed has been diverted... " message came up followed by a lift click and "MacKinnon."

"Thank you for answering, Seargent Major MacKinnon. Can you please ask the Major-General if I may stay at Challenor's Aske House tomorrow and over the weekend."

"Certainly, its Commadore Charmliss, isn't it? He is at his billet. I will patch you through."

A dialing tone.

"Treagh"

"I am sorry to disturb you, Denzil. Please may I have tomorrow off and the whole weekend? I am at Challenor's Aske House near Sperstow with Bella Queenborough and son-of-the-house Duncan Heldrew."

"Chuck, I am delighted. Take the three days and enjoy yourself. You deserve a break."

"Thank you, Sir. Arnoldina and I are teaching Bella and Duncan how to have a successful marriage."

Treagh laughed.

"Best of luck with that one, Chuck", and rang off.

I turned to Heldrew.

"Duncan, can you show me where the nearest lavatory is preferably with a bath and shower, and then organise a hot meal in the atelier. Arnoldina is a vegan and we need you to order plenty of fresh bath towels."

I think he knew that Arnoldina was vegan already, but of course the servants may have been ignorant of the fact.

Heldrew performed these chores. The bathroom included a WC and adjacently there was a separate WC with a washbasin. These facilities where of cast iron, porcelain and brass and evidently predated the Second War if not the First. The bath had a separate metal shower draining into the bath. I tried the shower taps.

Copious hot and cold water issued. I was thankful. Both these rooms were three or four doors down but we did not expect to be disturbed once the meals had been delivered.

Heldrew was absent for a good ten minutes and I went back to the studio to entertain the ladies. I went to my suitcase and retrieved a packet of disposable safety razors.

"Remove your clothing, and request Baroness Sperstow to remove hers", I requested Arnoldina.

Bella had already started. Lady Sperstow proved natural.

When the two women were naked I handed Arnoldina a razor and a towel, and I accompanied both to the bathroom. There were no surprises.

"Shave Bella and trim yourself. Don't forget the armpits", I ordered.

Arnoldina was of course a doctor of medicine and a registered nurse and Bella knew her womanhood was safe in Arnoldina's hands.

Fortunately both were in the bathroom when servants brought four hot meals one of which was rather unimaginatively sprouts, peas and potatoes sans the beef and Yorkshire pudding. There was nothing to drink except that an unopened bottle of premium brandy had staged a miraculous appearance. Duncan made to breach it and pour drinks. I quicky covered the stopper with my left hand and gave him a look.

"Thank you, Chuck", said Heldrew meekly.

The two women returned the very picture of flushed feminine innocence, which indeed they were.

"Put your chairs together and take your meals in fellowship", I ordered, "I shall hand you the duvet to wrap yourselves."

I took the damp duvet from the bed and wrapped them as they stood.

The four of us bolted our meals.

Arnoldina tapped me on the arm and said:-

"Charles, a word in the corridor"

I rose and followed her out of earshot.

"Bella is an intact virgin"

"Thank you for that, My Love. I should know and value that."

"Have you briefed Bella that her first Sacred Union will be painful and bloody and that she will be sore for days?"

"Yes, Charles"

"Thank you, Arnoldina."

We returned to the lovers.

"Are you a virgin, Duncan" I asked the man.

"Yes, Sir" was the immediate reply.

I realised this was an encounter of some delicacy.

"Okay, Duncan, let's strip and shower."

We stripped before the women and picked up towels.

We returned and I took the duvet and replaced it on the bed. Now all four of us were perfectly naked, and Bella had lost her make-up. Arnoldina never used it obviously. As I remarked earlier, she was a good puritan.

"Politics. Don't you love it?!" I remarked.

"Duncan, do you believe in capital or corporal punishment?"

"Neither, nor caning in schools"

I turned to Bella:-

"I think if you take life, you should forfeit your own. I have no opinion about flogging or birching."

"Method?" I queried.

"I think the prisoner should choose between hanging and lethal injection."

"Take the case that a prisoner, a murderer, was offered a choice between death and a life sentence with a non-torturous but very humiliating corporal punishment that he would never recover from psychologically: Is it ethical and what should he choose?"

"I think it is a complex question, and it depends upon the background and circumstances", said Bella.

"You see how difficult it becomes straight away. I have very definite views but even I am not always right, though I like to flatter myself that I am perfect."

(a titter of appreciation)

"Friends, you are wise if you leave public concerns at the threshold, and run your household by reference to private Love, Trust and Mutual Respect only", I pontificated.

"Duncan and Bella, you are countryfolk. Now, heaven forbid, your seven-year-old has been caught skinning rabbits alive. Duncan, notwithstanding his declared position, says he should give the lad eight strokes of the cane on the bare behind. What do you say, Bella?"

"I defer to my husband"

"You defer to your husband, not because you are cowardly or evasive, but because ultimately a child requires a final and unique arbiter if the integrity of the whole family is not to be compromised. If necessary the child can stand in the corner for thirty minutes whilst Duncan and yourself decide the matter in private. You are very fortunate to have servants who can supervise the child's safety and compliance whilst you deliberate the issue. It is dreadful for the rabbits, but your job is to maintain and enhance the mental and spiritual progresses of your child", I said.

"Returning to the points Arnoldina adumbrated, Bella, would you like to be a shrewish, sluttish woman always at loggerheads with your husband, even arguing in front of the children?", I continued.

"Charles, the predicament sketched is too vulgar to be worthy of reply."

"I am very glad to hear it, My Lady", I responded.

"Suppose you insulted your husband at a public gathering, would he be justified in privately spanking your bottom as long as you were undressed and the penalty was exacted in a very reverent, respectful and loving manner?"

"I do not know, but if it improved his behavior and mine and enhanced our marriage, I would tend to obey and suffer the correction."

"And on your side, Duncan, and I know this would never happen, if you slept with another woman would you submit to a similar correction at the hands of your Wife?"

"No, I would come to my Wife, strip, bathe myself and insist that I was punished, but afterward forgiven and that the lapse was never referred to again."

"You are both very practical people of goodwill, and were you to wed I anticipate very few problems. Arnoldina and I will demonstrate the mechanics if it helps. I shall send complementary copies of my books on marital sex and Holy Sacraments within marriage, but there are many helpful books available on love and marriage, inevitably of variable quality", I promised.

"You are very wise to study these matters before you commit to a binding contract involving the State or the Church", I asserted.

"Friends, you have had a very stressful few hours. It is nearly 2300 and I propose that we put our clothes back on, have a little brandy, say our prayers for a sound night and for those with no home, and that the ladies sleep in the bed, Duncan has my bivvy bag and I shift for myself. It is not warm", I attempted to conclude.

"I have a better idea", stated Duncan bluntly, "Challenor's Aske has eighteen double bedrooms, three of which are currently occupied. After brandy and prayers, I shall sleep in my own room, Bella sleeps in the Yellow Room and yourself and Arnoldina in the Blue Bedroom. Does that make more sense?"

"It makes eminent sense, Duncan, and my Wife and I thank you delightedly. You are most generous."

A thing I noticed: The higher you go up the English social scale, the less the prudery and pudicity.

The Blue Room was very spacious. It was also light and warm as there were external wall windows and the accommodation faced South, and being on the piano nobile benefited from the heated ground floor. There was an ensuite bathroom, and further lavatories along the corridor. I discovered latter that the Yellow Room was next door.

I do not know why Duncan had invited us into the atelier. Perhaps it was some sort of test.

The vast double bed was something else as they say. My Wife and I luxuriated in it.

During the night eerie calls appeared to emanate from the terrace.

"What is that, Charles?" asked my Delight.

"I don't know, Dear" I replied.

We cuddled more strongly under the duvet.

In the corner was a small round breakfast table that had been set for four.

We got up and Dina went for a shower. I put on my hiking fatigues and debated with myself whether to shower after Arnoldina had finished. I actually needed to defecate, so I put on my shoes and found a lavatory further down the corridor.

At 0700 there was a diffident knock. I answered the door to find Duncan and Bella beaming. They were dressed for a country walk.

"Come in and have a seat", I said, "there is no breakfast yet so we can wait and discuss plans for the day. Arnoldina will join us shortly."

"Jolliffe will bring the breakfast shortly", confirmed Duncan.

"Dina has been rather long. I shall check if she is okay", I announced.

As I rose I heard the bathroom latch turn and Arnoldina emerged like a goddess of the golden orient.

The company was open-mouthed.

Arnoldina clapped her hands and bowed to me. This startled Bella and she jumped visibly as she sat at table. Duncan gazed expressionlessly as he would have been trained at school.

"Holy Husband, I have sinned", said Arnoldina with quiet authority in her magnificent contralto.

At that very moment the butler barged his food trolley through the door without announcement. As he entered Arnoldina calmly faced him and lowered her arms to her side.

"I am very sorry, My Lady. Please excuse me", Jolliffe said.

"Good Morning, Sir", said Dina, "the error is mine. Please take the food away and return it in thirty minutes."

"Yes, Madam. Thank you Lieutenant-Colonel Feng."

Obviously, his address book was out-of-date already.

The impression was unbelievably grand. Arnoldina stood naked in the towering eminence of her 148 centimetres, her golden skin catching the harvest promise of the slanting morning sunlight, her cervine eyes sparkling in its rise and her raven hair now reaching down into her lovely gluteal cleft. She was like a goddess on some heathen temple, but stately, chaste and Christian.

I rose and sat on the edge of the bed.

Arnoldina joined me there and assuming the position took a pillow from the head of the bed.

"What would you like to say today, Loveliness?" I said softly but audibly in the country silence.

I rested my right hand comfortingly upon Arnoldina's right buttock.

"I have lusted for my kind host the virgin Duncan whom I should have honoured", stated Arnoldina.

"My Sacred Wife, please do not succumb to the whispers of Satan, for they lead to temptation and destruction. It is our Fallen nature to lust, but we must armour ourselves, with the help of Christ and our friends."

"Darling Wife, would you like to say a Prayer audible to those friends?"

"Yes, Sir"

My Darling Saviour who gave a harlot hope, please expunge my mortal sin of lust. Please console and protect the men I have wronged and console the good woman that I have offended and betrayed. I crave her forgiveness. Intercede for me my only Lord as I suffer under the righteous hand of my master.

Unexpectedly Bella started crying.

She and her man rose from the table, slowly approached and checked themselves.

I closed my eyes and said:-

My Holy Saviour, my only Lord and King, keep my thoughts and acts pure. Still and calm my anger as you stilled the sea. I love my Wife. All comparison is invidious and tempts us further to sin but I also love the man and woman she wronged. Make me think straight and strike soundly but with mercy in a halcyon soul. Let the restitution of Arnoldina be condign, building, lasting.

"Are you comfortable, Arnoldina", I asked.

Of course I received no reply. Arnoldina is no harlot.

I spanked only the lower buttocks and pulled my blows. Arnoldina cried. Bella stepped forward and seized my arm with all the strength of a professional horse-breeder.

"Stop, Charles, this instant!"

I had little choice. I turned to Bella and said:-

"Madam, you are profaning a Holy Sacrament."

Bella released and withdrew to her former position.

I posed theatrically with my hands in the air and stared at Bella as much as to say "This is a consenting adult on my lap. She is free to leave."

I returned my left hand to Arnoldina's waist and placed my right on her thigh.

Then I resumed the strikes and Arnoldina wept distractedly and gasped 'Oh, Jesus' and then 'Yes!, Yes!, Yes!' and she collapsed to the bed.

Arnoldina's climaxes are usually quiet and refined, like those of my first Wife back in 80V. I think she was hamming it up a bit for the students.

I turned Arnoldina onto her back.

I tenderly kissed her lips and said:-

Dear God, Bless this pure woman with your strength and forbearance always

Then I slowly moved to her portal of life, kissed and said:-

In the Issuance of Life, grant my Wife Arnoldina life perpetual

I Crossed her body and took her in my arms.

"Thank you, Sir, for your Ministry, for your Prayer and for your Holy Correction. I apologise for my sin, I loathe it, and I ask our Lord to take it from me and to annihilate it utterly", said Arnoldina.

"I love you, Arnoldina, and I Correct you with the deepest loyalty and respect, Arnoldina, and I cherish your every act of obedience."

There was a pause.

Duncan turned to his Betrothed and said:-

"That was very impressive indeed. They have taken something abusive and transfigured it to something very beautiful, very reverent."

"Yes, Duncan, but it is not for us", Bella said coldly.

I looked away from my Wife's tearful but serene face and at Bella.

"Bella, the day may dawn when you have to choose between a sore bottom and a marriage. Choose wisely. Take no thought for the morrow, but indeed the evil is sufficient unto the day thereof", I stated.

Ever practical my agricultural host Duncan offered:-

"I will get you a cold towel, Dina. After breakfast Bella will give you a rub with some ibuprofen gel and we will all go for a nice walk."

"No thank you, Duncan. I shall forgo the soothing. I shall reflect on what I have earned."

We had breakfast.

Ever a man to squeeze a sunbeam from a dark cloud Duncan asked:-

"Did you see the Blue Lady last night!"

"I find it difficult to see something blue moving against a blue background", I responded with my usual impertinence.

"Anyway, my lady is plenty blue enough for me!", I added.

Duncan and Bella tittered with embarrassed appreciation.

"Arnoldina and I heard very eerie calls last night, Duncan. What caused them?", I asked.

"Foxes on the terrace. It is their season."

Duncan had considerately provided black coffee, oat milk and hazelnut spread rather than butter or sugar, for our sunflower-oil baked croissants and toast; and for all four.

I nursed my arthritic wrist with my left hand as the pain became severe.

"Charles, can I get you a surgical strop and some cooling gel for your wrist. I am sorry for what I did.", offered Bella.

"It is okay, Bella, it will soon be okay with rest. I accept your apology humbly and with gratitude. You did what you did for your friend as you saw fit. Can more be asked of us?"

"You are very quiet now, Arnoldina. What are your observations?" Duncan asked.

"With very great respect to you, Lord Heronbridge, I have nothing to say to you this morning. This is Bella's day and for good or for evil she shall remember it all of her days more vividly than all days except the day she bore her first child, because today you inseminate her under God whose chosen instrument you are", replied Arnoldina.

I think we all hoped or dreaded this outcome, but it took Arnoldina to declare it in unambiguous terms, and leave little scope for honourable demurral.

Arnoldina continued:-

"For you, Bella, I have this: My Husband has never, ever, rejected any suggestion or request I have made to him, nor I wager shall he. There was once the one occasion when my husband contested my *implied* will in public and I admonished him in public in the most obscene terms. I was Corrected promptly. I was Corrected correctly, Corrected efficiently, and rightly Corrected with the sacred reverence due to that cherishment. I obey my husband willingly and explicitly, my husband obeys me implicitly for to honour me. Bella, you shall be Mistress in your own home because you will be correct at all times. Marriage is a two way street, Bella, and the most equitable of gaming-houses, because you win what you submit."

I felt sure that Duncan and Bella would know to what Arnoldina alluded, even if they were not present at the Albion Hotel that morning.

Bella turned to Arnoldina and said:-

"Would you not like to dress, Arnoldina. It is chilly in here and I am afraid servants might enter again."

"My nakedness is part of my Penance, Bella. It is for the regard of God only."

Thus admonished, Bella seemed abashed, but Arnoldina drove home:-

"Bella, may I ask a special favour of you?"

"Anything you want, Dearest Girl. You have only to ask. Would you like a racehorse?"

"No thank you, Bella, but that is the thing I wanted to talk with you about. Will you please stop whipping your horses?"

"I never strike livestock. It is most unprofessional", responded Bella shirtily.

"No, Lady Sperstow, but the jockeys you hire do. Order them not to."

"It will be done, Dr Mrs Charmliss."

"Arnoldina, may I ask a very personal question?" added Bella.

Arnoldina gave no response.

"Dina, do you always climax when your husband spanks you?"

"Bella, I orgasm at the first sight of him, and again if he touches me."

"Bella, I thrill. Bella, I thrill, again and again and again. It is often difficult to work and sometimes to sleep. But I am happy with my Faith, with my Portion and with my man."

"Duncan I have a further request if I may of yourself", asked Arnoldina.

"Arnoldina, I am privileged and delighted. What is it?"

"This is the first time I have really visited the English countryside and it is most lovely, even or perhaps especially as Winter comes. Your father's house and its grounds are very splendid and as a foreign guest I say very well managed, if that is not an impertinence."

"It is a very high complement and I am very moved. Thank you.", Said Duncan and then:-

"I say, you don't want my estate do you!" Duncan teased with a laugh.

"No, Duncan, that is Betrothed to another."

The table sobered up.

"My best understanding is that your father owns horse-pasture and woodland that extends for some miles", continued Arnoldina.

"I like to think I have a few acres in trust for my posterity and my people."

"A few days ago, though it seems decades, I made my husband a promise. I said that if we ever went walking in a private or remote place I would walk naked by his side. Will your father oblige me?"

Duncan took out his mobile and rang his father to relay the question.

"Dad says that you may but only if he may watch through his field glasses. He jests of course", added Duncan with a giggle.

"Duncan, I must walk with you in the same state in sympathy with my beautiful friend", stated Bella.

"Are you speaking of me, Dearest", spoke Duncan with another slightly embarrassed little giggle.

"Do you mind if I satisfy my curiosity at your expense, Duncan?" I said.

"Go ahead!"

"Your fathers surname is Heroncourt, and you are Viscount Heronbridge and yet your surname is Heldrew?"

"Yes, the Heldrews live in Argentina, and when Mother divorced Dad and married Mr Heldrew it was agreed that my name would be Heldrew for Argentinian and UK official purposes. Viscount Heronbridge is just a courtesy title. I am an only son and I will become the 4th Earl of Chamberfield in due course, if such tom-foolery persists. Weirdly, as Earl my surname would remain Heldrew."

"I see. Thank you, Duncan"

"*De nada* as Mother says"

As we rose from the table Bella undressed and put most of her clothes on a chair. Then she replaced her skirt and her shooting jacket. She was already wearing clean boots.

I retrieved Arnoldina's mourning dress from her case and hoicked it over her. She put on her synthetic belt and her walking boots.

Duncan and I shouldered small sacks and we set off across the vast tree-studded lawn which Duncan called a "park."

After a couple of hundred metres, when the terrace obscured the eyeline from the windows, Duncan ordered:-

"Strip, Ladies!"

I noted with satisfaction that he was learning to be master in what would become his house.

Duncan and I took our respective women's clothes in ready hand.

The women clung closely to us.

I could not have been happier and I think we all rejoiced in the innocency, the nature, the windless warmth and the falling, golden leaves. And of course the happy anticipation of sex discharged in obedience to God's purpose in Man.

The women clung closely in their primeval conditions, partly for warmth, mostly for protection against private demons, or in propitiation of their lovers. There was much laughter from all, and the exquisite squeaks of creatures revelling in their defiance of Fallen authority.

We entered the dripping woodland by a stile that presented several competing visions of the portals of paradise and strode forth into a garden of punk bats and fungus. Momentarily, the sun glimmered and spotted the women's skins with pantherine spots that shifted and shimmered in the glades, as if to compliment with light the matte camo dapples of the male attire. There were few nettles but those that stung the two naked females the women bore with Stoic grace.

I smelt woodsmoke and handed Arnoldina her dress and belt which she replaced with a shrug and a clasp. Duncan gave Arabella her skirt and jacket which she put on. Gingerly we approached the source of the fumes.

Presently, we entered a small clearing where a small fire of dry tinder burned before a green tarpaulin rigged as an extemporary shelter. The hovel appeared to be guarded only by the tiniest and most disarming toddler with blond curly hair. We stopped and stood in silence as he stared back with circumspect innocence, gently rocking himself from side to side. He held to the corner of his closed lips the very filthiest of formless toys, perhaps a well-loved teddy or soft toy rat. The boy was as filthy and as regardless of filth as innocence allowed.

His gaze fixated upon Arnoldina. Perhaps this was the first time he had seen a Sinitic visage in his short life. Perhaps like us all he was simply entranced by her extreme beauty. Perhaps he was becharmed by both.

After a few assessive seconds his little face beamed with delight as he ran to embrace Arnoldina's calves. Arnoldina stooped then knelt among the nettles as she smilingly cuddled and kissed the dirty little trespasser. Then Bella knelt and cuddled them both. Directly his mother appeared.

"Good Morning, Ladies. He is lovely isn't he. He is my little son James. I am Martha Selby."

Mrs Selby was as matted in dirt and smoke as her son, if that were possible.

The women rose and shook hands.

"I am Arnoldina Charmliss and this is Arabella Queenborough", stated the eldest.

"I know you Ms Queenborough, you are the horse lady, aren't you?"

"That's right", confirmed Bella.

"I am amazed that fine ladies with expensive clothes would cuddle and caress my little tyke."

"Children are children", stated Arnoldina, "I can arrange for you and your son to have a bath and to have clean clothes", committed my lovely Wife, but presuming the sanction of the landowner.

"That would be lovely. Thank you very much, Madam."

"We have not washed since my husband was sacked by the fucking Magonians four weeks ago. We lost our wages and our rented home overnight."

"I am a fucking Magonian", advised Arnoldina veritably.

"Yes, but you are a lady. I am very sorry I spoke so offensively. You are beautiful and you treated my little son very kindly. I shall remind him of you as long as I last."

"He will remember me anyway", prophesied Arnoldina, I thought with a touch of the ominous.

Presently, a disheveled man beyond his age appeared out of the woods dragging a dry and dead sycamore branch.

"Good Morning, Your Honours", greeted the man as he parked his stolen bough and commenced to break it.

He approached Duncan and I and declaimed:-

"I am Martin Selby, and you have met my wife Martha and my son James."

Selby offered offered his filthy hand. Duncan seized it manfully and said:-

"I am Duncan Heldrew and that is my fiancée Arabella Queenborough."

"Are you then his Lordship's son?"

"That's right"

"I am sorry I have trespassed and stolen. I am destitute and I shall move on, Sir."

"And you, Sir, whom do I have the honour of meeting?" continued Selby.

"I am Charles Charmliss and the lady with long hair is my Wife Arnoldina (née Feng)."

"I am honoured to meet you all and I apologise for my crimes and for spoiling your walk."

"This is wartime and I accept your apologies. I need an under-gardener. I can lend you a small cottage with water and electricity until you find your feet", stated Duncan to Selby.

"Be careful about modern slavery, Darling", counselled Bella.

"And you will get a small wage", segued Duncan.

"You are most generous and most forgiving, My Lord, I gladly accept for my Wife and little son."

"Have you got a shovel?", Duncan asked Selby.

"Yes, Sir. I shall bury the fire before we follow you."

"Good man. Thank you", replied Duncan.

"No. Thank *you*, Sir"

We installed the Selbys and the servants gave them suits of clean clothes. The butler showed Mrs Selby where to find a washing machine and she washed the family's own rags.

Then we four repaired to an early supper.

It was Duncan and Bella's trick so we ate at a table set for four in the Yellow Room.

I retrieved the brandy from the atelier and took the liberty of ordering Mr Jolliffe to prepare and deliver a vegan supper for four and bring it to the Yellow Room, but that within the next two hours would do.

We convened at the table without changing, though we left our muddy boots at the entrance and changed to house slippers.

"What are your thoughts of the day?" I asked no-one in particular.

"I thought the Holy Correction of Arnoldina was superb: Loving, respectful, Christian and kind just as such should be. It is important to lovingly correct and adjust, not to punish in vengeance. That would be self-indulgent. I accept that such rites should only benefit the penitent", was Duncan's appreciation.

Duncan turned to Arnoldina and said:-

"Arnoldina I am desperately sorry that I was the occasion of your suffering. In future I will try to behave with more decency and decorum."

"Duncan, I humbly accept your kind apology but the sin is not yours. You are innocent in all senses of that word. The evil is in my mind though not in my heart, my good friend", responded Arnoldina.

"Did I speak too much, and was my little lecture too long and self-serving?", I asked.

"Not at all, Charles", answered Bella, "and your Prayers were lovely. My only criticism, and it is probably informed of ignorance, was that your castigations were too harsh."

"Nonsense!", exclaimed Duncan, "anyway Arnoldina enjoyed it and has got the intelligence to learn from it."

"Don't be vulgar:- and stupid, Duncan", Bella answered.

I thought it was time to get some sparkling water and pour the brandy. I played waiter serving the ladies first. I gave everyone a quarter of their tumblers and left the mineral water on the table in its bottles, with the remains of the premium brandy.

"Was the walk satisfactory?" Duncan directed at me.

"It was idyllic. I have not enjoyed such a fine walk for years, nor such fine company. I greatly appreciated your fiancée's support of my Wife."

"It was the very least I could do, and it delighted Duncan", admitted Bella.

"Do you think the Selby's will find their feet?" I asked.

"Time will tell", said Duncan, "but they seem pleasant people, apologetic and courteous. They are clearly good parents. I hope I prove to be."

"Me likewise", I said.

"When Jolliffe brings the food, I shall order more drinks. What would you like Arnoldina?", offered Duncan.

"Can I have a Bloody Mary without Worcestershire Sauce, please Duncan?"

"Jolliffe has procured some vegan Worcestershire Sauce. Would you like to try it?"

"Yes please, Duncan."

"I will have a cold pint of Cornish IPA, please Duncan, if available, otherwise local IPA", I said with my usual porcine sense of precedence.

"Bella?"

"Get me a Pina Colada, please."

"I will have the same as Chuck", Duncan completed.

Jolliffe arrived.

It was tomato soup of the type thickened with corn flour followed by frankies, Arnoldina's favourite.

"Thank you, Duncan, you are a very considerate man", said Arnoldina.

Duncan blushed.

"It was your Husband's doing. He ordered", Duncan confessed.

"Charles, you are a treasure!" Arnoldina told me with an angelic smile.

"I am learning a great deal every hour, how to be a wife and how to be a hostess, even though I have had formal training for the latter, and wish I had had for the former. You are great teachers, both of you", stated Bella.

"I once worked for an egregious organisation whose motto was *always learning*. Well, Bella, we are all always learning until we die. You and Duncan have by a natural and unmeditated exchange taught Arnoldina and I about what life could be. I don't mean the land and the horses: I mean about friendship, love and trust. My wife and I love you both and wish we could stay with you forever. But war is war and we have duties, also to others.", I counselled in my usual way.

Bella said:-

"We love you too, Charles and Arnoldina, but I doubt that I have the inner strength to follow your stringent path. I Believe, but my Faith is not strong."

"Bella, you and Charles are novices. Give God time. His Mercy will rain upon you", I consoled.

"Bella, Duncan, please do not be offended by the things I say. You must think much of it very patronising and pompous, but through many years of teaching adult students I discovered that I could assume nothing and that angry students would often come to realise that they had been hasty and that amongst all the nonsense there were gems of wisdom that they could apply", I excused.

"Chuck, when I was at school, I mean 'School':- Eton College, I was taught to keep my mouth shut, my ears open, and my mind clear, unless I could crack a joke or make some pleasantry to lighten the mood, and *accurately* judge when the mood needed lightening. It is a big secret, but I hope to prove a good listener and a thinking student. I am acutely aware that you are not being paid. I shall find a way to honour your Wife and yourself", explained Duncan.

"The payment is not your hospitality, Duncan, kingly though it is. It is your love and your trust. Few couples would stand before me naked and ask to be taught about sex and marriage", I answered.

"For my part, friends, I was privately tutored", admitted Bella, "but I have a business to run, employing between thirty and fifty according to season. I was of course a student of Harper Adams Agricultural University, but my real education has been provided gratis, by the many men and girls who help me with their skills, their labour, their advice and their trust, and indeed by the animals they marshal."

I responded:-

"With regard to this morning's Holy Correction, I am quite aware that you both dismissed it as a lecture demonstration. But none of us are defilers of sacraments. We all have lustful thoughts. We all offend God who only meant us to use his furniture for propagation. If your Beloved Intended, Bella, did not imagine dreadful things for my most eminently fuckable Wife then I should feel mine own honour insulted. We are men not animals, we have a Contract with the Almighty, and if animals also have Free Will then it is men who exercise it. This, Bella, you have learnt."

"You both perceived, I doubt not, that I struck very moderately and mostly on the fatty but muscular flesh at the base of the buttock. My Wife is older than you guess, and her bones are likely brittle and my blows are calibrated to minimise risk of injury, by agreement with Arnoldina of course. She sobs in regret for her wickedness. She is not a child and she does not cry for pain."

"Castigation is never done to injure either the body or the mind. It is done to service the soul. It is painful but it is not intended to torture. It is always meant to propel the Penitent into a state of mind in which he is Corrected by God and sincerely, deeply regretful, which is what the Penitent wants to be. The Penitent concludes his experience by saying in the voice and the spirit, or in the spirit only "I hate my sin and I reject it with loathing." In a sense of speaking this licenses Christ to seize the offending object and annihilate it. Thus Free Will is not abridged. All this lays the groundwork of personal reformation. If you spank or otherwise exact any pastoral penance then you must do so with love, humility and the deepest respect even if the penitent is a stranger or an enemy. If you hate the person on your lap, then you must refuse to Correct. The Penitent needs and should get a Confessor who honours him. For her part, Arnoldina will not suffer in the presence of Duncan again, even if they are both naked."

"It is not easy, and it is not for selfish people."

"It is because we abhor to injure the mind that we never strike and much less spank children. They lack the mental maturity to process the sexual undercurrents of violence. If you strike children there is a real risk that you will curse them with the perversions of sadism or masochism for life. Evidence is too abundant. Always present a united front to children, any children, and settle any disagreements in private."

"Chuck, I have a hard question...", said Bella, "well I think it is hard at any event...with the most immense respect, Charles, you are not a large man. I have wondered what sex must be like with you. My transgression is at least insolent, and I ask that you Correct whatever sins you identify. I do not mock, Charles: This is a serious and for me disturbing request."

"Bella, I am not insulted and you may rest calm. I am gratified by your intelligence and the immense courage you show in broaching this dangerous question and enduring the psychic perils likely to result. I am not myself sure whether you have committed lust or whether it is mere intellectual curiosity, a thing correctible only through sin. For these reasons alone I could not correct, but in any case a Confessor cannot hear a Confession in which he has self-interest. Your Fiancé is entitled to Correct you if he can identify a sin, but he must do so *for your benefit only* **not** because he is angry and certainly not because he wishes to resolve his own speculations."

"I shall let it pass, Charles, Bella is a woman, a real woman, and I flatter myself that I am a man", Duncan intervened.

"Thank you, Duncan, you are more than a man", I replied.

"Bella I have a hard question for you, somewhat off the track we have trodden, but I think germane. May I ask it?"

"Charles, you may ask anything"

"Thank you. Take the case that you are alone walking a country lane not far from the stud and dusk is falling. A man with a knife emerges from a hedge. You have not brought your pistol. You decide to submit. This evil man breaks your hymen.

Bella, are you still a virgin?"

"I should hope to die", answered Bella.

"I would pursue the bastard and kill him!" interjected Duncan angrily.

"Friends, understandably neither of you answered my question", I persisted, "The answer is that Bella is still a virgin, because sexual intercourse is an act of intentionality subject to Free Will. Bella's acquiescence was not consent and her intention was not to lose her virginity. The physical injury is irrelevant and any issue is Bella's and hers in entail. The man has lost all rights to his son or daughter."

"Suppose the man just buggers her?" asked Duncan, still angry at the very thoughts.

"In England today the man would rightly be charged with rape, but from a theological point of view the man is guilty of buggery and not rape because his sin was not procreative. The man is a sodomite and subject to the spiritual and temporal penalties appointed for ordinary sodomites. If he breaks the woman's sphincter he is subject to penalties earned by acts of Grievous Bodily Harm. He is of course guilty of Battery and False Arrest in any circumstance.

From our point of view, the fact is again that Bella did not consent to penetration or any corporeal disturbance whether of a sexual character or not.

Consent is not Implied by submission. Consent is implied by search, and Bella did not search for the rapist or sodomite with intent to defile herself.

Duncan, you have searched for a lady to share your life and you have found one. Your Implied Consent is as live and actual as is her Implied Consent to her body", I replied to Duncan.

I continued:-

"Fellatio, cunnilingus and buggery or not procreative acts and frustrate God's Design for the procreation of species. They are ugly names for sordid things. Therefore, all are forbidden to Christian people. It is not a matter of doctrine or denomination. It is a matter of Discipleship.

I do not mean that you have to have seven or fourteen children.

You are not here to despoil the planet or induce famine.

Once you have the two or three lovely children whom you cherish forever, and who will love you beyond death, you may use contraception or any sensible measure that does not beggar your neighbours.

Sacred Union is unique. You excite tumidity, at least for the man's penis, and he carefully inserts it into the woman's vagina and gifts the Seed of Life as near to her cervix as he is able. If he is patient, skillful and lucky the woman will climax as he himself inseminates and both parties will relax in loving connection.

This is something God wills, and neither it nor its preparations are sinful.", I lectured.

"What is cunnilingus?" asked Duncan innocently. Fortunately he was calming down a bit now as I was starting to leave thoughts of brutality.

"Cunnilingus is when you masturbate the woman's clitoris with your tongue to bring her to orgasmic emission without necessarily depositing your Seed in its proper place. That is sinful because it frustrates God", I explained.

"A tender kiss on Bella's vulva or just a lick of her clitoris is not cunnilingus and Bella will thrill to it and become moist enough for painless Sacred Union."

"In your first act and your first days you are both tight and must expect pain. But persevere. A little blood may run."

"But the day will come when each Holy Union is a soft and luxuriant delight as a Merciful God meant it to be, and you will rush to the joy of each other's arms to fulfil a lively act of love, to think of your babies to issue, and to behold the sparkle of sunlight in your spouse's eyes. And as you consummate in body the love for each another's spirits you will drowse content and fall asleep in your Beloved's naked arms, twined in their legs, two mortal things in one."

"Sacred Union stands unique as a Sacrament of God that no man can disown or corrupt. In another world My Late Mother, who was an atheist, told me as I became old enough to fuck a woman that sexual intercourse was 'Sacred' using that word. She told me several wrong and very baleful things, but she was right about that and I remained a virgin until I found the woman I would marry", I added.

"Charles, these theological concepts and medical words bedazzle my mind, I'm afraid. I am just a horse-country farmer. You will have to show Bella and I how to act in practical terms", said Charles.

"Arnoldina and I will do as you ask. We are not ashamed of our love and neither should you be of yours."

"Duncan.", Bella said, "Don't you think Charles puts things so well and straight-forwardly but with such decency?"

"I certainly think that, Bella, there is no denying that whatever else Charles is or is not he is a wordsmith."

"Thank you friends. It is already 2100. You have a very heavy day tomorrow if you hold me to my word, and Arnoldina is both willing and able."

"I am willing and I am able tomorrow", affirmed Arnoldina in plain hearing, "sleep in assurance, Bella, that my Husband will do nothing demeaning or indecent to either yourself or Duncan."

"I accept your guarantee with gratitude, Dina, but accept mine that I should never imagine such eventuations", replied our veritable lady of a hostess.

Bella stayed in the Yellow Room and Duncan accompanied Arnoldina and me quietly to our own. I called Duncan in and said:-

"Please order Jolliffe to deliver a cold vegan breakfast for four to the Yellow Room at 0800 tomorrow. I should be obliged if you would join us at 0830, if you will."

"I shall act precisely as you say, Chuck."

Duncan left for his room. If I had been skillful it would be the last time he would ever sleep there.

Arnoldina and I retired.

"Arnoldina", I asked from my pillow, "Do you *really* fancy Duncan?"

"Don't be silly, Charles. Now who is profaning the Sanctity of the Confessional?"

Saturday dawned. The traditional day of marriages. I married my Wife of 80V on a Saturday. I worked in a civil engineering consultancy at the time and labours ceased at 1700 on the Friday.

Arnoldina and I went to breakfast with Bella in the Yellow Room.

We did not waste time.

"Today, Bella, we believe that Duncan may deliver his Seed of Life to your cervix. This is the consummation of Holy Marriage in any rite. Notwithstanding that, such a wedding is not recognised by any Church or State. Is this your free will, Arabella Queenborough?" I clarified and asked.

"Yes, Dr Charmliss, it is."

"Then if Duncan consents, and I shall ask him if he does, Arnoldina and I shall stand Witness to the Holy Sacrament, and if necessary show you in practical terms how to complete the act."

"Bella, do you promise to love, honour and obey Duncan?"

"I certainly love and honour Duncan. I am not sure about the obey bit."

"If you accept Duncan's Seed you submit to his will. But this is not a matter for me. It is for a husband to control his wife. Duncan is a humane but firm man. I have seen him in action. And you protect your fiancé from potential peril. I have seen you in action."

"This morning it is a good idea if you address your Betrothed in a very simple manner as 'Sir' or 'My Love'. No elaborate pet-names, endearments or titles, and no long protestations. Arnoldina and I will lead prayers and you may voice your own."

"Now, Bella, visit the bathroom. If you have a tampon please remove it. Try to defecate and urinate if you can. Have a shower and return here. Do not dress but go and kneel on the bed and wait."

At 0830 dead there was a knock on the door. I thought it was Duncan, but it proved to be Jolliffe.

"Yes, please clear the things, Mr Jolliffe", I said, "and bring, along with still and sparkling water, one bottle of red house wine and four fresh bread rolls."

"Yes, Commadore Charmliss"

As Jolliffe bustled out with his trolley, Duncan appeared at the door and I beckoned him in:-

"Good Morning, Heldrew", I greeted formally.

"Good Morning, Dr Charmliss."

"Are you willing in principle, and not withstanding difficulties, to deliver The Holy Seed of Life to your Fiancée's cervix in procreative expectation?"

"I am"

"Do you understand that this is a rite of Holy Matrimony in God's Sight delivered of the Spirit and that you are bound to this woman, and only this woman, forever."

"I do"

Bella came out of the bathroom and went and knelt on the bed.

I asked Duncan:-

"Do you understand the gravity of these proceedings and do you consent to your part therein?"

"I do"

Turning to Bella I said:-

"Come here" that abruptly.

Bella left the bed and took a seat at the breakfast table beside her husband-to-be.

"Do you affirm to love, honour and protect your woman for the rest of her days", I addressed to Duncan.

"I do"

"Do you, Arabella Queenborough, affirm to love, honour and obey Duncan Heldrew for the remainer of his days."

"I swear to love and honour Duncan Heldrew for the remainder of his days", replied Bella.

"Friends, only Quaker Members are authorized by the English State to solemnise marriages, I was a mere attender. I am not a priest or a registrar in any jurisdiction and I cannot grant a Certificate.

But as you consent I celebrate your Marriage in the Sight of God our only righteous judge.

Your friends witness your Marriage in love, if Marriage is what you make it.

My Wife and I are here to serve, teach and protect you for as long as you want those things. If you need practical assistance we shall provide it reverently and decently.

Today titles, names and endearments should be minimal. "Sir", "Madam", or "My Love" are more than adequate. This is a time for silence, action and prayer. You may pray aloud or in silence. Arnoldina and I will voice prayers."

"Now, and it is the last time I shall use this form, Lord Heronbridge, retire to the bathroom, urinate, defecate, shower and return to this table naked."

"Yes, Sir"

After Heronbridge had returned to sit at our table, Jolliffe entered with the water, wine and bread.

"Ah, Jolliffe", Duncan said, "please leave the things on the table before us." Both Heldrew and Bella were of course stark naked.

"Yes, Sir", Jolliffe replied without visible reaction, and pushing his empty trolley departed.

"Go and sit on the side of the bed, Sir", I ordered.

Duncan complied.

"Bella go and sit on his lap and steady yourself with your arms round his shoulders."

"Yes, Sir"

Bella complied.

I rose from the table and said "Strip, Arnoldina" as I removed my own clothes and placed them on an armchair.

I approached the couple and fell to my knees before them, folded my hands, closed my eyes and bowed my head:-

My Dear and Holy Saviour, my only Lord and King
I beseech you to
Bless this Marriage of two good people
with many serene years of
delight in the sanctified alliance of one another;
with happy children;
a prosperous home with ample but not excessive provision;
and death in the knowledge of a godly life well lived and a
common wealth well served.

I rose, bowed to the couple, and in the Latin Crossed myself and was followed by Arnoldina who stood before the couple, put her hands together, clapped once in that startling Oriental way, bowed deeply and then knelt:-

Bowing her head with folded hands she softly said:-

My Darling Jesus Christ who endured the arid desert winds
and strode the stormy sea, and saw it obey I beseech you to
Bless this Marriage of two good people with children who
laugh without mockery, smile without sycophancy, speak
with sanctity and act with obedience, that they may light
every minute of their parent's harmony with lives lived in
kindness and love of all, to the delight of their Father and
Mother in this World and the hereafter.

She turned her lovely face skyward and clapped. Then Crossing in the Greek manner as taught by Nestor she rose with the grace of a gazelle and returned to me as I sat on the bed edge.

"Duncan and Bella", I said, "watch and do as Arnoldina and I, but with reverence and tenderness of your own. If you dislike our actions or think them indecent then forbear but please do not comment or complain."

I chastely kissed Arnoldina on the lips and took her left breast in my right palm and gently massaged it in a slow circular action.

From the corner of my eye I could see that Duncan did as I did but with the ample breast of his Bella.

I told Arnoldina to climb onto the king sized double bed and lie prone. I gently massaged her now-dry buttocks and back.

The Betrothed couple climbed beside us and did likewise. Bella made little groans and squirms of developing ecstasy.

Then, Duncan waddled to the other corner of the mattress and turned to face Bella. She looked up in surprise at the sudden desertion. Duncan smiled to her and offered out his right hand. Duncan was still kneeling a metre from Bella. He smiled to her and said "Come here."

Bella hesitated.

Arnoldina said "Obey him."

Bella rolled to her lover and took his hand.

Still kneeling on the bed, Duncan gently placed her prone and held her hands behind her back with his left hand and placed his right tenderly upon her right buttock. Duncan closed his eyes and prayed aloud:-

Darling Jesus, make me a good Husband to this truly lovely woman who shall bear my children in pain and smile. Make me kind, considerate, protective and righteously proud of my Beloved Bella but make me also liberal and supportive. I love Bella deeply, and ever shall whether we marry or not. But I hope to witness her first parturition and welcome my longed-for child to life.

Duncan paused and then he said:-

"Everything I do I do for Bella, and I *shall* be obeyed in my own house."

Then Duncan said:-

"Do you wish to pray, Bella?"

Bella replied:-

"I cannot better your Prayer, Duncan, only echo it. I hope to face childbirth with courage for an infinite benefit. My prayer is only this":-

God, I thank you for this man

"Are you comfortable, Bella?" asked Duncan.

Bella was a robust countrywoman and she was a multi-millionairess and did not care much what anyone else thought.

"I am comfortable, Duncan."

Duncan delivered five of the very softest pats to each buttock. Bella laughed throughout, as had a wife of mine when she thought she deserved Correction, but was suffering punishing blows.

Duncan took Bella in his arms. Bella spontaneously said:-

"Thank you, Duncan. I needed that. I shall promptly obey in future, because I love and trust you."

"Bravo, Bella!" Arnoldina and I chorused.

"Bella, you have thanked Duncan of your heart, but will you please repeat these words after me because I am a silly stickler", I said, "'thank you, Duncan, for your Prayer, for your Ministry and your Holy Correction'".

"Thank you, Duncan, for your Prayer, for your Ministry and your Holy Correction.", repeated Bella verbatim.

"Is there anything else you would like to say to Duncan this morning?" I asked Bella.

"He means would you like to say sorry", Duncan whispered in Bella's ear.

Bella turned to face Duncan with a broad grin and gently said:-

"Dearest Duncan, Sir, I am very sorry for defying and disrespecting you. I really do respect you Duncan despite my stupid ways."

Duncan seized the woman in his arms and snogged her powerfully. Forgive my crude word, but that is the only way to describe it.

As I watched congratulating myself, Arnoldina softly called:-

"Charles"

I looked round. Arnoldina made a face and pointed to her own vulva, the Portal of Life.

I quietly replied "Go Ahead"

Arnoldina parted the lovers and said:-

"Excuse me, Bella. I need to make a little examination. Please open your legs a little."

Bella lay as Dina parted her labia and peered inside.

Arnoldina unhanded Bella and turning to me nodded.

I placed my left hand on Duncan's right shoulder as he knelt on the bed, obviously tumid.

"Okay, old man, do this. Grasp Bella's ankles firmly and part her legs. Intromit and complete Sacred Union."

"Yes, Sir"

Duncan required no second prompting but somehow he seemed to miss the mark.

"Help him, Bella", Arnoldina ordered.

Bella seized the glans and pushed it past her threshold.

Duncan made seven mighty thrusts.

Bella gasped and screamed.

It was over.

As far as Arnoldina and I were concerned Duncan and Bella were man and wife and were now to be treated as such. We would instruct no further unless requested.

A little blood came from Bella's portal, though the pair were still coupled. They fell into each other's arms.

"Dina and I will now leave you to your love-making and your sleep. We will go for a walk and return here for dinner at 1900", I advised.

Duncan said "Thank you." Bella was still in a swoon.

Arnoldina and I returned to the Blue Room and showered. I rang Jolliffe and told him Mr and Mrs Charmliss would not need lunch, but that we would return to Mr and Mrs Heldrew in the Yellow Room for dinner at 1900.

Jolliffe replied with a simple "Yes, Sir" and no query.

We put on our walking kit and left the house. We more or less walked at random and mainly along narrow tarmacadamed lanes.

The cool Autumn sun threw the transfigured woodlands into a sharp relief. Rabbits and squirrels danced in the adjacent pastures. The electric overhead cables arced in the lifting mist. Horses grazed in sparse and distant splendour like figures from the Eocene. It was another idyllic Mercian vision in the midst of a world war and a likely British Revolution.

After a mile or two we came to a large village where there was a fork in the road and of all things a fish and chip shop. There was a public house at the fork, but we did not go in. Instead I went into the fish and chip shop whilst Arnoldina rested on a bench by an old-fashioned red call box.

I purchased one large cod and chips for myself, and large chips and peas for Arnoldina. It was not exactly vegan of course but Dina ate ravenously. I had also bought a bottle of zero cola and we shared it.

After our meal I put the wrappings in a convenient garbage bin. Arnoldina handed me a wet-wipe and we wiped the grease from our hands.

We ambled along the right-most of the forking streets enjoying the afternoon sunshine. Presently we came upon a small knot of people in earnest conversation outside a small building with green painted eaves and a notice board outside.

A little apart a man in camo trousers and a puffer jacket stood looking at the crowd as he leant with both hands supporting himself on his sheep-stick. A fine border collie sat panting at his side.

"What is going on here?" I casually enquired.

The man's clothes were filthy. Both trousers and jacket were caked in animal excrement and he stank. Only his smart green wellingtons appeared clean. He himself could have enjoyed a shower or even a bath. Admixed with his other smells was cigarette tobacco, tobacco ash, human castoreum and days or weeks of sweat. I thought I smelt alcohol on his breath.

I stood back a little, and Arnoldina further.

"Fucking sod-busters. They think they have got problems. I am sick of them. Fancy a half pint and a sandwich before you walk on, Your Honours?"

I was amazed that a man's opening word to strangers would be such an expletive, one of the strangers obviously female, and he with such a fine, well-bred voice, obviously an ex-public school boy. I was also astonished at hearing the American pejorative applied to Englishmen.

"No thank you, I replied. We have just eaten."

"Splendid Chinky wench you've got there, Mister, must run like a fucking train?"

"That is enough", I said curtly, "Go and sleep it off"

The bore ambled off in the direction of the pub, swinging his crook at unseen crows with his dog trotting beside admiringly.

We gently pressed to where some of the crowd were entering the small hall. A man at the door was selling tickets.

"1000 crowns entrance per attendee for the Palatine Farmers' Fund please Sir, Madam."

I took out a 2000 crown note in exchange for our tickets.

The interior was a very bare deal-panelled affair I would have said 1920's. Then I noticed the fascia above a small proscenium: "Sperstow War Memorial Hall, 1922", the year of My

Late Mother's birth. The acoustics was dreadful and the echoes of two hundred voices hurt my ears. A plump, very agricultural-looking woman sitting next to Arnoldina wanted I think to make conversation with her exotic neighbour.

"Ammonium Nitrate", she shouted, "lethal stuff. Store it in a dry barn it explodes. Heap it outdoors, the rain dissolves it away."

"Why don't you use superphosphate?"

"Can't afford it"

The woman broke off and faced forward, perhaps a little offended.

I thought that with no ill will Arnoldina had possibly fallen into the trap of the queen who when told the peasants had no bread replied "Let Them Eat Cake."

Presently a man at top table stood between his two sitting comrades.

"Er,...Ladies and Gentlemen,...Thank you for coming, and believe me we are very grateful for all your hardship contributions."

A small public address system squealed in feedback.

"The agenda today...Hang on a Minute."

The speaker retrieved his reading glasses from a jacket pocket and closed the case with a metallic click.

"The agenda today:-
(A)   The Loss Gap on Roots
(B)   Magonian Requisitions
(C)   Power Supply and Power Cuts
(D)   Charitable Activities and Relief
(E)   Non-Supply of Diesel"

"Oh, hell", I thought, "I dropped a bollock here. We will walk home in the dark."

"Without further ado, Mr Palmer", said this chairman

"Thank you Mr Chairman, I have rung around the county and the latest mean delivery price of swedes is 987 crowns per tonne with summative production costs of 17834 crowns per hectare which equates to a production cost of 1567 crowns per tonne. Potatoes: delivery at the farm gate, 534 crowns per tonne, production cost 1237 crowns per tonne. 60% of root farmers estimate that they will be bankrupt within three months and 85% within six. Without DEFRA it is difficult to know who to complain to. Our Chairman, Mr Hollingrake, sent an email to the High Suzerain and Mr Treagh wired back to say that he was not empowered to interfere in UK economic affairs, so I emailed our Cabinet Office in Ithaca. The message reflected from the interface. I even sent a report to the King. The system processed the email and its attached PDF but there was no response as yet."

"Thank you Mr Palmer", Hollingrake interrupted, "we must make progress. We will doubtless return to Roots in questions from the Floor. Mr Walters!"

Palmer sat and Walters stood. Hollingrake maintained his sedentary position.

The floor was as silent as a vigil.

"Thank you, Mr Chairman. Again, county-wide and the dairy sector is of course mostly cheese in peacetime but we have curtailed supply to creameries by 80% since the Occupation. The Magonian Army takes our milk at a mere 2.734 centimes per litre and gives us not cash but these War-Substantive Promises of nominal value 10000 crowns each but are too heavy [he meant as a financial unit] and not redeemable at market. If the Magonians leave or are defeated we have lost an entire year's income."

Mr Walters picked up his Promise and brandished it in the air. It seemed to be a sheet of A4 printed in yellow and black inks. I fancied that I glimpsed the Magonian "Phi" symbol but I was some distance away so could not be sure.

I did some quick mental arithmetic and concluded that 10000 crowns was around $750 US and therefore chicken-feed, at least in pre-war British farming circles.

Walters put his prop back on the table before him and turning to someone in the front row softly said:-

"Mrs Dyer" as he gestured an arm of deferment to a fat middle aged woman who rose and stood at the right corner of the table as Walters sat:-

"Hello, every one, I am Nancy Dyer and I am the Director of Nursing both at the Countess of Congleholme General Hospital and at Witherspool."

Mrs Dyer was not in uniform but in a slightly frumpish cardigan and skirt and her ample breasts were covered by a light blue blouse with a fussy, frilly collar.

"Since the Occupation we have been unable to obtain cow's milk for babies and invalids and have had to fall back on vitamin-fortified oat milk, and imported baby formula when the odd lorry brings it from Ireland. But the oat harvest has failed this year due to Europe-wide bad weather and in any case ships are uninsurable in

European waters due to the War. Of course, our good ladies help out where they can but even they starve..."

You could have heard a pin drop as Mrs Dyer continued her jeremiad except that I could hear a woman softly sobbing beside me. It was Arnoldina. I put a hand on her arm in restraint and consolation. Suddenly Arnoldina rose to her feet and shouted through fluid weeping:-

"I am so sorry, I am so dreadfully, dreadfully sorry."

A low whispering filled the room.

The Ammonium Nitrate lady gently took Arnoldina's forearm and said:-

"There, there, dear. It is not your fault. Sit down and hear the rest of her report."

The dais and some on the floor gaped in astonishment.

I rose and grasped Arnoldina by the upper arm.

I shouted at the top table:-

"I am very sorry. My Wife is not well. Please may we leave?"

The Chairman Hollingrake rose to his feet and shouted:-

"Of course you may leave. Madam, I am very sorry we have upset you. We will of course refund your entrance."

I held up my open palm to Hollingrake as much as to say "No, that is okay, give it to your poor".

People pulled their legs in and as we bustled out a man on the corner stood and asked:-

"Are you staying locally?"

I turned and said:-

"Yes, why? We are staying with Mr Heldrew at Challenor's Aske House."

It was the man at the door who had sold the tickets.

"I will drive you over"

"No, Sir, please remain and hear the presentations", I objected.

"It is okay, mate, I know what they are going to say. I need a break. I know where it is. I will drive you and your good lady over."

Arnoldina was still crying into her paper hankies.

"Thank you very much, Sir", I conceded with secret gratitude.

We got in his car and were at Jimmy Heroncourt's grand portico within fifteen minutes.

We alighted and thanked the gentleman very profusely. He replied:-

"It was a pleasure, friends. I find the War very depressing. I will see you in Church tomorrow."

We entered the palatial country house and went straight to our Blue Room. It was 1600 in mid-November and essentially dark.

Arnoldina was still crying.

I took her in my arms and kissed her.

"Oh, Charles you must Correct me."

"Why?"

"Because I was rude, disruptive and assertive and I spoilt their important meeting."

"Arnoldina, none of those things are true and I want all the English to know that few Magonians are callous, unfeeling or exploitative. Do you think that I am so very unchristian or so very the hypocrite that I would castigate my Wife, or any woman, for expressing her compassion for babies or indeed for anyone else?"

Arnoldina started weeping heavily again:-

"Do you remember the three cardinal virtues of womanhood, Arnoldina?"

"Courage, compassion, cheerfulness", she replied.

"So cheer up, Arnoldina. You cannot help the babies by being miserable."

"Arnoldina, you are unspeakably brave, now be strong. Dear Wife, I do not know how I could live without you. You are old and cold. We will take off our hiking clothes and shower together beneath the warm, vivifying stream. Then we will dry each other and go to bed for a couple of hours.

I will give to you what you *really* deserve.

When we awake we will bathe again, put on our dressing gowns and dine with the happy couple."

"Oh, Charles. I was truthful. You thrill and amaze me with your every touch."

After Sacred Union Arnoldina and I lay drowsily beneath our duvet.

Arnoldina said:-

"That awful man with the nice dog, what did he mean when he said I must run like a train?"

"Now that is very low stuff, you do not have to think about that, Loveliness", I answered.

"No, Charles, tell me, I want to know."

"Well Englishmen think that all Oriental women are very submissive, obliging and really satisfying in bed."

"That is very silly, Charles. Am I very submissive, obliging, and really satisfying in bed, Charles?"

"You are loving, thoughtful, intelligent, compassionate, generous and you understand the meaning and value of godly sex as every Christian woman ought."

"Thank you, Charles, but I am intelligent enough to realise that none of that is true. But, Charles, you have not answered. Am I good in bed?"

"You are very good in bed, Arnoldina."

"I rather think we should speak to Duncan and perhaps his father about local arable issues and the likely onset of eventual famine", I suggested.

"Yes, but try to be tactful, Charles"

"I will do my best, Squirrel"

Arnoldina grinned with glee and cuddled me close.

At 1900 prompt we adjourned to the Yellow Room in our dressing gowns and slippers. We knocked and a beaming Bella opened the door similarly clad and ushered us to our seats at the dinner table, the same four-seater little table as that at which breakfast was served, but this was set of course for dinner, and cold champaign was already half consumed upon the table.

Presently, a smiling and notably relaxed Duncan issued from the bathroom in his gown. A further knock on the oak.

"Come in , Jolliffe!" hollered Duncan.

The butler bumbled in with his trolley and served the first course, hot tomato soup with a knob of butter and a bread roll. Delectable.

"Please Mr Jolliffe, in future could you not serve me with dairy products please. I do not need them. Others have greater requirements, though I say so as a vegan", admonished Arnoldina with surpassing gentleness.

"Dr Mrs Charmliss, I am so very sorry. I forgot your preferences. I will serve a bowl without butter immediately."

"Do not trouble, Mr Jolliffe. I accept your apology with thanks. I shall content myself this evening."

I knew this was a very great sacrifice for a very scrupulous woman and the impossible happened: My respect for my Wife deepened.

"Duncan, I had the privilege this afternoon of being able to attend a local farmers' meeting with Arnoldina", I said.

"Yes?"

"It seems that there is an arable depression part due to climate issues and part due to war requisitions. I am fearful of popular famine, if that is the right phrase. Roots and oats seem to be at a critical position. Do you think there is scope for putting more land to the plough, for the duration of the War only of course?"

Duncan paused in thought as he masticated.

"It is an interesting idea, Charles, I will see what is possible. I will have to consult with my Father and with arable experts of course. Leave it with me."

"Thank you, Duncan"

"I, too, am very grateful that you will consider this matter, Sir", said Arnoldina.

"Charles, you are *not* to plough your beautiful game park", stated Bella imperiously.

"Ah, the deer, yes, I forgot all about them. Charles and I will go out tomorrow and shoot them and give them to the people."

"No-one will be shot tomorrow, Duncan, we shall go to church as a foursome and first honour The Fallen. Then we shall stay behind and pray Thanks to God for the sanctity of your Everlasting Union and if the priest happens to be seen we shall confirm the details of your Church Wedding in the spring", softly commanded Arnoldina, knowing full well there would be no Spring.

I sat back in wonder. "What a clever, clever, woman. The Army lost a genius when it relieved her of her Commission. The Fallen: of course, tomorrow is Remembrance Sunday. How stupid of me."

CHAPTER TWENTY-THREE
REMEMBRANCE

Duncan stated that the local Anglican church where the service of Remembrance was to be held was that of Nether Chamberfield, a hamlet less than four hundred metres distant.

He went on to suggest that we walk along the connecting tarmacadamed lane rather than take the car as it was a pleasant morning and he expected the tiny parking-place to be congested. Duncan stated that the Service would commence at 1100 sharp on this nearest Sunday to the eleventh hour of the eleventh day of the eleventh month. Duncan said that Remembrance Day was one of many Indo-European fire festivals to mark the onset of winter and compared it to Samhain, Diwali, Halloween and Gunpowder Day (November 5th). I remembered this little disquisition because it was an unusually mystical touch for Duncan.

Duncan said he would knock for us at 1030 because although the walk was very short we should pray at the war memorial before taking seats in the pews.

I readily agreed and when Arnoldina and Bella had finished their porridge and coffee, Arnoldina and I went to the Blue Room to shower and change.

I drew the curtains and looked out of the window. The wan late Autumn sun was shining through the mist, caressing the still fronds of long grass and informing the tawny splendor of the distant deer. There was a frost on the grass.

I turned to my Wife and said:-

"It will be cold out today, Loveliness, you may wear underwear under your mourning dress."

Though it seemed like many years it was still only a few days since we received wire of Mr Feng's passing. I stood at the window and wondered how Arnoldina and I would get to the funeral in China when anything that appeared in the sky was automatically shot down by the "iron domes" of the respective powers.

"I did not bring any underwear, My Love", replied Arnoldina, as she placed her silver crucifix about her gorgeous neck.

"In that case, please wear your black puffer jacket, Beautiful."

"Thank you, Charles, I shall."

Arnoldina was putting on her formal black court shoes which have a raised heel.

"You can't wear those", I advised, "you will stumble and sprain your ankles on the icy tarmac."

"But I have nothing else suitable, Darling."

"You will just have to use the black hiking boots, Delectable. They are perfectly respectful."

"Thank you, Husband."

Arnoldina was the paragon of Christian obedience but she had worked hard to achieve it. I had little doubt that Mr Feng had been strict but loving.

We four arrived together at the War Memorial cross before the church. It had inscribed the names of the Fallen from both the previous World Wars and a single name from the Korean conflict. As yet no man or woman of the parish had died in the present global conflict.

We prayed in silence with bowed heads. I do not know what the others prayed for but I prayed for love and peace in the rejection of doctrine and all other manifestations of pride and egotism.

After my brief prayer I waited idly for the others to finish. I wondered what the Fallen had seen as the aspects of life and liberty worth fighting for. My thoughts turned to my custom. I wondered what others thought of Holy Correction, whether it was a Sacrament or a heresy, whether they saw it as merely silly or as obscene, whether they saw it as something for them, or as something for others, like naturism. Many of the Fallen would have seen wife-beating and husband-belaboring as a routine feature of married life, hardly godly, but something natural, though to be side-stepped if possible. Attitudes had rightly changed and both the man and the woman could now contemplate marriage without violence. But the rejection of violence carries its own penalties as the sorry state of our world amply demonstrated.

That was the point at which I had abandoned organised Quakerism as I thought the ideal of pacifism just that: An Ideal. In our Fallen world we should not picket nuclear bases because, a Satanic irony, we need to keep the peace. Treagh had forced me to carry a pistol and it had saved my life.

That pistol was now of course in my room at Challenor's Aske. I was not in uniform: I happened to wear a black breathable waterproof windcheater over a conservative white collared shirt, the collar open, with black storm trousers and black shoes. But I realised that I needed to be ready to leave or act immediately if the call came and determined to sit at the end of a pew.

There were no wreathes or poppies on view: The Royal British Legion was in Oxnard with the King.

Duncan and Bella looked up and it was clear that they had finished at the Cross. Arnoldina and I Crossed ourselves in our equal but opposite traditions. We then walked into the church and sat down at the end of a pew in the middle of the nave.

A spruce-looking middle-aged man paced down the aisle with a border collie dog whose claws clicked delicately upon the floor tiles. Astonishingly, it was the stinking shepherd who had offered us his hospitality in Sperstow. This man was transfigured. He had bathed, brushed his hair and seemingly changed his underwear. He wore a black suit and a black veteran's bonnet. Across his chest were five gleaming campaign medals, including, I noticed, the octagonal Polar Medal. The dog continued admiringly to consult the man's face, but there was no woman.

Man and dog took their posts at the organ.

Shortly thereafter a man in an ordinary gray office suit with collar and tie mounted the pulpit and started fiddling with his papers as I had watched a nervous Hitler do as he prepared to address a rally in a pre-war newsreel. At the front of the pulpit was one of those brass reading lamps with filament strips, possibly Fifties vintage, pantographically-mounted on two vertical brass tubes. It was illuminated. Presently the thing collapsed as I remember they tended to do at lectures in Manchester. The poor fellow in the pulpit attempted to wrestle with it with trembling hands, before he withdrew them reflexively on grasping hot brass.

I turned to Duncan and said:-

"That is the fellow who sold us tickets to the farmers' meeting yesterday."

"Yes, he is Patrick Enoldius, the local vicar, everyone calls him 'Pat'."

This was clearly going to prove a very different Church of England service to the ones I knew and despised in my boyhood.

Pat left the dratted lamp in its decumbent position and switched it off at the socket. Fortunately it was a brilliant morning and enough light penetrated the lead-camed windows for him to read, and for us to read the order-of-service crib sheets thoughtfully provided at our places.

Enoldius looked up from his papers with a gentle smile and said:-

"Friends and neighbours, please stand for the National Hymn."

We did as directed.

The organist skillfully struck up the brief prelude as his dog howled an antiphony.

Then we sang:-

I vow to thee, my country, all earthly things above,
Entire and whole and perfect, the service of my love;
The love that asks no questions, the love that stands the test,
That lays upon the altar the dearest and the best;
The love that never falters, the love that pays the price,
The love that makes undaunted the final sacrifice.

I heard my country calling, away across the sea,
Across the waste of waters, she calls and calls to me.
Her sword is girded at her side, her helmet on her head,
And around her feet are lying the dying and the dead;
I hear the noise of battle, the thunder of her guns;
I haste to thee, my mother, a son among thy sons.

And there's another country, I've heard of long ago,
Most dear to them that love her, most great to them that know;
We may not count her armies, we may not see her King;
Her fortress is a faithful heart, her pride is suffering;
And soul by soul and silently her shining bounds increase,
And her ways are ways of gentleness, and all her paths are peace.

This is taken from the poem *Urbs Dei/The Two Father Lands* (1912) by Sir Cecil Spring-Rice. The music was "Thaxted" by Gustav Holst (1921).

Many in the audience, including myself, were trying to stifle sobs.

"Please sit", said Enoldius.

Then he prayed over we below him:-

"Our Dear Saviour Lord Jesus Christ,
The scorched,
allay their pain, smooth their scars,
heal them
The blinded,
restore their sight
for the smiles of their beloved,
the glory of an autumn sunset,

> **The strivings of their arts**
> **The deafened,**
> > **make them delight in birdsong,**
> > **the twitter of their children**
> > **The call of a wife once more,**
> > **and ever in paradise**
> **The broken**
> > **set their bones, let them climb**
> > **to their feet and walk again in**
> > **Your path as they follow the Furrow**
> > **you Ploughed**
> **Bring us to Peace and Safety in Love and Honour**
> **Above all, Dear Jesus, make us forgive.**
> > **Amen"**

*"**Amen**"* we echoed.

Enoldius commenced his sermon:-

"Esteemed Brothers and Sisters, we gather today for The Fallen. Many of you wonder, what was it all for? Today England is beneath an alien yoke, so what was achieved by the deaths of so many, from England and so far?

Our defeat was engendered by *our* weakness, *our* cowardice, *our* ill-preparedness and *our* hedonism.

Our fathers died in honour for the things they held dear and the sins of the sons are not the sins of the fathers. They have their portion.

For whatever reasons the Magonians have occupied this Sacred Land and placed us in fealty to them, but they are clement rulers and it is not our place to hate them or any man, it is our place to love and obey.

These foreign people have not sinned. They have done what they had to do for their own safety, acting with courage, sacrifice and forbearance.

Love and respect them."

It is a cliché but I use it again: You could have heard a pin drop. There were some nervous throat-clearings, and not a few scowls, seen from the corner of my eye.

Enoldius continued:-

"Dearly Beloved, I am indebted to Loren Skinker for this compilation of Holy Scripture which we shall find edifying. Please forgive me reading the script like a schoolboy. I do not wish to stumble.":-

But as for you, ye thought evil against me;
but God meant it unto good, to bring to pass,
as it is this day, to save much people alive.
If I rejoiced at the destruction of him that hated me,
or lifted up myself when evil found him:
Neither have I suffered my mouth to sin
by wishing a curse to his soul.
When a man's ways please the LORD,
he maketh even his enemies to be at peace with him.
Say not thou, I will recompense evil; but wait on the LORD,
and he shall save thee.
Rejoice not when thine enemy falleth,
and let not thine heart be glad when he stumbleth:
If thine enemy be hungry, give him bread to eat;
and if he be thirsty, give him water to drink:
For thou shalt heap coals of fire upon his head,
and the LORD shall reward thee.
Ye have heard that it hath been said,
Thou shalt love thy neighbour, and hate thine enemy.
But I say unto you, Love your enemies,
bless them that curse you, do good to them that hate you,
and pray for them which despitefully use you,
and persecute you;
That ye may be the children of your Father which is in heaven:
for he maketh his sun to rise on the evil and on the good,
and sendeth rain on the just and on the unjust.
But I say unto you, Love your enemies,
bless them that curse you,
do good to them that hate you,
and pray for them which despitefully use you,
and persecute you;
But I say unto you which hear, Love your enemies,
do good to them which hate you,
Bless them that curse you,

and pray for them which despitefully use you.
Then said Jesus,
Father, forgive them; for they know not what they do.
And they parted his raiment, and cast lots.
Bless them which persecute you: bless, and curse not.
Dearly beloved, avenge not yourselves,
but rather give place unto wrath:
for it is written, Vengeance is mine;
I will repay, saith the Lord.
And be ye kind one to another, tenderhearted,
forgiving one another,
even as God for Christ's sake hath forgiven you.
I exhort therefore, that, first of all, supplications, prayers,
intercessions, and giving of thanks, be made for all men;
For kings, and for all that are in authority;
that we may lead a quiet and peaceable life in all
godliness and honesty.

"Dear Friends, if you find my words bitter and hate me, then so be it. I cannot stand in the pulpit and lie or dissemble. Of what value is Freedom of Speech if we cannot find Truth in profound subjection, or Knowledge in the depths of disaster?"

"Please stand for our prayer for our rulers", said Enoldius.

Dear God, please support King George and Mr Treagh in the taxing and onerous tasks of power. Give them wisdom and lightness, justice and mercy, and as you favour them let them favour others. Give them the succour of the balm of your Holy Love, cleansing their hearts of all fear, all anxiety, all Satanic things that prompt to excess and lead them to allow us our portion of the Earth as you guide them to prosper in safety.

There were load but not necessarily hostile murmurings.

"Please remain standing for our next song, friends", said Enoldius.

We read and sang haltingly the fine tribute to The Fallen written by Frank John Musker and set to the music of Michael Kamen.

Then Enoldius said:-

"For our third and final hymn I would like you to sing with me, if you would, a very ancient English tune which was first documented in the middle of the Sixteenth Century but has passed through the hands of several poets in the succeeding half millennium. The Church records it as "Kingsfold" which is where Ralph Vaughan-Williams says he first heard it, but if you are familiar with..."

Our organist glanced at the priest:-

"E Minor, Adriolis", Enoldius shouted to the loft.

"...'Five Variants of Dives and Lazarus' that Vaughn-Williams wrote in 1939 you will know the tune. These words 'I heard the Voice of Jesus Say' are by Horatius Bonar and are Victorian."

Patrick Enoldius nodded to Tramp and we sang:-

I heard the voice of Jesus say,
"Come unto me and rest;
Lay down, thou weary one, lay down
Thy head upon my breast":
I came to Jesus as I was,
Weary, and worn, and sad;
I found in him a resting place,
And he has made me glad.

I heard the voice of Jesus say,
"Behold, I freely give
The living water, thirsty one;
Stoop down, and drink, and live":
I came to Jesus, and I drank
Of that life-giving stream;
My thirst was quenched, my soul revived,
And now I live in him.

I heard the voice of Jesus say,
"I am this dark world's Light;
Look unto me, thy morn shall rise,
And all the day be bright":
I looked to Jesus, and I found
In him my Star, my Sun;
And in that light of life I'll walk
Till travelling days are done.

"Please remain standing", continued Enoldius.

Our Father, which art in heaven,
hallowed be thy name;
thy kingdom come;
thy will be done,
in earth as it is in heaven.
Give us this day our daily bread.
And forgive us our trespasses,
as we forgive them that trespass against us.
And lead us not into temptation;
but deliver us from evil.
For thine is the kingdom,
the power, and the glory,
For ever and ever.
Amen.

We repeated every sacred line of Christ's Prayer after the Vicar of God.

A quiet murmur marked the end of the brief but very moving service as the congregation filed out.

Arnoldina strode to intercept Enoldius before he left.

"Please, Holy Father", opened my Wife.

"Please will you guide my friends and I through the Holy Eucharist."

"I would be delighted to", Enoldius answered with a smile of surprise for his exotic interlocutoress. "Let us retire to the sacristy where we are unlikely to be disturbed."

There was only one chair, so the five of us knelt on the floor in a little circle.

Enoldius almost immediately stood again and said:-

"I have forgotten the bread and wine. I will just nip to the rectory and get some. I won't be long."

"Do not trouble, Father", continued Arnoldina, "I have some wine and fresh bread together with some little plastic cups in my shoulder bag. I am a Nestorian."

As Enoldius took these accidentals he said:-

"Well, My Child, I do not know where Nestoria is but you are most welcome to England. I am sorry we upset you yesterday."

"Do not apologise, Holy Father. I was weak and disruptive and it is I who should apologise", responded Arnoldina.

"What is your name, My Child"

"I am Arnoldina, Sir, this is my husband Charles, and these are our friends Duncan and Arabella."

"Thank you, Arnoldina. Yes, I know Duncan and Arabella."

"As we kneel, Holy Father, and before Communion, I beg you to bless Charles and I, and Duncan and Bella in our common-law marriages which we consummated by Sacred Union yesterday", requested Arnoldina boldly.

"I should be highly delighted, Arnoldina. 'Try before you buy' is always what I say", Enoldius replied startlingly, "I know that I shall be churching Duncan and Bella in the spring, but of course that will require their continued consent", seeming to echo my long held opinion that knowledge was not certainty.

"I am sure that consent will persist", I contributed unnecessarily.

Yes, I was sure this was not the Church of England I had known and unloved so long.

Enoldius rose and placed his hands on Arnoldina's head and mine and pronounced:-

Dear Jesus, please Bless this good couple Arnoldina and Charles with the balm and content of Your love as they struggle through joy to live as man and woman as You wanted them to live in Love and Trust of one another, improving their skills day-by-day in the love of each other and the love and nurture of their children until the day You call their souls to the long rest of heaven. So help them God.

So help us God

The priest moved to Duncan and Arabella and placed his hands on their heads:-

Dear Jesus, please Bless this good couple Arabella and Duncan with the balm and content of Your love as they struggle through joy to live as man and woman as You wanted them to live in Love and Trust of one another, improving their skills day-by-day in the love of each other and the love and nurture of their children until the day You call their souls to the long rest of heaven. So help them God.

So help us God

At that juncture there was a diffident knock on the sacristy door.

Enoldius shouted:-

"Come in!"

The organist shepherd sidled in sheepishly:-

"I am sorry to interrupt, Pat, I just wanted to apologise to the young lady."

"Which young lady?" responded Patrick Enoldius.

"The Chinese young lady"

The shepherd did not seem to realise that the 'young' lady of whom he spoke was 976 years old.

Hesitantly the old man wrung his service beret in his hands as he approached Arnoldina and bowed as a peasant caught poaching might bow to a duchess sitting on an Assize bench.

"My Lady, I am mortified and very sorry that I was so rude and spoke of you so filthily yesterday. I know it is not an excuse, but I had been drinking all morning and did not know what I was saying."

"Sir, you are forgiven. The only words of censure I shall say: Keep off the bottle, it is a source of disaster", responded Arnoldina as she rose to stand and shake his hand.

"Thank you, My Lady. I knew you were a woman of breeding as soon as I saw you. I am Adriolis Tramp. Friends call me Adie."

"Well, Adie, I am Arnoldina Charmliss", exchanged my Wife as she resumed her obeisant position.

"Why don't you stay for Communion, Adie?" asked Enoldius.

"No, Sir, I am unworthy"

"What bloody nonsense! You must stop beating yourself up, man."

With hesitancy and great humbleness the shepherd knelt in our midst as the priest and I sidled aside to admit him.

Enoldius spread a sheet of clean office A4 paper on the floor tiles before each of us six celebrants and, after washing his hands, placed a morsel of bread upon these together with a plastic cup with a little red wine in each.

Enoldius elaborated the Prayer, as we all six responded:-

The Lord be with you

All **and also with you.**
Lift up your hearts.
All **We lift them to the Lord.**
Let us give thanks to the Lord our God.
All **It is right to give thanks and praise.**

It is indeed right,
it is our duty and our joy,
at all times and in all places
to give you thanks and praise,
holy Father, heavenly King,
almighty and eternal God,
through Jesus Christ your Son our Lord.
For he is your living Word;
through him you have created all things from the beginning,
and formed us in your own image.

[*All* **To you be glory and praise for ever.**]

Through him you have freed us from the slavery of sin,
giving him to be born of a woman and to die upon the cross;
you raised him from the dead
and exalted him to your right hand on high.

[*All* **To you be glory and praise for ever.**]

Through him you have sent upon us
your holy and life-giving Spirit,
and made us a people for your own possession.

[*All* **To you be glory and praise for ever.**]

Therefore with angels and archangels,
and with all the company of heaven,
we proclaim your great and glorious name,
for ever praising you and *saying:*

All **Holy, holy, holy Lord,**
God of power and might,
heaven and earth are full of your glory.
Hosanna in the highest.

Accept our praises, heavenly Father,
through your Son our Saviour Jesus Christ,
and as we follow his example and obey his command,
grant that by the power of your Holy Spirit
these gifts of bread and wine
may be to us his body and his blood;
who, in the same night that he was betrayed,
took bread and gave you thanks;
he broke it and gave it to his disciples, saying:
Take, eat; this is my body which is given for you;
do this in remembrance of me.

[*All* **To you be glory and praise for ever.**]

In the same way, after supper
he took the cup and gave you thanks;
he gave it to them, saying:
Drink this, all of you;
this is my blood of the new covenant,
which is shed for you and for many for the forgiveness of sins.
Do this, as often as you drink it,
in remembrance of me.

[*All* **To you be glory and praise for ever.**]

Therefore, heavenly Father,
we remember his offering of himself
made once for all upon the cross;
we proclaim his mighty resurrection and glorious ascension;
we look for the coming of your kingdom,
and with this bread and this cup
we make the memorial of Christ your Son our Lord.

"*Amen*" said we all and each drank the wine and ate the bread.

As in all Eucharists of my limited experience a pall of calm seemed to fall upon the company. It was the Presence of Christ in Person. It is not something that is explicable in rational terms. It is the Spirit, the Bread and the Wine. It is unique.

There is no prospectus, as there is in Marriage, Confession or even Funeral. There is just submission, acceptance, the surrender of sin. Unconditional.

CHAPTER TWENTY-FOUR
ATONEMENT

We walked back to Challenor's Aske through the noontide sunlight. The parked cars had gone and the War Memorial Cross was deserted. We returned to our respective rooms, showered and put on our best clothes. At 1300 we all went to lunch with Lord Chamberfield, Jimmy.

The four off us settled down to a vegan luncheon with Jimmy.

Grace was omitted but Duncan said:-

"Father, may we plough the Park and the other pasture in order to plant oats and roots for the local poor, purely as a wartime expedient of course?"

"Yes, that seems quite sensible. I will see Masterton tomorrow and no doubt he will employ the right experts and workmen. If we don't lend our land we might lose both the land and our heads, what?" said Jimmy looking around with a nervous giggle.

"What about the deer?", asked Arnoldina.

"We will drive them into the woods. They enjoy eating tree leaves and there is plenty of long grass and chicken-of-the-woods for them to eat", Jimmy replied with a smile. I could see he was trying to spare Arnoldina's feelings.

"I don't want them to hurt the chickens", said Arnoldina.

Duncan lent across to Arnoldina and whispered:-

"Chicken-of-the-woods is a yellow bracket fungus."

"Oh", said Arnoldina with shy embarrassment.

"Thank you very much, Gentlemen", said Arnoldina and continued:-

"Bella, the local hospitals have run out of cow's milk and nothing else is suitable for neonates. Will you please allow milch cow's to share land with your horses so that the people can provide milk to Mrs Nancy Dyer and her staff", requested Arnoldina.

"I find you request extraordinary for a supposed vegan. No I shan't and anyway horses do not get on with cows", answered Bella.

"Bella, you will withdraw 'supposed' this instant!" Duncan intervened.

"No, I say what I mean and mean what I say", said Bella in open defiance.

"Bella, withdraw the whole statement and apologise to Arnoldina, or Correction awaits", said Duncan, turning the screw.

With that Bella set down her cutlery in an over-controlled way and flounced of to the Yellow Room.

Duncan rose to follow. His father grasped his arm.

"Sit down and finish the meal for our guests, Duncan", ordered Jimmy, "and never threaten a woman: Act or keep silence."

"She defies me, Father"

"That is a matter for you. In the meantime we have company to entertain."

"I am very sorry to have offended Lady Sperstow, Lord Chamberfield, may I leave to go and apologise to her?", said Arnoldina.

"No, Madam, please keep your seat. I say, do you drive?"

"Well, for many years I drove an Army Ambulance as part of my work as a field nurse, and indeed I drove one until my recent dismissal."

"Splendid! I am looking for a driver!", grinned Chamberfield with a sly wink, and continued:-.

"Dr and Dr Mrs Charmliss, I am more grateful than I can express for what you have done for my son, always a shy and diffident lad, but a true Christian. Thank you both, and especially thank you Dr Mrs Arnoldina. We love you always."

"Thank you, Jimmy, I said. You too have a special place in our hearts, as do your Son and his bride-in-God", I replied.

"Splendid! I will get Duncan to drive you home"

"What about Bella?", I queried.

"Oh, I will go upstairs and spank her myself!" Jimmy said with a wicked laugh.

"No, I will get Jolliffe to go up and pack her things and then I will either drive her to the stud myself or get Masterton to do the honours", Jimmy clarified.

It was getting dark as Duncan's Bentley draw into the car park behind the Presidium and beside the old Judges' Assize Lodging in which I was billeted.

Duncan parked and switched on the courtesy lamps. Then he turned to me and said:-

"Do you recall what you said to Christ in your Prayer of Witness?"

To be honest I did not, and I hesitated.

"You asked that Christ grant me **ample but not excessive provision**."

Duncan removed his car keys from the ignition and offered them to me.

"The Registration Documents are in the glove box", he added.

"Thank you very much, Duncan. I greatly appreciate it. You are most generous", I said taking the keys.

"*De nada*. I will pick up a new one tomorrow."

"How will you get home?" I asked.

"I will catch the commuter bus"

I was too stupid to offer to drive him back to Challenor's Aske.

"Please do not castigate Bella. I shall ask Charles to Correct me for spoiling our dinner and hurting Bella.", begged Arnoldina.

"Darling Arnoldina, I promise not to beat Bella", responded Duncan.

We got out of the car and Duncan unloaded our suitcases and shook hands. He walked out toward the bus station in the gathering gloom.

Arnoldina decided not to return to her flat but to stay the night with me in my billet.

We opened the heavy oak door and entered.

"My Love, I shall not Correct you for you have not sinned. Bella has sinned but it is Duncan's option whether to Correct her in the loving and respectful way we taught him, sanctified by prayer and contrition. Nevertheless, I always respect your Confessions, Arnoldina, and I wish you to prepare for Holy Correction in the normal way."

"Prepare for Holy Correction, Arnoldina", I said.

Silently, without haste or reluctance, she stripped and went for a shower.

I stripped naked as all Husbands should out of respect for God and their Better Half, and waited on the bed edge.

After drying herself, my perfect, perfectly devout and obedient woman assumed the position. I placed my right hand on her bottom.

"Is there anything you wish to say, My Love."

"Yes, I offended Bella and spoilt her luncheon with us. She must be very unhappy."

I commenced:-

My Darling Jesus Christ
Comfort my good Wife through the ordeal to come, guard
and strengthen her, and may all evil fall down before her
and vanish like the mirage of sin that it is. So help her God

So help me God

Then Arnoldina prayed:-

Dear Jesus, help the suffering babies and their distraught
mothers. Lift oppressions from the poor and needy and
guide my lovely friend Bella to find a Way. Lord, make me
find the Way.

"Are you comfortable, Arnoldina", I asked.
No reply.
I tenderly lifted my Wife to sit beside me. I cuddled her naked body, and kissed her lips with abandoned passion as I held our heads together with my right hand. She put her arms about me. I lifted her a little and intromitted.
"How can I bless such a saint?" I asked.
I was of course about to do just that in the natural way of a man.
Arnoldina was too ecstatic to answer.

By 0725 I was back in my office. At 0730 Edmonson rang and asked me to report to Treagh in the enormous room.
Treagh asked:-
"Did Arnoldina and you enjoy your weekend with Duncan Heldrew and his fiancée?"
I wondered how he knew. Perhaps I had told him.
"Yes thank you, Sir. It was excellent. I learned a great deal, Sir. Throughout the Palatinate there is a critical milk shortage affecting hospitals and neonatal units. I was told that there are Army milk requisitions which are aggravating existing production dearths. Is it possible to suspend requisitions, Sir, until supply conditions stabilise?"
"No, Commadore Charmliss, I am very sorry but I am not authorized to interfere in British economic affairs. I would be court marshalled."
"Please at least place a 14-day moratorium on Army requisitions, otherwise children may starve", I replied.

"Leave it with me, Charmliss"

"Yes, Sir, Thank you, Sir"

Treagh continued:-

"Over the weekend, Charles, I have had other experts examine this matter of the Holy Atonement or *amende honourable* or whatever they wanted to call it. Firstly, the candle. Experiments showed that a dumpy one-kilo votive candle fitted with a saltpeter-impregnated wick formed a hollow pipe of wax which exploded half way through, spattering burning wax everywhere whilst the wick burnt on like a powder fuse. On the other hand, a thin taper of a large candle quickly burned down until nothing remained of the wick dripping molten wax everywhere. Ordinary candles stayed alight as long as no draft or shower snuffed the wick.

One hundred athletic female volunteers were canvassed from Army PTIs and gymnasts. They were instructed to hold one kilogram at arms' length standing; and then walking slowly. Standing, the posture was sustained for a mean of 458 seconds; when walking for 245 seconds. So the tolerable carry distance is a little under 330 metres.

The distance from the Ladyfair to the cathedral altar is 650 metres. I am determined not to botch this exercise with the World watching. The length of Congleholme Abbey Cathedral is 88 metres, under cover.

Goodleague will be fitted with a temporary surgical splint to make it possible for her to walk and kneel.

I shall order Goodleague to be walked this distance or less carrying an ordinary votive candle one kilo of dumpy aspect ratio to me at the altar unless you object, Commadore Charmliss", Treagh briefed.

"I have no objection, Sir, and if I may I commend your promptitude and diligence."

"Goodleague will have a hempen noose round her neck, and it will be your task, Commadore Charmliss, to carry the free end without danger of strangulation."

"Yes, Sir"

"Thank you, Charmliss. If Goodleague completes this exercise, and the candle arrives at the altar lit, and I forgive her, then I shall ask the justices to acquit her and to give her comrades eight years to life as common murderers. Do you approve, Charmliss?"

"I do, Sir"

"I have had three candles cast. I want you to use the rest of the day rehearsing this exercise with Seargent Geraldine Wong and

Seargent Major MacKinnon sitting in my place behind the altar. MacKinnon is carrying the paraphernalia. Any questions, Commadore?"

"None, Sir"

"Very good. The Abbey is closed to the public but you are to allow television men and other journalists to prepare their work. A car awaits at the main entrance. You will wear your casual rig whilst rehearsing and change into No.1s before you are picked up at 1930 in your billet for the start of the ceremony at 2000. You must wear your commadore's cap with the crown and anchor to show you are British. Sorry, Chuck."

"It will be dark, Sir", I remarked.

"All the better for seeing", answered Treagh.

"Now are there any further questions, Charmliss?"

"None, Sir"

"Very well, dismiss"

I stood and saluted in my old RN manner:-

"Thank you, Major-General Treagh."

Wong, MacKinnon and I had time for twenty cycles of the rehearsal, some of which were filmed. Wong was naked except for an ankle-length linen shift, and I must say she acted the part of a contrite young woman with great skill, as good as any professional actress I thought.

The evil hour came.

Treagh's car dropped Treagh and I at the West Door. Treagh was also in full uniform with his medals. We entered to a wall of noise. There was a congregation of over a thousand with the families and friends of victims of the late atrocities at the front before the altar. Goodleague was in a linen shift. Two armed men and an armed woman guarded her. Goodleague was holding the unlit candle at ease.

I overheard a commentator with a Canadian accent remark that this was the first time an *amende honourable* had been witnessed anywhere since 1836 and the first time ever in England.

Treagh took up his station, rose from his seat and beckoned at me. A single bell tolled.

I lifted the free end of the rope. Goodleague held the candle to arms' length, the lights were dimmed, and the candle lit.

It burned with a tall steady flame without sputtering.

Alarmingly I could see nothing in the eerie silence: Only the three candles burning on the altar. I could also see Goodleague's candle dominating everything and barely marking the border of the file of seats beside us. There were pin-pricks of red or white lights on audiovisual equipment, and there were cables across the floor to be navigated. Neither of us were wearing goggles. They were thought redundant, as the candle did not sputter. When I occasionally looked up ghostly yellow shadows were seen to stalk the walls. Otherwise I studied the ground and warned Goodleague of wires and other trip hazards. I found it safer to hold her left arm and whisper rather than attempt to use the rope to encourage or restrain.

I had a sense of the historicity of the scene and its awfulness: Awful in both the old and the new senses of the word.

As my eyes grew accustomed to the low light level I became more confident and led Goodleague to the steps of the altar where I told her to kneel and speak. First, she placed the still-lit candle on the centre of the alter with the others.

Goodleague knelt on the lowest step, placed her hands together and said:-

Dear God, I am very sorry for my crimes and especially for my murders of many people and the injuries of multiple others. *I abhor my sins and I reject them with loathing.* I wish to become a good person who loves. Please god, forgive my comrades and show them the way to lead with love and toleration. For my part I beg you to chasten my spirit and forgive my wickedness. I shall never use violence again.

As far as I was concerned this was enough, but I continued to stand holding the noose. Next Goodleague looked at Treagh and said:-

"My Sovereign Liege, King George, I am deeply sorry for attacking your subjects and your foreign surrogates *in loco* and for the murders and mayhem I have perpetrated. I accept your punishment with gratitude and beg you to acquit those whom I wickedly misled. Please forgive them and my evil self."

Treagh looked on with no visible emotion.

Then Goodleague continued:-

"My victims and your loved ones…"

She turned through one hundred and eighty degrees to face them:-

"Please forgive me. I am most truly, humbly sorry. Please forgive the men I led into violence and evil."

By now Goodleague was weeping and she prostrated herself before the gathering.

One or two people in the congregation shouted "I forgive you", or "We forgive you."

Whispers and titters began to degrade the solemnity of the Sacrament.

Treagh rose to his feet and pronounced:-

"On behalf of your King I discharge you."

I removed the noose as quickly as safely possible.

Acclamation became noisier but was still subdued. There was no clapping or whistling.

Goodleague remained prone on the tiles crying bitterly.

The candle was left to burn out.

The lights were raised and the doors opened.

I lifted Goodleague to her feet as she continued to cry with downcast gaze.

"You are free to go on Police bail", I said, "but if I were you, I would come with me to a safe place." Goodleague acquiesced as I led her by the forearm to an inconspicuous back door of the chancel.

Treagh was already in the car, and when Goodleague and I were aboard it departed immediately with Palatine motorcyclists sounding sirens and flashing blue lights. Goodleague was still lost in her remorse and humiliation. But I had thought I had glimpsed the beginnings of devotion and contrition.

When we arrived back at Goodleague's cell the Palatine Chief Constable no less was seated waiting for us, together with Lieutenant Slenderman:-

"Miss Goodleague, all terrorism charges have been dropped but you must still stand trial as a murderer. You and your associates no longer face whole life tariffs but you may be sentenced to life, which usually means eight years before parole. You are young people with lives and marriages ahead of you. The Palatine Police will argue for your personal acquittal but the decision is up to a jury and you will be tried at Preston to minimise local bias. English Law does not officially recognise remission by reason of *amende honorable*. You may travel freely, but I do not think it is sensible to go back to your house just yet. It is under Police guard. Stay here for a few days and then travel to stay with friends for a week or two, or at a hotel, in an out-of-the-way locality. Do not grant interviews. You are on Police bail and if you do not turn up for your trial you will suffer consequences. Do you have any questions?", rehearsed the Chief Constable.

"No, Sir. You have been very clear. Thank you, Sir.",
Goodleague answered meekly.

The Chief Constable left without valediction to any.

I turned to Slenderman and said:-

"Lieutenant Slenderman, please ring for a female guard."

"Yes, Sir"

A female guard arrived within seconds as she was presumably loitering in the corridor.

"Miss Goodleague, please remove your shift and your prison outfits", I requested.

Goodleague complied, and the female guard stated:-

"You will find your clothes in that blue bag in the corner. They are new and similar to the clothes you wore at arrest. Your actual arrest clothes are seized for evidence. Dress."

"Yes, Madam"

"Have a shower first", I ordered.

"Yes, Commadore Charmliss"

After the murderess had showered and dressed, the female guard ordered:-

"Sit at that table and await your late supper. Lights out is at 2300 unless Commadore Charmliss varies."

"Yes, Madam"

"As I said, you are on bail, and if you are stupid enough you are free to leave", I reminded Goodleague.

"Please may I remain, Commadore Charmliss", begged Goodleague.

"The door is fully unlocked. You may leave but others cannot enter, except for guards. You are not currently under arrest and you are entitled to your Bible, a newspaper, other literature and a television. Would you like any of these things?" I advised.

"Thank you, Commadore Charmliss. Please may I have my Bible, a television, a biro and some writing paper and a bottle of water?"

"Certainly, Lieutenant Slenderman will arrange these things. Have you been well treated?"

"Yes, Sir"

"Then eat your supper. Your things will be brought at 2230 and lights out is at 2300."

"Thank you, Commadore Charmliss", replied Goodleague.

Slenderman and I left with the guard who set the lock mechanism to permit cell exit and then slammed the cell door shut.

I learned later that milk requisitions ceased that very night.

CHAPTER TWENTY-FIVE
NOVEMBER CALM

I woke up to the doorbell of Arnoldina's flat at 0905.

I had overslept and thought blearily that Treagh must have sent a car and he would be furious not to have me in his office for de-briefing.

I lifted Arnoldina's lovely arms from my shoulders and hurriedly donned some trousers.

Whoever it was was now thumping loudly upon the woodwork.

I opened the door to behold the strange sight of a garage driver immaculate in a green chauffer's suit with a matching green peaked cap:-

"Does a Dr Mrs Charmliss live here?", he enquired.

"Yes, that is my Wife."

"I have a delivery, Sir. Is she available to sign, Sir?"

"Dina! Dina! It's a delivery man", I shouted into the interior.

My Wife emerged as she struggled to put on her dressing gown.

"Yes, what is it?"

"I have been ordered to deliver this car, Madam, and this greetings note."

Arnoldina tore the note open:-

Dear Dr Mrs Charmliss,

This is just a starter, ha ha.
(At least I hope it starts!)
This firm usually builds tanks,
not the thing you want
for modern shopping or getting
about on country roads!
It is a small token of my

Son's and mine undying gratitude.

Love from,

Jimmy

"Here are the keys and the Reg documents, Madam", said the driver and departed for his pick-up.

The car was parked outside on the road.

It proved to be a brand-new Rolls-Royce Cullinan automatic hard-top in British racing green.

"Oh, Charles. What a lovely man! We will have to go for a drive and then go and thank Jimmy!" exclaimed the loveliness.

"Yes, Dear. Aren't you going to put some clothes on first?"

"No, we will go naked!" said Arnoldina cheekily.

We went indoors. Arnoldina showered and changed into her mourning dress and put her crucifix round her neck. She had bought some sensible underwear and put it on because the weather was getting cold. I am not a complete wowser and Arnoldina had my tacit permission to wear it. The thing I really detested was that dreadful police uniform. I only had the No.1s I had worn to entertain Goodleague. I had to ring Treagh.

"MacKinnon", answered the voice at the other end.

"Seargent Major MacKinnon, please tell the Major-General that I have to take the day off. My Wife has had a delivery."

"Oh, congratulations, Chuck! Is it a boy or a girl?"

"No it's a Rolls-Royce"

"Ha Ha well congratulations anyway. I'll send her a card!"

"You're a card yourself, Teddy", I responded.

"Anyway, the boss is not here either. He found yesterday very stressful. He has gone out on a date."

"Well bravo for him!", I replied. "Thanks, Teddy", I said and switched off.

"Arnoldina, drive me to my billet. I will change into my camo hiking gear."

Arnoldina found the bijou roller no trouble at all and we were at the Lodgings within ten minutes.

"Before you switch off check we have some petrol, Loveliness", I counselled.

"The gauge says half-full, Charles."

"That should last the day", I remarked as she carefully parked next to the Bentley Duncan had given me.

I showered and changed into my camo kit and rejoined Arnoldina in her new car.

"Let's drive to Merehill and look at the river and the ships!" said Arnoldina breezily.

Arnoldina drove us sedately to a broad slip beside the Mersey that had sailing dinghies on trailers parked on it. But there was ample space to park the SUV whilst we watched the river and its commerce.

On the other bank was a city that stretched as far as we could see, but appeared mostly to comprise gleaming steel oil refineries rather the grand buildings of its 80V analogue, Liverpool. When I died the Britain of 80V was essentially non-industrial but it was already clear that the Britain of 78V was highly industrialised, or at least this corner of it.

"That over there is Hatton Dypsidorian, a city of over one million people. Most of the workers roost amongst the metalwork with their families", stated Arnoldina.

"Don't they have houses, shops, schools, hospitals?" I queried.

"The middles classes have these things in the suburbs, and Congleholme is really just a glorified suburb, but ordinary workers live on site with their families though they usually have private cabins.", said Arnoldina.

There was clearly a different aspect to 78V Britian that had eluded me in the quasi-paradisial world of Congleholme and Sperstow.

As we sat in the Cullinan viewing the wide estuary and the city on its far side the metal installations gleamed in the sun and I remarked to Arnoldina:-

"Over there in 80V there is a city about as extensive called Liverpool but it was never industrial, but a great port city with very slight shipbuilding which latter died out by the 1880s, when Liverpool handled forty percent of global trade. Liverpool built the fast paddle-powered blockade runners that ran the Union blockade during the War to end American slavery. As a port it was cosmopolitan and built many splendid streets and buildings, including two of the World's great cathedrals and the only significant English theatre culture outside

London. Liverpool had a scattering of shallow, Triassic oilfields but they never amounted to anything."

Arnoldina replied:-

"Hatton Dypsidorian sits on an enormous Permian oilfield similar to those in Texas but did not develop until the 1880s. It is a good city, founded upon aspiration and progress, with prosperity for all. Liverpool was an evil city. I am not speaking of the Slave Trade which came centuries later, but of Bad King John who built it as a jumping-off point for the subjugation of Ireland."

"Hatton is dominated by oil and petrochemicals. Amongst smaller outfits, the multinational firms Stonnard-Fox dominate the North and Ward-Victoria the South", added Arnoldina.

I started to appreciate how the detail of physics is reflected in the grosser measures of geology, which in turn commands the fate of nations.

I wound down the window and listened to the wavelets lapping on the concrete of the slip and the quayside. There was a small and ancient-looking ecclesiastical building immediately south but mostly we were surrounded by dry docks, slipways and cranes. Two or three seagulls mewed and fought their desultory fights.

"We are amidst the shipyards of Irrebarran and Lonsdale, the warship makers. The MFS *Dypsidorian* was built here", continued Arnoldina.

"The what?"

"MFS *Dypsidorian* is one of seven Magonian bucentaurs or super-carriers that have a flat top from which to fly drones or land aeroplanes if you are brave enough, but the main armament is guided missiles. They also have nine hundred-centimetre guns in three turrets, mainly for show", Arnoldina defined.

"What tonnage?" I asked.

Arnoldina thought a while.

"Displacement? One point four million tonnes?"

My Wife was obviously describing something enormous, much bigger than any ship conceived of in 80V.

"You have described 78V and 80V to me very well, Arnoldina, but you have never alluded to 79V. Why?"

"79V is a magmatic world, at the co-ordinates of Congleholme a vision of hot lava flows, boiling seas and creepy creatures who predate the scorching desert sands. There are no chordates. The laws of physics are nearly the same as here or 80V", stated Arnoldina.

"Is 79V Hell, Arnoldina?" I asked.

"If you say so, Charles"

"Is it possible that I may go there after my life here?"

"Yes, but you would not survive long, and you would soon get another deal of the deck."

"Arnoldina, in little more than a month you have taught me more than I would ever have thought possible", I said.

"I am here to serve, Charles"

"Even after your dismissal from the Army?"

"Especially after my dismissal from the Army, Charles"

"Arnoldina, my good Wife, please may I ask you something. Please don't be offended and please do not be angry with me. I love you so."

"Ask"

"Sometimes you climax during Holy Correction, even when you are being spanked. Please believe I wholly approve. Pleasure should admix your pain because I believe that assists your spiritual development more than does something purely negative. Also it prefigures the delight and the suffering intrinsic to parturition which I consider the acme of woman's Mission on Earth. Maybe I am too man-centric? Am I, Arnoldina?"

"Not at all, Charles, you are a man and that is an end of it. But I do enjoy my spankings as do most men and women who are inured and the total package of Confession, Prayer, Castigation, Blessing and Husbandly consolation helps me to grow and refine as a devout Christian person. This is not to say your strictures are ineffective. Any reasonable person thinks twice before repeating their sin, not because they are a coward, but because they realise that what they have done is an anti-social error."

"You truly are the most devout and saintly woman I have ever met, Arnoldina."

"We love each other too much, Charles, and are blind to our mutual defects."

"Dear Wife, may I propose this? In addition to our Corrections when we merit them, can I experiment with a formula like this: You or I lie naked across the other's lap, but instead of rigour we have prayers together and then I give you a tender massage of your thighs, bottom and back to bring you to climax and then I turn you over and kiss and cuddle you and we have Sacred Union for another orgasm. Would you like that?"

"It sounds absolutely delightful, Charles, but before we get too excited and before it gets too dark, we shall drive over to Challenor's Aske and I shall thank Jimmy in person."

"Wonderful, let's go!" I exclaimed boyishly.

At the portico of his great house Jimmy broadly grinned and greeted us and shook Arnoldina's proffered hand with his both arms. Arnoldina thanked him with profuse sincerity.

The gloomy November afternoon was already darkening and there was a moist chill in the air.

"Stay for dinner. I have had your room aired and heated for the night. Duncan and Bella are sleeping in theirs. I will tell them you are here", the 3rd Earl of Chamberfield invited.

"Thank you, Your Lordship. That would be delightful", responded Arnoldina before I could demur.

"Have you forgotten already? I am Jimmy!"

"Today we have tomato soup, followed by frankies and then vegan coconut cake and non-dairy custard", stated our most considerate, and prescient, host.

"Oh, frankies are my favourite" Arnoldina reminded us.

Duncan and Bella appeared. The ever-diligent Jolliffe had rung them.

Bella knelt at my Wife's feet and pleaded:-

"Dear Arnoldina, please forgive me for the evil, spiteful thing I said to you. I really am very sorry. It is untrue and I withdraw it wholly."

Arnoldina knelt herself and took Bella in her arms saying:-

"I forgive you, Bella. Now stand up and we shall dine together with the menfolk."

"Arnoldina, I did not know if you would ever come back. I wrote this for you. I was going to post it tomorrow."

Bella reached into an inside pocket of her dressing gown and retrieved a sealed envelope marked "Dr Mrs Arnoldina Charmliss, 47B Pencordan Way, Congleholme."

Arnoldina tore the letter open:-

My Darling Arnoldina,

I am so very sorry for the wicked, spiteful, unwarranted things I said to you. Please forgive me. I love you as a sister and I want to be your friend forever. You are literally the woman who taught me how to fuck in the best possible way if you will permit the word used in its correct, sacred, sense.

I am a proud, insolent person and I need to mend my ways, and I will try to with the help of my Darling Husband and yourself, Arnoldina.

Duncan Corrected me in the way you showed because I asked him to. He did so with firm manliness but also great sanctity and reverence. He delights me and I love him.

With regard to the cows and the babies, Mr Masterton and Mr Hollingrake have agreed to help me with the paddocking and the logistics of milking and delivery. The Selbys will help with the milking twice daily. I have no pasteurisation facilities but Mr Hollingrake says he can organise it. The first milk should reach the Countess hospital on Friday.

With Love and Esteem,
Arabella

The two women fell into each other's arms, weeping profusely.

"Now that's enough of that, the soup's getting cold", Jimmy objected.

CHAPTER TWENTY-SIX
PANIC

I have postponed this further writing for many days. Even now, though a full universe separates me from those times, I find it difficult to talk about. I do not know how long ago it is, maybe thirty or forty years by the reconning of 80V, so I suppose this is about 2076AD but affectively it gets no easier. I was born in 1952 so I suppose I am 124 or thereby. I am not the impotent diabetic myasthenial I was in 80V. In fact my health is excellent.

Treagh rang me at about 0340. I had left my mobile switched on.

"Hello, Chuck. I need to see you immediately in the Presidium. Don't worry. For once, neither you nor your wife are in trouble. Come in uniform."

"I am at Challenor's Aske, Sir. What is the problem?"

"I cannot say, Chuck, this is not a secure line. Have you a car?"

"Yes, Sir. Arnoldina's Rolls-Royce is here."

"Drive now and be with me in uniform by 0500."

"Yes, Sir"

"What is the matter, My Everything?" asked Arnoldina, waking with drowsy concern.

"Treagh wants me uniformed in his office by 0500."

"Darling, I shall drive you and we shall present together", said Arnoldina.

"Thank you, My Love", I replied.

I had brought no uniform, so I put on my fatigues. Arnoldina was also naked, so she put on her mourning dress and a puffy black anorak.

We did not shower. We picked up some chocolate biscuits and two plastic bottles of fizzy water and departed without valedictions. We wished to disturb neither the family nor the servants.

There was a thick November fog and Arnoldina drove gingerly through the narrow lanes and darkness, but fortunately no-one else was abroad, not even it would seem the Palatine Police.

We arrived without mishap at 0445 and parked at my billet. We went in and I changed into my No.1s as a Magonian Naval Commadore.

Arnoldina left her anorak in the Lodgings and we left for Treagh's office as a couple.

As we approached it became increasingly obvious that something was very wrong.

There was abnormal bustle for 0500 hours, and as we passed the hermetic room where the communications servers were installed we found it brightly illuminated with the door wedged open and the aircon running full pelt.

"Mind the cables, Commander!", someone shouted as my Wife and I picked our way over wires strewn across the corridor. Whoever he was, he had seen my cuff rings, but was uncertain of my exact rank.

I stopped a corporal passing in the opposite direction.

"What's going on?" I enquired.

"They are preparing to send it up", he replied and hurried on.

Soon Arnoldina and I were with Treagh.

We sat before his desk. He was standing holding the handset of an archaic green dial telephone connected to somewhere with plaited wire. He put the handset on his desk to keep his connection live.

Treagh sat.

"Analogue landline only now, Charmliss."

"Yes, Sir. What is going on, Sir?"

"Do you want the good news first, or the bad."

"Good news, please Sir."

"Dr Mrs Arnoldina Charmliss has been re-instated to full Lieutenant-Colonel rank with honour and with immediate effect. She has back-pay. No uniform can be provided at this time, nor a revised ID document", declared Treagh.

"Yes, Sir. Thank you, Sir", I replied, and then without missing a beat, "Can she have a pistol, Sir?"

Treagh opened a desk draw and reaching in produced a Wrortlemonger and Bierce 9mm semi-automatic identical to my own and two spare clips which he chucked across the desk at Arnoldina. She rose and took the weapon and ammunition.

"She will need it. My policy was always to issue identical weapons, and the Rolls-Royce of pistols so that my men and women always had reliable guns and sharable ammunition."

"Very wise, Sir", I remarked with my usual patronising fatuity.

"I am glad you agree", replied Treagh.

"And what is the bad news, Sir."

"The Russians have entered the War."

"What?!, Why!?, On whose side?"

"On the Russian side", said Treagh, "They are in Gainsborough."

"Gainsborough? Why?"

"I suggest you ring and ask them. They are on the end of that line", said Treagh with an impatient sarcasm very unlike him.

"Major-General, I speak fluent Russian. Would it help if I do just that?", offered Arnoldina.

"I am sorry, dear. I think things have gone beyond that today. I do not want any lady to be rebuffed, possibly with bad language", replied Treagh.

"Charmliss, I need you to take charge of the destruction of all police and intelligence records in such a manner as to render them forensically inreconstructible, and then assist with the burning of this building."

"What about the prisoners, Sir", I objected.

"Release them"

"Yes, Sir" I agreed.

"Sir, you cannot destroy the Old Assize. It is a Grade One Listed Ancient Monument."

"Chuck, old friend. I shall not hazard the life of a single man for the sake of any building, not even the Sistine Chapel."

"Thank you, Sir. You are very right, Sir", I replied.

"Now, Lieutenant-Colonel, go to your Husband's billet, change out of your mourning, and dress in fatigues", as Treagh said these words Edmonson threw a shoulder holster into her lap, "Pack bags for your Husband and yourself and await his orders. You, Charmliss, set about your work."

"Yes, Sir", my Wife and I replied together; rose, saluted in our respective conventions, and departed.

When I arrived at my office, MacKinnon was standing there with our trusty sledge, the same as that with which I had scuttled the *Conwell*, and a broad grin on his face.

"We better be systematic, Seargent Major", I commenced, "We will need to brake the hermetic seals of hard disks and smash the wafers of all SSDs. The optical disks and paper records we can isolate for burning", I advised, "Leave no data readable."

"Yes, Sir. I mean 'No, Sir'", replied MacKinnon.

We had breakfast and had finished with the computers by 1000. MacKinnon and I then took the boxes of combustible records on a trolly down the nearest elevator and onto the Ladyfair for ignition. Fortunately it was not a wet day.

I paused and looked at the grim scene beneath the mid-November overcast. Some piles of confidential paper were already afire upon the pallets strewn upon the pavement for aeriation.

It occurred to me that these may have been the first fires to disfigure that parade ground since Mistress Maisie, Margaret Hogg, suffered there nearly five hundred years before.

I saw that many APCs and military lorries had leaguered in the streets beyond.

We returned to my office for a last scan around. I was in the act of removing the spare ammunition from my desk, and my spare pistol loaded with a fresh clip of course, when a most surprising thing occurred.

Goodleague paced in wearing her prison-issue civilian outfit.

"Not now, Goodleague", I said dismissively, "We're busy."

She handed me a white envelope and knelt before me, folding her hands.

I tore the missive open and read her letter, written in blue biro on prison-issue note paper:-

Dear Commadore Dr Charmliss,

Thank you for everything you have done for my Fellow Prisoners and Myself. I owe my life to your Wife and my Liberty to you. I love both of you. I am very sorry for all the trouble I have brought you and all the evil things I have said about and to you. If I could erase the past I would.

I shall never again use violence to achieve my aims.

Go with God.

In Humble Love and Respect,

Felicity Goodleague

I put the letter back in its envelope and the envelope in an inside pocket.

"Here", I said, "Take this", handing her my spare pistol. Goodleague burst into tears.

"I am glad you now abhor violence and repudiate it. But you will need the gun. The Russians are coming.", I advised.

I offered Goodleague a seat and she remained until she had composed herself and then left. I never saw her again.

I assisted with the last of the files-burning and with the setting of further explosives within the Presidium. Lunchtime at 1300 was approaching. I rang Arnoldina down in the Judge's Lodging and told her to prepare our meal and take some white wine from the refrigerator.

"Charles, come at once. Something is going down", said Arnoldina.

I did as I was told.

As I opened the oaken door of my billet I was surprised to see Jimmy with Duncan and Bella.

"Hello, friends, what is going on?", I asked.

"Charles, the Russians have reached Derby we think and the Magonians are retreating.", stated Duncan.

Of course, I knew this last: After all I had just assisted that retreat.

"We are rounding-up the other members of The Albion Club plus the Selbys and Messrs Hollingrake, Masterton and Enoldius, with others. These are all people of skill and experience, essential for survival in a refugee community, as are Arnoldina and yourself. Will you join us?"

I hesitated.

Jimmy intervened.

"We know, Commadore, that you are reluctant to, as you see it, betray the men who helped you adapt to our World, but *au fond*, if you will forgive the expression, you are an Englishman and fate made you so at birth, without choice or culpability. Your Wife is now an Englishwoman and a very esteemed one. There is nothing now for her in China. Now my son is a farmer, you are a soil scientist with I believe teaching experience and your wife is a very experienced medic. We are almost all scientists or other professional men and our skills are needed for communal survival. We all have cross-country vehicles and enough petrol to reach Ireland or France. If and when the War ends we can, with other patriotic associations, form the essential nucleus of a provisional government with a view to a modern, free, British republic."

Jimmy stopped speaking. Jimmy, the 3rd and very possibly the last Earl of Chamberfield watched and waited.

"Do come", spoke Bella, "we love you and we need you."

My Wife approached and knelt at my feet. She folded her hands and looked imploringly into my eyes:-

"Commadore, give me my orders", she softly demanded.

"We come", I decided.

Arnoldina rose beaming and our visitors smiled with tearful eyes and approached to hug Arnoldina and I, to kiss us as if a much respected uncle and aunt and to shake our hands.

CHAPTER TWENTY-SEVEN
THE HARD YARDS

Life is a hard trial. Life is a Pilgrimage through time and space full of meetings and partings and bereavements. We are not privy to its Purpose, if any, nor can we prophesy its vicissitudes.

Arnoldina and I packed our few things and took our little cases to my Wife's capacious and robust car. Wherever we were going I decided also to take my Bentley that Duncan had so generously given me.

Jimmy and his son and daughter-in-law had gone but it was clear that others were either in or near their own vehicles and I recognised Shrigley's little car and Pratley's long wheelbase Land Rover.

I could hear the ominous booms of distant artillery from the East. Of course, the noise may have arose from exploding missiles or drones rather than cannon. I did not know who was fighting whom or care, so preoccupied was I with my own destiny and that of my new Wife and the child she might bare.

I did not want to leave Congleholme, one of the few places where I was truly happy, respected and fulfilled, where I enjoyed a second marriage to a much older and more experienced woman with her own version of Christian joy, and I had a chance of posterity.

I bitterly, bitterly regretted what I saw then as a lousy betrayal of Treagh, Ionescu and the other brave, unselfish men who had graced a foreign army with their considered and idealistic allegiance. I know what it is to have Freedom of Speech, and the good and evil uses to which I have put it, and that despite all it is worth dying for. I felt like a coward and a traitor and remembered that Arnoldina was again a Magonian officer. I cannot imagine how she felt beneath the mourning dress she had resumed and the mantle of wifely obedience she had embraced.

It was a sunny afternoon on the cusp of late autumn dusk and the Sun was very low in the West before its early retirement. The guns, if that was what they were fell silent, and then a most extraordinary thing happened.

A shadow of intense light:- Yes I know that is a contradiction but I don't know how else to describe it:- A shadow of intense light seemed slowly to process around the walls and pavements with sharp arrises of ordinary shadow, and intense reflections from windows. Whisps of vapour rose lazily from wet tiles. There was a weird buzzing sound which may have been small arcs in ionised air between the wires twisted along telephone cables, or some other recondite electrical effect.

Then the light abruptly ceased and also the buzzing.

Shrigley had materialised behind me in his old, annoying manner, perhaps to re-iterate his version of welcome.

I turned to him and said:-

"What the fuck was that?"

Shrigley replied:-

"They have nuked Hatton"

Looking back, if I may use that expression, it was a good job the majority of us were on the Southern side of a large stone building or our exposed skin would have been badly burnt.

I checked that Arnoldina was okay and we walked through the brick tunnel onto the Ladyfair and looked to the North.

I noticed that the Magonian convoy had already departed in its entirety. I could see no-one anywhere.

A stately column of what appeared to be gray volcanic ash or it may have been water vapour appeared to have already formed above where Hatton Dypsidorian should have been maybe twelve miles away. Above an enormous ball of fire roiled. I say ball but it was more like a dodecahedron or icosahedron whose soft edges were an intense black and its faces a glowing red-orange if that makes sense.

Somehow, on this clear evening, the high stratosphere seamed to answer with a cirrus-like halo of vapour.

And then, as if further to perplex this vision of almost supernatural wonder, the very air seemed to fracture like a limitless crystal. As a man with crystallographic training I wondered idly whether the hanging fragments were monoclinic or triclinic: Their faces met at different but uniform angles.

And then growing tori of soft white cloud grew from the column like the balconies of a satanic fungus whilst barbs of dirty dust and vapour grew groundward from the column. It was a Plinian vision of a Classical inferno, geological, Vesuvian, Biblical.

We stood enthralled.

Suddenly Terring appeared from nowhere.

"You stupid fuckers", he addressed my lady Wife and I, "It will fucking blind you!"

He switched his Geiger counter on. The thing screamed its head off.

"Get back in the fucking tunnel now!"

"Yes, I am very sorry Professor Terring", I apologised stupidly.

We did as he instructed and he of course accompanied us. As we entered the structure the counter changed to a minor key and Terring switched it off. Terring removed his glasses and crouched against a wall with his mouth open and his hands behind his head. Arnoldina and I aped him.

There was an almighty explosion. My ears rang and I was temporarily deafened. Bricks tumbled at the Ladyfair entrance. Then I remembered the sappers and their timed detonation of the communications servers.

Terring remained cringing.

So Arnoldina and I remained as he.

Then there was what I can only describe as a concussion. My cranium seemed to contract and my brain ache within it. My fillings started to bleed. I cannot really explain it to make sense. I lost my hearing for a time and my eyes jiggled up and down as they did during my myasthenial attacks in 80V, but here more violently and as I was squatting in stillness. I thought I would lose consciousness or perhaps die. A handful of seconds or minutes later a hurricane swept by, so loud and singing I could hear it from deep in the tunnel, and then suddenly all was quiet and still.

I know this is a most inappropriate analogy but it was as if the planet had passed an orgasm and this was its quietus of calm.

Terring rose and tapped me on the shoulder. Arnoldina and I stood also. I asked my Wife:-

"Are you okay?"

She mouthed a brief response, but I was too deaf to know what it was.

As we made for the crawlable car park portal of the tunnel it became clear that other survivors had sheltered in the tunnel. Terring had replaced his glasses and he crawled before us, carefully pushing his precious counter before him.

As we reached the car park behind what had been the old Assize Court building shattered glass carpeted the ground and the cars had been dented to one degree or another by falling masonry. We would have to ascertain which remained drivable.

I turned to Nicklous Terring and shouted:-

"We owe you our lives"

Terring grabbed my right forearm and squeezed roughly. He turned and looking into my eyes his own dissolved to tears. He said nothing. He released me and removing the glasses he had remounted wiped away his tears with the back of his hands.

Arnoldina remained strangely unaffected. She had seen a lot in a long life and a thermonuclear explosion was another outrage to be taken in her stride. A spanking might be a cause to weep, an atom bombing just another bloody thing.

I was too stupid and two stupefied to be much bothered, at least in this shocked state. It was another interesting and mildly exciting anecdote for my memoirs. I had died once already and to me everything here was just bonus and I was no longer in pain or perceptibly ill or dependent and I was relishing every second of it.

As we regained daylight and the car park the crisp crunch of glass answered our each tentative step and the shards were as treacherous as ice. The Old Assize Building was a Grade One Listed structure and the windows of the rear lodgings were of late Georgian and early Victorian rolled Chance glass. It was not safety glass such as that in our cars and broke into dagger-sharp shards. It was clear that several loitering in the lot had been impaled by falling glass and that already some had lost or were losing sufficient blood to be beyond recovery.

There were low cries and groans of uncertain provenance, rather so to say, like the singing of cavies in their tribes, and almost as musically melancholy as the closed-mouthed serenades of those charming rodents.

As regard our cars it was clear that most of the windows had crazed into the opaque nodules of safety glass. Arnoldina's roller was an exception. It was very expensive and very new, designed like all Rolls-Royces with half an eye upon military service. Similarly my heavy Bentley was nearly unscathed, but the glass in Pratley's Land Rover had fractured to small shards so that the windows were still transparent enough to drive, with due caution.

Falling debris had scratched and dented the car bodies. Shrigley entered his small French car with some difficulty and turned his key in the ignition. Nothing happened. None of the glowing annunciators on the dashboard illuminated. The starter motor stayed silent. The whole vehicle was dark and silent. Shrigley reached under the fairings and pulled the hood catch-release. The hood popped up and Shrigley lifted it to disclose an impenetrable loom of coloured cables.

Pratley appeared and speaking to Shrigley said:-

"'Got a fucking starting-handle, Pott?"

"No"

"You'll have to leave it then. You, and your missus and lads can travel with Jeany and I if mine is good. I will try it now."

Shrigley's lads proved to be in their late twenties so assuming it moved at all it was going to be a Tardis.

Pratley tried his self-starter and there was no response so he retrieved the starting handle and cranked his motor. The Land Rover coughed into life.

Arnoldina tested her car and she had instant ignition without recourse to hand-cranking. Belatedly I tested the Bentley. It started no problem. We now had at least three operable escape cars. None dared to switch off their motors.

Suddenly someone turned into the entrance in a blue Phantom with its windscreen punched out. Nine or ten dirty adults and a toddler emerged. Duncan was at the wheel and the others proved to be Jimmy, Bella, Joliffe, Masterton, Mr and Mrs Selby with James, Enoldius and a couple of others I failed to recognise. How the hell Duncan packed them all in I shall never know.

Shrigley had failed to take me into his confidence but it appeared that this car park was an emergency rendezvous for The Albion Club and its hangers-on whether with Treagh's permission or not I had no idea.

Someone parked carelessly behind Jimmy's roller in a black Galaxy. Ionescu emerged followed by Maggi Landheart, Jason Warble, Ennias Mickawber and unbelievably Bunny Balfour with her husband Thomas and two teenage girls I could not identify.

So according to my arithmetic we had 19 men, 7 women, 1 lad, 2 lassies and an infant making thirty persons in all.

It was lucky that Warble's car was so big that ten small people could cram in at a pinch. Ionescu had had the sense to to idle the engine.

Terring and Arnoldina approached Pratley and I, and Pratley spread a motoring map of North Wales on the hood of Pratley's Land Rover. There was now no perceptible wind. Terring briefly switched on his counter and showed the red read-out to Pratley:-

"X and gamma are 210% the Congleholme ambient and we must leave within twenty minutes", he remarked.

"The Presidium is 15.5 GC miles from Marcus Square, and Mancuvering [apparently "Man-soo-ver-ing] is 67 GC miles from Marcus. According to the Inverse Square Law if ambient is the same in Mancuvering then HE radiation will be 5.4%. Is that correct, Nick?" claimed Pratley, seeking confirmation.

"Agreed. Ambient is negligible at both locations", responded Terring.

Suddenly I felt very ignorant.

"Where is Marcus Square?", I asked, "and what is GC?"

"Marcus Square is the nominal centre of Hatton. It was Ground Zero, and GC is Great Circle Distance", clarified Terring patiently.

"Go to your car and type this into your GPS: MU3 2QF. Then wait for an allocation and follow my car at 40 mph.", ordered Pratley.

"Yes, Sir" I replied instinctively.

"If you get lost, ring my number 07768 234788. Expect to re-rendezvous in one hour and twenty minutes."

"Yes, Sir"

"Tell your wife to get into her SUV and await an allocation."

"Thank you, Sir", pre-empted Arnoldina, departing on a heel.

"Oh, and change into your fatigues and driving shoes", Pratley shouted after her.

The trunk of Arnoldina's Cullinan was a mere thirty metres on the other side of the lot and she opened it, opened her little case and without turning a hair stripped her dress and court shoes (perfectly obedient so no underwear remember) and donned her fatigues and driving shoes. Then she patiently set her GPS and waited, as her engine idled.

My Bentley was naturally parked next to Arnoldina's car and I noticed that Pratley had dispatched the women Queenborough, Landheart, Mina Shrigley and the entire Selby family to Arnoldina. Little James was so delighted to be re-united with my Wife that he clung to her shins beaming to her face so impedingly than Arnoldina took him in her arms, kissed him and handed him over to his mother so that Arnoldina could safely drive.

Tactfully, Shrigley gave me charge of the entire Balfour family, and Mildred's boyfriend Maxwell Fortess plus two men I did not know and Enoldius. With nine of us in the old Bentley it was of course very intimate.

The remaining fourteen (if my arithmetic is uncharacteristically correct) Pratley split between himself in his long wheelbase Land Rover and Warbles's Galaxy.

Before we moved Pratley had his men sweep and shovel the worst of the broken glass from the entrance before we inched our way out.

Pratley and Shrigley had obviously researched this route of escape meticulously. Pratley led at steady speed along the inland dual-carriageway D235 carefully avoiding the main coastal motorway M372a which would be likely to be clogged with refugees and military convoy under these circumstances. As it was, there was virtually no west-bound traffic though the eastbound carriageway was jammed with Magonian convoy presumably heading East to engage the Russians. There were no tanks, "crawling coffins" as I had always thought of them, but numerous APCs and half-tracks as well as logistics and communications lorries. Their predicament seemed ghastly and very ill-officered, sitting ducks for any passing Ithaca or Russian drone. Having said that the continuing existence of ballistic "iron domes" and the fact that spy satellites had long been shot from the sky hampered aerial operations. I wondered if it would not have been better to send the light armour overland but admittedly the North Wales landscape is hardly helpful to tracked vehicles.

Shortly, we passed a large road sign saying "Welcome to the Semi-Palatinate of Angarn." I marvelled that the British had not remove it immediately before War was declared. One of the youngsters said, "We are in Wales."

Months later Duncan told me about the contractor and his tractor which Jimmy had hired to plough the Challenor's Aske park for roots as we had agreed. The plough was configured for a land (straik) of five furrows. The contractor's driver made two lands up and down the park, that is nine furrows with the dead overmould and then slopcd into the trees to defecate. No sooner had he waded into the scrub when there was an almighty detonation. The tractor and its tackle apparently vapourised and was replaced with a large blackly-smoking pyre. The consensual interpretation of this startling event is that a cruising Russian drone programmed to annihilate any large metal object just happened to find this contractor's tractor.

The trip to Mancuvering was largely uneventful. My passengers were very subdued, even the teens, and most slept most of the way. No-one requested a comfort break, possibly because they knew it would not be indulged.

As we advanced the terrain became wetter and more mountainous, with settlements sparser but larger. Although place-name boards and directions had been removed by The British at the War's inception it was nevertheless clear that the Welsh language had never been used in these parts, most differently to the similar locations in 80V.

I discussed this anomaly with Arnoldina that night. The Chinawoman was as familiar with the arcana of English history as she was with that of Russia and of course China, and the languages of all three of those reactionary powers. She said that Edward the First had made a point of extirpating the Welsh language in his campaigns of 1277AD so that almost all placenames in Wales were in "sensible" English as opposed to the Brythonic sister-land of Cornwall's condition, where the Cornish language coexisted with English to die naturally in the late Eighteenth-Century. The result was risible Cornish hybrid placenames such as "Sticker", "Maybe-Burnthouse" and "Come-to-Good." Notwithstanding that, I could not imagine anywhere in England proper being called "Mancuvering" and I would defy any untutored Englishman to pronounce that correctly. 78V was of course subtly different in its physics and evolution to 80V.

Pratley led us into a large suburban parking lot. There was a large Sainsbury's, several German supermarkets, a carpet shop, and lots of other large shops ranged around a vast car park. The ASDA had a petrol station, as did the Sainsbury's. Interestingly there was also a Land Rover dealership, and a showroom of Rolls-Royce and Bentley cars, though these had long be made by different makers. I suppose Mancuvering was about the size of Swansea but unlike that Glamorgan city of 80V it entirely bestraddled the Lleyn Peninsula rather than partly occluding the Gower.

Some of the shops were boarded and all were closed.

The car park was almost deserted of cars and we saw no-one, not even security staff though I suspected some were lurking.

Pratley got out of his Land Rover and made a wrist signal as much as to say "Switch off your ignitions", and then a gathering gesture to say "Alight and draw near."

The thirty-odd of us gathered closely in the car park and Pratley briefed us:-

"Tonight we return to our cars and sleep until 0400 hours when we rise and gather provisions for six weeks. Those provisions will include canned food, baby milk, clothing, footwear, medication and tanked gasolene. We are already cramped so we will also liberate one Land Rover and a capacious van, a seven-tonner if we find one.

At 0800 exactly we will return to our cars and make along the F267 single carriageway for CN5 6YU following me at 30 mph.

ETA is 0900.

Charles Charmliss: Follow me

Pott Shrigley: The Supermarkets

Arnoldina Charmliss: Liberate Medicaments

You do have your pistol, I take it, Dina?"

"Yes, Sir", replied my Wife, "and I agree to gather essential medicines, Sir."

"Nick, what is Gamma and X for this location?"

Terring switched on his machine.

"High, but only 5% of the Presidium value."

"Good, we leave at 0600 exactly for an ETA of 0700."

"Any questions"

Silence.

We dispersed to our vehicles and urinated and defecated in the ornamental bushes as the shops' lavatories were inaccessible.

Only a few of us had sleeping bags but the cold November night was in any case notably cozy, even intimate, as we slept in our respective cars in the arms of each other and the windows partly drawn down.

At 0345 sharp, as if by telepathy, the thirty odd rose, relieved themselves and set about their appointed tasks.

Pratley and I climbed into his Land Rover.

Pratley used a hammer to knock the remaining shards of glass from the windows.

Pratley then drove us at speed straight for the plate glass window of the Sainsbury's and turned through 180 degrees. He then reversed into the window crazing it, and the opaque sheet of glass tipped bodily and fell.

Two uniformed men approached shouting.

Pratley removed a pistol from a concealed shoulder holster and shot one man dead. The other ran away.

Pratley replaced his pistol, put the car in forward first gear and positioned it back on to the Land Rover dealership window to achieve his second breaking and entering.

"Get in that car, fill the tank and then load up at the Sainsbury's", ordered the erstwhile computing lecturer.

"Yes, Sir" I replied.

I was astonished to discover the keys in the ignition of the factory-fresh Range Rover. I climbed in and drove to the Sainsbury gas station. I hoped that the thing ran on green mixture and draw up at an appropriate pump.

I put my credit card in the slot and the pump remained silent. I checked the liquid crystal annunciator. It was blank and the backlighting was off. I took out my mobile with the stupid idea of contacting the Sainsbury's helpline. There was no signal.

Just then a man in overalls came out of the dark payment booth.

"Excuse me, mate. I will have to pump by hand. Wait a minute", he said.

Wielding a bunch of keys he opened a panel of the pump fairings, inserted what looked like a canal lockkeeper's windlass, and started cranking. Gasolene mixture slurped slowly into my tank.

After a couple of minutes I replaced the cap and turning to my benefactor said:-

"Get in this car and I shall take you to a place of safety."

"I am not leaving without my wife and daughter, Sir."

"You have thirty minutes to get them to this very spot. Leave the pump open and the windlass here", I said.

"Thank you, Sir. We will be here."

The pumpman got in a small car and sped off.

I started the Range Rover. Fortunately, it sounded healthy enough. I drove round to the Sainsbury's.

By now the women had gathered trolleyfuls of canned goods and beans, and ten-kilo sacks of rice and Enoldius had arrived with a seven-tonne white van, a Mercedes I think, and was helping Shrigley to load it. A young man and woman I had not noticed before were sitting in the van.

I went up to them and opened the van passenger door. I presumed they were the owners of the vehicle.

"Excuse me", I said, "can you please help the others load your vehicle?"

"Yes, mate"

The couple threw their own cargo onto the rink and loaded the provisions.

Arnoldina was standing disconsolately with a trolley full to the brim of medicine. In a plastic bag on top were separated packages and glass bottles of stuff. I looked inside. I took out one marked "Toujeo 25" and brandished it before my Wife's eyes.

"How the hell are we to store insulin?" I queried.

"We will make do, Darling", she replied.

I found another cardboard box of syringes that was marked "Diamorphine." I presented that to my Wife and looked into her eyes. She stared back with a chilling look I had not seen on her beautiful face before. She said nothing. I put the pack back in the bag.

"Put the whole trolley in this car you have stolen, and pack the rice around it with the little fridge. Plug the fridge into the cigar lighter and put the insulin, the lidocaine and the eye drops into the fridge", Arnoldina ordered.

"Yes, Loveliness" I obeyed.

Arnoldina then assisted me to load the further rice.

I then went in search of Pratley. He was assisting Jimmy, Duncan, Bella and Jolliffe to get petrol into the blue roller. It seemed to take ages. The pumpman was cranking and an unknown woman and little girl looked on, I presumed the pumpman's family.

"How is your tank, Charmliss?", asked Pratley.

"Three-quarters full, Sir."

"And your wife's?"

"Just off full, Sir."

"The pumpman and his family will travel with the van owners. I have briefed them on the rendezvous", stated Pratley.

"Thank you, Sir", I replied.

"Who will drive our cars?" I enquired.

"The same as drove out, except that Enoldius will drive the liberated Range Rover, and Mr Miggins will drive his own vehicle", replied Pratley. I supposed Mr Miggins to be the owner of the white van.

By 0538 we had stolen as much as could be carried and we set off in convoy, Pratley leading in his Land Rover.

No-one and no vehicle were encountered on the way, not even a dairyman's tractor, though cows and sheep were abundant and apparently healthy.

CN5 6YU proved to be a National Trust car park at a place called Tripant. There was no evidence of three hollows, the spot being an especially windswept patch of bleak plateau with a couple of bird-watchers' hides.

I think that this place identified with a place called Porth Felen in 80V. There was a lifeboat station beneath the cliff and a minor tarmacadamed road led down to it. People switched off and alighted. Shrigley and I convened with Terring in Pratley's car.

Pratley drove cautiously down to the tiny harbour that accommodated not only the lifeboat station but three open fishing boats and an iron pontoon drawn ashore behind a moule.

The place was deserted. We entered the lifeboat station and the rescue vessel proved to be a capacious Shannon type vessel. Terring made to start the engine and it roared to life. Terring switched off and rejoined us on the floor.

There had been a quarry behind the harbour in previous centuries and it might be possible to park cars whilst people and provisions were transferred to the lifeboat, we thought. But they could not be leaguered here because of exposure to sea damage during storms. We had no idea whether the slipway would bear such a load or whether the boat would founder at launch.

"You are our only sailor, Charmliss, and you must command loading, sailing and disembarkations", ordered Pratley. I was terrified at the mere suggestion, but kept silence. I also noted the man's degree of confidence in my competency.

"We will have to launch light, and I shall motor to the lee of the moule and we will load from there", I remarked.

Pratley seemed a little disconcerted at my address.

There appeared to be a large mountainous island offshore maybe 3000 metres distant. I gazed at it.

Pratley said:-

"That is Monk Island there are four farms because the distal side is some square miles of arable and pasture with minor woodland. On this side is a large hill of Upper Paleozoic formations in which there are old coal, lead and limestone mines in which thirty people can shelter, both from radiation and from the weather. There are the ruins of an old abbey and above its graveyard a large rectory and a small Methodist chapel. Between the abbey and the chapel are rows of single-story cottages which accommodate pilgrims in season. Now is off-season. Expect six permanent inhabitants: The far lighthouse is automated. There are also derelict bunkers and observation posts from the Second World War."

This place sounded to me very much like the Bardsey Island of 80V but the hill on Bardsey is Lower Paleozoic, I think, and I know there are no mines.

"How big is the island", I asked, "and is there a harbour?"

"The island is 28.64 square kilometres, call it 11 square miles, and the nominal side length is about three and a third miles", Pratley clarified.

Our self-appointed and universally-acquiesced leader had clearly supplanted Shrigley, however tacitly or tactfully, but I pressed neither man, preferring that I would address the nature and position of the harbour at some other time.

We drove back to the car park above the cliffs and escorted the rest to the harbour. Fortunately there was little swell and the tide was high. Masterton and I launched the lifeboat and motored to the lee of the moule. We made fast to some old cast iron bollards. Pratley organised the relay of the provisions to the boat. Arnoldina, disconnecting the little refrigerator from our car, gently lifted it and a stolen suitcase full of drugs aboard. She reconnected the fridge to the boat's supply. Our nurse and doctor installed herself and kept vigil over these precious necessities.

I checked the load line. There was still plenty of freeboard but thirty odd people were yet to embark.

"Return your vehicles to the car park. Stay with them and allow passengers to board the lifeboat", barked Pratley at the assembled company.

"When most are on the boat we shall check the load line again, Charmliss", Pratley quietly assured me.

"Yes, Sir" I replied.

We checked.

"Come with me", Pratley ordered me, and we returned to our cars to follow stragglers back up the cliff road to the NT car park.

Pratley intercepted me as I emerged from the Bentley and we boarded his Land Rover to go where I knew not.

He drove a few hundred metres to a farmstead that had clearly been an RN Fleet Air Arm observation outpost during the Second World War and beside sundry bunkers and concrete roads there were dilapidated huts and three large well-maintained aircraft hangers. There was a modern farmhouse at some distance.

It was at such an establishment, but on the Atlantic cliffs of Pembrokeshire that my Parents, both RN meteorologists, had met in 1947, and it was the site of HMS Goldcrest to which my Wife and I consigned their ashes in 2021.

Pratley visited each hanger in turn. The first two were empty except for hedgehog and fox skeletons and rafter pigeons who scalded us as we walked below.

The third structure contained an expensive new tractor and sundry farm machinery.

As we turned back to the car an angry middle-aged man in dirty dungarees strode up:-

"Get out! Thieves! If I see you here again I shall shoot you!"

Pratley calmly took out his pistol and shot the man through the heart. It was his second murder in twenty-four hours.

We got back in the car and drove to the farmhouse. There we discovered a distraught middle-aged woman in a cotton dress and a hysterically-weeping teenaged girl.

"You murdered my husband, you coward. You killed our coxswain.", she stated.

This last reference to the coxswain perplexed me for some days until I realised that she spoke spiritually, perhaps an old endearment, as well as literally.

"Take off your clothes", ordered Pratley to the two women.

The older woman fell to her knees and clasping her hands begged:-

"Oh, please don't rape us, Sirs!"

This was exactly the tearful, submissive behaviour that would have guaranteed rape at the hands of younger men. But I was an ill eighty-four year old. I had no idea about Pratley but he looked sixty in 80V terms and may have been ten times that in this cosmos.

"We shall not rape you. We are married men.", I explained stupidly.

"Let them come as they are.", I said.

Pratley abruptly turned to me with a scowl of surprise.

We drove the women to the lifeboat fully clothed and with anoraks and sleeping bags. We left the farmer where he lay for the crows, the foxes and the badgers.

I took the two women below to Arnoldina.

"These are bereaved prisoners.", I told my Wife, "Please look to their needs. They shall accompany us to the island."

"Yes, Holy Husband", was the surprisingly formal answer.

I returned to the moule.

Pratley was waiting for me.

Suddenly my wife emerged and shouted:-

"Charles, there are children in their farmstead!"

Pratley said, "We will go and get them."

We went back to the farm and found a boy about six, a girl of maybe eight and a baby in a cot.

I said to the little girl:-

"Are there any more babies, children or people here? Your mummy is waiting for you in the lifeboat and your daddy has gone to Heaven to see Jesus."

"Where is my sister?", asked the young lady, I thought with great presence of mind, especially in the circumstances.

"She is with mummy", I assured.

The little woman shook her head solemnly.

She retrieved the baby from his carrycot and cradled him in her little arms.

I lifted the carrycot and led the children to the Land Rover and said:-

"Look at the floor, children, until we reach the boat."

They obeyed in silence.

You can imagine the scenes as the family were re-united, though without the husband and father, so I shall leave them undescribed.

I stepped up the companionway and climbed onto the moule.

Pratley was waiting for me.

"Earnest", I said, "I do not like what we do or what we have become. Are we really marauding banditi and low highway robbers who exploit the misfortune of others and who depredate the countryside?"

"Look at this, Chuck", replied Pratley. He drew a handful of Magonian thousand-crown notes from his pocket and scattered them to the wind.

The particoloured scraps of worthlessness decorated the shorescape like so much confetti at a wedding of Satan with Fate.

"Look, Charles, I'm sorry. I know we have never got on. I am sorry for what I said to you on our first meeting and I am sorry for everything that has happened since. I wish you were my friend. I have always admired you. Your Faith and your Devotion to the things you believe in: I wish I could believe. Your humility and your willingness to sacrifice your own principles to the good of all. I love you, Charles. I am a married man as you said. You know that I mean no insult", said Pratley.

"Charles, what do you want? We have families to feed and to keep out of range, so far as is possible for any creature of flesh. What do you want for the men I have killed, do you want them to die slowly in the agony of radiation sickness, their skin burning into blisters and being sloughed in flame without fire, vomiting their hearts out when no vomit will come, weltering in their own shit like animals, knowing they will die but not when, or if they will be sane enough to know, or sighted to see? Or do you want them to die promptly and with honour, defending their family and their property as they swore they would?" continued the sometime computing lecturer.

"Chuck, what I would give to return to the work I hated back in the Hatton that has gone forever. I am not a murderer or a thief and I want none of this. I feel that my soul and spirit have been raped, not by my dismissal by foreign occupiers but by the whole circumstance of this new world with no credit, no courtesy, no trade and no culture. A new world of privation for Erny, for Chuck, for Jeany, for Dina and all: Even for the very enemies you say we should love."

"Earnest, I do not know what to think, or even what I want, beyond my Sacred Wife and the child I hope to beget", I admitted.

Pratley grabbed my right hand in his and squeezed painfully. He fixed his left hand to my bicep. Tears ran down his cheeks and into his beard as he stared solemnly into my eyes. For a moment etched into my memory a shaft of sunlight transfigured his tearful, manly face as a seagull shrieked and swooped past. Pratley hugged me close and then released and turned back to his car.

I followed him.
I said:-
"Earnest, we must bury this man."
"Charles, you are right. It was the first and most sacred duty of the first men and forever divorced them of other animals", the murderer and altruist agreed with a surprising piety.

We drove back to the body. The corpse had not yet begun to stink or perceptibly to decay but rigor mortis had passed. A pool of frozen blood sparkled in the sunlight and overspread the tarmac. We found a one thousand kilo empty fertiliser bag and a man-sized wooden crate in the adjacent hanger and placed the poor farmer therein and respectfully lifted the makeshift coffin into the back of the Land Rover.

"I think we should go to the farmhouse to retrieve clothing, cash and keepsakes to console the bereaved women", I suggested.

"Yes, that is very kind and thoughtful of you, Charmliss", said Pratley, "we shall drive across."

Pratley and I spent half an hour gathering things.

We returned to the moule and hoisted the coffin aboard and placed it on the little patch of deck that must do service as a quarterdeck. Pratley unclipped the Union Flag from the sternstaff and draped it over the crate. We persuaded Arnoldina to take the clothes and heirlooms, including photographs of their late husband and father and give them to the lady of the household.

"Program this into the autopilot", ordered Pratley, handing me co-ordinates jotted in blue biro on a journalist's notepad sheet.

"Yes, Sir", I agreed and adjourned to the cockpit to do it.

I returned to Pratley standing on the starboard gunwale and he said to me:-

"Muster all on this moule. Tell drivers to follow me to the hangers and park their vehicles and then to report here at 1000 hours."

I said "Yes, Sir" and did as instructed.

The last driver arrived back on foot at 0946.

I ushered the last aboard and satisfied myself that the thirty-eight of us were present and correct.

We cast off and when we had cleared the moule and the boat pointed vaguely at the island I went to switch on the autopilot. The sea was clear and I switched off the centimetric radar for a reason. I returned to Pratley.

"Captain, this vessel is yours and so are we people", proclaimed my ersatz pilot, not exactly my friend, not precisely my enemy, a murderer and a man of sound morals, like myself a puritan republican, but an atheist I would then have most gladly Confessed, though I would never hear the blissful Request.

The sea sparkled in the sun and the crisp effervescence of the wake's cavitation sang like champagne. The sea was calm. The boat rolled slightly as it changed azimuth, and righted. The gulls mewed. The slow throb of the engine beat a muffled orison. I was nervous of our trim, knowing that if the lifeboat capsized it would self-right but that the people who stood or sat upon every tenable square inch would be in the water. There were no records of sea life attacking humans in Wales, but the winter sea was alive with sharks, orca and jellyfish. But this was academic: Most of us, including the Love of my Life, were non-swimmers and hypothermia would pre-empt drowning.

It was a halcyon sea, an ocean ready to surrender its dead.

Enoldius and I climbed the service ladder to the radar gantry. He held his Prayer Book and I my Bible as we entwined in its stanchions.

I proclaimed:-

𝔄nd a certain scribe came, and said unto him, 𝔐aster, 𝔍 will follow thee whithersoever thou goest.

𝔄nd 𝔍esus saith unto him, 𝔗he foxes have holes, and the birds of the air have nests; but the 𝔖on of man hath not where to lay his head.

𝔄nd another of his disciples said unto him, 𝔏ord, suffer me first to go and bury my father.

𝔅ut 𝔍esus said unto him, 𝔉ollow me; and let the dead bury their dead.

𝔄nd when he was entered into a ship, his disciples followed him.

I closed my Bible and Enoldius opened his Anglican Book of Common Prayer and read the Order for the Burial of the Dead to the assembled company:-.

Man that is born of a woman hath but a short time to live, and is full of misery. He cometh up, and is cut down, like a flower; he fleeth as it were a shadow, and never continueth in one stay.

In the midst of life we are in death: of whom may we seek for succour, but of thee, O Lord, who for our sins art justly displeased?

Yet, O Lord God most holy, O Lord most mighty, O holy and most merciful Saviour, deliver us not into the bitter pains of eternal death.

Thou knowest, Lord, the secrets of our hearts; shut not thy merciful ears to our prayer; but spare us, Lord most holy, O God most mighty, O holy and merciful Saviour, thou most worthy Judge eternal, suffer us not, at our last hour, for any pains of death, to fall from thee.

Forasmuch as it hath pleased Almighty God of his great mercy to take unto himself the soul of our dear brother here departed: we therefore commit his body to the sea; earth to earth, ashes to ashes, dust to dust; in sure and certain hope

of the Resurrection to eternal life, through our Lord Jesus Christ; who shall change our vile body, that it may be like unto his glorious body, according to the mighty working, whereby he is able to subdue all things to himself.

As Enoldius pronounced "body to the sea" fit young men cast the coffin hence. It sank like a stone. The flag of our nation floated like flame upon the glistening waves.

The farmer's wife and her daughters wept inconsolably.

So did Earnest Pratley.

CHAPTER TWENTY-EIGHT
MONK ISLAND

The lifeboat swung round the island's southern headland, slowed and turned towards a tiny port. It was much the same as that at Tripant except that it was backed by flat arable hinterland rather than cliffs. There was a masonry lighthouse and its whitewashed support complex on a rocky headland to our larboard.

I noticed that about two miles ahead a steep elliptical hill rose and near its foot what may have been whitewashed buildings.

I switched off the autopilot and took the helm.

As we neared the lee of the moule in the little harbour, I was making one or two knots. The boat hit the weed-bedecked ashlar with a bump and men lept ashore to make fast the berth.

"I am going ashore to see if I can borrow or steal a useable tractor or trailer", volunteered Duncan. Bella decided to stay with Arnoldina on the moule as the others disembarked with hand baggage.

I tried my mobile for a signal. It was of course dead, so I visited the weather-battered GPO call box a hundred metres up the road. It was of course without a tone.

"We are alone", I shouted to anyone interested.

Presently a man I did not recognise and was conceivably a resident farmer arrived on an aged tractor towing a very convenient flat-bed trailer.

He turned off his engine, alighted and shouted:-

"Who is in charge here?"

I volunteered. As had previously been pointed out to me, I was the only refugee with senior police experience.

"You are trespassing. Landings have been prohibited since the War started."

"Please, Sir", I begged like a child, "we are refugees from a nuclear attack near Congleholme and we are looking for shelter away from the weather and nuclear radiation."

I did not wish to christen our landfall using Pratley's method.

Just then Terring materialised at my shoulder with a suitcase and his Geiger counter in the other hand.

"Yes, Sir.", he confirmed, "This machine I am holding is a radiation counter and if you require I shall turn it on to read the radiation level here."

The farmer studied Terring suspiciously.

Terring turned on his counter and it made a low whine as it started to tot figures on its glowing red annunciator.

Terring consulted it and pronounced:-

"Sir, the radiation is only 4% what it is in Congleholme but it is still very dangerous. We propose to walk the lee of the far hill and shelter in the old mines until the radiation is at a safe level for agriculture, and eventually to return to our homes."

"Well the adits are open but there is plenty of abandoned or empty property. Sort yourselves out, and we will discuss rentals later.", replied the farmer.

"Thank you, Sir, you are very generous", I conceded, "but we are destitute and our cars are on the mainland. But we can pay with our labour."

"I have been farming here since before the War and I have heard and felt nothing.", declared the farmer.

"No. Weak but dangerous radiation is painless but, with respect Sir, I am a particle physicist and I advise that you take your family to shelter in a mine.", counselled Terring.

"Okay, I will consider it and we will discuss things later. In the meantime, would you like to hire myself and my equipment for a few crowns?"

"Yes, Sir. I am about to take a banknote from an inside pocket, not the pistol", I assured as I reached into my jacket.

The farmer looked very alarmed.

I removed my wallet, took out a 10000 crown note and gave it to him. He looked pleased and relieved and even smiled.

The farmer, Duncan and the other men transshipped the provisions from the lifeboat to the trailer whilst the women and youngsters, together with Shrigley, myself and other old men slowly wended our way towards the hill and some adit.

It was clear that several trailer loads would be necessary as well of course as unloading at the other end.

It was now 1145 and I fretted about the late November light.

"Do not worry, Darling Husband.", said Arnoldina to the fraught look on my face, "we are in God's hands and this is a new Deliverance."

I turned and smiled to my fellow hiker. I did not think it an appropriate walk or fitting weather to test her obedience!

An ever-admiring Bella graced my Wife's other flank, and Duncan had neither ordered her naked. It was a sunny calm day but cold though clothing did nothing to protect from gamma rays.

It was with such pleasant thoughts and an occasional prayer that we reached the ruins of the old abbey. There was a large home farm with extensive steading immediately to the West across a cobbled lane, and rows of pilgrim cottages, empty out of season, to the South plus a few static caravans, lashed down to concrete footings against the wind. The pilgrim cottages faced the abbey graveyard across another lane set at right-angles to the first.

This lane was a slight acclivity leading to a small, intact Methodist chapel and a large vicarage or rectory of maybe sixteen bedrooms, a building I would ever think of and refer to as the "manse" as I did such dwellings during my Scottish youth.

Behind the manse, and further up the hill the lane entered a sequestered quarry in which grew small deciduous trees beside a large clear pond over which a small waterfall fell. On the far east of this pond a small clear effluent issued from the open adit of an old lead mine and a little up the hill at a different horizon was a coal adit and on from that on the hillside a concrete look-out station of the Second World War.

The geology was as noted different to the Lower Carboniferous plumbiferous limestone facies of, say, Clwyd or Northern England, and utterly different to the Bardsey lithology back in 80V. This stratigraphy was more similar to the Upper Carboniferous transition geology of East Cumberland or South Northumberland as exemplified by the Oakshawford horizon and its supercumbent coals. The Oakshawford coal is, if I remember correctly, the English manifestation of a Scottish cannel coal, whilst the others are bituminous coals of one quality or another. At any event, these are Lower Carboniferous as are the massively-bedded blue limestone strata of Pennine England, Clwyd and the Mendips.

But the physics of 78V is different to that of 80V and the geology of the two universes reflects those distinctions.

I was contemplating this idyllic grove within a paradisial island when Terring appeared beside me and took a reading.

"It is 1% over Congleholme after the blast, and three times ambient here.", Terring told me, "But we may as well live in the buildings as it is 1.76% in the Abbey graveyard, and the dank conditions of a disused mine or any bat-roost are more likely to injure health than being exposed to radiation no worse than that in a granite townhouse."

"Thank you, Professor Terring", I replied, "that is well worth knowing and I shall advise the people accordingly."

I told Arnoldina to arrogate a set of rooms with a kitchen and bathroom within the manse, and shortly thereafter Terring joined us in another room, as did the Heldrews and Jimmy with Jolliffe in a granny flat; and slightly later the Shrigley party and Enoldius elsewhere in the building. Pratley and his wife Jeany chose to accept one of the cottages along the lane, as did Masterton and the Selby family. In Abbeyview Cottage, the Balfours took up residence with their daughter Mildred. Mildred's friend Mary Lane stayed in one of the caravans. Their mutual friend, Max Fortess often visited but slept in the Home Farm as did Ennias Mickawber, Fishy Hotcarp and other single men.

Jason Warble and others of the old Albion staff occupied another pilgrim row cottage.

All the manse bedrooms had a petitioned-off fireplace and also the whole vicarage boasted oil-fired central heating.

Before the manse, on the sunny western side was a lawn and behind a small orchard abutting the hill with some dilapidated sheds and a greenhouse to the rear.

In view of Terring's late radiation assurance it was decided not to store the provisions in mines but rather the dry of the Home Farm steading, where, in fine weather, meals might be prepared, rationed, and communally enjoyed.

It was so like Bardsey, but bigger and more commodious.

On the whole, we avoided empty properties nearer the harbour and this was proved to be wise.

I was surprised to see an electric lighting system. I tried the switch in the bedroom and an LED ceiling bulb of I guess 100W equivalent lit instantly. I switched off. I switched on the three bar electric fire. All three of the 1Kw elements slowly lit cherry-red, but feebly.

Presently there was a knock on the front door.

Arnoldina was still in her hiking strip and she answered the door.

"Good afternoon, Madam. I am Truby Waters, the farmer your Husband met at the moule. I have come to brief him about the electricity, water and other utilities."

"Thank you so much, Sir. You are most considerate. Please have a seat in the kitchen and I shall fetch my Husband, Commadore Dr Charles Charmliss. I am Arnoldina, Dr Mrs Charmliss.

Would you like a glass of cola or sparkling water? I am afraid it is all we have."

"No, Thank you, Mrs Charmliss, but I have brought a bottle of red for your courteous and most generous husband."

The door of the bedroom was open and I overheard this conversation. By the time I came down Waters had set three tumblers from the Welsh dresser and poured three libations. I wished he had not. Arnoldina and I needed something for Communion.

Waters explained that there was a tiny Pelton wheel in a concrete shed on the way to the mine and though rated for 6Kw it only generated 2 or 3 depending on the rains, as it mainly took run-off filtered from the hill. The bulk of the power for the tiny Abbey hamlet came from a wind turbine on the crest of the hill rated at 10Kw but which struggled to yield 6Kw in a brisk breeze. However, there was a battery-rectifier-inverter set next to the turbine shed which stored 150 KwH and provided power continuity given responsible use.

As to the potable water, that came via a galvanised pipe under pressure from a spring half way up the hill and was reliable.

Sewage was by septic tank adjacent to properties.

Only bottle gas was "available" and Waters asked us to economise and likewise the central heating oil.

Interestingly, there was, in Waters' estimation, enough thin coal to sustain a community of forty souls indefinitely if the manpower and means could be found to work it.

In a concrete shed in the orchard behind the Manse, Waters divulged that forty rechargeable AA batteries were on trickle charge. He said ten LED lanterns and torches were here and there, usually without batteries, but when the AA batteries were fitted the lamps were good for three hours, which should prove adequate for access to the moule on foot. The lantern maker said not to use rechargeable batteries, but they had been found to give no special problem and better duration.

There was, due to occlusion by the hill, only a poor television signal.

I walked over to the telly, picked up the phasor, and tried BBC1: No signal. Then GBNews: No signal. The same for Blaze and every other channel I tried. On one channel there was a trace of some Irish transmission in the English language but it tended to falter.

I again checked my mobile: No signal.

"No, there is no cellphone signal, even before the War", confirmed Waters.

I thought "This must be paradise." Of course, I knew from a scientific point of view that it was not, though it was a damned nice place if you were in good health.

"Is there any way we can monitor power production without going down to the turbine shed through the weather?" I asked.

"Yes, there are repeaters in the downstairs pantry. They show wind production, water production and battery charge status. They also display potable water pressure. The potable water comes out of the Corn Well by gravity. It never fails. I will show you", Waters said, meaning the repeaters.

Waters led Arnoldina and I to the pantry and showed us how to read the liquid crystal annunciators.

Arnoldina turned to Waters and asked:-

"Mr Waters, now there are so many of us on the island will you need assistance to plant and harvest crops, or milk cows? My Husband and I will ask the others to help whenever you need us."

"That is very kind of you, Mrs Charmliss, I will bring more paddocks under the plough as long as I have fuel, and when needed I shall plant oats, turnips and potatoes, as well as cabbages and carrots. My own family and I can milk the kine for the foreseeable future. There are sheep, and we can cut their wool for spinning and weaving if you stay here for years."

"Mr Waters", my Wife continued, "I am a qualified physician and nurse. I shall set up a surgery here, and you and your family, as well as others can approach me whenever you need medical support. There is no charge."

"Thank you, Dr Charmliss. You are most generous. For the moment, Mrs Waters and I and our children are healthy, but who knows what this foul and evil War will bring?"

After half an hour Waters said:-

"Well I must let you get on. If you need me walk half-a-mile down the lane towards the moule and you will see a brick farm with blue windows marked 'Rowan Farm' amidst some mature trees. Knock on the door and my Wife will tell you where I am."

"Thank you very much for all your kindness, Sir", said Arnoldina by way of valediction.

We drained our wine and shook hands. Waters mounted his tractor and departed shorewards.

The November sun had passed noon and whilst it lasted Arnoldina and I resolved to check out the mine adits and the plunge pool before the lead mine.

We walked about one hundred metres, maybe a little more, through a most sheltering and sequestered grove of small trees and scrub toward the sound of plashing water.

Presently we arrived at a most lovely clear pool of cool water between mossy banks, shaded by trees and fed not only by a dubious trickle of clear but limonitic mine effluent but a slim, tall waterfall of copious fresh water. Dace and other small fish, maybe bottom-feeding gudgeon, graced the water, the bed of which was of clean cobbles. The cutest quarter-moon of a sandy beach led down from this southern path side.

Arnoldina and I glanced at each other with adolescent smirks, stripped and waded in to our necks. The water I knew must have the chill of late November, but weirdly I was not cold or even shocked. Arnoldina's skin was not of burnished gold as per normal: It was of a bronze tan with no lightening where one may expect clothing to occlude the sun's rays. Then I realised that whilst clothing absorbed infra-red radiation, gamma rays and x-rays ignored fabric and my Wife must be badly scorched by atomic radiation.

"Why are you so red, Charles? Why is your skin pealing. Have you sun-bathed naked?"

I felt sick. I changed the subject.

"Arnoldina, can you swim?"

"No, Charles"

"I will teach you now"

"Yes, Charles", my Wife replied skeptically.

I waded fifteen metres to her east and swam the crawl towards her. I took her in my arms and kissed her.

"Watch me very carefully as I return to where I was."

I taught myself to swim in this fashion in the sunlight of the swimming pool of my Parents' Hampshire nudist club. I was ten. They were RN. Southern Hampshire was all RN in those days and RN half-tracks would pass by on the scorching A3 tarmac, chewing up the metalling, dark blue vehicles emblazoned in white "RN." I watched the adult swimmers carefully and aped them. Presto! I was water-born and never looked back. Once I had the confidence I taught myself the butterfly and the breast-stroke, but I always preferred the crawl.

Arnoldina lunged and crawled. She was safely swimming and reaching me gave me a deep wet kiss. I held her buoyantly and intromitted. Arnoldina groaned in ecstacy.

"Bravo!" shouted another contralto from the shadows, and clapped. I looked to the southern bank and saw against the sun two figures with a basket, dressed for a picnic.

Suddenly, as one, they too disrobed and ran to the water. It was Duncan and Bella.

We splashed each other like children and the women screamed and giggled.

We were water babies and I was deliriously happy, as I knew my Wife and friends to be.

It was late November and the Winter was yet to come. Here on Monk Island there would be the most fickle snow but raging storms and even the occasional hurricane could be expected. I feared that our little though robust craft might be beached and damaged, and I knew that the weakest of our number would succumb to hypothermia if heating oil ran out, unless the strongest cuddled them close to the detriment of long-term community survival.

Hence the need to hew coal and plenish the long-partitioned-off fireplaces.

I went to inspect the coal adit to the south and a few metres uphill of the waterfall.

The adit was still open but the timber lintels of the portal were rotten and part collapsed. There were mounds covered in broom and gorse before the adit on a flat topped half-cone of waste against the hillside. I suspected that the mounds were stockpiles of coal ready for the winter of 1937 when the last last non-clerical fishing and farming folk, except for the Waters family and two or three others of the southern plain had departed for ever.

It would have been around that time that the Church of England and the Methodists would have installed oil-fired heating and rudimentary hydropower for seasonal pilgrims.

I used a mattock to remove some of the overgrowth and my conjecture proved correct, at least for this exploratory exposure. The coal seemed to be as fresh as when dug, except that it was sodden with water. I saved the broom and gorse brash for kindling. If all the volume of these mounds was coal then it was likely that the forty-odd of us, including the Waters family, would have enough to heat one room throughout the worst months.

It seemed to me that re-opening the underground galleries would be highly dangerous unless there were two men at minimum and at least one was a competent mining engineer with hydraulic props and timber baulks. Or with explosives we could dynamite the whole hillside and screen coal from the debris. But these were capitalistical dreams fit only for a civilisation that no longer existed. I left my mattock where it was and returned to the manse to get a wheelbarrow from the orchard. When I arrived back I was filling the barrow when I was surprised to be approached by Ionescu, not in the uniform of a Magonian Commander, but in camo fatigues like mine.

"Good Morning, Commadore", he greeted.

"Good Morning, Commander Ionescu", I replied formally, "have you come out for a constitutional?"

"Well, I suppose in part, Charmliss, but I am very interested in the derelict observation post, pill-boxes and gun emplacements, and their potentials as look-outs or as nuclear shelters."

"That is a very excellent and prescient idea, Eugen", I remarked.

"Thank you, Chuck. Despite what I flatter myself are youthful looks I am even older than yourself, and am fit only to play sentry.", said this very humble and modest man.

"You are fit for many things, Eugen", I assured.

"Eugen, after the War, will you go back to your old professorship?"

"No, Chuck. Younger men are much better than me and deserve the chairs. They know about computers and things. Anyway, I am certain my country is back under Russian occupation and they are not people who favour free speech activists!"

"But what about your family, Eugen, do you not want to die amongst your loved ones?"

"I have no family, Charles. Mother died in 2000 and Father in 2006. I never married. The people of the Albion Hotel, the staff and the residents, are my family, and that is why I deserted the Navy."

Ionescu sat on a rock. As his clothing tensed I noticed he was not carrying his pistol. I still was as I feared that special forces of one side or another could land at any moment and they might not be friendly.

Then to my astonishment the ninety-seven year old male officer burst into tears.

I stooped down beside him and embraced him about his shoulders.

I said:-

"Have a really good cry, Eugen. God knows we all need one. You are truly right. We really are your Family, all forty-five of us. For all we know we may be the last humans on Earth, and for good and evil a new Genesis."

I started to sob myself. I said:-

"You are not a deserter, Eugen, and you most certainly are not a traitor. You have been given a most evil set of alternatives, through no fault of your own, and of those evil choices you have selected the most life-affirming and become a Father of the Spirit though you are not one of the flesh. It is the Spirit that persists though the flesh departs."

"Charles, you are a most saintly man, and your Wife most holy. I do not know the correct response in the Quaker religion. I am a Roman Catholic. What I say is 'Thank you for your Ministry'."

"That is exactly right, Eugen, and it is a great honour for me to console a man of your quality, under God. Now, Eugen, let us go and inspect the old emplacements and you can advise me about their usefulness whether for observation, storage or whatever. I wish I was as good a man as you think I am."

We followed a sheep track to the first of the interesting concrete structures. It appeared to be a reinforced concrete observation post with an overhanging roof like an enormous sun visor but which was possibly intended to shield observers from shrapnel, and would have been just as efficacious against driving rain.

I estimated that we were now about two hundred feet above the sea, but without maps it was difficult to be precise. If that was approximately correct then the horizon would have been at twenty-three miles in the visible western arc. I thought it an excellent observation post though it was only a fifth of the way up the hill. In World War Two it would have given forty minutes notice of the approach of any ship and even today might give enough warning to gather people into hiding if provisions were previously stashed in shelters.

The face of the emplacement was now obscured by ash saplings, broom and gorse and I doubted that it would be readily identified by passing traffic.

"What is your opinion, Commadore?"

"It is an excellent and very well sited post, Commander Ionescu", I replied, "neither too remote, nor conspicuous at or near a skyline, nor likely to be above an ordinary cloudbase. On the other hand, it would be sufficiently above a sea fret for the observation cabins and antennae of capital ships to be visible at distance."

Ionescu had stopped weeping. On the contrary, he was beaming like a schoolboy on a new treehouse adventure.

"Those are sailorly thoughts, Commadore. This shall be my home. I do not wish to live for a thousand years. I wish to die happy here protecting my people."

"You are a very noble man, Commander Ionescu. I wonder what is behind that steel door?"

"I do not know. Mr Warble has brought a hammer and a set of metalworker's tools. I think that Professor Terring has a sledge. When I return to the village [it was hardly a hamlet] I shall ask he or Pratley if I may borrow one.", replied Ionescu.

Knowing Ionescu's habits and his careful diplomacy it was most unlike him to elide an honorific.

"Stay here please Chuck, whilst I go and get my glasses and a flashlight. I will see if any gentleman can lend me tools."

I did as requested. Sure enough a sea fog formed like a ghost in the still, damp, sunny air. After half an hour of my fascinated gaze upon this evolving formation the sprightly Ionescu emerged with Warble and Terring.

"Good Morning, Dr Charmliss, it is good to see you again. I am sorry about what happened at the Albion", remarked Warble.

"Good Morning, Mr Warble", I replied, "that is all right. I was in the wrong, and I apologise to you."

Terring offered no salutation but after switching on his counter remarked:-

"We are down to only 1.25% of the Presidium level here."

Ionescu tried to depress the handle on the steel door. It would not budge. He took the heavy hand hammer that Warble offered him and tapped the resisting lever. It yielded stiffly as if seized in caked grease, which may have been the case. The lock seemed to have been machined from marine brass which had hardly corroded after a hundred years in the cold salt air.

The door opened outwards and so what we really needed was a wrecking bar or better still a five-foot crowbar.

"I will go and see Mr Waters and ask if I can borrow a crowbar", volunteered Warble.

He departed whilst Terring, Ionescu and I huddled together in a corner of the parapet. The fog was having its effect on the air temperature. After all it was almost December and we were lucky there was no storm.

After around seventy-five minutes, Waters and Warble returned up the hill. Waters had a crowbar and Warble a wrecking bar and an LED hand-lantern, the sort that works from non-rechargeable batteries.

Waters offered his crowbar to the doorframe as I held the lock lever down to the maximum angle that we had been able to tap it.

Suddenly the heavy door sprang open. It had proven to be unlocked and was made of half-inch steel, which may have been adequate against shrapnel or small-arms fire.

Warble switched on his lantern and gingerly led the way. Something flew past my head and I ducked instinctually.

"Bats.", remarked Terring, "There must be another entrance, not necessarily big enough for human access."

The concrete walls were saturated and we could hear water dripping into a puddle somewhere, but there was no issue at our feet so presumably the water eventually drained to a winze or stope. Here near the entrance at any event there was concrete flooring and walls.

Ionescu switched on his flashlight torch and shone it down this corridor or gallery I suppose you might style it. It seemed to lead a few metres down to another, lighter, door which was fitted with small wire-reinforced glass lights.

The gallery was about 125 centimetres wide and on the left were hooks where fire precaution sand buckets may have rested. Interestingly, there was also a wind-up telephone which Ionescu tried: It turned freely against the resistance of its magnets and I wondered if a bell might be sounding somewhere habitable below.

We levered the inner door open and found a concrete chamber about four by five metres and another light door offset on the other side with smashed lights through which a cold draft blew.

Terring switched on his machine again and announced:-

"0.3% above ambient. This is no worse than being in Cornwall. You could live here indefinitely."

I thought with amusement of my 80V Wife who hated Cornwall. She would have thought this dripping dungeon infinitely to be preferred.

In the stark light of Warble's lantern we saw some provisions canisters in wooden pallets. The food may have been beans, bully or soup. Some of the cans were intact and others burst and the food long since turned to soil. There was also a pair of Pusser's high-powered binoculars complete with folded tripod, and larger drums of what may have been diesel of which the entire complex stank. There were three or four cases of ammunition, but it would have been unlikely to suit our light foreign weapons.

The potential as a radiation bunker, or even a blast shelter, was obvious. Ionescu was boy-happy. I think he entertained fantasies of this being his new home. He must have found life with the Albion staff tedious, despite his right good will, and theirs.

The usefulness of this gallery would be even greater if and when we broke through that third door. I almost felt like George Herbert, 5th Earl of Carnarvon: "Can you see anything?" to which Carter's alleged reply was "Yes. Fucking wonderful things."

As I have said, Ionescu was even more excited. After the first and second doors were opened, Mr Waters immediately left with his tools to attend his farming duties. We heard his tractor depart from the turning space by the Methodist Chapel about one hundred and fifty feet below. Ionescu said to Terring, Warble and I:-

"I shall tidy this place up and salvage anything useful and hand it to Mrs Charmliss for medical approval and safe-keeping for everyone. I shall air and repair the shelter and lay in emergency provisions for all for seven days after a nuclear attack. I shall move my bedding and kit up here and mount a 24-hour watch. I shall mount and recondition the old binoculars and bring also my own glasses [hand binoculars, he meant] and report any anomaly promptly."

It was an interesting if somewhat breathless prospectus, and I immediately resolved to give him whatever assistance he required, if he consented.

"Would you like me to heave stuff?" I asked.

"Yes please, Commadore", Ionescu agreed.

Then I suggested:-

"If yourself, Professor Terring and Mr Warble agree to crank the telephone handle in shifts I will walk round the village trying to hear any bell that responds. If you permit I will do it now. Give me ten minutes to descend."

"That is a good idea. Thank you, Chuck", the three seemed to accord.

When I got to the "village" I systematically walked around but heard nothing but the gulls and the far sea that was now softly breaking and blowing the fog eastwards.

I then went to the manse to tell Arnoldina to prepare a lunch for four hungry men.

As I entered I said:-

"Loveliness, I am with Terring, Ionescu and Warble at an old lookout about a quarter of a mile up the hill. It is already about 1300 if my watch is right. Please prepare lunch for four men now."

"Yes, My Holy and Beloved Husband. There was an old-fashioned electric bell ringing in the scullery a few minutes ago, Darling. Kindly look into it. There may be refugees at the lifeboat station."

"Yes, My Love. But it may be to do with Ionescu hand cranking a telephone dynamo at the look-out."

Just then Waters unexpectedly arrived back on his tractor.

He entered unceremoniously and announced:-

"The air raid bell in the closet has been ringing. We did not know that it still worked. Get everyone into that bunker of Ionescu's."

We immediately vacated the manse to discover Water's wife Kate and her children Faith and George in an open crop trailer behind his tractor. The family had brought bedding and bags of food and toiletries, and notably two cavies.

"Where were you when the bell was heard?", I enquired.

"In our dining room at Rowan Farm", Waters answered.

"I think you can stand down.", I advised, "I think it was Ionescu testing the alert system in the observation bunker. But I will get my glasses and go up to the crest of the hill to see if there is any activity at Tripant or elsewhere on the mainland."

"Don't bother to climb", said Waters, "I will take you along the old quarry road that faces Tripant harbour, and if you bring binoculars you can check for yourself."

"Excellent", I replied, and went to get my field glasses. I had noted that Water's had taken the precaution, probably at the start of the War, to paint his bright red tractor in blotches of brown and green as an extemporary woodland camouflage.

Waters uncoupled his trailer and I said:-

"Tell your family to deposit their kit in a dry room of the manse. My wife Arnoldina will show them where. Then they will be ready to carry it to the bunker up the hill if we have trouble."

"Thank you, Sir", replied the farmer.

"I am Charles Charmliss, a retired soil scientist and superintendent of police, and my Wife is a Magonian Lieutenant-Colonel, a qualified medical doctor and nurse. I am technically a Magonian naval officer. I suppose we are even more technically deserters."

It occurred to me that Waters was across these details already but I thought it would do no harm to remind him of our experience in case it should become useful.

"Yes, I am Evelyn Truby Waters, farmer and former zinc smelter calcining foreman", replied Truby Waters, proffering his hand which I shook. Waters added, "I do not care about your military antecedents or disloyalties as long as you are honest and industrious contributors to our collective survival."

"I promise that all of us shall be that, Sir", I affirmed.

So the two of us boarded the tractor and bumped over the level road round the North of the island until we arrived at an old quarry that overlooked Tripant across the strait.

I noted several delipidated buildings of concrete blocks with intact galvanised or asbestos rooves and more or less sound Crittall windows which I thought might serve as accommodation or storage.

When Waters parked I lifted my glasses and noted with even greater interest a half-track and a military truck at the tiny port beside the empty lifeboat station. I assumed that the troops would have conjectured that some party had absconded to Monk Island employing the lifeboat to do so.

My heart sank as I further noted the "empty star" markings something thus ☆, the recognition emblem of the Russian Army in this War. The old soviet Red Army had displayed a red star and the WWII American Army a white. The Ghanaians use a black star and several countries a yellow one. But the "empty" star was simply a yellow fimbriation printed on the natural background colour of whatever bore the device, in these cases North European Forest Camouflage.

I turned to Waters and said:-

"The Russians have occupied Lleyn."

Waters remounted his tractor without comment and we returned to the Village.

Arnoldina gave the now seven of us a slap-up meal of frankies with five cans of liberated tomato soup, inevitably shorter commons than would have greeted four men, but very welcome to ravenous folk, who left with heartfelt smiles and handshakes.

The short day was already darkening and Arnoldina and I enjoyed a tepid shower in our warm embraces and turned in.

"The Russians are at Trepant", I advised from my pillow.

Arnoldina received the news sombrely but without comment. She knew a thousand years of Russia very well, and spoke Russian fluently.

I do not wish to be misunderstood.

The pentagram (known heraldically as a mullet) is an Ancient symbol of Satan. Heretics were burnt wearing it. It is a beautiful and mathematically very interesting device. It appears on the arms of many families (it denotes a third son) and the flags of many nations. It betokens intellectual ascendancy. The Three Wise Men followed a Star of Wonder to find the Promise of Christ. As we steal Evil from Satan to make it Good: Why should we not steal the pentagram and make it a safeguard and an ornament?

All men are evil. If the pentagram is a symbol of both America and Russia the peoples thereto are no more evil than anyone else. The Americans have devised many wonders as have the Russians. The latter are a notoriously handsome nation, melding the European and the Oriental. More importantly they are great creatives: In literature, science and the performing arts. Their political tradition is autocratic but like all men their best efforts are emulable.

I hoped and prayed that in their treatment of whomsoever remained of my dejected people they would prove as humane and as forgiving as the Magonians had been in their time, better and more compassionate than either the British or the Germans had proven.

Jimmy, Duncan and Bella were at the manse. Later Mr Waters came in a battered Land Rover. There was no rust on the aluminium of its old bodywork but it had clearly seen better days, its dirty shattered windows held together on the inside with sticky tape against the driving rain. I did not know he possessed vehicles other than his tractor but I noted that this car had a useful power winch on its fore fender.

The four convened in my study and I found light chairs for them and for myself. I think that they wished for neutral ground for negotiating some sort of agreement.

"I ask Mr Waters, please to borrow some of your cattle and breed them on the three paddocks nearest the Home Farm that we may provide milk for the infants and young people, that exist and might follow in our small community. Also that we may breed some of your sheep upon the waste of the high hill to give us milk for cheese and wool to weave", Jimmy craved.

"I shall lend you two tups and fifty ewes to graze Goony Myney and a bull and ten milch cows in one paddock, which should prove adequate initially. I realise that you are destitute. Therefore, in addition to your labour freely given I shall take 25% of the issue by way of compensation.", promised Waters.

"I find that most reasonable, Sir", agreed Jimmy with a pleasant smile.

"I am glad you are pleased, Your Lordship", responded Waters.

"Call me Jimmy, please"

"Goony Myney is a rather amusing name to my English ears", I remarked with my usual lack of address, "Does that extend to the whole of the uncultivated hill, and how did it get that name?"

"In the ancient language of the Welsh the phrase *gwyntog mynydd* or rather *mynydd gwyntog* meant 'windy hill' and 'Goony Myney' is an Anglicised rendition. The word 'Goony' may be influenced by the Cornish 'Goon' meaning 'moorland'. The servicemen of the last War had ruder names for it", clarified Waters helpfully.

I rose to pour my guests a very parsimonious measure of liberated cognac and placed a pitcher of tap water from the holy well before them.

Duncan entered the discussions:-

"My Wife and I would like to plant three of the fields north of the village that you now hold as ungrazed pasture for potatoes, turnips and oats in order to supply our people over the winter and the spring."

Waters looked to Duncan with a scowl:-

"I object to the word 'now'. I hold the freehold of all Monk Island in fee entail except for tiny pockets ceded to Trinity House, the Admiralty or the Church. The RSPB and the NT are tenants and they pay. Withdraw your presumption."

"I do beg your pardon, Mr Waters, I misspoke. I withdraw my presumption with deep apologies", groveled poor Duncan.

This appeared to mollify Waters.

Just then Arnoldina came in and standing asked Waters:-

"What would you like for lunch, Mr Waters? I am afraid it will be vegetarian."

I noted that Arnoldina said "vegetarian" rather than "vegan."

"Oh, that is most kind of you, Dr Mrs Charmliss, I will leave it totally to your discretion. Please do not make anything splendid. I will content myself with short commons as their Lordships enjoy. There is a war on of course."

Arnoldina left to prepare the food.

Waters continued:-

"You may borrow my tractor, plough and seed potatoes, as well as seed grain. You must source turnips for yourselves. Realistically, you are too late for a winter harvest, but you may get a small spring yield. I have no fertiliser but the fields have not been tilled since the War:- I mean the Second World War. Again I shall take twenty-five percent by weight."

I took a journalist's notebook from a tit pocket of my fatigues and a black biro. I remarked:-

"Thank you, Mr Waters. You are most generous. If we were to forage the waysides or the wastes of Goony Myney could we gather fruits or roots that were nutritious and safe to eat?"

"At the field margins and hedgerows you may find various Allia at this season including the three cornered garlic betrayed in calm weather by its smell, as also sea beet and wintercress. From the hill you may pick bracken fronds that must be dried and pickled. They will stink your house out. But the season is May, and the tough fronds are difficult. Good King Henry is available here and there. On the coast there is rock samphire and inland wild carrot. Burdock and dandelion roots are very nutritious but may have to be roasted as they are tough. Again, the hill is good for thistles all of which can be eaten once the spines have been stripped, and nettles which are a good salad once they have been steeped to remove irritant acids.

I have no time to forage, but my daughter Faith, though only fourteen is an expert, and she can guide you to the best places.

Rabbits and puffins are plentiful if you are prepared to kill them. If you can acquire rifles the rabbits can be shot, and the puffins trapped with nets."

I made running notes and when Waters finished I replied:-

"Thank you, Mr Waters. I do not think we would survive the winter without your generous help and advice."

Presently Arnoldina came in with five steaming bowls of creamed rice garnished with golden syrup and a little salt. She went away and returning distributed five 500ml bottles of cider to me and our guests. I found the cider as welcome as the hot rice.

Though the conversation was brief I think we had the beginnings of a modus vivendi that would tide us over at least until the summer of 2037 as long as there was no great influx or hostile raiding.

Later, when our guests had gone, I asked Arnoldina where she had precured this real and hungrily devoured treat. She said she had found a 5kg catering can of creamed rice and the syrup in the rectory pantry, possibly for the entertainment of pilgrims.

Pratley was installed in one of the pilgrim cottages a few doors down from the Balfours. Arnoldina had visited and Jeany gave Arnoldina the cider which Pratley had liberated from the Sainsbury's.

The next morning, very early about 0530, Pratley called by knocking on the manse door. No-one had yet been able to raise a cellphone signal. Terring was not with him because Terring, besides assisting Ionescu, had found a short-wave radio. It was analogue and he could not detect any transmission using it, but had spent hours tampering with it. It seemed impossible unless he could steal a digital short-wave radio from the Mainland of Great Britain.

It was raining heavily.

"Commadore, we will take the boat and forage today." said Pratley peremptorily.

We had all lapsed into the wartime euphemisms of "forage" to mean theft, and "liberation" to mean stealing.

"You are not in command here, Pratley, or indeed anywhere else. We are a free republic of equals and I decide what *I* am going to do today", I responded.

"Well, I am sorry you feel that way, Charles. There is no need to be defensive because as I said when we first met neither of us have ought to defend. Jeany and I love you, and we both greatly admire Arnoldina. I am sure that your wife's dispensary would greatly benefit from any medicines or surgical equipment we might steal, whilst the rightful owners, most probably dead, are in no position to benefit of it."

"We must see that our women successfully bear, and that the young grow and prosper. Unfit and unwanted we are the New Patriarchs, respected friend", concluded the professor.

I saw the sense of Pratley's words, and respected his temperance.

"You are right, Sir. I am sorry I spoke so offensively. I shall get my Wife and our car keys and we shall come."

Pratley grasped my arm as he had on the moule at Tripant and gazed into my eyes with his sad and briming stare.

"Thank you, Commadore. Terring and Enoldius will accompany us in Arnoldina's vehicle if that is okay. Please permit your Wife to drive her car. I shall drive my stolen Range Rover and Mr Miggin's will follow in his white van in case we get lucky. I will try to steal Semtex and automatic weapons and Enoldius will literally go for gold. There are three chemists and two surgeries and a cottage hospital in Restingheuse [say 'Rest-ing-hughs': apparently] and it would be silly to go further if it is not necessary.", Pratley briefed as he stood in the blue dawn of the Welsh rain.

Arnoldina and I put on our breathable waterproofs and hiking boots and picked up our car keys and pistols. It was clear that Pratley was an excellent exponent of espionage. He clearly had a real talent for it, unlike either Arnoldina or myself.

"Yesterday Waters and I saw two Russian convoy in the harbour of Tripant. I do not know whether they are still there", I commented.

Pratley stood in the rain and thought for a few seconds.

"Are you feeling athletic, Chuck?"

"Yes??"

"Get your glasses. We will march to the top of the hill via Eugen's place and recruit him and his binoculars. We will scan Tripant and the visible countryside for signs of potential hostiles. In the worst case we will have to sail direct to Restingheuse harbour, steal cars and work from there. Arnoldina can stay here and make us flasks of hot chocolate to take aboard."

"That's capital, Earnest", I replied, "let's go!"

There was a track all the way to the summit of Goony Myney presumably beaten by pilgraims and sheep. At the summit there was a trig post and Pratley, Ionescu and I leant against it as we scanned the Mainland.

The rain was moderating and sunshine was trying to break through but we kept our hoods up, as much to protect our lenses as our heads.

I saw a small gray township at the head of a sandy bay on the south side of the Lleyn about three miles from Tripant and maybe seven statute miles from this vantage. It seemed to be much the same as Stonehaven, and if so would have had a peacetime population of six or seven thousand I supposed.

"What is that settlement?", I asked Pratley, pointing.

"That is Restingheuse. It has the pharmacies I spoke of and two Asian jewelers believe it or not. It also has a gunsmith. He may have rifles, not automatic, and more likely 9mm ammunition for our pistols. If I can steal shotguns and cartridges we can hunt rabbits.", continued Pratley ever the optimist.

There was no sign of the Russian transport in Tripant harbour or life or light anywhere.

We turned and scanned the western seas. There was no ship or life of any kind in sight. What I surmised to be the distant Irish coast was blue with rain and enlivened by no light, not even navigation bouys. I could not expect regular lighthouses as we were now beyond astronomical dawn. I know that the Monk Island light scanned at night strongly enough to shine through our bedroom window.

"We will go to Tripant and hope our cars are still there", determined Pratley.

On arrival at Tripant the six of us moored the lifeboat to the moule and climbed the cliff to the old RNAS hangers.

Our cars, including the stolen Range Rover, were still there but interestingly someone else had removed the farming equipment including the tractors.

"Actually, I think we can leave Dina's car", said Pratley, "and Dina can drive the liberated Range Rover whilst the rest of us pile into mine."

I was relieved to hear this as I did not want Arnoldina's new Cullinan so much as scratched.

Pratley spread a 25000 OS map on his car bonnet [hood] and pronounced:-

"Okay, follow me and set this into your GPS: MU7 5GF. It is the Town Square car park in Restingheuse. If you sight a hostile who appears to shoot or be otherwise over-interested in us, sound four horn blasts, make for the Tripant Maule at good but safe speed and board the lifeboat without further ado."

We went to our respective cars: Arnoldina and I to the "liberated" Range Rover; Mr Miggins to his van; and Terring, Enoldius and Pratley to Pratley's Land Rover.

Restingheuse was a mere three and a half miles and I wondered how we had missed it on our trip from Manceuvering. We arrived at the Town Square car park without incident and there were a surprising number of shops but little sign of looting. We had seen no-one and no transport since leaving Monk Island. Once we turned our engines off the atmosphere was very ghostly. Terring switched on and took a reading.

"3%", Terring muttered perfunctorily.

"Okay, the Michael's of Hatton chemists shop is down Eggborough Street over there, Arnoldina and Charles, and the Boots just beyond it down Codd's Row. Do your damnedest and if there is time we will raid the hospital for any remaining instruments. Enoldius and I will raid the gunsmiths and jewellers. Arthur [Miggins], go and do the Tesco at MU7 6ER", specified Pratley, and continued:-

"We reconvene here at 1145 hours. If someone has not arrived by 1215 we travel in convoy to Tripant Maule for 1300, load the boat, and leaving the cars in the quarry, depart for the island. Any questions?"

"Can Mr Miggins get a case of cider and a case of vodka", I asked for some reason. I have had bouts of incipient alcoholism since boyhood. Maybe the stress was getting to me again.

"Will do.", replied Miggins, "Also there is a seed merchants by the Tesco and I will raid it for oat grain and root seeds."

"Very good thinking, Sir!" Pratley congratulated him.

Arnoldina drove me in the stolen Range Rover to Michael's of Hatton and I used a fireman's axe to break through the plate glass. It was in darkness and I could not find the switch. Arnoldina switched on her flashlight and we made our way to the stockroom. I made to break down the door but Arnoldina arrested my forearm:-

"It might be unlocked, Charles", she said. And when my Wife tried the door handle it opened without difficulty.

To me it was a treasure trove. To Arnoldina's expert and selective eyes it was a resource.

"Bring that, that and that. And get the Potassium Iodide", said my Wife, pointing at cartons and crates that could literally have contained anything as far as I was concerned.

"We need headlamps, but that reminds me, we will liberate some AA and AAA cells when we come back", I remarked.

"Yes, Sir", said Arnoldina.

We stacked the loot in the Range Rover and returned for the batteries, the band aid and bandages; and also the contents of the refrigerator including insulin, lidocaine and anti-gloucomics.

"Get the Isodur before we leave, and anything else you can carry", ordered Arnoldina.

"Yes, Madam"

After stacking this we noticed a large outdoors and mountaineering shop next door. I forced an entry. We quickly stripped the shelves of anything breathable and waterproof: Jackets, rain-trousers, bivvy bags, hiking boots and briskly piled them into the Range Rover, not forgetting all the headlamps we could find. They also stocked alkaline dry cells and we lifted them and, stealing the supply of bags-for-life, packed them and the headlamps.

"What is the time, Arnoldina?"

"1120"

"Right, let's hit Boot's and then back to the rendezvous", I ordered.

"Yes, Sir"

We wasted three minutes trying to find Codd's Row.

I backed the Range Rover through the plate glass window which crazed to safety cuboids which sagged but hung in sheets upon their plastic substrate. I removed this debris with my axe.

Arnoldina ran for the strongroom, and I followed.

I laboured at the door, but it would not budge. Then my Wife noticed that there was an emergency intercom by the door and its emergency warning light was glowing red.

Arnoldina pressed a button and shouted:-

"Hello, anyone there?"

And released.

No response.

"Hello, anyone there? I am a Magonian policeman. We have come to take you to a place of safety. We also need your medicines to treat people damaged by radiation", I added, shouting into the speaker-microphone.

The door unlatched electronically and we were confronted by a chubby man of around forty pointing an old Webley service revolver at us. He was accompanied by two women, about 40 and 25. They were all wearing white coats and were of South Asian race.

"Please put your gun away, Sir", I requested, "my Wife and I wish to take you to an island where you will be safe. If you stay here the Russians will kill you and ill-treat your ladies. If you are lucky they will simply leave you in peace to die of radiation sickness. We want you to help us load medicines into our car for our people before we go."

"Do you have chloroform or diamorphine, Sir", asked Arnoldina.

"I cannot say, Madam", replied the male.

"Look, we have no time to argue. If you refuse to co-operate Mr Pratley will shoot you out of hand. Put your gun down and help us load.", I said.

Reluctantly, the man pocketed his old gun and said something to the women, perhaps in Hindi or Urdu which I was told are mutually-intelligible. Neither my Wife nor I spoke it.

Then the three lifted boxes and made to take them to the car. Arnoldina also lifted strategically-chosen drugs and followed them. I took out my Wrortlemonger and Bierce.

When the man had deposited his load I said:-

"Take out your gun and throw it to my feet."

He did so.

I picked up the weapon and pocketed it.

"Now the three of you, get in the car", I ordered the South Asians.

I joined them on the central bank of bucket seats of the 7-seater SUV, having first buried them under cartons of drugs and re-distributed the cold goods to the front passenger seat.

We were crammed full. Only Arnoldina, in the driver's seat, was relatively unencumbered.

By the time we reached the Town Square it was 1148.

The Miggins and Pratley parties were already there and fully-loaded.

Only Pratley left a vehicle and came over to me. I wound the window down.

"What's with the wogs, Charmliss?" asked the Professor.

"My Wife liberated them from the Cash Chemist's strongroom", I declared.

"Kill them"

"No, Sir. They have co-operated and I promised to take them to a place of safety", I answered.

"Follow me, we will hit the hospital on the way back. I want only Arnoldina and I, to identify and forage essential instruments", said Pratley without emotion.

"Yes, Sir" I replied.

We stopped for a mere ten minutes and Arnoldina returned carrying armfuls of clean non-offensive waste bags stuffed with scalpels and forceps in boxes as well as other portable paraphernalia and further strops and bandages. Pratley appeared to be carrying an ophthalmoscope and an electronic microbalance.

The pair dumped these in Pratley's Land Rover and we set off in convoy.

We had hardly driven a mile when the narrow road ahead was blocked by a small personnel carrier with the Russian "empty star." Our three vehicles halted and we wound down our windows.

Pratley was leading but as far as I knew he did not speak Russian.

We were between Pratley and Miggins, who was of course thus in the rear.

An officer in Russian uniform approached us whilst some young soldiers fixed us with automatic rifles.

As remarked earlier, Arnoldina spoke fluent Russian and lent out of her window and shouted:-

"господин, господин"

This, in Roman phonetic is "Gospodin, Gospodin":- "My Lord!, My Lord!" which I understand, rightly or wrongly, to be a very polite form of address.

The officer approached her, and I said:-

"Tell him we are taking essential medicines to Russian detachments in the Lleyn and the others are transporting valuable contraband for bribing Irish smugglers. And that we work out of Monk Island."

Arnoldina imparted this information in rapid Russian.

The officer turned to me impassively and said:-

"Papers" in English.

I proffered my British passport, the same as I had left 80V with.

The officer looked at it skeptically, glancing up to my eyes several times, presumably doubtful of the photograph.

The man said something.

"You are a hostile?", Arnoldina translated.

"No, Sir. I am a British native and bear no ill-will: I co-operate."

Arnoldina relayed this to the officer.

Then in perfect English this officer said to me:-

"Apply for papers as soon as possible"

"Yes, Sir"

Then he said something into a chest-radio and listened for replies.

"I have ordered a cutter to intercept your lifeboat docked at Tripant. Six men will help you transfer goods to it and the cutter. You will then be assisted to unload at the island", continued the officer in English.

"Thank you, Sir. I am most grateful for your help", I replied.

The Russian signaled his troops to move the personnel carrier aside and we slowly processed to Tripant, the Russian vehicle following at a safe distance.

On arrival at Tripant harbour we found the Russian cutter moored beside our lifeboat with its crew of six occupying the later. The sailors came ashore onto the moule as we drove up.

The officer and four men climbed out of their carrier which they parked behind us, preventing escape. They then unloaded the vehicles *for us*, splitting between the lifeboat and the cutter. I ordered the three Indians to board the lifeboat and sit below. They did. The rest of us assisted the Russians to trans-ship.

At the conclusion the Russian officer said:-

"You, the lady and the men. Park your cars in the quarry, leave the keys in the ignitions, and board your boat. Follow the cutter to the island quay."

"Yes, Sir. Thank you again for all your help, Sir.", I grovelled.

For the sake of politeness, Arnoldina translated my words into Russian.

The officer bowed Germanically.

We obeyed implicitly.

We crossed the mild sea without mishap. No-one had eaten. The sea was choppier than when we first came and held the funeral of the farmer Abel Lloyd, but no-one was seasick.

At the moule on the south shore of Monk Island the Russians helped us unload the stores and then motored away.

We secured the lifeboat and went to borrow Mr Waters' tractor and trailer. We were lucky. A vespertinal breeze was starting to pucker the waves and rain was threatening. We rode back in Mr Waters' battered Land Rover and his son George drove the tractor with attached trailer. We unloaded the goods and took it to the Home Farm steading in two shifts, the latter by lantern light, as the lighthouse scanned mesmerically through the darkling, developing fog. Suddenly, the fog horn started to sound, which startled me.

"The refrigerated goods must go in the Home Farm fridge immediately", Arnoldina reminded me.

"Why not the fridge in the manse?" I asked.

"Three reasons: The manse pharmacy fridges are full. If any machine breaks down and all the insulin and latanoprost is in it we lose all these essentials. Also if one building is bombed and the other survives we still have life-saving and sight-saving resources, at least for the winter."

"You are so intelligent, Arnoldina, my Love. I wish I was like you."

"I know I am intelligent. But you do not wish you were like me. I am a woman, and it is much better to be eighty-four and male rather than nine hundred and seventy-six and female.", remarked Arnoldina reverting to her cybernetic mode.

We reached the Home Farm steading which had to function as a warehouse until a proper audit could be done on the warm goods in daylight.

Pratley strode up to Arnoldina and I with a face like thunder, the more lurid for the shadows of the LED lanternlight. I thought he was going to bollock me for letting the three Asians live.

"Fucking bastard, fuck…I was going to raid a quarry and liberate its Semtex just round the corner from where those bastards stopped us.", complained our frustrated professor.

"Never mind, Earnest", I consoled, "some other time, perhaps. Anyway, we should be grateful they let us live", I added pointedly.

"Do you think my Wife deserves thanks for mollifying armed men in their own language, and for expertly procuring vital medicines?", I added, turning the knife.

"Of course she does", conceded Pratley, turning to the Oriental he despised. "Thank you, Lieutenant-Colonel Dr Mrs Charmliss for all your kindly and successful strivings."

I do not know whether Pratley more greatly valued kindness or success: You decide.

"Thank you for your guidance, Professor Pratley", replied Arnoldina, making it sound almost like an insult.

Pratley flounced off to his cottage, his dinner and his grateful wife.

"Have a Venus Bar, Charles. Keep your sugar up. I will have one myself."

"Thank you, My Love. Let's go home with our lantern, romantically eating our chocolate as we pass the spooky graveyard!" I teased.

The day dawned bright but overcast. There had been a ninety mph hurricane during the night. They are common on the North Wales coast in winter, and structures are built for them.

Truby Waters turned up outside the manse on his tractor towing a trailer full of wet dimension timber. I saw that there was mostly deal in 100 by 100 by 2400 lengths but also a admixture of what seemed to be American Oak, a fine structural timber in 200 by 200 by 4800 baulks.

"Good Morning, Chuck", said Waters, "offload this into the steading and gather some men and I'll take them to the harbour, there is plenty."

"Yes, thank you Mr Waters, and Good Morning"

We rode two hundred metres to the Home Farm barns, and between ourselves and the tractor's power winch stacked the load.

There was still intermittent driving light rain. Waters and I went from cottage to cottage canvassing male volunteers with promises of a share of what they handled. Some men were reluctant but came in their storm jackets and waterproof trousers. Pratley, Shrigley and Terring were all with me, as was Mr Miggins and Ennias Mickawber, for once not in his drafty Roman uniform. We boarded the trailer and were at the tiny island harbour within minutes. Mrs Waters and her son George were already there in the lashing spray and rain.

We all dismounted and I fell to my knees in a puddle and prayed:-

Dear God,
Thank you for the Power of Your Creation and for
Turning Evil to Good Effect
Thank you for this most timely
Gift of Wood
God teach us to Build and not to Burn
Give us Strength, I beg You

I Crossed myself, rose and joined the other men to help them load. Mr Waters took one third of the timber to his own premises and the Fellowship took the rest. Individuals were allowed to appropriate up to half of what they gathered and some men did though Enoldius and I forewent. Mrs Waters worked at least as hard and as effectively as any man. Tom Balfour and Eugen were conspicuous by their absence, though of course Eugen was in his look-out though he may have neglected to see the flotsam because of sleeping. Certainly, he did not spin the bell, or if he did Arnoldina did not hear him.

Whatever the facts, it was clear that I would have to organise a relief roster for him.

I prayed again as I worked:-

My Beloved Lord Jesus Christ
I am most sorry for my callous neglect of
My Darling Comrade Commander Eugen Ionescu
Please make me find him two reliable and responsible
Fellow Watchers in Warning for our Tiny Fellowship.
So help me.
Sir, I do not know the occasion of this Gift
Please Comfort and Preserve the men and women of
The good ship that has Lost or is the Loss
In Your Holy Name.

I hoped, as was likely, that this was mere deck cargo, washed away by the late storm, but of course I knew that the whole ship may have been sunk, whether by the force of nature or the malice of men.

I saw that there were also three forty-foot containers on the shore, washed high, two seemingly intact and one very battered.

We moved and distributed the wood in five shifts, and by the time we had cleared the beach it was too dark to investigate the containers.

Mrs Waters had kept tally and we had gathered 87 lengths of 100 by 100 beams totalling 2.088 cubic metres; and 42 lengths of 200 by 200 totalling 8.064 cubic metres.

The team of us agreed to reconvene on the morrow at 0830 to address the problem of the containers, if the weather was operable.

Fortunately, the new day dawned sunny with a gentle breeze from the South. Mr Waters turned up with tractor and trailer which bore a steel contraption which proved to be a hydraulic cable cutter powered by the tractor. This made short work of the security seals on all three containers.

We opened the container doors on the two intact boxes, but had problems with the damaged container because the doors had jammed.

The first intact container seemed to be filled with cardboard boxes with various labels and logos on them. The sizes appeared to be pretty standard: 60*60*60 cms and 60*60*120 cms.

Terring did a quick calculation and estimated that if the whole content was such boxes then we could expect 175 such boxes.

We held a quick confab in the field and decided to load all the boxes and deliver five to every residence on the island, whilst a ration of five and any superfluous would go to the Waters Family. The families would open their boxes and identify the contents. Later, the adults of the island would convene in the "War Room" to allocate common property and organise beneficial exchanges. Clearly, and by way of illustration, Arnoldina would demand and almost certainly be given all pharmaceutical or medical equipment, whilst the agriculturalists would receive boxes of seed, etcetera.

After all, it was Christmas!

The next day, at 0900, the 34 adults of our scratch Fellowship convened in the "War Room." Arnoldina had deputed Ananta Anand to babysit the eleven teens, children and infants in the ground floor surgery and ward area with a promise that the Patels and Arnoldina would settle the distribution of medicines later. Ananta had her work cut out, especially as swapping and haggling was expected to extend for three to four hours.

Early on Terring's announcement that he had a case of ladies' Christmas themed lingerie caused universal mirth, but this was quickly trumped by Ionescu, a ninety-seven year old male virgin [all were kind enough to accept his word for it], boasting a case of blow-up latex dolls. Being the kind of man I am, I proposed that Terring and Ionescu should collaborate to make the dolls decent.

Fortuitously, Arnoldina and I had been delivered a box of assorted packet-of-three condoms, which elicited predictable pleasantries, and which Arnoldina seized immediately for the pharmacy.

It was clear that these, and a case of fancy paper tissues, had been a consignment to the same Glasgow sex shop, a fact confirmed by the identical dispatch labelling.

Bunny pointed out that the dolls could be tailored to produce waterproof capes and awnings, handy in a Welsh winter whilst any lingerie not useful as underwear could be used to stuff quilts if bedsheets could be found.

The Heldrews were promptly able to submit four boxes of blankets and bedsheets of Indian manufacture for the common stock and Bunny and Jeany promised to collaborate to make quilts, more properly I suppose described as duvets.

Masterton had received a case of chocolate bars and generously distributed them as Christmas gifts for Ananta and the children, taking the cardboard box bodily down stairs for Ananta to distribute. This of course Masterton had carried to the building with him, but most packages had been left at the dwellings where they were delivered for later pickup and re-assignment, handwritten paper chits sufficing as promises. Most importantly several cases of seeds and other agri-related materials had been identified or surmised and the Heroncourt-Heldrews and the Waters Family assigned these amongst themselves.

The exchanges dragged on until 1400 when Ananta was able gratefully to surrender several very sleepy and queasy children.

Three boxes of very light 3kW motor-generator sets had materialised but the only petrol on the island was in the tank of Waters' battered Land Rover since his tractor used diesel of which Waters had an adequate reserve.

Pratley came to me as we adjourned and proposed:-

"Chuck, what do say you if Shrigley, Terring and we take the boat to the mainland when the weather is calm and drain the tanks of our cars. I have got a length of neoprene pipe, a knife, an axe and we have liberated three large cases of fuel cans. I don't see why the Russians should have it when we have got generators."

"It sounds good to me", I agreed.

"Where is the NT lawnmower and its fuel kept?", I asked.

"That is a good question. Chuck. When you have a minute, hunt it."

"Yes, Earnest"

The morrow rained. Enoldius, myself, Pratley, Shrigley and Terring put on our rain clothes and set off to empty the second intact container. Again Waters helped us with his tractor and trailer, and after five shifts we had relocated another 175 or so cardboard packages together with a few spools of enameled wire and eight reinforced plastic crates of what we guessed to be arms or explosives. We relocated the bulk of this kit to the Methodist church next to the manse, but the putative explosives we left in a derelict barn on the way from the village to the Northern quarry. We also identified five boxes of what we thought might be digital radios or short-wave radios which Terring carefully set aside in case he could rig them to receive news from the outside world, if an outside world existed.

The next day was also rainy and windy, but Pratley and I went with a crowbar to investigate the putative explosives and weapons whilst Terring stayed at home to work on the radios.

We broke open one case disappointingly to discover New Year's Day fireworks.

I was about to turn my attention to another crate when Pratley said:-

"Hold on a minute, Chuck"

He pulled out the fireworks and threw them into the rain to reveal a solid bed of Semtex packed into 500 gram blocks separated in polythene wrappers. A bonanza, certainly for miners. Taking the crowbar to a suspiciously heavy crate, Pratey broke it open. Absurdly, the top of the contents was a mass of tiny teddy bears of the kind that people dangle from car mirrors, or award to children at fairgrounds. Pratley swept them out with the backs of his hands to disclose 48 boxes of Wrortlemonger and Bierce 9mm semi-automatic pistols, exactly the same model as those that Treagh had gifted to Arnoldina and I.

Pratley broke a box to see if the pistols had live magazines fitted. The specimen did not.

We broke a third heavy box which was filled with unmilled rice in which we found embedded 200 9mm clips of fifteen to fit the pistols.

Pratley remarked:-

"We must gift a pistol and four clips to each of the 21 male adults whether he is armed or not and cover the remainder with hay bales here in the dry. Also, there must be compulsory pistol training for all adults. I would be honoured if your wife would teach mine.", stated Pratley.

"Yes, Professor Pratley", I assented, rather formally.

I took the crowbar and levered open the remaining two crates. The first contained three Muebler 9mm sub-machineguns of the exact type that Goodleague had used when she shot at me in, ironically of all places, that furniture store on the Hodgate.

The final box contained 90 9mm clips to fit the Mueblers.

"We will each have a Muebler and fifteen clips, and the third we will give to Ionescu because he is isolated and may be assaulted by SFs or paratroopers", said Pratley.

"That is wise and most considerate, Earnest", I acceded.

"Those are qualities that better describe you, Charles", replied the Professor.

A warm, sunny winter's day dawned with a very slight breeze. There was no urgent business and I thought it would be pleasant to take Arnoldina to the plunge pool where we had picnicked with the Heldrews and resume her swimming lessons. We would swim naked of course and delight in every moment!

We marched up the little valley with alacrity and stripped gleefully. The water was cold but bracing and with our exercise we became acclimatised. I had Arnoldina swim to me practicing her breaststroke. The style was aptly called for her lovely dugs seemed to swirl charmingly as she approached, as if they had a mind of their own, whilst her rounded and womanly bottom spread and clenched behind her.

As she arrived she stood on the shallow sandy pond bed and wrapped her arms about me.

Arnoldina calmly and chastely said:-

"Charles, I am pregnant"

My heart lept. I did not know what to say. I had yearned for this moment, this message, for seventy years and in two universes. To hear it of my woman, either woman, knowing that in 80V it was impossible and here in 78V highly improbable. But for Jesus Christ nothing is truly impossible.

A gentle squall swept the bare trees and ruffled the water surface as the waterfall maintained its steady drone.

I clasped my Wife to my body and rocked her to and fro. I kissed her abandonedly.

"Arnoldina, Thank you. I love you desperately and I long to meet our son or daughter and love him and feed and teach him, and above all to guide his Immortal Spirit in freedom."

Arnoldina eased her grasp and stepping back smiled tenderly.

Then she resumed her cuddle as the chill water swirled around our legs and fondled our private parts with its cold caress.

I voiced what I thought:-

My Darling Lord Jesus Christ,
My Only Lord and King,
Thank you.
I cannot choose the words I need.
Make me the very best of fathers
Excepting only Your Own.
Make me loving, tender, smiling and protective
Respecting my Child. Never raising my voice.

Never striking.
Just loving, teaching, supporting and encouraging
Delighting in his every tentative step and essay.
So Help me Christ.

So help us Christ

Echoed Arnoldina.
Then I said:-

Dear Jesus,
Please aid and comfort my good Wife
Through the Pain and Joy of Pregnancy
And the Supreme and Blissful Agony
Of Childbirth.
Let nothing perturb the gestation
Or the Sound Health of Our Child
Make me a good comforter
And attentive always.
Please help her Jesus.

Please help us Jesus

Responded Arnoldina.
Then Arnoldina prayed:-

My God,
King of Creators and Sure Artificer
I love you.
I love my Husband.
I loved his prior, now at your Holy Hand.
I love my Son. I know not where he is.
I hope and pray him safe in this global conflict.
He has survived so much with Perfect Fortitude.
Now I beg you
Support and Console my coming Son or Daughter
That My Charles longed to hold
During a Long and Happy Life
Free of Sin and Frustration.
So help Him or Her, My Lord God

Help Him or Her, My Lord God

I echoed.

We held hands as we kissed, standing in the bubbling, sedately streaming pool.

"How long, Arnoldina?"

"This is 78V. Four months is normal for a human."

"Thank you, Arnoldina. He will be an April baby, like his father. It is getting chilly. Let us dress and return home.", I suggested.

The gutter was backing up. A conduit that normally had to convey the copious discharge of a cave was now threatening to overspill in the torrential rain and flood the cottages. Cobble sized shards of limestone had swept down and dammed the little ditch, cemented by the mud of the fields.

I took a mattock from one of the sheds. I was fully dressed in one of my waterproofing-steeped hiking suits, complete with pistol in case of hostile paratroopers or other insertions. But I was soaked to the skin. The rain was warm and there was the promise of a clearance to sunshine.

I swung at the rubble in the ditch though was making but a slow impression, what with my bad shoulder, my advanced age and all.

I knocked on Bunny's door, the nearest.

"Is Thomas in?" I asked.

Bunny turned to the interior and hollered:-

"Tom, It's Commadore Charmliss."

Thomas Balfour presented at the threshold. I said:-

"Mr Balfour, can you please help me clear the ditch. It may overflow and flood your house."

Always a quiet and passive man, rather than taciturn or sullen, Balfour expressionlessly and without greeting left his abode and followed me the few metres to the locus of the problem.

He stood looking at the blockage in a vacant taurine manner.

"Get a pick or mattock and clear the debris three metres downstream from where I am working, please, Mr Balfour."

"Call me Tom", Balfour at last remarked almost like a cowboy at a stand-off in a corny old film.

The rain was now a fine drizzle in the sunshine and a double rainbow formed over the abbey ruins. The ditch torrent was unabated.

For some reason, probably simple desperation, or anger at the man's dumb insolence, I took out my pistol and pointed it at Balfour.

To my surprise, he did not turn away to get a spade, or grovel, attempt resistance, or even turn sideways to minimise the target area. He turned full frontal with his hands at his side and cocked his head back.

Suddenly a tiger cat of hell materialised.

"You coward! You absolute yellow bastard!", Bunny Balfour screamed in my face as I held the pistol lowered beside me. "Threatening an unarmed man, my Holy Husband with death! How dare you! How fucking dare you! You arrogant bastard. You think you are so superior!"

Thomas pushed between his wife and myself and took her by the shoulders.

"Don't, My Dearest. He is not worth it. Please go home and cook the girls their dinner. I will deal with him. I will do as he says", said Thomas to his wife with calm tenderness.

"No, you fucking won't. He can do it himself. He is very good at beating shit out of women and threatening unarmed men. He has not got the guts to fight you man-to-man. He is a fucking coward."

I put my pistol back in its protective shoulder holster and removed my sodden jacket and throwing it to the ground threw the weapon on top of it. The safety catch was on throughout but neither Balfour nor his wife knew that.

I think Balfour thought we were about to settle with fisticuffs because he started to remove his own jacket.

Then to the open mouthed astonishments of my adversaries I removed my trousers and flung them aside also.

I was now standing bollock naked in the lane, like a drowned rat, clad only in plimsolls.

There was a large weather-worn block of ashlar near, perhaps a mounting block in long-gone centuries, and I pointed at it.

"Go and sit there", I ordered Bunny.

She complied.

I lay awkwardly across her lap, backside skyward, and supported myself by grasping the edge of the block.

"What now, Charmliss?!" the woman asked.

"Madam, I have committed the sins of pride and wrath threatening your Holy Husband with a lethal device whilst he was not armed. Please pray for me."

My Most Sacred Saviour,
commenced this most devout prostitute
Teach this arrogant, cowardly, hypocritical, sadistic, bully bastard fucker, sorry my Lord for my profanities, I mean *person*, the real meanings of courage, kindness and humility as exampled by my Holy Husband Thomas consecrated by You.

My Holy and only Lord and King Jesus Christ,
I prayed
Please console Mr Thomas Balfour and his good wife and family whom I most grievously insulted today. Please continue to grant them the love and protection of Your Holy Spirit and the souls of one another, and cleanse me of my foul minacity born of pride, fear and anger. Make me a better leader, quick to help and slow to anger. So help me God.

So help him God Bunny responded and gave me one almighty spank on my right buttock. I winced. She paused.

"Get up", she said almost spitting the words with contempt.

I climbed from her lap and said:-

"Thank you, Madam, for your Prayer and your penalty. I am sorry I insulted your Husband and wasted your time."

I was ignored.

Whilst all this was going on, Jimmy, Duncan and Mr Jolliffe had materialised with spades and picks, and gazed open-mouthed in incredulity.

Bunny turned to them angrily and declaimed:-

"What are you fuckers gawping at? That was a one-off. The usual rates apply to you, *'gentlemen'*", said the whore with a sneer.

Bunny returned to her cottage and slammed the door.

Thomas went to his shed and coming back with a spade immediately set about clearing the stream rubble from where I had indicated. I returned to mattocking the large stones upstream of him. Within five minutes I had removed the dam, and Balfour had cleared the mass downstream, so that the ditch gushed forth in clarity and the water's height subsided.

I always carry an intact packet of Bonanzas and a cheap lighter so that I can socialise with smokers. I had discovered as a boy in Stockholm that these and the local Jim Golds were the best cigarettes anywhere.

Taking the soft pack from my pocket I tore off the cellophane wrapper and discarded it. I offered a cigarette to Balfour and he accepted it. I lit it for him as he instinctively cupped his hands about mine to shield the light from the breeze that was not there. I took a cigarette myself and lit it, inhaled deeply, and put the pack and lighter back in my pocket. Balfour took a long, grateful draw looking vacantly across the abbey graveyard without making eye contact.

"Thank you for helping me clear this ditch, Tom", I spoke.

"Not at all, thank *you*, Commadore Charmliss, for my family and I are the beneficiaries."

I put the pack in Balfour's jacket pocket and turned to walk back to the manse.

Upon arrival Arnoldina seemed instinctively to know what had happened, unless she had been watching developments through her field glasses.

"Strip, Charles", she ordered, "I shall not ask you to shower since notwithstanding the late deluge water is cold and precious here. You are thoroughly washed anyway. When you are ready join me at the marriage bed."

"Yes, Madam"

I had a perfunctory shower anyway and after drying I walked to our bedroom. Arnoldina was sitting on the side of the bed naked and I crossed her lap.

"What will you say to me this afternoon, Darling Charles?"

"My Lovely Arnoldina, my Wife under God, I have this day sinned against our Lord and Saviour through pride, fear and anger. I threatened an unarmed man with my pistol. His wife gave me the benefit of Holy Correction but was most merciful. I come to you now in abjection. Please cleanse my spirit."

"Thank you for your candid Confession, Charles. You have been most remarkably and unexpectedly sinful for a man of peace, and strikingly irresponsible and immature for an eighty-four-year-old scientist, sailor and diplomat. I shall confiscate your gun until you are responsible enough to carry one. If you visit the mainland with the other men I shall allow you to carry it whilst you are off the island."

"Thank you, Madam, for your admonishment and for your concession."

My Holy Saviour, please restore to my devout and holy Husband his lofty principles of pacifism and love for all creatures. Please cleanse him of every vaulting vanity and restore to him the courage and kindness for which all have held him in the highest esteem, *so help him God*

prayed Arnoldina.
So help me God I responded.

Jesus Christ, my only Lord and King, save me from pride, fear, wrath and all the mortal perils that flow therefrom and protect all from my wickedness. Cleanse my everlasting spirit of all cowardice and malice so that I may reach your Holy Cross and become the man you want me to be.

"My Master and My Holy Wedded Husband, are you ready?"

"Yes, Madam"

Despite my Wife's age, her unarmed feminine hand, her pregnancy, and her slight frame I received the very licking of my life, most richly merited.

Through my storm of wailings and tears I eventually received the intimate Blessing.

Arnoldina remarked:-

"I am glad you are crying, Charles, you deserve to, and it will give you the catharsis that you need and have long had to live without. I love you beyond any reason and any merit of us either. I do not know what I could do if you left me, Charles. I rely upon Christ utterly."

Arnoldina was nursing her arthritic wrist by cupping it in her left fist and rotating the right.

"Shall I give you some analgesic gel?" I offered.

"No, Charles, we must suffer together"

Arnoldina took me in her gracious arms and kissed and cuddled me.

I said:-

"Thank you, Madam, for your Ministry, for hearing my Confession, for your Prayer and your most condign Holy Correction. I will do as you ask and try to be good."

"I shall help Our Saviour to guide and comfort you always, My Husband, as I have sworn of the Spirit. Now, Charles, I am yours. Lead me through the Lord's Prayer."

I did as instructed and we dressed.

The morrow dawned overcast. I decided to take a wheelbarrow up to the old colliery adit and to load it from the pre-war stockpiles and wheel downhill to a cottage and leave a Fellow load for the start of winter. The coal heaps were of course pre-World War II, rather than pre-this-war, if you follow my meaning. So the coal had been weatherside for a hundred years.

I had not been shoveling for ten minutes when much to my surprise Tom Balfour approached the adit with a wheelbarrow and a load of dimension timber of the sort lately washed up near the harbour.

"I thought this might be useful if you decided to re-open the gallery, Chuck", stated this shy man quietly as he began to unload the wood at the adit portal. "I picked it up from the beach yesterday afternoon", Balfour went on to explain.

He then paused this work and offered me one of the Bonanzas I had given him. As I said Tom was a shy man, but modest and brave, and very unassertive. Not at all as prejudice would imagine a whore's husband. I liked him. His hands trembled slightly. I took a cigarette gratefully and he lit it with his own. I took a deep draw. I, too, was nervous. I did not know what to expect.

Tom turned from my face and exhaled.

Then Balfour said:-

"I am sorry about yesterday, and I am sorry about the language. I want you to know that Bunny is a most excellent, Christian, woman, and she respects you. We both do. Your job, whether self-appointed or not, is not easy. I had a job at Stoat and Geeling, the lead refinery. I was a fork-lift driver. When they closed we had no income to support ourselves and our young daughter. I could find no more work. Bunny stepped in. She did what she is best at, she did it with honour and great sacrifice, suffering many humiliations and abominations, and made more than a just income for us all. We want our daughter to have a steady profession, respected, not the trade. She is interested in nursing, but we cannot afford to send her to university, even if universities still exist."

I was astonished. It had never occurred to me that there was no Social Security in the Britain of 78V.

"Tom, it is I who should apologise to you. I am deeply sorry. I am sorry for the obscene thing I did, and I am sorry that all these things have happened to you and your ladies. I wish you better times", I averred.

"Chuck, I could not help noticing as you lifted your shovel that the bulge has disappeared from under your jacket. Have you stopped carrying your pistol?"

"Yes", I replied, "The Wife confiscated it."

We both giggled spontaneously like boys.

Tom took off his day-sack and started to rummage in it. He retrieved two 500ml cans of 9% strong lager, now virtually illegal in Scotland, but which Tom must have liberated on the way to the island.

He handed one to me.

"Aren't you going to save them for Christmas?", I asked, regarding the holiday days away.

"This *is* Christmas", replied Tom, "Christ has Redeemed His final pledge. Christ is with us."

I burst into tears again. I do not know how often I have wept in this universe, in its weird but interesting war, an inferno for some, a tutorial for others.

Tom and I were about to lift our barrows and descend the hill when Ionescu ran from the opposite direction and paused by us. He was out of breath and looked nervous. He was holding his binoculars.

"There is a warship hove too by the lighthouse", said the Magonian Naval Commander and look-out. "Come to the Eyrie and have a look."

We raced uphill the fifty metres or so to Ionescu's WWII observation bunker.

"I think it is the USS *Malcolm Scipio*, a light guided missile cruiser. It has the Union Jack on the jackstaff and the 'black spider', the ✳ recognition mark, a stylised British Union Flag denoting a ship of the Ithaca Coalition. The actual British White Ensign is flying from the crossyard", Ionescu tentatively identified.

"When you say 'Union Jack on the jackstaff' do you mean the British national flag or the US Union Jack of fifty mullets on a Prussian blue field", I asked.

"I mean the US jack", clarified Ionescu.

As we watched an RIB foamed away from the ships side heading for the island's harbour. Through Ionescu's glasses it appeared to have four men aboard with some red or orange boxes which may have contained explosives. We were too late to attempt a defence of the moored lifeboat, Water's farm or anything else at that position, about two miles away.

"What are your orders, Commadore?" asked Ionescu.

"We will play possum. But Tom, go and tell Pratley what has happened. He has a sub-machine gun. Then help him round up the twenty-one women and children and take them to the dell with the waterfall. There is an old mine adit behind it. Gather them in the dell with notice to walk through the fall to the adit if invaders enter the village. Men are to assemble in the dell with guns."

"You do not wish to rush to the arms of your gallant compatriots then, Chuck?" replied Ionescu, with very uncharacteristic sarcasm.

"I do not", I replied, "someone once told me that our Fellowship was his people." I added pointedly.

Tom had already run on his way.

"Permission to speak, Commadore", said Ionescu.

"Yes, what is it, Commander First Class Eugen Florin Maria Ionescu?"

"I propose to remain in this look-out and enfilade any hostile who approaches the dell. If the hostiles and their ship make way I shall descend to the dell and pass the all-clear."

"Permission granted, Commander."

I thought about staying with Ionescu to await developments but instead ran down the hill to the manse to alert Arnoldina.

When I arrived she was already standing in the front doorway porch in full camo fatigues with ammo pouches. She had my Muebler slung over her shoulder and the obvious bulge of her pistol augmented her already adequate breasts. Her belly was especially noticeable in this kit. It had already begun to swell with child. As I approached she handed me my own Wrortlemonger in its shoulder holster.

"Where the bloody hell have you been?" the Loveliness greeted me.

I pointed at her with a smile and said:-

"Spanking later!"

"I will be happy to give you one", Arnoldina quipped back ambiguously.

"Run round the village telling all the men to arm themselves and that all must assemble at the church door at 1345 hours to follow you to a place of safety. I am going to run to Rose Farm and tell Waters to gather his family and guns and go to the church by Land Rover", I specified.

"Do you mean Rowan Farm."

"Of course I fucking mean Rowan Farm", I responded bad temperedly.

"You shall run nowhere, Charles. I shall order Mr Fortess to run and bear that message and return with the Waters'."

"Thank you, Lieutenant-Colonel. I shall go to the steading and look for another good runner to back him up."

Suddenly there was a booming detonation which seemed to reverberate from the hillside without echo. Not that I am an expert, but it seemed too puny for a nuclear explosion.

Professor Terring ran past and said:-

"Don't worry. It's conventional"

And hurried away on some errand, presumably to take gamma readings: It may of course have been a tactical "dirty bomb."

We parted hurriedly, and as Arnoldina left Ionescu arrived panting.

"Come up the hill with me, Chuck", he ordered.

We bounded up the hill as fast as old men could and paused halfway to the Eyrie when we thought we had sufficient vantage to follow events at the harbour.

Ionescu put his glasses to his eyes.

"The fuckers have blown the lantern off the fucking lighthouse", the Commander stated unambiguously.

"Why?"

"Why don't you fucking radio and ask them?" said the formerly most demure of my male friends, handing me the glasses with a scowl.

It seemed to me that the all-important lifeboat was undamaged though I could not see the waterline. Certainly the lantern was missing and the ancillary old Trinity House engine and compressor sheds were on fire as were the maintained but uninhabited lighthouse-men's family cottages. I could not detect any activity at Rowan Farm but a runner was already half way there.

Ionescu and I walked the rest of the path to his look-out bunker at a more gerontion pace, and Ionescu handed me some spare binoculars and used his own to study the South.

We could see that the RIB was motoring back to its mother ship, and four men were aboard without the red and orange boxes.

"We will wait until the cruiser is underway", I ordered.

"Yes, Commadore", Ionescu answered.

There was an uneasy silence. Ionescu seemed worried about something. I hoped that the late visitors had not left us a nasty surprise.

"Charles?", asked Ionescu diffidently and interrogatively.

"Yes, mate" I responded.

"I am very sorry about my insubordination and filthy language. I pray God that you will forgive me", said Ionescu.

I grasped him above the elbow and he turned and looked into my eyes.

"I forgive you, Eugen Ionescu. I love you. You are the least foul-mouthed and insubordinate man I know. We are brothers and we are at peace."

His eyes filled and he lifted the glasses back to them, perhaps to conceal the spurious shame of his tears. It was no good telling him not to cry, or even have a good one. That would only have brought fluid tears and embarrassment for my esteemed, and very masculine subordinate, who was stressed today beyond what a man should bear, weltering in a shame and guilt that were not rightfully his.

"The RIB has been lifted aboard and the cruiser is going starboard", announced Ionescu.

"I shall go and stand the others down", I replied.

I did not do a roll call but as I entered the swimming dell it seemed that all were present except the Water's family, Fortess, Martin Selby and of course Ionescu. There was a hushed hubbub and I decided not to shout incase acoustical monitoring was deployed from the cruiser or indeed other hostile shipping.

Arnoldina was sitting with Bella and Duncan.

The latter greeted me and Arnoldina looked up from her position seated on a grassy bank and smiled. She asked:-

"What passes, Thundermouse?"

I was delightfully startled by this new and very American endearment.

"Please stand everyone down, Arnoldina", I requested, "The British have left though they have destroyed the lighthouse for some reason."

I was compellingly reminded of the 1798 poem *Inchcape Rock* by Robert Southey. The poem fascinated me as a boy, with its evocation of gratuitous evil and the Retribution thereto.

As I walked to the harbour, carrying both my pistol and my sub-machine gun in case of infiltrators I met the Waters family in their Land Rover with the runners and Faith's delightful cavies. I told them I was going to inspect damage as the marauders had returned to sea.

Remarkably the lifeboat was afloat untouched but the lantern of the lighthouse blown away. Bits of dovetailed ashlar littered the lighthouse yard and the ancillary buildings were still burning fiercely.

I discussed this strange occurrence with Arnoldina when I returned to the manse. She said she could not explain why the lifeboat was untouched whilst the lighthouse had been destroyed. Her best theory was that because the lifeboat was owned and run by a charity, the Royal National Lifeboat Institution, it was spared by some humanitarian treaty: Whilst the Brotherhood of Trinity House collected tolls from shipping and was thus a private enemy corporation, eligible for plunder or destruction. I still could not understand the mentality of men so scrupulous to do this selective evil when there was no GPS signal and no Decca intersections, because the requisite satellites and transmitters no longer functioned. But I suppose that is the nature of Evil: It is selective yet ubiquitous.

I later learned that both the RNLI and Trinity House are registered charities, and my perplexment grew and persists.

It was a night of a full moon. There was a cloudless sky but occasional cold zephyrs that rattled the windows and caused an owl in the abbey ruins to hoot. Occasionally some other more distant bird would reply. The atmosphere in the large old rectory was very ghostly, as were the ruins when I looked from the window, and the ledgers of the graveyard were starting to dissolve like stone in smoke. As I breathed a film of ice formed inside the glass. The lead cames cast lattice shadows that crept over the carpet and up the bed like succubae. A gauzy wraith of white mist was starting to develop on the lower ground and the rooves of the Home Farm were beginning to take on the aspect of disembodied displuvic prisms floating above a calm lake of candour.

Arnoldina slept naked as I insisted but now she nestled under three duvets as she softly snored in contented slumbers.

Suddenly the Air Raid Precautions bell sounded.

I hurriedly dressed and mounting my pistol took up the Muebler and raced downstairs where I fumblingly laced my boots. I grabbed a flashlight and hurried as fast as my legs would take me to Ionescu's Eyrie.

The Commander handed me his binoculars without greeting or comment and pointed toward the island harbour.

I lifted the glasses to my eyes and beheld a great conning tower with snorkels and antennae standing black against the mist. I thought I could descry the Russian "Empty Star" recognition mark, but whatever it was a larboard running lamp was glowing red amidst the gloom. I was amazed at this incredible lack of wartime precaution.

I handed the glasses back to Ionescu.

"Get your Muebler and two flashlights and we will make our way cautiously down the road", I ordered.

"Yes, Commadore"

By the time we reached Pratley's cottage, the Professor was standing there with Arnoldina. Both we fully kitted and armed, and Pratley was carrying his sub-machinegun, and inexplicably his shotgun. Perhaps he designed to pot a stray peasant along the way?

The four of us continued our cautious walk seaward, lights off and walking on the grass verges to minimise the sound of boot-strike.

Presently a dark ghost issued from the fog. It was Waters. He joined in silence and the five of us slowly walked toward the harbour.

Just then we heard the sound of a light outboard motor, which stopped. We took cover in the ditches and waited.

After two minutes four black figures materialised from the seaward fog as they silently walked toward our village.

Ionescu emerged from his cover and said:-

«Добрый вечер, господа. Могу ли я помочь?»

At the approaching foursome.

They abruptly arrested themselves in startlement.

«пожалуйста, отведите нас к своему командиру»

replied a middle-aged man in a gruff sailor's voice.

Ionescu beckoned them to follow him and then said in English:-

"They want to speak with you, Dr Charmliss."

"Thank you, Professor Ionescu.", I replied as I emerged onto the road.

A middle-aged man in a Nazi-style leather trenchcoat stated at me:-

«Мы хотим купить картошку и водку»

"What did he say, Eugen", I asked.

"I thought he said he wanted potatoes", Ionescu replied.

Arnondina joined us and said:-

"He wants to buy potatoes and vodka."

«У нас есть золото», continued the man in the coat.

I thought I recognised the word "zoloto": Gold.

"He says he has gold", confirmed Arnoldina.

"Tell him to come with us to Rowan Farm where we can discuss trade."

The Russian officer must have suspected that we were enemy officers, or Magonian deserters, but no attempt was made to kill or arrest us. The Russian sailors were carrying obvious pistols but were otherwise unarmed.

When we reached the farm Mrs Waters was awake and she switched on the kitchen-diner lanterns and gestured to the Russians to take seats at the dining table, which they did.

Waters and his wife took the other two seats and Arnoldina drew up a set of foldable kitchen steps as a stool and sat between the Russian officer and Waters as interpreter. Pratley, Ionescu and I stood around leaning our backsides against the kitchen counters, I hoped not in a threatening or provocative way.

My Wife said something at length in Russian.

Her interlocutor said: "Da, Da, Da" and nodded.

Then the Wife added something else, and then looking up to my face said:-

"They basically want one tonne of potatoes and or parsnips, and all the vodka we can spare."

I turned to Waters and said:-

"Mr Waters, can you provide our guests with 1000 kilos of potatoes to take with them. I will drive to the Home Farm and get them some cases of vodka."

"Mr Charmliss, I have got a stock of 430 kilos of potatoes but only 57 of parsnips. Our visitors can take all to their ship."

On the way I had seen several clamps of root vegetables of unknown species.

"Thank you, Sir. You are most unselfish. May I borrow the keys to the Land Rover?"

Waters reached into his pocket and handed the keys to me.

"Arnoldina", I asked, "can you please tell these gentlemen that I am Charles Charmliss, the island magistrate and deputy pastor, and that you are my Wife. That we can give him 430 kilos of potatoes and 57 of parsnips and also 25 litres of vodka. Tell him that I apologise because the vodka is only *millésime du Warrington*. That we can help his men load the provisions onto his boat."

Arnoldina translated all this and the officer smiled.

Pratley and I drove out to get the vodka.

On arrival Pratley and I loaded six cases of six 70cl bottles of 38% vodka into the car, almost our entire supply, and we returned to the farm within fifteen minutes.

We parked in the farmyard and re-entered the house.

One of the Russian officer's men in ratings' kit complete with anti-macassar was also smiling: Presumably because he spoke English and understood, at least in outline, what I had said.

«Кошерные ли они?», asked the officer looking at the smiling rating.

The latter nodded, and he and the officer strode out to inspect the car. The officer returned with a bottle of Warrington vodka.

He poured the contents equally into two 500ml soft drink tumblers and throwing his arms wide shouted "Comrade" and embracing me in a bear hug kissed me on the lips as my bad arm felt fit to break again. He offered me my glass and exclaimed:-

«Вашего крепкого здоровья!»

I took it from his hand and took a polite sip.

"Cheers!", I replied limply.

The Russian drained his glass, threw it to smash on the kitchen flags, and seized my right hand in a crushing shake.

Mrs Waters briefly left to check that the children were still asleep. Suddenly there was an aethereal whistle that seemed to come from under the kitchen sink. The Russians braced in alarm as their leader strode forward to investigate. He lifted a kitchen towel to disclose two guinea pigs in a cage.

The burly Russian turned with a smile of delighted relief.

«Морские свинки», he advised everyone.

Then the Russian said something else and reached into his tit pocket. He placed something on the table. It proved to be a 100 gram bar of 99.9999% Russian gold.

Before the War, and in 80V, this would have been worth around seven thousand sterling or roughly $8750.

We helped the four Russians load their RIB with what we had promised them, and they motored into the fog.

I never saw a Russian again.

CHAPTER TWENTY-NINE
MILDRED

One of the larger second floor bedrooms of the manse had an en-suite bathroom and the Church of England seemed to have fitted the bedroom out as a kind of conference room-cum-council chamber with a big committee table, a computer desk and a telephone extension. Satellite communication was impossible, either because the satellites had been switched-off or shot from the sky. But there was an undersea cable across the short strait to Tripant and onward to England. This too appeared dead as there was no dialling tone. So anyone who wished to employ the computer had to use the existing installed resources or bring his own disks, and Terring had materialised as a major user, working on his census, his audit of skills, and his plans for postwar democracy.

The room was large and a single bed with bedside console had been set against a wall opposite the fireplace, perhaps for a duty observer. It appeared unslept-in.

I always thought of this common ground as the "War Room", in a side-ways tribute I suppose to the Laginas and their crew. But of course we were indeed fighting a war whether we liked it or not: A war with the monarchists, the Americans, the Magonians, the Russians, the native fascists, each other, isolation, the weather, the sea: All Comers.

One afternoon Jimmy, Duncan, Bella and Mr Waters all turned up having inspected the seeds that Mr Miggins had liberated from Restingheuse in order to discuss the logistics of planting and harvesting and they wanted me to attend as *de facto* police minister of our tiny forty-five person community, since brief conscriptions might be necessary.

We trooped upstairs and entered the "War Room" where Terring was busy.

Terring rose from his seat at the computer.

"There's no need to go, Nick, we will only be an hour. And you may be able to contribute thoughts on agriculture", I said.

"No, I need a break anyway. I will have a walk to see Ionescu, take a couple of readings, and come back this afternoon.", Terring replied.

The rest of us settled around the table.

No sooner than we had done so but Pott Shrigley strode in. He had been keeping a low profile since we had left Congleholme and we had seen little of him or his family. I think he was afraid.

Possibly afraid of being roped-in to a forage on the mainland? Afraid of confrontation with Pratley? Afraid of armed men generally? Just scared? Your guess is as good as. Certainly he looked worried and haggard. He had lost weight even in the month or two I had known him, and he was never fat.

"Hello, Pott", I greeted, "we are about to discuss planting and harvesting which might involve all forty-odd of us. Pott, would you like to have a pistol and a shotgun? Maybe you could Pott some rabbits?", I offered, sniggering in self-congratulation at my capital pleasantry.

Shrigley did not seem consoled either by my greeting or my drollery.

"Chuck, I am very worried about the demographics of our community."

"Yes, Pott?" I queried.

"Nick has done a mini-census, more an audit, and he has discovered that we are 24 males and 19 females with two male infants. Only nine are of marriageable age and status of which six are girls."

I was well aware that, historically, castaway populations with a preponderance of one sex tended to self-exterminate through violence even before Lotka-Volterra effects or famine did their work, but our community was clearly not in such a state, at least not yet.

It was also clear that rivalries, especially sexual rivalries, might lead all to disaster.

These Malthusian considerations were certainly no grounds for complacency, but I sensed that Shrigley really wanted to discuss something else, some much more proximal problem.

"Pott, what have you *really* come to talk about?" I wheedled.

"Is it okay if I talk about one of the teenagers in her absence?"

"Of course it is", I re-assured, "we are all adults and intimate friends."

"We have to apply the laws of England in our microcosm", pronounced Shrigley. I suddenly felt grateful that Pratley had found business elsewhere that morning.

"What is the issue, Pott?" I asked

"Mildred Balfour knocked Mary Lane, her 'friend' to the ground and then kicked her, bruising Mary in the upper right thigh, the left buttock and the anal region. Mildred may have been trying to kick the vulva. Mary also has a black eye."

"Where is Mary at the moment?"

"She is staying with Mina and the boys."

"Has anyone got cellphone photographs of the injuries?"

"Better than that, Charles. I took several pictures of the bruising using my digital SLR", said Shrigley.

"Okay, Pott, bring your photographs and Mary Lane to the ground floor reception lounge now. Farming lady and farming gentlemen, please may we adjourn our meeting until Thursday? You may remain and accompany me if you wish to observe and advise."

"I cannot speak for Mr Waters, but Bella and I would prefer to remain as I am sure my Father would. Bella and I have still much to learn."

"Thank you for your support friends", I said.

"I better return to work, Mr Chairman", said Truby Waters, talking to me.

"Thank you, Mr Waters. I am sorry that I have inconvenienced you", I said.

Waters nodded an acknowledgement and left.

Duncan, Bella, Jimmy, Arnoldina and I re-convened on sofas and chairs by the blazing coal fire in the reception lounge, which had an old back-of-grate boiler for domestic hot water:- A welcome oil-saving feature.

Arnoldina and Bella briefly went to the kitchen to boil tea using a bottle gas stove and came back with tea and biscuits for seven.

Shrigley went to retrieve his camera and Mary.

Just as the women brought the tea and biscuits, Mary came in with Shrigley and his camera.

"Let me see the injuries, Pott", I said.

Mary was badly bruised. I passed the camera to Arnoldina for her professional assessment of the injuries.

"I need to take Mary to the bathroom to check her over as she is now", declared Arnoldina and my Wife and Mary adjourned for five minutes.

On return Arnoldina said:-

"Mary confirmed that the bruises are three days old. They are sensitive in places and Mary finds excretion very painful. But no flesh is broken, Mary is still intact, and I assess that there will be no pain after a further two days", said Arnoldina.

"Thank you, Arnoldina. Mary, tell me what happened."

"Mildred had been rather moody ever since we came to the island. I think she missed school. I came to visit. Max was already there. I mean in the rear sitting room of Mr Balfour's cottage. Mildred called me a whore, and that she was going out to gather wild garlic. I started crying and Max came onto the sofa and cuddled me and held my hand. Then Mildred came in unexpectedly and struck me in the face with her fist. I rose to defend myself and she pushed me over and started kicking me. She only stopped when Max grabbed her and held her. Then Mrs Balfour came in and said that Max and I must leave immediately."

"After you left what do you think happened to Mildred?" I queried.

"I do not know. She would not have been punished. The Balfours were always very indulgent."

"I see. Can I ask Mr Shrigley and yourself to stay here, with Lord Chamberfield and his son and daughter-in-law whilst I go and bring the Balfours for separate interview? Help yourselves to beer and biscuits.", I said.

"Yes, we shall stay", answered Shrigley.

I walked the hundred or so metres to the Balfours' pilgrim cottage.

The door was answered by Bunny.

"Good Morning, Mrs Balfour. Please come to the vicarage immediately with your husband and daughter."

Bunny seemed uncharacteristically sheepish and subdued.

"Yes, Commadore."

I took the three up to the second-floor "War Room" lately vacated by Shrigley and the agriculturalists. The rest followed us. I did not request those to return to the fireside.

"Sit over there by the window, Mr and Mrs Balfour, and Mildred you sit at the big table opposite me. Everyone else sit against the windows and walls, please. Except Mr Shrigley, you go and get Maxwell Fortess and bring him here."

"Yes, Commadore Charmliss."

Ten minutes later Shrigley arrived back with Max Fortess, by common consent Mildred's fiancé.

When they arrived the roster was: Mr and Mrs Balfour, and Mildred; Mary Lane; Arnoldina; Jimmy Heroncourt; Duncan and

Bella; Shrigley and Fortess and myself. Eleven of us occupying eleven of the twelve chairs in the Conference Room.

I took the opportunity to observe the company.

There was a general air of uneasy anticipation.

It is likely Arnoldina and the Heroncourt family were confident they were about to witness a Holy Correction. Tom and Bunny would have guessed that something along the lines of corporal punishment was brewing, given my previous reputation and behaviour. Mildred, Mary, Max and Pott would not have had a clue.

Mildred was at that difficult age when a girl becomes a woman, or a boy becomes a man. She was a striking young redhead whose thick, wavy tresses tumbled to her slender shoulders, framing a pale, lightly freckled face that progressively blanched in the fidgety silence of the room. A rosebud mouth pouted below her aaquiline green eyes and her pert nose.

Mildred was dressed in a cotton shirt with a denim jacket that seemed too small for her already ample chest, and a pair of loose jeans with turn ups. She also had men's socks on her feet and Doc Marten's style boots.

After Max was seated I commenced:-

"Good Afternoon, Miss Balfour."

Mildred maintained her sulky demeanour, looked fixedly ahead and voiced no response.

"May I call you Mildred?" Silence.

"Miss Balfour, you are not quite a woman yet. You are sixteen…"

"I am seventeen", I was quickly corrected by Mildred herself.

"I am sorry, Miss Balfour, it was my mistake. Because you are seventeen the laws of England and Wales specify that you may participate in sexual activity and may marry if your parents permit, and that you may court your betrothed, if you remain free. Within less than a year you will be able to have sex and marry without reference to anyone but your intended. I know you think I am a rambling old man, perhaps a dirty old man, but I want you to bear these things in mind as I ask you some more questions. You do not have to say anything else, but it may help you and the man you love if you do."

"Would you like anyone present to speak for you and guard your interests whilst I interrogate you?"

"Yes: My Daddy and Jimmy"

"Very good, Mildred. This afternoon you must call Medrington Heroncourt 'Lord Chamberfield' or 'Sir'; My Wife is to be addressed as 'Aunty Dina' or 'Madam' and I am 'Uncle Charles' or 'Sir'. I know you think I am a patronising old fool who wants to treat you as a child. Believe me, Madam, that is not as I think of you, but I must make concessions to your age, as you must concede to mine. I shall call you 'Mildred'. This is not said to humiliate or belittle you: It is said with very great respect and if today you behave as a woman and not a child I for one will respect you forever.

Your name is a name of honour, and you shall live up to it.

Do you have any questions so far, Mildred?"

"I do not believe in Lords, Uncle Charles. Only our Lord Jesus."

"I agree with you, Mildred. I do not want lords in England either. But today is a special occasion and we will call Jimmy 'Lord Chamberfield' because he is a respected friend and we want to make him feel great. Do you have any further questions or objections, Mildred?"

"No, Sir"

"Thank you for helping me, Mildred. Mary Lane alleges that you assaulted her in your family home. Would you like to tell me what happened that day?"

"Miss Lane had been coming-on to my boyfriend since we left Congleholme. She has no respect for the love of Max and I. Max is a man. He will fuck any woman who comes on at him. I came back from picking garlic because I needed a bigger bag. Max and Mary were kissing on the sofa, and Max was trying to pull her trousers down. I went over to her and hit her in the face with my fist. She stood up and grabbed a lantern thing to hit me with. I pushed her and she fell holding it. Then I gave her a good kicking and she cried and Mommy came and threw them out."

"Thank you for your very clear account, Mildred", I said.

I looked to Fortess and said:-

"Do you love Mildred, Fortess?"

"Yes, Sir"

"Then why did you attempt to have sex with this other woman, Mary?"

"Because I was selfish and thought I could have them both, Sir. I am very sorry for what I did. I love Mildred and if she will have me back and Mr Balfour permits I shall marry her."

"Now there's a proposal, Mildred! Do you love Max?"

Mildred was sobbing.

"With all my heart, Uncle Charles."

"Aunty Dina, can you get the young lady a box of tissues, please."

"Yes, Sir"

Mildred blew her nose and looked to the floor disconsolately.

"Mildred, would you like to have a cup of hot chocolate and some biscuits, or go to the toilet?", I asked.

"I would like a cup of hot chocolate and biscuits, Sir."

I looked up and raised my eyebrows to Arnoldina but the perfectly obedient Loveliness was already on her way.

"Mildred, when you kicked Mary did you aim for any particular spot?"

"Yes, I tried to kick her cunt, but she moved and I hit her arsehole", clarified Mildred truthfully if indelicately.

"Mildred what you did was very wicked. If you broke Mary's sphincter she would have dribbled excrement unstoppably for the rest of her life. No one would employ her and no man would marry her. Is that really what you want for your friend?"

Mildred burst into fluid tears.

"No, Sir", she sobbed.

"Well then, Mildred. You have committed the crime of Actual Bodily Harm, often known as ABH. You are liable for up to five years imprisonment in a Young Offenders Institution and if I were sitting on the bench I would send you down for four years, which would reduce to two years and eight months with good behavior.

I do not have penal facilities here on this island, but I can ask Commander Ionescu to find a bunker or mine gallery and chain you to the wall, or I could find an old quarry building. You would have a bed, a chair and a mosquito net but it would be very damp. In neither case would you enjoy much light or exercise for your thirty-four months and the inevitable bats and spiders might make your life extra unpleasant. You would have to urinate and defecate into a bucket and take it to a sump for disposal. Every so often myself or one of the other men would take you to the sea, strip you and bath you, even in winter.

That is your legal entitlement in Wales. I cannot award that myself. I would have to empanel a jury of twelve adults to try you and Lord Chamberfield and your Father would have the thankless task of defending your hopeless case without the benefit of a barrister's fee.

There is an alternative. Because you are a young adult but not quite of full culpable age I can offer you the Sacrament of Holy Correction. That exposes me to very grave personal risk but I will do it for yourself, your parents and your manfriend if you consent. All these must witness. I shall not play the hypocrite. In this instance it would be a corporal punishment, and I would be profaning a Holy Sacrament. But it would be over in hours and you would walk away a free woman, in my eyes an actual woman. It is a highly sexualised but religious procedure. It would not compromise your virginity. If you are interested I will give you details, otherwise I shall arrange a trial.

You said you believed in the Lord Jesus so, Mildred, do you believe in God?"

"I believe in God, Uncle Charles, and I wish you to tell me about Holy Correction."

"Very well. Aunty Dina would take you to the bathroom and give you a warm shower and shave your body hair. She would lead you to me as I sat on that bed and lay you still naked across my lap with your bottom uppermost. Then I would ask you to confess your sins: Not the statute crime of ABH, but the theological sins involved in its commission, such as anger, jealousy, pride and lust. Then I would say some voiced prayers and you would say some prayers. You need not voice all or even one of your prayers if you wish not to. I shall ask you if you have finished, and when you have I shall spank you with fast, heavy blows, twenty-four on each buttock. I shall use only my naked right hand, but you will be beside yourself with pain. Then we will have a short break for extra prayers, a drink of water or a visit to the toilet. Then I shall give you another sixty spanks and we will have another break. By now you should be *really* sorry for your attack on Mary: Not just in your mouth but in your Immortal Spirit and ready to do anything to compensate her. Only when you are unselfishly contrite you must tell Jesus that you want him to take all your sins from you and annihilate them. Then I shall turn you over and make the sign of the Cross over your torso. We will then say the Lord's Prayer together and maybe extra prayers. I shall ask Max to come and Bless you by kissing your lips and your portal of life. Then I shall lift you in my arms and take you to your Father. You will be physically able, but you will never hit or kick anyone ever again, so your liberty will be justified."

"Mildred, what do you want to make of your life", I asked.

"I want to become a nurse, Uncle Charles."

"It is a very fine vocation. My Wife is a nurse as well as a doctor of medicine. When you leave prison, or your briefer punishment, would you like Aunty Dina to train you for nursing?"

"Oh, yes, please Uncle Charles!", said the young person with conviction.

"Please, Uncle Charles, what is my portal of life?"

"It is the vulva through which babies pass when they are born, or when your husband gives you the Seed of Life. It is very Sacred. You called it a 'cunt' which is to use the word in a correct but very vulgar way. Never use the word 'cunt' unless you mean to refer to the Portal of Life."

"Thank you, Sir"

"May I ask further questions, Commadore Charmliss?"

"Yes you may. Please call me Uncle Charles if you remember."

"Uncle Charles, I understand a bare bottom spanking, but why must I be quite naked?"

"There are many reasons, Mildred. First of all, you are not a prostitute, and you do not appear in front of males partially-clothed to titillate them. Your total nakedness is a Gift of God received at birth that you can display without shame: Though not with pride or hauteur because God made your body, not yourself. I am not a canting hypocrite so I shall say this: Myself and all the other men here are heterosexuals and they would delight in seeing your young naked body, because it has sexual allure for them, but you rise above all that because you are pure and you intend no prurience.

Secondly, your skin would be grasped and struck with force. If cloth interposes bacteria and spores would drive into your skin, causing irritation at best and infection at worst. Also pathogens would become airborne for yourself and others to breath. The bathing or showering after you disrobe cleanses the skin augmenting the antiscpsis.

Thirdly, your full nakedness lends you a sense of vulnerability and submissiveness. Surprisingly, this is an advantage for you because that and the actual spanking promotes the secretion of the sex hormone oxytocin in your brain. That makes a person feel like loving and hastens their progress toward spiritual contrition. You may feel a strange sexual pleasure when being spanked. That too is a Gift of God to help people have babies, and it is very much not something to be ashamed of. This is one of the reasons we can speak of penitents *enjoying* their Holy Correction.

Fourthly, the Confessor who spanks must be able to see the condition of your skin and circulation at all times, both for safeties sake, and to adjudge when to cease spanking.

There are plenty of other mutually-independent reasons but I mean to teach not to bore.

You have a right to demand that I as Confessor am also naked, on the grounds that we are people praying in God's Sight, and that He is entitled to our innocent earnests of Good Faith. We have nothing to hide from God or Man.

But I understand that you might be offended or frightened by the idea of resting upon a naked old man, so if you wished I would confess you fully clothed, or wearing underwear."

"Thank you, Uncle Charles. I appreciate you talking to me as a woman, mature enough and intelligent enough to value your explanations. I obviously have a lot to learn."

"Mildred, when I was seventeen I had a lot to learn, but I had forgiving masters and wise instructors, so though I deserved several beatings, I received only kindness and encouragement. I intend to submit to you as you to me, and to offer kindness and encouragement, though in a harsh way."

"I also wish to add this, if I may. I am glad that you are crying, not because I hate you, quite the contrary. Tears cleanse the soul of its pride and spite, and also promote oxytocin and other beneficial body chemicals to enter the blood stream, improving both the speed and the quality of your Confessional experiences. I spank hard and fast to make both men and women cry more abandonedly, because they are better off for it. Crying is a sign of strength, not of weakness, and Uncle Charles and Aunty Dina often cry, whether they are spanked or not. It happened that another Wife of mine, in a previous time, laughed throughout her castigation. That was not because I am a soft hitter or she disrespectful. Strong emotion comes in many forms and my Wife of those times benefited greatly from that Correction and never offended in the same way again."

"Mildred, this interview is very important for all forty-five of us and I am not trying to shoo you away, but I think you should take forty-eight hours to go away, discuss these choices with your Mother and Father, and come back to me with your decision."

"No, Uncle Charles. I have made up my mind already because I respect the integrity of your advice and I Trust you. I have read on the Internet that sanctified spanking is both an Act of Trust and a spiritual tonic. I wish to suffer and enjoy Holy Correction."

Then I said:-

"You will have a rough few minutes, Mildred, but you will never regret your decision. You are a very courageous woman, devout, patient and willing to learn. I love and respect you, as every person here admires you, whether they like you or not. You have made the wise and the womanly choice, that benefits both your family and your community.

Now please go to the bathroom with Aunty Dina, remove your watch and any jewellery, and your crucifix and chain and hand these things to my Wife for safe keeping. Nothing shall be round our necks, and I shall remove my wedding band and my watch. Try to urinate and defecate if you can, and then have a warm shower taking care to remove all your make-up, pins and hair conditioning.

Do you want me to shower myself, and work naked, Mildred?", I added.

"No thank you, Uncle Charles. I mean no offence. Your body has the grace and dignity of any man, but if you remain clothed in your soldierly fatigues it enhances your Authority as a man under God."

"Thank you, Mildred. That is a very intelligent observation, tactfully delivered."

Arnoldina led Mildred out of the bathroom with a kindly arm around her shoulder. Heartbreakingly, but quite naturally Mildred had buried her downcast face in her hands and was weeping softly.

"Thank you for your courage and your trust, Mildred. We all love you. Please come and settle on my lap", I invited, as I held out my arms and smiled, I hope in a consoling and kindly manner.

Mildred lay prone and Arnoldina set a pillow under her head and another under her portal of life, guarding the latter with a folded dry towel. Arnoldina knelt by the bed and crossed Mildred's ankles and gently held them, remarking:-

"Mildred, you are free to leave at any time and go to trial. Just say and Uncle Charles and I will unhand you and take you to your Father. I am here to stop you rolling onto the floor and hurting yourself."

"Thank you, Aunty Dina. I wish to stay."

"Lord Chamberfield, please draw up your chair and place your right hand on Mildred's head to comfort her", I requested.

"Mary, if you truly love and forgive Mildred, then come and kneel at her right hand and hold that hand", I added.

"Dr Charmliss, I have loved Mildred since we were babies, and I forgive her everything, and I obey with delight", replied Mary.

Both obeyed.

Mildred was now sobbing fluidly. I placed my right hand on her right buttock and gave a gentle squeeze.

"May God Bless you and comfort you throughout your ordeal and bring you a prompt and complete relief. Now please confess your sins, Darling", I commenced.

"Sir, I struck Mary as she sat and when she rose I knocked her to the ground and kicked her, badly bruising her."

"Yes, My Love, but did you commit the sin of Pride?"

"No, Sir. And please don't call me 'My Love' or 'Darling'. Endearments are for my Parents and my man."

"Mildred I accept your admonishment and I apologise. But I shall say many silly and annoying things until we are finished. Only then may you complain and I will say sorry. I do love you, I hope in the way an uncle loves a young niece, and I say these things to help us both endure this harsh but sacred rite.

With respect to Pride, is it fair to say that you thought your idea of love was better than Maxwell's Will and that you sought to impose your imagined rights to him against any wish he had to hold Mary?"

"That is fair, what you have said, Sir"

"Now did you envy Mary?"

"Yes, Sir. I was jealous and I wanted Mary for myself alone."

Max

"'Yes, Sir' is quite sufficient, Mildred", I counselled, "You are not here to be humiliated or to abase yourself."

"Thank you, Sir"

"Mildred, did you commit the sin of lust?"

"Yes, Sir"

"And did you commit the sin of Wrath?"

"What is Wrath, Uncle Charles?"

"It is anger, Mildred"

"Yes. Very much I did."

"So you are jealous, angry, lustful, and prideful. You are a very wicked woman, aren't you Mildred?"

"No, Sir"

I gave her another little squeeze and said:-

"You are a very wicked woman, aren't you Mildred?"

"Yes, Sir", Mildred sobbed.

"Mary, can you please get a tissue and dry your friend's tears and hold the tissue whilst she blows her nose?"

"Yes, Sir." Mary obeyed, as all men and women should to benefit another.

The company gazed fascinated in awful silence.
I closed my eyes and prayed aloud:-

My Holy Saviour, comfort your suffering daughter Mildred
Let her know that through her anguish
A larger light shall dawn
Magnified through her clear tears

My Holy Saviour
Award your daughter Mildred fortitude
The courage to endure and the strength to pray
Let her pain be light and the
chastening of her spirit complete
Take her sin and set it at naught
Restore to her the Innocency that her trespass adulterated
Forgive her now and forever
And prompt the forgiveness of those she wronged

> *Please help her God*

"Now, Mildred say this little prayer after me":-

My Holy Saviour
> *My Holy Saviour*
Guard and keep the purity of my confessor Charles
> *Guard and keep the purity of my confessor Charles*
Let him enjoy no profane delight
> *Let him enjoy no profane delight*
In my pain or exposure
> *In my pain or exposure*
Make him shrive me with apt words and sincere prayers
> *Make him shrive me with*
> *apt words and sincere prayers*
Timely, prudent and useful
> *Timely, prudent and useful*
And let him strike without stint and without spite
> *And let him strike without stint and without spite*
But with completeness and compassion
> *But with completeness and compassion*

> *Please help him God*
> **Please help me God**

"Now, Mildred, I have suffered corporal punishment and I have abhorred it all my life. But I must not be a hypocrite. What I am about to inflict is corporal punishment. It is Satanic. But if you are strong, and I know you are, you will invert it into a Blessing of Divine Penance.

Mildred, are you ready to endure?"

"Yes, Uncle Charles"

I revert to my old cliché: You could have heard a pin drop.

I paused.

I lifted my hand from her right buttock and delivered twenty-four mighty open handed blows to each alternate nates as Mildred screamed, gasped and wept abandonedly.

I paused and placed my hand on her thigh..

Mildred squirmed, stretched and muttered under her breath:-

"Oh, fuck"

"Please do not swear, you Delightful Lady. A fuck is a most holy thing, created by God to produce a baby. Always speak of it with reverence. Do you wish to reply, Mildred?"

"Yes, Sir. You are right, Sir, and I am sorry for what I said."

"Very good, Mildred. Thank you. You are doing fine. You are a very brave, religious and patient young woman. You will not only survive, you will be triumphant and you will thrive beyond my lap and most likely for the rest of your life", I counselled. "We will now have a short break. Do you wish to visit the lavatory?"

"What is that, Sir?"

"It is the toilet"

"Yes, please, Uncle Charles"

We unhanded the young woman and Arnoldina accompanied her. Mildred had started to sweat and tense her gluteal muscles. Arnoldina would have given the young woman a warm shower and for all I know an anti-sudorative like picrotoxine. I had given no specific instructions: After all I am not medically qualified but I doubt my Wife would have used ibuprofen because of its analgesic effects. I decided to cover Mildred with a duvet when she returned, until it was time for beating to restart.

Whilst they were away I asked Jimmy:-

"Jimmy, is 1500 okay to resume the planting discussions on Thursday? If so I will go and see Waters and clear it with him."

"If it is okay with you, Charles, I will offer Waters that time and date myself, and also a choice of 1030 Saturday morning or 1530 Sunday with prayers, all here. Then I shall tell you and Duncan."

There was a general hubbub of conversation which I found annoying, but I forbore to call for silence, since I was myself so flagrantly abusing a Holy Sacrament, and, arguably, abusing a young woman.

"That is brilliant, Jimmy", I agreed.

I looked at Tom Balfour as I scanned the room. He gazed back sternly and made a thumbs-up sign. Bunny was as impassive as usual.

"Jimmy", I said, "can you please go and clarify what Tom means by his signal. Does he want me to Bless and stop now, or to continue with the next sixty or less, or what?"

Jimmy went and bent before the seated Tom to ask. Tom said something that I could not catch. It was a relatively long consultation: Maybe thirty seconds. Jimmy returned and stated:-

"Tom is satisfied so far and wants to continue as normal. If his daughter is excessively distressed he will simply rise and take her from your lap, he says."

"That is fine, Jimmy, thank you.", I replied.

I looked across to Tom who was looking at me. I nodded and gave two thumbs up. Tom nodded back.

My right hand felt as if it was on fire. The arthritis in my wrist was hurting terribly and the shattered upper arm and shoulder, repaired so badly in 80V were giving me hell. I must have looked grim.

Just then, Arnoldina returned with a very fresh young Penitent and re-installed her across my lap. I covered Mildred with the duvet.

"Blood sugar is 2.9", remarked my Wife.

"Get her a cup of hot chocolate with extra sugar, and a Venus Bar", I ordered.

"Yes, Sir. Charles, you must use an instrument", my Wife pleaded with a very earnest face.

"No, Madam. Never", I answered gruffly.

"Uncle Charles, I feel really, really happy. I feel empowered. I know it is a funny thing to say. I feel calm, like a mighty seabird, not flying, but sailing, if that makes sense. Nothing seems like effort any more, and I don't care what anyone thinks. Am I wicked? Am I a pervert?"

"You most emphatically are neither, Mildred. You have been what theologians call transverberated. It is a type of religious sexual ecstacy mediated by your hormones. Things can be described in both scientific and religious terms: There is no inconsistency. In spiritual terms Christ has visited you in Person to confiscate your sins and give them to Satan who collects such gifts to play with. And to be the Toy of Satan is to not exist, so that effectively the sin is annihilated. To be without sin is to be an Imitation of Christ. You have joined Him in Union. That is the very opposite of perversion or wickedness."

After minutes, Arnoldina returned with a tray of hot chocolate for Mildred in one of those spill-proof containers for babies and elderly people, two Venus Bars, a liberated pack of chocolate digestives, and two vegan cappuccinos for Jimmy and myself. It was all most welcome and the liquids were drained by all three of us.

Mildred had settled a little and was only sobbing intermittently.

"I hope you have not given her painkillers", I half-admonished Arnoldina.

"No, Holy Husband", was the reply, "I want Mildred to profit from her experience."

Jimmy smiled at the young Penitent. I preferred to think of her as a willing penitent rather than as a compelled, or as in this case, a blackmailed prisoner. Jimmy placed his hand gently upon her hair, as it had been before.

"Do you know any good jokes, Mildred?" he asked softly.

The young woman looked up to him with a smile of delight.

"I know some hedgehog jokes, Lord Chamberfield."
"Please can I hear them?" softly asked the old earl.
"How do hedgehogs play leapfrog?"
"I don't know, Mildred"
"Very, very carefully!", said Mildred with a little giggle.

"That is a good one", said Jimmy, "I have one for you: Why did the hedgehog cross the road?"

"To show he wasn't chicken!", answered Mildred with triumph. I had no idea whether that was the correct answer or not, but I was glad that Mildred was not being crushed by this outrageous assault as I had been by mine.

"Do you like hedgehogs, Mildred?" asked Jimmy.

"Rar-thur! I love them. I hope to see one, one day."

"That day, we will walk the island together with Geoff and see if we can find one without frightening him.", offered Jimmy.

I equally had no idea who Geoff was, but I presumed one of Waters' dogs and perhaps Jimmy had visited Waters' farm on business.

"Mildred, shall we say a little prayer for the hedgehogs and for the other animals of England, whoever they are?", offered Jimmy.

"Oh, yes. Let's Uncle Jimmy!"

My Holy Saviour   commenced Jimmy
　　My Holy Saviour　　responded Mildred
Our Only True Lord and King
　　Our Only True Lord and King
Preserve in Peace the Hedgehogs and the
Animals of England
　　Preserve in Peace the Hedgehogs and the
　　Animals of England
Give them Many Happy, Healthy Babies
　　Give them Many Happy, Healthy Babies
Protect them From the Guns of Hungry Hunters
　　Protect them from the Guns of Hungry Hunters
And from the Futile Loss of Speeding Cars
　　And from the Futile Loss of Speeding Cars
- And not forgetting Faith's Guinea Pigs:
　　Martin and Chuzzlewit

Jimmy interrupted himself. Mildred turned her head and beamed at Jimmy with a giggle of delight:-

　　- And not forgetting Faith's Guinea Pigs:
　　Martin and Chuzzlewit
In the Name of Our Most Holy Father Creator of All
　　In the Name of Our Our Holy Father Creator of All
Amen
　　Amen

Mildred had stopped crying and contentedly returned to sipping her re-filled hot chocolate.

I looked up from Mildred's ruddy bottom to Jimmy.

I said:-

"Thank you, Jimmy. That was much appreciated."

Jimmy nodded in smiling acknowledgement.

"Charles, would you like ibuprofen gel on your wrist, covered by a surgical strop?" asked my Wife.

"No, Thank you, Arnoldina. I must suffer with the youngster."

"Can I give you a local lidocaine injection?"

"No", I responded impatiently.

"Mildred, get up and go to the toilet and be sure to shower afterwards and wash inside your portal of life. I will come and collect you", ordered Arnoldina.

"Yes, Madam." Mildred rose and retired to the en-suite.

When she was out of earshot Arnoldina said:-

"Charles, you must ease back, or else you will be Corrected by Another, less caring-handed than your Holy Wife."

"*I* am in charge of this Correction", I responded pridefully.

"And so you are, Holy Husband. I meant no insolence and I defer with the greatest reverence and respect. Please soften your blows I beg, that all may be chastened and become the people that God wants them to be. Shall I retrieve the Penitent, Sir?"

"Yes, please Arnoldina"

Mildred settled back, prone on my lap.

"Mildred, I am very sorry but I shall shortly give you softer blows than you need or deserve, and likely fewer than sixty, because I am weak."

"No, Sir"

"What do you mean, *No?*", I answered with stupid affront.

"I mean that you are strong, Sir."

I burst into tears.

Then Mildred said:-

"I love you, Dr Charmliss. You are a real man. Your blows torture you at least as much as I, in both Body and Spirit. Your tears become you as mine become me, for they are earned. Hit me."

Jimmy said:-

"You have Contrition, Charles. You must either try this woman or acquit her."

I ignored him.

I said:-

"Mildred, say this prayer with me":-

𝔒𝔲𝔯 𝔉𝔞𝔱𝔥𝔢𝔯, 𝔴𝔥𝔦𝔠𝔥 𝔞𝔯𝔱 𝔦𝔫 𝔥𝔢𝔞𝔳𝔢𝔫,
    Our Father, which art in heaven,
𝔥𝔞𝔩𝔩𝔬𝔴𝔢𝔡 𝔟𝔢 𝔱𝔥𝔶 𝔫𝔞𝔪𝔢;
    hallowed be thy name;
𝔱𝔥𝔶 𝔨𝔦𝔫𝔤𝔡𝔬𝔪 𝔠𝔬𝔪𝔢;
    thy kingdom come;
𝔱𝔥𝔶 𝔴𝔦𝔩𝔩 𝔟𝔢 𝔡𝔬𝔫𝔢,
    thy will be done,
𝔦𝔫 𝔢𝔞𝔯𝔱𝔥 𝔞𝔰 𝔦𝔱 𝔦𝔰 𝔦𝔫 𝔥𝔢𝔞𝔳𝔢𝔫.
    in earth as it is in heaven.
𝔊𝔦𝔳𝔢 𝔲𝔰 𝔱𝔥𝔦𝔰 𝔡𝔞𝔶 𝔬𝔲𝔯 𝔡𝔞𝔦𝔩𝔶 𝔟𝔯𝔢𝔞𝔡.
    Give us this day our daily bread.
𝔄𝔫𝔡 𝔣𝔬𝔯𝔤𝔦𝔳𝔢 𝔲𝔰 𝔬𝔲𝔯 𝔱𝔯𝔢𝔰𝔭𝔞𝔰𝔰𝔢𝔰,
    And forgive us our trespasses,
𝔞𝔰 𝔴𝔢 𝔣𝔬𝔯𝔤𝔦𝔳𝔢 𝔱𝔥𝔢𝔪 𝔱𝔥𝔞𝔱 𝔱𝔯𝔢𝔰𝔭𝔞𝔰𝔰 𝔞𝔤𝔞𝔦𝔫𝔰𝔱 𝔲𝔰.
    as we forgive them that trespass against us.
𝔄𝔫𝔡 𝔩𝔢𝔞𝔡 𝔲𝔰 𝔫𝔬𝔱 𝔦𝔫𝔱𝔬 𝔱𝔢𝔪𝔭𝔱𝔞𝔱𝔦𝔬𝔫;
    And lead us not into temptation;
𝔟𝔲𝔱 𝔡𝔢𝔩𝔦𝔳𝔢𝔯 𝔲𝔰 𝔣𝔯𝔬𝔪 𝔢𝔳𝔦𝔩.
    but deliver us from evil.
𝔉𝔬𝔯 𝔱𝔥𝔦𝔫𝔢 𝔦𝔰 𝔱𝔥𝔢 𝔨𝔦𝔫𝔤𝔡𝔬𝔪,
    For thine is the kingdom,
𝔱𝔥𝔢 𝔭𝔬𝔴𝔢𝔯, 𝔞𝔫𝔡 𝔱𝔥𝔢 𝔤𝔩𝔬𝔯𝔶,
    the power, and the glory,
𝔉𝔬𝔯 𝔢𝔳𝔢𝔯 𝔞𝔫𝔡 𝔢𝔳𝔢𝔯.
    For ever and ever.
𝔄𝔪𝔢𝔫.
    Amen.

As if by reflex, everyone present responded to the Prayer of Christ, and at the conclusion many or all were lachrymose.
    Then I said:-

My Holy Saviour
Accept I beg you
The pain of your daughter Mildred as
Reparation for her Sin
Remove all distress from her mind and spirit
Prepare her to amend and recompense her evil
And please exact no further penalty on Earth

Or in The Life to Come

"Mildred, this is very serious. You must not, I repeat *not*, say this following prayer, the Act of Contrition, unless you are truly, deeply sorry and you will do what you can to expiate your crime, such as for instance by giving the woman you kicked free medical care for the rest of her life. If you say this without meaning it you could burn in Hell, though I don't actually believe you would because God is merciful. That is why he sent his Son to Redeem us. If you are not ready and you wish for a criminal trial or further spanks, that is fine, and it will be done. But if you are Contrite under God, say the prayer after me. Which is it, Mildred?"

"I am truly sorry under God, and I will care for Mary and her babies for their lives to the best of my ability, without payment. Mary is my life's friend and I love her", replied Mildred.

"Mildred, say this prayer after me":-

My Dear God, I am sorry for my sins with all my heart.
My Dear God, I am sorry for my sins
with all my heart.
In choosing to do wrong and failing to do good,
In choosing to do wrong and failing to do good,
I have sinned against You
whom I should love above all things.
I have sinned against You
whom I should love above all things.
I hate my sins and I reject them with loathing.
I hate my sins and I reject them with loathing.
I firmly intend, with Your help,
to use the pain of penance
I firmly intend, with Your help,
to use the pain of penance
To sin no more, and to avoid
whatever leads me to sin.
To sin no more, and to avoid
whatever leads me to sin.
Your Son, Jesus Christ, suffered and died for us.
Your Son, Jesus Christ, suffered and died for us.
In His name, my God, have mercy.
In His name, my God, have mercy.
Amen
Amen

I turned Mildred onto her back. She winced as her sore bottom contacted the rough towel.

"I am sorry.", I said, "Would you like myself or Aunty to rub some soothing gel onto you."

"No, Uncle Charles. No thank you."

"Please wait whilst I say a Prayer of Blessing.", I said.

"Yes, Sir"

Our Holy Saviour, who walked from the
Garden to Golgotha
Forgive this good woman her evils
The sins confessed and those known to
her spirit but not her mind
But guide her to find and confess
her further acts of wickedness
And renounce further sin
Listen to her prayers always and make her keep them holy
Exacting of her no perpetual forfeit.
Accept her Sacrifice of pain as Imitation of Christ
Strengthen and Console her
In your Holy Name I commend Mildred to you,
my only Lord

I Crossed myself.

Then I took the fingers of my right hand and softly placed them on her scalp and lifting took them and placed them on her Portal of Life. Then I lifted and placed them first on her right nipple, then on her left.

"Mr Fortess, come here please." I ordered.

Max Fortess came and stood as Mildred remained supine.

I prayed:-

Please God Bless this your daughter Mildred
with a long, content and fulfilled life

"Now very softly and dryly kiss Mildred on the lips", I said.

He did.

Then I prayed:-

Please God Bless the Progeny of your Daughter Mildred with happy, healthy lives that they may Propagate and Progress your Plan

"Now kiss Mildred on her Portal of Life and briefly caress her with your tongue", I requested of Fortess.

Fortess looked at me in startled astonishment.

Then he did as bidden.

Mildred climaxed.

I lifted Mildred in my arms. Jimmy and Arnoldina rushed forward to support me physically. Tom Balfour rose abruptly and paced forward quickly. I gave him his daughter into his arms.

Most inappropriately, some started to clap. I looked around shaking my head and saying "No, please don't."

Three days later I went to visit the Balfours. I took Arnoldina with me. I knocked on the cottage door. Mrs Bunny Balfour answered.

"Come in friends. I will put the kettle on.", said Bunny.

"How is Mildred?" I asked.

"I think you should ask my husband."

Bunny led us into the back parlour, the same as where Mildred had kicked her friend almost sterile.

"Have a seat on the sofa and I will call Tom in."

Tom entered and proffered me his hand and we shook. Then he bowed to Arnoldina and said "Lieutenant-Colonel Dr Mrs Charmliss."

"Dina, please", my Wife replied.

"Tom, how is your daughter?" I asked.

"See for yourself"

"Mildred! Visitors", bawled her father.

Mildred ran to us beaming and wrapped her arms round me.

"Daughter, Respect!" ordered Tom.

Mildred stood back, still smiling, curtseyed to me and repeated to Arnoldina.

"Welcome, Uncle Charles and Aunty Dina. I love you."

"Thank you, Mildred. We love you too."

"It is a different world, Chuck. Since her spanking, I mean Holy Correction, Mildred always awakes with a smile, helps with the cleaning and has stopped answering-back and swearing at the Wife. She is a different girl. She is still just as talkative but it is 'Uncle

Charles' that and 'Aunty Dina' this and constant talk of Uncle Jimmy and his hedgehog prayer", explained Tom.

"Oh, Mildred. Never swear, especially at the woman who gave you life. You know that it is most unchristian and unwomanly. You know the Fifth Commandment of God and that you must obey those who care for you. So never answer anyone back. Do not state opinions, only your advice for action, and if that advice is rejected the correct response is to leave or to say 'Yes, Sir' or 'No, Madam'", I ministered.

"I no longer answer-back, Uncle Charles."

"What did you just do, Mildred?", I asked with a smile.

A look of horror overspread the fair face.

"I just answered-back, Sir. I am very sorry."

"Mildred, you said you loved me. So do me this favour, please", I said.

"What is it? I would do anything for you, Uncle Charles."

I suddenly realised, and the horror was mine, that even if this woman lived for a thousand years she would still think of my Wife and I as "Uncle Charles" and "Aunty Dina" and refer to us as such when reminiscing. And that she would never see a hedgehog, or any hispid thing, even a hairbrush, without remembering Medrington Heroncourt, perhaps when both hedgehogs and earls were long extinct.

"Kneel down before your Mother and put your hands together. Look up into her eyes and beg her to forgive you for your swearing and your insolence."

"Yes, Sir"

The young lady did so without demurral.

Bunny replied as Mildred knelt:-

"I forgive you, my daughter, everything but this: You have not thanked Dr Charmliss for his Holy Correction that has so greatly benefited yourself and your parents, and neither have you apologised for wasting his time and causing his bad arm to suffer such pain."

Mildred rose and kneeling before me clasped her hands again:-

"Dr Charmliss, Uncle Charles, please forgive me. I thank you with all my heart for your Holy Correction, for taking the time to hear my Confession and making me deliver it correctly, for all your prayers and Ministry, for the safety and comfort of your care, including the painful smacks which stung and smarted but which were richly deserved and I apologise for wasting your time that I know you needed for urgent business, and I am sorry for the torment of reviving old wounds.

Dr Charmliss, Commadore, I know that you are a conscientious objector, both to violence in general and to corporal punishment in particular, and I thank you for your many sacrifices and concessions for the benefit of our island Fellowship, knowing that you can gain nothing for yourself.

I shall learn. This is my promise."

"Thank you, Mildred. My Wife Aunty Arnoldina has something she wishes to say to you."

Mildred rose and knelt before Arnoldina.

Arnoldina looked down and said:-

"Mildred, I know you are interested in becoming a nurse whilst I need the help of an apprentice.

If you wish you may come and live with Charles and I on call always as a trainee nurse and I shall teach you what I know about nursing whilst you help me on the job. You cannot play the fine lady. You will have to learn to manage blood and excrement without showing disgust, to handle needles and to see death and other evils, to change beds and do all manner of unromantic things. You will have to wear a nurse's uniform over Army fatigues or else nothing at all, unless I tell you that you can vary your dress. If you swear or wear make-up or do anything unprofessional or unwomanly I shall Correct you myself. You will not be required to work on a Sunday but will be expected to practice your Devotions that and every day, or to visit your parents or a manfriend. Peoples' lives would depend upon your work. You must obey me promptly and without question, except when the question is needed to relieve your ignorance.

Any payment will be at a token level.

In return you will receive the basics of a nursing education free of charge, a bed and vegan board at my table, clothing without charge if I approve it, medical care for yourself at no charge, and firm but Christian treatment.

The apprenticeship will last between two and three years and I shall provide you with open testimonials.

Do you accept these terms?"

"Yes, Madam, and I thank you for your kindness and your trust."

"Then you will come with me now and you may return here for your things in a few days' time. Mildred, is your bottom still sore? If so we can medicate it when we reach the surgery."

"No, Madam. Thank you for asking. The pain and redness both vanished after a long sleep and there are no bruises."

"That is another advantage of hand spanking, and a youthful, healthy constitution", observed my Wife.

"What a brilliant education you are getting, Mildred", remarked Bunny, "I hope you appreciate it."

"Mother, I do"

CHAPTER THIRTY
THE DAWN OF HOPE

The day dawned limpidly clear with brilliant sunshine and a deep blue sky, 'aethereal' as Addison put it.

Arnoldina had installed Miss Anand as her pharmacist and told her to shelve the drugs in the surgery anteroom according to an agreed system. In return Ananta Anand fed at our table and we clothed her and provided accommodation in the old servants' quarters in the attic. The Patels, meanwhile, had been awarded one of the pilgrims' static caravans. I was not sure what the Patels did, but we tended to leave them alone, not I hope out of snobbery or racism, but they kept themselves to themselves and we did likewise.

I suppose Anand was about twenty-eight or thirty with the chubby face and raven, wiry hair of a Punjabi. She wore Western fashions with a good-quality cashmere cardigan against the cold, and went abroad with a puffer anorak. I think she had always been single, but of course I did not pry into the sex lives of my Fellows. I believe she was vegan or at any event vegetarian.

We had given up worrying about such issues as modern slavery, and we felt guilty about our flagrant breaches of rightful and required English laws. For myself as a Quaker I was especially disconcerted as I remembered the four-hundred year history of our unarmed campaign in England and British North America for principles of freedom and humanity against the torturers and hangmen of inflexible States. I did not wish, with a new tribe of forty-five others, to establish a new Dispensation with a collective Original Sin.

We were no more entitled to rule than Anand and the Patels, just because we were Christians and had guns. We consoled ourselves in self-congratulation at our magnanimities.

It was the lead-up to Christmas insofar as the Yule meant anything in our penury and isolation in the midst of a grand atrocity.

I cannot remember whether it was the 19th or the 20th of December. My Wife and I were loitering in the surgery in that sleepy ennui of an English Advent. We had an open bottle of liberated sherry on the table between us with some factory-made mince pies that Arnoldina had thoughtfully stolen from the Sainsbury's.

All I recall is that it must have been a Friday because Ananta appeared before Arnoldina, curtsied and said:-

"Madam, may I please have time for my Devotions today for it is the Muslim sabbath. I must pause for a few minutes five times today to pray to Allah."

Arnoldina knew that Ananta was UK-trained to Masters level, and something of an expert on British and Irish wild medicinal plants.

Arnoldina responded:-

"Yes, that is fine, Miss Anand. Take a walk on the hill and in the lanes with Mildred, pausing and praying with my apprentice whenever needful. Allow Mildred to worship according to Christian rites, but do not hesitate to discipline her if she is insolent or disobedient. Identify and name any medicinal plants you find and make Mildred draw them in her sketch book, noting their names and clinical properties."

"Yes, Madam. May I make a suggestion please, Lieutenant-Colonel Charmliss?"

"Yes, Ananta, what is it?"

"I still have charge on my mobile. I can photograph the plants to best advantage, and when we return this evening I can scroll through the frames and Mildred can draw and describe the herbs on her student pad."

"That is an excellent idea, Ananta. But nothing teaches of natural things like meticulously drawing them with one's own hand. Make Mildred draw the herbs in the field, *and* draw them again in the comfort of this surgery. When you return with our student you both may have a little wine and cake, if your Faith permits.", said Arnoldina.

"Thank you, Madam. The exercises will be performed your way. I am not a bigot and I will be delighted to honour the Birth of your Holy Prophet in whatever way you deem fit.", replied Ananta Anand.

The South Asian Muslim then addressed Mildred.

"Come, Mildred. Put on your puffer jacket. Put a bottle of water, two mince pies and your sketch pad and pencil in your day sack. Then hold my hand and we will start our learning of the sacred arts of medicine."

"Yes, Miss Anand", replied Mildred, a rosy and enthusiastic picture of contented obedience.

By 1530 the Welsh winter was darkling and the herbs were folding their leaves and going to sleep. A cheerful pair of young medics returned to us volubly, sat, and drank their sherry with further mince pies. Then Arnoldina and I left the table and adjourned to the the extempore ground-floor ward of three beds that attached to the surgery through a glazed door. As yet there were no in-patients and my Wife and I took off our boots and dozed in the Easternmost bed otherwise fully clothed.

Whilst the two young ladies were engaged in field studies, my Wife had prepared a meal for four for our dinner: Frankies with tinned tomato soup (what else?)

1800 arrived and Anand wrapped-up the tutorial and Arnoldina and I could re-occupy the Formica-surfaced surgery table.

Arnoldina reheated the meal and served it. Then she poured some chilled cola for herself and the girls, and an IPA for me.

Unexpectedly the expectant silence was broken.

Ananta Anand bowed her head to the table and prayed:-

Allah Most Merciful,
Thank you for the Peace of this Fine Meal among Friends
Thank you for their Hospitality and their Kindness
And for the Cheerful Application of Our Good Student
And the Bracing Day we spent in the
Study of Your Creation.
I love you. I love them. Bless them all.

Then Mildred put her hands together and closed her eyes:-

Dear God,
Thank you for Ananta and her Patient Lessons
Thank you for her Good Fellowship as I learn at her Hand
Thank you for this fine vegan Meal
And the Love my Mistress poured into it.
Bless my Mother and Father, and
Aunty Dina and Uncle Charles
And give them a Great Christmas in
Your Holy Care.
Amen

"*Amen*" the three of us echoed.

It put me in mind of Grace at the home of my doctoral supervisor, a Scottish Presbyterian elder, on the day after I had successfully defended my thesis. I worshiped the man, though at that time I was a proud atheist and did not participate in the prayer with which he, his wife and numerous grown children honoured me and honoured their God.

But these this evening were not formulaic prayers of routine, but were felt prayers consecrated by the moment, steeped in love and not doctrine.

Mildred unfolded her camp bed in this little surgery, removed her uniform and fatigues without pudor and donning her nightdress retired to sleep with her teddy bear. Anand kissed her forehead and took her leave.

It somehow seemed that Mildred had recovered her virginity intact, as had maybe her mentor. I do not mean in the physical sense: Such was never doubted in either woman. I mean the recovery of a lost innocence natural to all men and women, a precious condition that people like Pratley and I had resigned.

The next day also was a splendid winters day of calm and sunshine. I thought I should get up off my backside and prune some of the fruit trees in the small orchard behind the manse.

As you possibly recall, there were neglected fruit trees sheltered between the house and the hill, with dilapidated sheds abutting the later.

About 0945, as I began work, I heard the alarm bell ring in the manse. There was a sudden commotion in front of the Methodist Church. A number of people were jabbering and pointing. Ionescu came running down the declivity from his look-out:-

"Charles, come up and look at this."

I followed Ionescu up the hill at the double. Half way to the lookout we paused. We did not need our glasses. There, sitting in the sea, almost motionless, was the most enormous ship. It may have been a full one and a half nautical miles offshore.

"It is the bucentaur MFS *Dypsidorian*, one of only seven in the Navy", Ionescu declared authoritatively. He meant, of course, the Magonian Navy of which both he and I were officer deserters.

"Do you think they will come ashore, Eugen?", I asked disgracefully.

Ionescu paused and took up his glasses.

"I wouldn't", Eugen said with seamanlike deliberation.

I stood and marvelled. It had nine 100cm guns with gleaming gold plated bronze flash cones lately defiled with films of carbon. So she had obviously fired on something recently, maybe a merchantman or a shore installation. I had heard dull concussions in recent days and the ship may have been bombarding Russian land forces at extreme range. These guns were largely propaganda weapons built to impress. Clearly, she did not rely upon guns in this technical age. The nuclear-powered battleship-cum-aircraft carrier hybrid mostly siloed drones and ballistic missiles, its principal means of attack and defense.

"They say it could sink the whole of the RN with its auxiliaries without recourse to nuclear warheads", boasted the Romanian.

The general design seemed to echo the architecture of pre-war cruise liners. Towers, antennae and general tophamper were conspicuous by their absence and it was not clear to me how the vessel was navigated or ranged. The top of the ship was a long flight deck. If you were brave enough or stupid enough you could land a squadron of modern fighter-bombers on it, but sane sailors would use the surface to dispatch and receive drones. As I gazed rapt like any son of RN ratings the thing emitted the soft hum of industrial fans and a soaked and soiled ensign dangled from the crossyard on its enormous theatrical bowsprit. To augment the import of that jack flag an enormous black φ Magonian recognition mark defaced its gleaming larboard hull.

I borrowed Eugen's binoculars to study the hull's ports. It was clear that these were for launching missiles or even managing loads rather than offering guns.

"I wonder if Slummers is in charge. I wouldn't like to navigate such a mass in close waters, almost hove to in hostile seas", I mused.

"Nor I", responded the Commander First-Class.

"It was built in Merehill. I have always wondered why the RN did not build one or two, whatever you could have afforded", mused Ionescu.

"Answers on a postcard, Eugen", I responded.

The Commander turned and looked at me in bemusement.

"Fucking politicians", I clarified.

The *Dypsidorian* was by far the largest ship I had ever seen, of any type or class. Even the great tankers were tiny by comparison. Presently the great warship turned slightly to starboard and picked up speed. A bow wave developed and within a few minutes I would have guesstimated its speed at about 25 knots.

Arnoldina and Mildred had materialised at our side, with Bella.

"Come on, Ladies. Let's go back to the surgery", I requested in impotent guardianship.

I was pruning the trees when a brilliant flash like sheet lightening suffused the orchard. Some of the small dry leaves at the tops of the trees smoked and smoldered, or maybe it was just water vapour. But the flash lasted some seconds which of course lightning does not. There was that strange buzzing sound like an old-time make-and-break for an inductor. As with purported ghost sightings it was difficult to say whether the buzz was an objective acoustic sourced from an external agent, or whether it was an intracranial auditory or neurological effect triggered by who knows what. Since all is mediated by the brain definitive answers elude us.

The buzzing noise ceased with the light. I knew instinctively that a thermonuclear detonation had occurred not too far from me.

After the light and the buzz suddenly switched off a most frightening thing happened. A vast tawny-coloured plate of rusted iron some ten metres long and possibly three wide, with marginal rivet holes, some of them torn, landed on the hillside above the sheds, and sliding down, arrested against a shed shattering it.

I supposed that whatever had detonated had torn a hole in the sea, and some Victorian wrought iron ship, probably a sailing trader, had been ripped from the sea bed and sent skyward piecemeal like a spray of volcanic bombs.

Within a minute, Terring, ubiquitous in such emergencies, was with me holding his gizmo.

"Radiation is 25% what it was during the blast we experienced at the Presidium. I recommend convening the people in the waterfall dell as a precaution", he advised to the Fellowship's ersatz magistrate.

No sooner had he finished this counsel than we were struck by an almighty concussion which knocked us off our feet. Fortunately, the orchard grass was long and tussocky and we were in shadow from the sea, so no old men were injured in this particular scene, except that we were too deaf to hear each other's exclamations or explanations.

As we rose tentatively, Terring tapped my shoulder:-

"We go see Eugen", shouted the professor in a strange pidgin.

I made a thumps-up as I levered myself from my seated position.

We briskly paced up the hill to the look-out eyrie. We found Ionescu lying amidst debris with blood on his face.

"Help me. Please help me", this very robust ninety-seven-year-old officer pled pathetically.

"I am blind."

"Don't worry, old man", said Terring kindly, "Charmliss and I will carry you to the hospital."

When we arrived Arnoldina was ready with her apprentice beside her. Arnoldina stripped Ionescu and dressed him in pyjamas. Ionescu was a tall man and Arnoldina had been considerate enough, in stealing supplies, to err on the side of largeness.

"Mildred, Commander Ionescu has two black eyes where his binoculars fell against his face, and he is bleeding from facial cuts. Go and get a basin of hot water and put five grams, just five grams, of boracic acid in it and stir with a plastic spoon. Bring the basin here and I will show you how to clean the Commander's face and eyes."

"Yes, Madam"

"Eugen also has bloody hands where he tried to save himself", I remarked.

"Yes Charles, we will clean the rest later."

Mildred arrived and Arnoldina showed her how to clean Eugen's closed eyes and wipe the blood from his face. Mildred turned out to have a very gentle, if somewhat tentative, touch, not at all like a violent young thug.

"Mildred, we are going to go to the dispensary and you will help me find 0.4% Oxybuprocaine; Uveitis; Latanoprost and Viscotears. When we return I will carry the medicines and a disposable syringe and you will bring your pencil and student pad."

"Yes, Aunty Dina"

When the two lady medics returned Arnoldina said:-

"Mildred, I am going to instill oxybuprocaine into both the gentleman's eyes. It is an addictive and very dangerous drug that can actually blind. So I must put in only three drops into the conjunctival sacs. Watch what I do very carefully and make notes on your notepad."

"Yes, Madam. Why are we giving him this drug?"

"So that when we inject him he will feel little pain. We must wait ten minutes for it to take effect. Now, Mildred, pick up the uveitis bottle and squirt a little into the barrel of the syringe."

The girl did as bidden.

"Uveitis is an anti-inflammatory corticosteroid for the eyes, Mildred, prepared for post-corneal injection. Make a note, Mildred, and give me your pad. I will draw the cross-section of an eye, and you must draw the needle in the correct position."

"Yes, Aunty"

After ten minutes Arnoldina retracted Eugen's eyelids and injected the corticosteroid.

"Why did we do that?" asked Mildred intelligently.

"It will reduce inflammation in the officer's eyes and relieve pressure on his retinas. A little later I will show you how to help by putting in Latanoprost drops whenever Commander Ionescu awakes, also to reduce intraocular pressure, and every six hours to instill Viscotears just to keep his eyes moist and healthy."

"Thank you, Aunty Dina."

"Thank you, Arnoldina, and you too Mildred. You are two saintly women", said Ionescu pleasantly.

"We are in the Hands of God.", replied Arnoldina, "But Mildred and I will do all we can."

"Eugen, what happened?" I asked.

"I kept my glasses on the *Dypsidorian* in case it fired back in our direction. It was a full hour. At the end the ship appeared to shimmer and float above the horizon. There must have been an inversion. I think it was still making way but it remained for minutes. Then I had a stabbing ache in both eyes, and was suddenly blind as I stumbled backwards against a chair and lost balance. As I fell to the floor the binoculars impacted my eye orbits, and I cut my hands trying to save myself.", explained Eugen.

"The ship may have been destroyed by a nuclear torpedo", I speculated, "a lump of Victorian plating presumably from a seabed wreck landed above the orchard a mere thirty seconds after I saw the flash", I added.

"Are you okay, Charles?" asked my selfless officer.

"Yes, I am okay, thank you, Eugen"

"I am going upstairs to get some shut-eye, Eugen", I said, "is there anything I can do for you before I go?"

"No, I'm okay for now, Chuck"

I held the man's hand and squeezed it. I then took the stairs to the bedroom Arnoldina and I shared.

It must have been the early hours. I was in bed and woken by an uncharacteristically worried and flustered Arnoldina.

"Charles, Charles, wake up"

Dozily I woke and said:-

"What is it? What has happened?"

"Eugen and Mildred are sleeping together. I cannot command your officer. I do not know what to do, Charles."

"What?!" I responded, "Explain what has happened."

"We instilled the drops at 0015 and I took Mildred to the surgery. I commanded her to take off her clothes and don a pair of rubber gloves and kneepads to clean the lavatory, sinks and shower. She refused saying cleaning was not a nurse's job. I told her not to be proud, to be obedient and prompt and to do as bidden. I would find spray and disinfectant for her, and she could shower afterwards and shower the commander in the morning. She again defied. I said 'Very well. You can strip and work naked for the next 48 hours. We are well-bred people and no-one will mock or jeer at you but they will think you a proud student showing that there is nothing special about you, that in truth you have only what God gave you'. Mildred took off her uniform and fatigues and sat naked by Eugen's bed shivering and clasping her arms round herself. I sat on the next bed to invigilate. Then Eugen said 'Get me a bottle of water, Mildred, and hold it to my mouth'. Mildred obeyed, and Eugen grasped her arms to guide them. Then he felt her hip. 'Why are you naked?' Eugen asked. 'Mrs Charmliss has disciplined me for refusing to clean the toilet, Sir', said Mildred. 'What nonsense! Come into my bed and keep me warm,' said Eugen, and Mildred has done so."

"Don't worry. Ionescu is a man of honour. He will not assault the girl", I counselled my Wife.

"It is not Mildred I am worried about. I am scared she might take advantage of him", replied Arnoldina.

Arnoldina was of course still fully clothed. I rose naked from our bed. I took Arnoldina by both hands. I softly said:-

"Holy Wife, let us kneel and pray"

We knelt together, facing as we held hands.

My Wife took the initiative:-

My Darling Lord and King Jesus Christ
Counsel me I pray.
Please forgive my cowardice and my cruelty in fearing
my student and
Overreacting to her adolescent insolence and pride,
lest she become truly dangerous.
Make me a firm but generous teacher, and a true Aunt.
Teach *me*.

Give me the strength to yield.

I said:-

Jesus Christ, my Only Lord and King
You know my Wife's heart and that she is brave and kind.
Please guide me.
Lend me the tiniest part of Your Wisdom.
I cannot command a Lieutenant-Colonel,
much less her student.
I can command my Commander,
but wish not too, for his sake.
Lord what shall I do?
Lord, you know I was never a Father, and grieve for it.
Teach me to be a good Uncle and a good Leader.
So help me.

So help him, Arnoldina echoed.

I squeezed my Wife's hands and gazed into her lovely eyes.

"Arnoldina, are you prepared to vary your orders?" I asked.

We rose as one, still holding hands.

"Charles, you cannot go like that!"

"Like what? Oh, okay!"

I dressed and we approached the cuddling twosome together.

"Wake up, Mildred", said my Wife.

"Mildred, you must not do the wicked, evil thing Aunty Dina did in Congleholme. You must never sleep with a patient. He is unable to give disinterested consent."

"I am sorry, Aunty", replied Mildred as she sleepily vacated Ionescu's bed.

Ionescu stirred.

"Go to the surgery and put your fatigues and your uniform back on, but not your socks and boots just yet. Then come back here and stand by", my Wife ordered the girl.

"Yes, Madam"

"Mildred, I shall remember this obedience. It is special to me", added my Wife.

"Thank you, Madam", replied Mildred.

Mildred obeyed.

"Commander Ionescu. Eugen", I commenced, "Will you do me a special favour as a friend?"

"Of course I will, Chuck. Anything"

"Leave your bed and stand before me. I will help you. Then I shall help you replace your fatigues over your pyjamas, and I will help you to the lavatory for a pee. Then I will help you back into bed and, I am fully-clothed Eugen, and I shall climb into bed beside you for body warmth against the cold."

"Thank you very much, Sir. I am in your debt."

"No, I am in yours, Eugen"

"Mildred", commanded the Lieutenant-Colonel, "we will climb into the next bed for the same reason, and whenever the Commander awakes you may instill Latanoprost, and an hour after Viscotears."

"Thank you, Madam. Thank you for your mercy."

"It is an honour", replied Arnoldina.

"Mildred, look at those men. They are not abominables. They could be sailors sheltering in a corner of a barbette soaked with blood and ice. You would pity such men.", added Arnoldina for her student's benefit.

"Aunty, what is a barbette?"

"It is an open steel enclosure on a warship, to shield the guns and the men from shrapnel and the sea."

"Thank you, Aunty. What are abominables?"

"Mildred, if you do not know I will not tell you, and I hope you never find out."

"Mildred", I called across the gangway between our beds, "tomorrow morning Uncle Charles will take off his clothes and show you how to clean the toilet and the shower, and we will bathe the Commander together."

"I love you, Uncle Charles. Please don't. Aunty can direct me."

I was very worried about Eugen. There was so little we could do for him. The man was obviously very cold, whether due to injuries, his age, his nutrition or all three. I knew that there was a case of rubber hot water bottles in the surgery. The bottles had been liberated from one of the containers, and Arnoldina had requisitioned them.

I knew also that there was a supply of three-season sleeping bags and breathable waterproof bivvy bags somewhere and that either Terring or Pratley may know where I could find them.

Presumably, Terring would be in the War Room using the computer at this hour. I went up and asked him if he knew where I could put my hands on a sleeping or a bivvy bag. Unfortunately, he did not possess either but offered his blankets. I thanked him, and promised to return if I was unable to source what I needed.

Therefore, I should have to canvass Pratley, not quite an enemy, but a man I distinctly disliked.

I arrived at Pratley's cottage and the door was opened by Jeany:-

"Good Morning, Jeany, is your husband in?" I asked.

"Good Morning, Commadore Charmliss", Jeany responded with a coy, sweet smile and a little bow in her reticent way. "I am sorry to inconvenience you. Erny is in the Home Farm amongst the communal assets looking for Christmas gifts to give the youngsters. He will return for his lunch at 1215."

Jeany was always like this and I wondered if she was a spanked woman. Another of those valuable lessons I learned as a tiny boy at the knee of my Late Father, whenever he was home from sea, was that women should be spanked regularly as "it softens their natures."

"Thank you, Jeany. I will stroll down and talk with him."

I reached the Home Farm stockrooms and quickly found the soft-hearted if murderous Pratley sorting through the boxes and cases.

"Good Morning, Earnest", I greeted.

"Ah, good morning, Chuck. I want to have a serious discussion with you."

"I am looking for a sleeping bag and a bivvy bag for Eugen to use in his sick-bed. He is very cold and it is only 3°C in the ward. Mildred and I give him hot water bottles, but that is inadequate", I responded.

"No problem at all, Chuck. I have not yet found any though I seem to recollect Mr Jolliffe mentioning a pack. I will give you mine. I have not used them and they are still in their hermetic wrappers. They are in the house and I will ask Jeany to give them to you as we pass by."

"As we pass by?", I said quizzically.

"Yes, we will walk to the church for our serious discussion", explained Pratley.

This was ominous.

Was Pratley converting to Christianity? Did he want my counsel or my Blessing as a pastor? I sincerely hoped he was not going to demand Holy Correction.

Atheists and agnostics are eligible: All you need is to be over eighteen, of sound mind, and be in current possession of a backside.

My doctoral supervisor, whose every word I worshiped, told me that if you wish to "put a man on the spot" you do not summon him to your office or your palace: You go to see him.

Jeany knew where the items were and readily handed them to me as we went. We reached the little Methodist Church.

Curiously, Pratley drew his Chanctonbury pistol and placed the weapon inconspicuously in one of the empty flower pots in the porch.

"Are you armed?" Pratley asked me.

"No, I no longer carry a weapon habitually", I said.

We entered and I placed the bedding on a pew, and Pratley and I sat uncomfortably beside it, but keeping a few feet between us.

"Dear Charles", Pratley opened with a tone of sincerity I am afraid I could not reciprocate, "Jeany and I love each other indescribably. We were at college together, slept together, and got married when we gained our doctorates. We have been married for forty-one years without a single cross word. I cannot tell you how much I love her.", completed Pratley redundantly.

"Why are you telling me this, Earnest?"

"Charles, you will not like to hear this. Jeany is a nuclear physicist specialising in weapons design. We have a long friendship with Nikolous from when we worked together at Daresbury. Jeany is a Christian. As you know I find Belief impossible. I do not know whether it is the Pauline Strictures or her natural inclination and have never had the courage to ask, but Jeany acclaims my every word and act, no matter how criminal. I have never struck her, neither would I ever. I prefer death", continued Pratley.

"Jeany really looks up to you and Arnoldina. She thinks you share a perfect Christian marriage though, intellectually, she knows that you are unblessed by any priest. We both look up to you and your Wife, Charles, I have told you before, and so what I am about to say comes hard, hard, hard to me as I love you as a friend and brother and I do not wish to lose your company or your counsel. I love you, Charles."

Pratley buried his face in his hands and wept. I was unmoved.

"Charles, I really appreciate your selflessness, your courage, your prudence, your co-operation. You are a violent man who represses his violence. But you are also a very hard man. The Balfours: They are not like you and I, Charles. They are literally of a different class, perhaps a better class of people. For sure they have virtues, virtues less well-canvassed than their vices. Charles, these are people who accept whatever you say and do because you are a better: You are a scientist, you are a naval officer, you are a superintendent of police, you are a whatever. If you told them to nurse a blind sentry, they would do it now. If you told them to part their legs and be fucked, they would do it now. If you told them to go to the Mainland and fight the Russians and not come back, they would thank you, ask if they could borrow a boat, and take unreasonable pride in their deference.", continued my weird admirer.

"Charles, I beg you as a friend, please do not beat the poor. Jeany and I are staunch liberals. We hate corporal and capital punishment, we abhor it, but we do not hate or abhor you, Charles. You are a very fallible man, as are we all, but you do your best for our beleaguered little Fellowship, as all must. I say again, I love you and I forgive you.", concluded Pratley.

I knew now that there was an unbridgeable gulf between Earnest Pratley and myself. I still could not bring myself to see Pratley as an enemy. If he was tried for murder I would volunteer as a witness for the defence, and be righteously proud to do so. Pratley was a good man and I was not. Pratley believed bravely and unmovably in what he did, as did I. I replied at last:-

"Earnest, I do not expect you to credit this, but I love you and I am your friend, not just your confidante. If I was not I would have shot you out of hand. I did not beat Mildred because she was young, vulnerable, working class or poor, or even because she was a violent thug in the making. I beat her as I would beat any: To evade greater evils. If you believe that I am a cruel man, Earnest, you do not know me. I am not political as you have discovered, but I believe that all men and women have a Place of Honour in society. Mildred's father admired his wife, but wanted his daughter to have a respected profession, and now his daughter glimpses such, and can aspire beyond our small provinces. Mildred is intelligent and will learn. Can you and I say we will, Earnest?"

"When I was a doctoral student", I continued, "I went with friends to see an opera. In that irrational and un-English entertainment a woman sang of her devotion to Faith and Art. Faith is born of suffering, Earnest. That I had to learn for myself, the hard way. Art *is* suffering. Art is an Act of Faith.

I once worked with men, and one woman, who designed bridges. To build a bridge, in figure or in the letter, is an Act of Faith. I admired them and wished I was as clever, and as altruistic. In the old days legators built bridges of stone, hoping thus to access paradise when they died, for they had Faith, and sought not Hell.

I admire you, Earnest. You are a bridge builder. We each seek to avoid Hell."

Earnest had stopped crying.

We rose together. Earnest looked into my eyes. We shook hands and left the little fane. I took Ionescu his warm bedding.

CHAPTER THIRTY-ONE
PREGNANCY

Human pregnancy was different in 78V to that of 80V. Physics and chemistry differed a little between the two universes, and that could have exaggerated effects upon intricate and finely-balanced systems, such as those of geology, botany and zoology.

In 78V, normal human pregnancy lasted between four and five months, not nine. So, for example, if I impregnated Arnoldina when we first enjoyed Sacred Union behind the rhododendron bush in mid-September, then the birth of our little one could reasonably be expected in mid-January to mid-February.

For another thing, women did not have periods on the Planet Earth of 78V. They ovulated at orgasm, and if fertilization failed the egg was resorbed by the uterus. I reasoned, in my usual captious way, that those who protested in 80V that no god would have awarded women periods, were here confuted by a System nicely fitted to obviate the nuisance.

But like 80V women, those of 78V had so many eggs in their ovaries that there was no danger of running out unless they were very old and very sexually active.

But it was now nearly Christmas and Arnoldina had a distinct hump of a tummy. The wide elastic waists of her fatigue trousers were now getting tight and the trousers had an annoying tendency, for Arnoldina, of slipping from her hips.

It had for a good fortnight been too cold for Arnoldina to inhabit the manse naked or wearing her dressing gown. In any case, with the teenager at large, it lent greater authority if my Wife was clothed. So I had instructed her to wear two loose petticoats under an unbelted gown and her down-filled puffer coat which came down to the shins, but if she was cold she could wear additional approved garb. Further, I encouraged her to take it easy, and to rest in bed where possible. I awarded Ananta the lionesses' share of the teaching and supervision, including Eugen's care, whilst I asked Jimmy and Terring to relieve me of day-to-day queries and admin whilst I tended to my Wife's needs.

One evening, it may have been Christmas Eve, I cannot remember: Hey, give me a break! I am after all well over a hundred, yes, it was Christmas Eve if I recollect, my Wife and I were lying in bed reading. Terring had lent me one of the his old Daresbury manuals about magnetohydrodynamics. Of course, I am too daft to understand such matter, but it was impossible to get *The Times* or the *Navy News* here on Monk Island, what with the War, the contending navies and all. It was freezing and we were wearing all our kit underneath the duvets. The coal fire, which Mr Jolliffe had very kindly made and mounted, dwindled.

Bored, I idly turned my head and quipped:-

"What is that, Loveliness? It looks like a dirty book to me!"

"Not at all, it is only slightly foxed and faded, with no superscriptions."

It is better not to trade pleasantries with a genius.

"Show me", I responded.

Arnoldina flipped the front cover shut using her thumb as a bookmark. The damp-looking cover bore the title "Perfect Obedience" and the author name "M Kenelm Ringstead." I smelt a whiff of that musty damp old book smell.

"The Foreword is written by some Brit admiral who alleges that his friend Kenelm or "Kenny" as he preferred to be known was a Chilian ex-Naval Intelligence man instrumental in helping him win the Falklands War", clarified Arnoldina.

"I wonder why he didn't use his first name?" I queried idly.

"For the same reason Mr Waters does not use his: Because it sounds effeminate", said my Wife.

"Oh? Well what is Mr Waters' first name then?"

"Evelyn", stated Arnoldina.

"And Ringstead's first name?"

"Marjerry"

"What kind of sadist calls his son Marjerry", I objected.

"There are some funny people around", confirmed Arnoldina.

"Where did you get it?"

"When Ananta took Mildred onto the hill to look for medicinal herbs I thought I would have a look around the Methodist Church to kill time. At the back I saw a dark blue baize curtain that appeared to be hanging down the wall redundantly and I wondered what if anything was behind it. I pushed the hanging aside to disclose a nice wooden door and when I tried the lock it yielded. Behind was a vestry – do they have vestries in Methodist Churches? and the little room was fitted as a library with capacious shelves and a table and chair, I suppose for pilgrims. I looked at the titles: They were mostly devotional or theology, or popular theology like this book. The title intrigued me so I have 'borrowed' it", said Arnoldina interestingly.

"Is there any medicine or nursing that might suit Mildred?" I asked.

"There is at least one book on first aid and one of those old medical encyclopedias that I might use in tutorials. Surprisingly, there is also a well-illustrated book about obstetrics and neo-natal nursing which may come in handy. It is the type of book useful for setting exam questions and for clinical draftswomanship. There is also a lot of elder care and pastoral stuff."

"In this book, Charles, there is a most delightful passage in the chapter "Mindful versus Mindless Obedience" about a perfectly obedient Christian couple who respect and assist one another with prayerful love. Would you like me to read it to you?"

"Arnoldina, My Most Lovely Espoused Creature, Mother-to-Be of that I yearn, I don't care if it's a bus timetable. I want to hear you read it just to hear your delectable voice."

"Charles, you're such a charmer."

My Wife flicked through the pages to find the right one. She found it and rehearsed:-

For example, a man and his wife are praying together.

They are kneeling unclothed, facing each other and holding hands. Their nakedness is a token of their candour to God and their Trust in one another. They have nothing to conceal.

They take a break from praying to discuss Sacred things.

"Dearest Husband, Sir" says Wife, "It says in Ephesians 5:24:-

"𝔗herefore as the church is subject unto 𝔠hrist,
so let the wives be to their own husbands
in every thing."
so should I obey you in everything?"

Her Husband replies:-

"I want to ask you a question. Suppose that I came to the kitchen and commanded 'Today instead of making our vegan omelette with parsley you must use henbane', how would you respond?"

"I should say 'No, Sir. Please suggest a different herb'"

"Why would you not explain that henbane is rich in hyoscine, a deadly poison?" objected Husband.

"Because, Sir, you would be embarrassed and guilty that you had made so dangerous an error, but suffer that guilt knowing that you had not sinned, but acted in ignorance so that shriving was impossible."

"Why would you simply not say 'Don't be so bloody stupid, you'll poison us all!' like many wives would?" says Husband.

"For two reasons, Darling Husband, firstly and most importantly because I would break the Third Commandment by taking the name of the Holy Virgin in vain. Secondly, the response would be most disrespectful of my Holy Husband and therefore of God his Master. I should expect and warrant the prayerful Sacrament of Holy Correction. Pride is thinking we are better than others. Pride is a sin. Pride leads to insolence and offence, which hurts. I should Confess both blasphemy and pride to the man in charge of my morals, as I care for his.

And as an observation, Sir, I am not 'many wives': I am an unique individual, your Holy Wife appointed by God to suit you, and you alone."

"Thank you, Madam, for your Ministry and your explanation. I am dreadfully sorry I asked that question, my good woman. I insulted you, and I beg your pardon."

"There is no insult, Lovely Husband, we must explore our faith frankly in order to continue our struggle toward the Cross", said the truly Holy Wife.

"Darling Husband, do I have your permission to ask another question before we resume prayer?"

"Of course you may, My Delight" permitted Husband.

"Is it true that muons can travel over a mile through solid rock to be detected at the bottom of a mine in Yorkshire?" asked Wife.

"I do not know, My Love, I barely know what a muon is, I am only a builder. You would have to ask a particle physicist or a geologist. But I can help you search the Internet to see if we can find relevant information. I love you so much, My Lady. You ask such penetrating questions, if you will pardon the pun."

"I pardon you everything, Sir, and you are not *just* an anything. You are a whole man and I love you."

"My Darling and very patient Holy Husband, may I ask to delay our prayer yet again?"

"Of course you may, my Holy Wife, because I know that you never delay out of cowardice but always from sacred regard for the Worship of God."

"Thank you, Sir. I wish to request Sacred Union, for though I know that we have agreed contraception meantime, and that I cannot procreate, I wish to enjoy sex that I may more closely approach the spirits of both God and His Deputy."

Husband and Wife stand and, with innocent little giggles, eagerly retire beneath the duvet. After their prayer-blessed copulation they sleep a little and then resume their worshipful positions. Wife makes no attempt to expel or remove her Husband's Holy Seed of Life, though she knows it of null biological effect, because she knows even better that it is an earnest of Husband's loving and respectful spirit.

"Thank You for your indulgence, Sir"

"No, Thank *You*, Madam, for the opportunity to express my unconditional Love for my unspeakably Holy Wife and for our mutual Creator, for Sacred Union is a voiceless Prayer beyond all corruption."

"Sir, I wish to Confess"

"Then my Treasure, we shall assume our positions", replied Husband.

Husband sits on the edge of the marriage bed and Wife lies prone across his thighs. As he comfortingly puts his right hand on Wife's bottom, Husband asks:-

"What do you need to tell me this afternoon, My Beloved Wife?"

"When we went to Holy Communion this morning and stood in the car park Mabel draw up in her new BMW and I envied her her car and answered her smiling 'Good Morning' very curtly and with a sullen, indeed surly, face."

"My Darling, jealousy is very sinful and you were right to confess promptly and without prompt. On this occasion of Correction I wish you to pray before I do."

"Yes, Sir."

My Darling Saviour, My Lord Jesus, my only righteous Lord and King, I beg condign Correction of your anointed Deputy for my despicable sins of envy, anger and insolence borne of my warrantless pride in my own entitlement. I abhor my sins and I reject them with loathing. Please cleanse my soul and console the woman I have wronged. I bitterly regret the

shame I have brought to the Husband who loves me despite my wickedness in traducing himself and our Holy Marriage in front of another.

Father forgive my Good Wife these hateful sins and cleanse her Sacred spirit to restore the innocence she sullied. When next we meet Mabel, please make her wish the lady 'Good Morning' or 'Good Afternoon' with a cheerful countenance, congratulate Mabel on her new car and wish aloud that Mabel has enjoyed driving it.

"Are you comfortable, my most Esteemed Wife?"
Silence.
"Are you comfortable,
 my Most Esteemed and Loved Espoused?"
Silence. A long pause.
"Darling Husband, aren't you going to spank me?"
"No, Madam. I shall not. I have left the matter in the Hands of God."
Wife abruptly rose to kiss and cuddle her Husband, with tears in her eyes but no crying.
"Lie supine this instant!", admonished Husband, "And take your Sacred and intimate Blessing."
"Yes, Sir."

"Charles, is that not the most beautiful thing?"
"Arnoldina, that is the finest Christian homily I can remember, outside of Holy Writ."
"Ringstead goes on to ask if there is 'anything deficient or ungodly in the Love these two share, or in the Respect they reciprocate?', is there, Charles?"
"No"
"Let us pray, and thank God for writers and the Freedom to Write", I invited.

CHAPTER THIRTY-TWO
PERCEPTION

It was what the British call Boxing Day, the 26th of December. I gazed from our bedroom window over the farmland and the misty Irish Sea. Imperceptibly, the nights were beginning to lengthen again but this far North the days remained short and sombre.

I watched as brief squalls breezed their way towards us across the little island plain. White veils of misty virga made ground, hiding this field and then that paddock as they fitfully progressed manse-wards. The impression was delicate and serene though strangely minatory.

The fields were lush and desolate. The grazing grass was largely devoid of livestock, whist the full-grown turnips painted patches of veridian that lent a subdued colour here and there.

It was every inch and hour a Welsh winter: Soft, cool, wet, enveloping.

When the sea was visible it too was wan and misty, empty and inscrutable. But not the Satanic sea of the Ancient Semites, the Sea of Jonah, to be feared and shunned. Rather a talking sea, with white wave combs breaking with a sibilant susurration upon the rocky beaches in the middle distance. A sea that spoke as it spoke to Arnold on Dover Beach, like a man who spoke softly and carried a big stick, a modest and self-confidant man whose puissance was undoubted.

It was a sea like my friend Eugen, equable, reticent, neither calm nor rough, a sea at peace with itself, though conveyor of evil purpose and bad tidings, like Milton's darkness visible, though none such were there today.

One Christmas, back in 80V, I told my Wife that my Late Father worshiped ships. He did. I do not mean that he prayed to the things, or sang at them, or anything like that. He reverenced the warship, body and spirit, the bigger and more powerful the ship the better. My Father kept the plaster crests of the ships he served in during the Cod Wars on his study wall. He used enamel paint meticulously to paint them in their heraldically proper colours. The last Christmas present I bought my Father was a book about ships, but he was too ill to enjoy it.

I believe in God, Father did not. But I share with Father a confidence that the warship is the culminating product of the Works of Men. The warship is no more an evil thing than a pistol. God gave us neither. Men are evil.

My Mother and Father were RN people. I thought of Navy men:- and Navy women. Mother and Father spoke of little else. I thought wistfully of the old RN, its bonhomie, its jealousies, its slippery decks and its blood-shod glory.

Presently, a little bluster visited my window and tapped the squares of leaded glass like the gentle rap of fingernails, as tiny drops of freezing rain impacted.

It was a calming scene. Entrancing. My Wife slept and snored softly. Our tiny hamlet slumbered.

I spoke to God:-

My Dear Lord Jesus, Our Holy Saviour,
Thank you for the Gift of Sight
Which like a careless and ungrateful child
I have always taken for granted
And very often abused
As a young landscape photographer gazing to the sun to
Assess the fall of light
Or in later life studying with lust images no man should see
Please guard and console your suffering servant Eugen
Who lost his sight to an obscenity
Seeking to keep others safe.
Restore his sight, I pray, or give him the strength to
Adapt his other senses to a ten-fold power that he might
See with his ears and find his way according to the
Lay and camber of the stones of our rocky roads.
So help him God.

I turned to return to bed.

In the silence, caressed only by that winter wind, there was a sudden commotion beyond the oaken door. A wild man burst in, closely followed by a silent young South Asian woman and her girl-like companion.

It was Eugen.

"Arnoldina, Charles, I can see!"

A blue dusk was setting in. The leaded panes formed, as it were, the yetts of carceration as in a fresco of Peter's waiting. Soft and distant thunder grated and groaned in the windward distance. Eugen was on his knees as the girls stood by. My Wife awoke and, sitting up in our bed, surveyed the raptured scene.

Eugen was bowed in prayer, his downcast head, mumbling softly, in what language I did not know. I was not sure whether I did not know the language or could not hear Eugen's soft reverences. It may have been Romanian. He was a linguist. It may have been Aramaic.

Unexpectedly, Eugen lifted his head and turning to Mildred, the younger of the girls, commanded:-

"Your Holiness, come here"

Mildred did as instructed and knelt at Eugen's right hand, she too facing our bed. Her obedience seemed to me incivil, unreasonable, contrite, almost servile.

The approaching storm was almost upon our island and its rising hill. As the low and hastening clouds met the little mountain they burst forth in large and copious tears. Lightning, the light the golden colour of electrum, flimmered and licked about the house to near immediate cracks of thunder. As Ionescu folded his hands and gazed ceiling-wards the dusty, aging Swan lamp above us flickered and faltered and re-lit. It was a scene not so much dramatic as if the Earth sought to outdo art: It was more a scene Baroque, half-barbarous, like a canvas of Caravaggio, or, more so, El Greco.

Then the Catholic Crossed himself in the Latin style and said:-

Holy Saviour
Thank you for the Gift of Sight
Lead me to Guard and Marshall it
The Better that I may Serve You and the
Everlasting Quests of Art and Science
That My Fellows may Wake neither in Fear nor Want
But in Laud and Awe of your Creation.
Thank you, You who Rose Again Resurgent
For the Holy Saints Arnoldina and Mildred
Ministers of your Love and Agents of Repair
Give them Long and Fruitful Lives,
Delighting in your every deed through Them.
Amen

Arnoldina and I were thunderstruck, though the manse our dwelling was undamaged.

"My repair is a Miracle of Christ", stated Eugen at any who might listen.

Arnoldina commented:-

"Eugen, your sight itself is a Miracle of God in his Creation, as are the imperatives of the evolution that engendered it.

Mildred and I are nurses. We nurtured and comforted you as good women should all afflicted. Eugen, your Body is of God, and your Body repaired itself. No Holy Saints are here."

Eugen Crossed again, and scooping Mildred in his arms rose and departed as the brief perfulgence passed.

The rest of the night was quiet and, tired beyond fatigue, we slept until the next day, was it the third of Christmas?

An abrupt raping of our oaken door woke us.

We were, you recollect, fully clothed and I drowsily rose to answer.

It was Terring.

"Sorry to wake you and your Wife, Charles, but I want you to help me repair the village electrical system before the others need the supply. I believe that the wind turbine may have burnt out or blown down, but we better start at the storage hut and look for clues there."

"Yes, Nick, I am no expert, but I will gladly assist if I can."

When we arrived at the rectifier-battery-bank-inverter hut Nick first checked the input and output circuit breakers, installed to protect all other line equipment from overload.

We noted that nine of the twelve input breakers had tripped, suggesting but not proving that the wind turbine was the origin of failures, whilst the little hydropower set was functioning normally. On the other hand, ten of the fifteen output breakers had tripped. As I said, I am no expert, but this puzzled me, since it suggested that some transient surge had passed from the batteries.

"I better re-set the outputs first, Chuck, if only to check the batteries are charged and useful."

I stood by like some very mature student, as once, proffering a pass, I had been accused by a bus driver when, as a fifty-one year old, commuting to a class for a second MSc.

Terring re-set the output breakers and then switched on the house lights of the cabin that were on one of the output circuits. The lights lit normally and Terring switched them off.

"Charles, go round the cottages and the Home Farm inviting everyone to check their power *but not to stay switched on*, then check if Rowan Farm is still on-grid. In the meantime, I will climb the hill to check the transmission on the way to the windmill. We will meet here at 0900."

I gave him a thumbs up and visited the customers. Half way through the canvass I entered Rowan farmyard to the soft hum of a diesel generator. I knocked on the door and it was answered by Mrs Waters.

"Good Morning, Mrs Waters, and Merry Christmas once again", I greeted, "I have come to check if you still have power. There was an outage earlier."

"Thank you, Commadore Charmliss. A Merry Christmas to you, Sir, and please convey our Season's Greetings to Arnoldina. Yes, when the power fails our backup automatically kicks-in in case there are cows parloured or lambs incubated. However, we have to reset it manually. Let me reset the generator, then I can test the power."

The lady led me to the generator, and stopping the engine, tried the lights in its housing. They lit. I looked to the house. Mr Waters or one of the children had risen and the kitchen and bedroom lights shone. A fraction of a minute later someone must have switched on an electric kettle because the remaining Swans dimmed whilst LEDs extinguished.

"All okay then, Mrs Waters. I must get back to Professor Terring", I said and with a wave returned.

By 0835 I was back at the battery hut and Terring was already waiting. The kettle had tripped an output breaker. I explained the likely reason and Terring reset the gadget.

"It was the windmill. It blew down, and the fiberglass vanes, still turning, shattered. It is a professional repair, one for the Ecclesiastical Assurance lads, and from now on we have 20% to 25% power exclusively from the hydro. We must ration to rechargeable lanterns, the vicarage and the church. Please convene everyone in the church, Charles, I shall go and tell the Waters' the situation."

One of my Glasgow hostel friends was, the last time I heard of him fifty years ago, the Chief Executive Officer of the Ecclesiastical Assurance Company. He was a Town and Country Planner by profession. I wondered if he was still alive. That was obviously in 80V.

"Thank you, Nick, I will go round the village, then, and tell everyone to gather. By the way, the Waters family have a diesel generator, if that helps."

"Charles, I prefer that they conserve diesel for the vehicles. They may have an allocation of four rechargeable lanterns."

"Okay, Nick"

The forty-five us us were in the church. Not just babes in parents' arms but also the likes of Mildred, and even Faith.

Nick stood in the modest pulpit and declaimed in his best lecture-hall voice:-

"Brothers and Sisters of our Island Fellowship. The wind turbine blew down and destroyed its vanes. Therefore, power must now be severely rationed, as we depend utterly upon our little Pelton generator. Each household must keep electricity switched off on all lights and appliances. Each household may have use of two rechargeable lanterns: One on charge in the charge shed, the other for use. Rowan Farm may borrow four since livestock may need emergency service at night. The Vicarage and the Church will have maintained power. This is so that medical services, convocation and public administration may progress uninterrupted..."

A man in the nave stood.

It was Mr Miggins.

"Mr Terring", Miggins commenced, "I am a time-served industrial electrician and a Registered domestic electrician. If I am useful I shall serve."

"Thank you, Mr Miggins, Arthur, I need you and want you. Please come and stand with me", said Terring. Miggins literally did just that, standing at the pulpit foot.

Another man patiently stood. It was Masterton. Terring shouted:-

"Yes, Mr Masterton?"

"Sir, there is in a back steading of the Home Farm an old showman's engine complete with dynamo. I surmised that it may have produced power to service the farm before the hydro was installed. There is a low-tension switchboard on the wall beside it. If Mr Miggins and other volunteers will assist me and there is coal available it should be possible to work it, at least to power the farm."

"Thank you, Josias", Terring shouted back, "Please come forward."

I wondered how such a heavy object had been shipped to this island until I remembered the rusting pontoon at Tripant. A showman's engine dynamo is only good for 7 NHP, say 4Kw, at 110 volts, so it would have to feed DC directly to the batteries on a pretty much 24/7 basis. It would be sensible to move it to a watercourse and wheel the coal down to it. Competent electricians were definitely required, especially as we lacked the skills and facilities to build an inverter, though the likes of me and Tom could cut and heave coal.

Ionescu was mobile and fully-sighted. He was clearly disturbed, I suppose you would call it PTSD, though like many such popular diagnoses the acronym is too freely bandied about. Arnoldina's more experienced opinion was that Eugen was borderline psychotic, hopefully in a transient way, but she told me she was standing by to administer aripiprazole injections. She said this was a last resort, as diabetic symptoms might ensue, and insulin was limited. She was keeping a syringe in her pocket, but the solution would have to be kept in the surgery refrigerator: We did not have a portable refrigerated case, whether for insulin, aripiprazole, or any other heat sensitive drug.

Ionescu was still bedded in the sick bay, and it was out of the question to return him to his eyrie.

By 1100 we had adjourned the electricity supply meeting. Terring went back to the battery shed to isolate the outputs to premises other than the manse and the church, and then returned to his own quarters in the manse, and presumably to his – I say "his" rather than "our" – because he was the only voluntary user – computer.

I took the opportunity to take a brisk walk to the look-out post and find Ionescu's Muebler and his pistol and bring them to the manse for protective safe-keeping. Ominously, I was unable to find the pistol.

Then I went to the War Room where I met Terring, already busy on his computer. I sat at my desk and read another book Terring had lent me. It was an old A-level physics text about sixty years old, an excellent book, and more at my level than magnetohydrodynamics.

Unexpectedly, Arnoldina opened the door and said:-
"Incoming!"

I ducked under my desk comedically, and my Wife positioned two chairs together, on the other side of the desk and in front of me; and two further away, I could not surmise who for.

"Shall I serve tea and mince pies for six, Charles?"

I wondered if she was still joking.

"Yes please, Dina, and bring some bourbon for me and Nick."

The perfectly obedient one complied to the letter.

As Arnoldina and Ananta brought the refreshments on trays they were followed by Mildred and Eugen holding hands. We were well within the Twelve Days of Christmas and I wondered if I was to be the victim of some practical joke.

The ninety-seven-year-old and the seventeen-year-old took their seats before me, Mildred at Eugens right hand. They did so without releasing hands. I had a feeling, not of revulsion, but of horror for the sake of two good people, and especially for the misfortune of Eugen, my junior officer, but so senior to myself in maturity and goodwill though a mere fifteen years divided us.

Though a wealth of learning and experience divided the lovers I knew that each was a virgin. Virginity is a state to be hallowed and guarded, though I am not sure that it is a healthy condition for persons of procreative age.

They were two very different people and I loved them both and wanted them happy. In my old world, the world of 80V, my Wife was seventeen years my senior. I cannot claim to have been a virgin when we married because I bedded her six months before our marriage though she was the only person with whom I ever United. I was twenty-seven, she forty-five. Your mathematics is at least as good as mine, and you know that Arnoldina was 892 years older than I.

Instinctively, I realised that if I was expected to play Registrar, then we needed a proper Priest.

"Ananta, please go and fetch Mr Enoldius for me", I asked.

As the young Muslim departed I uttered a brief and silent prayer to My Saviour that I should not require Witness of either her or the Nestorian.

Ananta returned with Patrick, who beamed at me and bowed to Arnoldina, who smiled and bowed back for courtesies sake. The rest of us were sombre. We had entered sombre: We had stayed sombre. All, that is, except Mildred, who only gazed at the face of her new beloved: Enraptured. Presently, she flung her arms about Eugen's shoulders and kissed him. She was not with us: In Body, of course, in Spirit, no.

I gestured to Patrick to take the chair to my right and to Arnoldina to sit at my left. Patrick's smile of greeting crystallised to the fixed simper of the professional and he proffered his hand.

"Happy feast of St John the Apostle!" greeted Enoldius, as he shook with myself and my Wife.

I cleared my throat.

"Happy Christmas", I replied weakly.

Enoldius placed his entwined fingers on the table in his familiar attitude, and moving his hands thus joined up and down quipped:-

"And what is this innovation, Charmliss, a yuletide betrothal?"

"I think my officer is about to explain", I replied.

"Commadore, Your Holiness", said Eugen, calmly if stiffly as he genuflected to Arnoldina. "We are privileged to be present with Saints, two of many who have graced this island, though not in modern times. One is with child. The other not yet espoused. My privilege, my duty, my delight, Commadore Charles and Holy Father Patrick, is to be the Chosen Husband of St Mildred and to be the unworthy and sordid agent of her bringing forth a race of loving people instilled by God of the Holy Spirit, that the Earth may replenish in the Will of Christ."

"I do not know where to begin, Eugen. So I will begin at the beginning. Congratulations! I cannot think of two more loving, intelligent, patient, modest and very devout people more worthy of Holy Matrimony, and my Wife and I acclaim your Betrothal in love. But, Eugen, please take care for the lady. She is consentable in the laws of Wales, it is true, but she is still very inexperienced in all things, as is Your Honour in matters of the marriage bed. I caution you", I counselled.

"Eugen", entered Arnoldina, "I also congratulate yourself and my student on your wise choices. Eugen, neither Mildred nor myself are saints, though I accept your reverence with gratitude, and I hope humility. We are two very fallible nurses doing what we can so that some of the last men in the world may live and multiply. It is normal for those blinded by intense light to regain their sight after days, whether gradually or suddenly as in your case. The Holy Miracle is the vision itself and the recovery and restoration of the retinal pigment."

"Arnoldina, you are a Holy Saint of Christ, I would not expect you arrogantly to take credit for my cure, or even a share of such."

"You cannot win with infatuates, Arnoldina", I thought unvoiced.

Mildred seemed uninterested in these careful debates. She tightened her grip around Eugen's slender but powerful shoulders, kissed his lips and swooned:-

"Oh, Eugen, I love you. Eugen, bind me with chains and I shall be yours forever."

"No, My Love", replied the Commander, "you are bird-free to soar as you will, suffused in my love wherever you be. I am not your gaoler. I am your lover, the father of your Blessed children to be. Kiss me again."

Then, looking at Eugen, Arnoldina said:-

"Eugen, men and women differ. It is not only a matter of anatomy. It is a matter of physiology, of our hormones and our psychic needs. This is the Will of God according to his irreproachable Design. Mildred may require you to effect her words literally, that she may fructify. Are you prepared to Correct Mildred in the holiest and most prayerful manners, truly to love and protect her, to shepherd her immortal Spirit as she invigilates yours."

A look of astonishment clouded Ionescu's face, as he gazed across the table to Arnoldina.

"My Lady, I have never imagined this. I have heard you use foul language, but I never expected this. What abomination! In what filthy gutter does a woman of quality learn such things?"

"Commander, please do not admonish my Wife", I countered.

Eugen turned his face to mine.

"You bastard!", he spat.

"Eugen, please do not insult your commanding officer."

"Permission to speak:- Sir!", shouted the Commander across the table at me.

"Oh, please don't, Eugen, I beg you", I replied as I folded my hands before him. "I have entered nothing in the log since we left Congleholme. Please don't make me. You will hang us all. Eugen, a friend begs on his knees."

I knelt. Only my head and my hands were visible to Ionescu across the table.

"Permission to speak, Commadore Charles Edward Charmliss:- Sir!", now with over-controlled calm.

I unfolded my hands and resumed my seat.

"Yes, Commander Eugene Florin Maria Ionescu, what is it?", I asked in resignation.

"Miss Mildred Balfour and I require to marry according to the rites of the Holy Catholic Church at once."

"Thank you for your request, Commander Eugene Florin Maria Ionescu which shall now be considered", I responded coldly, "Miss Balfour is under eighteen years of age. Do you have her father's permission?"

"No"

"It seems to me, without I hope insolence, that you assume the lady implies consent. Does the lady consent?"

"I consent to marry Commander Eugene Ionescu with all my heart, Commadore, Uncle Charles", replied Mildred.

"Ionescu, you should know that I was ever only an Attender. Only fully matriculated Members of the Religious Society of Friends are authorised to solemnise marriages in Great Britain."

"That has nothing to do with me, Charmliss."

"Commander Ionescu, I am truly sorry that I have offended you and that I have lost your friendship, that I valued dearly."

Ionescu stared into my eyes with anger.

Enoldius took over.

"Dear Brothers and Sisters, in this Season of Goodwill and on the Feast of St John I think of John and why it was that he ran naked from the garden. I suppose we will never know. Maybe he was distraught as he mourned the impending loss of a Friend, though under very different and more Solemn circumstances than the joys we here contemplate. Commander Ionescu, will you permit me to make a brief Reading and if appropriate say a prayer or two with you and your fiancée?"

Ionescu turned his head to Enoldius. Mildred was out of his face now, but still embraced.

"Yes, Holy Father, please do."

Enoldius retrieved his Bible from his day-sack and donned his reading glasses. Opening the Holy Scripture he flicked through the pages until he found the verses he wanted and preached:-

45 For even the Son of man came not to be ministered unto, but to minister, and to give his life a ransom for many.

46 And they came to Jericho: and as he went out of Jericho with his disciples and a great number of people, blind Bartimaeus, the son of Timaeus, sat by the highway side begging.

47 And when he heard that it was Jesus of Nazareth, he began to cry out, and say, Jesus, thou Son of David, have mercy on me.

48 And many charged him that he should hold his peace: but he cried the more a great deal, Thou Son of David, have mercy on me.

49 And Jesus stood still, and commanded him to be
   called. And they call the blind man, saying unto him,
   Be of good comfort, rise; he calleth thee.

50 And he, casting away his garment, rose,
   and came to Jesus.

51 And Jesus answered and said unto him, What wilt
   thou that I should do unto thee? The blind man said
   unto him, Lord, that I might receive my sight.

52 And Jesus said unto him, Go thy way; thy faith hath
   made thee whole. And immediately he received his
   sight, and followed Jesus in the way.

[Mark 10: 45-52]

"Brethren and Sistren , what does this mean?"
Silence.
"Sight is not just about perceiving the forms and
colours of material things, or of rejoicing in their beauty or avoiding
the ugly or the perilous. No, it goes beyond to discern the hidden
structures and underpinnings of things, their spirits, for spirits can
move without form or colour. Why did Bartimaeus cast his robe aside?
It was because robes occlude, and occluded things are obscured to sight
and covers confuse the apparent and the actual. It was the actual of
Bartimaeus that that blind man wished to disclose to his Saviour. You
would never judge a book by its cover. Well then? Do not judge your
friend by his intransigence. Today, I shall not invite you to disrobe in
the letter for it is not your Bodies in question but your Souls at stake",
Enoldius advised.
        "Friends, let us pray", requested the Church of England
Priest, "Say each line after me":-

My Holy Saviour
> *My Holy Saviour*

Give us the sight to see
> *Give us the sight to see*

Not only the Beauty of the Sea and the Land
> *Not only the Beauty of the Sea and the Land*

Nor of the fine Plants and Animals who Grace Your World
> *Nor of the fine Plants and Animals*
> *who Grace Your World*

But Also and Better
> *But Also and Better*

The Love and Beauty of Our Forgiving Souls
> *The Love and Beauty of Our Forgiving Souls*

That shall last forever in Your Holy Sight
> *That shall last forever in Your Holy Sight*

Resurrector
> *Resurrector*

Restore Our Friendships
> *Restore our Friendships*

One Thousand Times Deeper
> *One Thousand Times Deeper*

One Millions Times Better
> *One Million Times Better*

So Help Us God
> *So Help Us God*

The company looked up. There was a shuffling of feet and someone coughed nervously.

Mildred still garlanded Eugen's neck with her body.

Arnoldina requested:-

"Ananta, will you please take Mildred to the kitchen and prepare tea and biscuits for the seven of us, and cucumber sandwiches using the bread you baked yesterday. When you return, I would like you to manage the hot tea up the stairs, whilst Mildred can carry the cold goods in a basket."

"Yes, Madam"

"They could use the dumb waiter, Arnoldina.", I objected.

"Do not confute me, Charles."

"No, Madam. Sorry."

Ananta disentwined Mildred from her idol and the two young ladies left us.

Ionescu fumed even more. I did not think such possible.

"When the time comes, Charles, will you assist me in celebration of the Holy Matrimony of this pair?", offered Patrick with a genuine smile.

"Patrick, few things would delight me more. I am greatly honoured and privileged. Thank you", I replied.

"Well I am going for a piss, if it is alright with my commanding officer", remarked Eugen, as he rose from his seat.

"Certainly, the lavatory is over..."

Ionescu was already half way there before I could complete the sentence. A minute later he returned and threw something heavy on the table in front of me. It was his pistol.

Eugen resumed his chair and glowered at me. Evidently, this was a macho staring competition.

I pushed his pistol back at him and it fell from the table top on his side. He retrieved it from the floor and he pushed it back to me.

"I resign my commission", Eugen stated.

I pushed the weapon back to him.

"I do not accept. You are a valuable member of the Fellowship and your commission in the Magonian Navy is important to every soul on this island."

Eugen pushed the pistol back to me. It was scratching the lacquer. This time I took the precaution of removing the magazine.

"Coward!", Eugen exclaimed.

I returned the weapon.

"Commander Ionescu, you *shall* obey Commadore Charmliss", my Wife intervened, "My Husband is inferior to you in age, learning and intellect but he is superior in rank. My Husband's personal immaturity and tactlessness are not your concerns: They are mine, and it is mine to Correct those failings if and as I choose. I ask nothing for myself or my Husband, but please withdraw your resignation in the interests of the forty-three others who find themselves in our unlooked-for predicament. With regard to your fiancée, and it is with genuine sincerity and relief that I congratulate her on a fine choice, I insist that she finishes her apprenticeship with me before she marries. I estimate I shall need three years. Will you please help us?"

Eugen looked at the table, perhaps with contrition, I thought.

At last he looked up towards Arnoldina.

"Yes, Lieutenant-Colonel Charmliss. Thank you"

Arnoldina slid the magazine back to Eugen. He reloaded his pistol and returned it to his shoulder-holster.

"Thank you, Commander Ionescu. As always, I am again in your debt. May I ask please that you withdraw your aspersion upon my Husband's honour, and never again bring a firearm into my vicarage?"

"Charles, I am very sorry that I called you a 'bastard' and a 'coward' and I withdraw those epithets in shame. I also withdraw my filthy imputation against your Wife and I beg her to forgive me", said Eugen with contrition.

I reached across the table, and Ionescu and I shook hands.

Turning to Arnoldina he said:-

"Sorry, Madam, it will not happen again."

Just then Ananta and Mildred returned with the afternoon tea and serving those at table brought their own seats thither, the better to manage their refreshments.

I cannot recall that Enoldius once relaxed his smile of equanimity throughout these proceedings.

As he enjoyed his tea and sandwiches he flicked through his Bible again.

"Friends, may I Read again?"

No-one answered.

For my part, I was too busy guzzling the liberated chocolate mini-rolls that the young ladies had considerately brought with the tea, and they too showed healthy appetites.

Enoldius slowly crossed himself, and took a sip of his black tea. Then he read:-

23 And when he was entered into a ship,
   his disciples followed him.

24 And, behold, there arose a great tempest in the sea,
   insomuch that the ship was covered with the waves:
   but he was asleep.

25 And his disciples came to him, and awoke him,
   saying, Lord, save us: we perish.

26 And he saith unto them, Why are ye fearful, O ye of little faith? Then he arose, and rebuked the winds and the sea; and there was a great calm.

27 But the men marvelled, saying, What manner of man is this, that even the winds and the sea obey him!

(Matthew 8:23-27)

CHAPTER THIRTY-THREE
THE RUSSIANS APPROACH

"Am I really immature and tactless?"

"The fact that you pose that question means that the answer is 'yes'", answered Arnoldina.

The day looked grey and grim outside as the day dawned in a midwinter's fog. We decided to stay in bed.

"Men seek validation, especially against their rivals and that makes them susceptible to flattery. If I had failed to flatter the man to compliance I would have resorted to threatening Eugen with the withdrawal of medical support for life. And if that had failed I should have put a bullet through his heart. Spanking would hardly have been a practical route to obedience under the circumstances: Do you not agree, Charles?"

"I could not survive this new world without you, Arnoldina."

"I know. And you would not have come to my hand without Eugen. He saved your life.", replied my Wife.

"How come?"

"Shrigley tried to kill you as you sat friendless in the Albion."

"Why?"

"Who can descry the minds of men: Fear, jealousy, care for a leadership rôle he could not sustain? Eugen could read the signals and, leaving the bar room, re-entered by the rear staff entrance. As Eugen lifted the counter hatch to approach the knot of rebels around you Shrigley took out a knife and Heldrew and Hotcarp tried to get him off you. Eugen took out his pistol and shouted to Shrigley to back off, which he did. Eugen confiscated the knife and told Pott to treat you civilly in future. The knife had grazed your head. Eugen rang me in the nurses' hostel and I took over."

I mused in silence: "It is a bloody good job I refused Shrigley's offer of a lift."

The small, peripheral islands of Britain harbour many quaint and archaic features, here in 78V just as in 80V. Those which retained a tenuous inhabitation into the middle of the Twentieth Century were awarded a K6 telephone box each, one of the red Giles Gilbert Scott cast-iron glazed boxes that every foreigner thought characterised the country. We had one by the harbour. They were connected to the Mainland by undersea analogue cable.

By the same token, at least here on Monk Island, the old wired electromechanical ebonite telephones with heavy corded handsets, the kind replaced in the Sixties of the last century, survived not only in the kiosks but also in the houses. One sat beside our bed, on my side, in the master bedroom of the manse.

It startled me. There was a sudden loud burst of make-and-break bell ringing in the British burr-burr; burr-burr; burr-burr pattern. Instinctively I lifted the heavy handset and put the earpiece to my ear. A fast-talking male voice speaking what I guessed to be Russian rabbited at me. I leant across and handed the handset to Arnoldina and said:-

"It's for you."

Arnoldina took the set and said:-

"Arnoldina Charmliss-Feng, Da"

For some minutes that was the last talking she did.

At length, Arnoldina said something in Russian, and was silent for another few minutes; then another brief response, perhaps a question, and another five minutes of silence. I checked my Bolex chronograph. It was 0934.

Arnoldina and her respondent must have been on the telephone a good twenty minutes.

At last Arnoldina, tensing her arm to give me the handset, told her interlocutor:-

"Da, Da, Spasibo"

and handed me the handset.

I replaced it.

"That was the Political Commissar for the Angarn Oblast speaking from Wroclaw", stated my Wife.

"He has said that he will land a magistrate, a postmaster and a welfare assessor by helicopter on the lighthouse helipad next Tuesday, and simultaneously a motor pinnace will bring troops whom he wishes to billet for a while with us. He wanted the helicopter delegation to be met and briefed by 'responsible elements'.", said Arnoldina.

"How many troops?", I responded.

"He did not say. He says that an aid package will follow promptly when needs have been assessed."

"I better round-up some men and Waters' tractor and clear the pad of ashlar and blasting debris", I remarked.

"Did he say anything about our back-pay or pensions?", I asked venally.

"He said that the Magonian Government wished to interview Arnoldina Feng, Charles Charmliss and Eugene Ionescu on potential charges of Cowardice and Desertion in the Face of the Enemy. He said that the Russian authorities would naturally not co-operate but the topic may be raised at the committee stages of the pending Armistice Conference: A cease-fire was currently in operation. His superiors had an application from the FBI to interview a Eustace Batley regarding seven counts of First-Degree Murder and Grand Larceny. The Ithaca government-in-exile wanted the extradition of Charles Charmliss on possible charges of High Treason, Assisting the King's Enemies and Treason Felony. The Russians had explained to all enquirers that extradition is illegal in the Russian Federation. I told him we had no information regarding the Batley gentleman, and that Charmliss was dead, all of which is true, isn't it, Charles?"

"Yes", I admitted.

"I asked about the general war situation. The commissar said he had limited assessments, but that the High Command currently thought that the surviving Russian population was around twenty-five to thirty million of a world population of maybe 300 million rather than 11,000 million. He recommended that all persons remain on Monk Island, and that enemy officers would be debriefed there. Subject to good behavior and co-operation they would be allowed to remain. England and much of Europe is too radioactive for human habitation. I asked about London, Congleholme, and Xian and Moscow. He replied that London, New York, Xian, Paris and Moscow no longer existed and that he did not know where Congleholme was."

"We better bury our arms and ammunition", I remarked.

"Don't be stupid, Charles"

Suddenly Arnoldina threw back the duvet and grabbed her abdomen. She was flushed and sweating profusely. She was wearing several loose gowns and a padded housecoat. I was in full fatigues. It was very cold.

"Charles, I am in labour. We must go to the plunge pool.", My Wife advised.

Surely she did not mean to birth in the pool? At its warmest the water would be six degrees centigrade.

She grabbed her doctor's bag and we rushed downstairs and out of the door. A light icing of snow dusted the ground. The cobbles and sharp pebbles of the lane tore our naked feet. The island was silent.

At the pool, Arnoldina stripped and waded from the little sandy beach. She was an unhealthy red all over, whether from the labour or radiation damage I had no idea. She seemed to be making for the waterfall.

I stripped and waded after her.

Arnoldina stood below the full force of the fall. She slowly tilted her head back into the stream in seeming ecstacy. I embraced her and we stood below the cascade for an hour which must have been seconds. We kissed and then Arnoldina pushed me away and staggered towards the mossy greensward of the bank above the beach. Halfway there she swam and then waded to the grass where she lay on her back and gasped.

I lifted her ankles and she pushed and gasped and moaned and screamed.

Something issued of Arnoldina's portal of life.

And then a gush of blood that drained to the pool.

My Wife was still. My Wife was cold. My Wife by turns golden yellow or ruby red, was white.

I did not grieve for my Arnoldina. I was too shocked, too frigid to think. I was too cold to love. I never embraced her again.

I picked up the grizzling thing, our child.

It was a strangely hirsute issue, like a little chimp but in place of limbs it had strange little flippers like a sealion. It was truly tiny, and weighed no more than one and a half kilos. Its jaw jutted forth in a simian way and its eyes were an unnatural deep blue, but pleochroic and chatoyant, taking a purple aspect as it moved in the light.

I prepared to strangle it.

Then it smiled at me and said "Da-Da." It smiled and said "Da-Da" I swear it.

I clasped it to my cold heart, placenta and all.

My Wife was still bleeding to the pool.

Then I became aware of a spirit standing behind me, somewhat to my right.

It was Bella.

She knelt and took the child from my hands.

"It will be a brother or sister to my little one, to my expected", said our friend, her voice full of compassion.

"What do you want to call it?" asked Bella.

"Clement. That is what I want it to be."

"What if it proves female?" responded Bella.

"Clemency. That is what I want it to give."

Bella tied the umbilical cord with a fibre of her dress and placed the creature beneath her jacket, at her breast. Then she left.

I burst into a torrent of tears.

I felt like someone was pressing my chest with weights though I was kneeling on all fours. A sharp pain filled my left shoulder and seemed to radiate to my jaw and my left arm and hand. I vomited and took the pressure off that hand, rolling helplessly into the pink-stained pool.

EPILOGUE

As I lay in the bed gentle summer vespers blew through the slightly-open sliding window and made the lifted venetian blinds go shrim, shrim, shrim in the drag of the breeze. In sympathy but counterpoint the metal ferule on the occulting cord went a gentle tap, tap, tap on the off-white plaster.

Beyond, in the sunshine, was a beautifully-cut summer lawn with a lush green berm behind on which grew lovely birch and alder saplings dancing in the wind. "They must have underground permeation for the alders." I speculated idly.

It was a scene of extreme serenity, post-orgasmic, soporific, timeless.

Ranged between the window and my far bed were identical beds with the covers drawn up so there were no wardmates to talk to or swear at.

It reminded me of the moment I woke up in intensive care after a botched operation. It must of been four o'clock in the morning and all was silent. I was alone except for similar covered apparent cadavers. On the television screen was a single word: "Sunday." Presently a middle-aged woman dressed all in white approached calling "Mr Charmliss, Mr Charmliss." She looked uncannily like my Clerk of Meeting and I immediately thought she was an Angel of God, and that I was in some antechamber of the afterlife. I smiled at her.

But this predicament was somehow different.

There was no angel, whether of God or the other One.

Presently, a nurse bustled in, tampering with the pillows and covers of the other beds, I thought neurotically, as if evading intercourse.

"Where am I?" I asked through the silence.

"What do you mean, love?"

"Am I back in Congleholme?"

"No, love, I don't know where Congleholme is. But you are in Valchester."

Ah, we were getting somewhere, literally.

"Do you still do Ghost Tours in St Olave with men dressed as Roman Centurions?"

"Now you are a big boy, love. You know there are no such things as ghosts or romans."

I reached for the handle thing on its chain hanging from the standard iron gallows thing above the bed, the thing they have there for you to haul yourself sitting from a supine position. I felt the handle as I grasped it but I was weak as a kitten and could not haul myself up.

"Nurse", I said, "I want to go for a piss. Can you help me out of bed, please."

"I would have to get a man to do that. But you do not need it. If you are uncomfortable I can give you an injection."

"Don't fucking bother", I thought, "I will piss where I lie."

"Nurse", I further pleaded, "What year is it?"

"Now don't be silly, love. It is 2056 as you well know."

"Well where the fucking hell have I been for the last twenty years?"

"Now don't swear, Ducz. You are so lovely and such a gentleman. Why demean yourself with swearing? We found you on a park bench and brought you here. Ducks were sitting all over you for the warmth. So we called you Ducz. You had no ID. We don't know where you were but it was probably prison. But wherever it was it is all behind you now, love. It could have been Witherspool Hospital for the Criminally Insane because they remove ID before they dump patients. They will not say who these poor rejects are because of Data Protection and Privacy laws."

"I am Dr Charles Edward Charmliss, but you can call me what you like as long as you bloody stop calling me 'Love'."

"I am very sorry, Ducz. It is just my silly habit, love. I will try to stop. You are such a love, love."

A shill voice obtruded from the corridor outwith:-

"Lizi, Lizi, coffee time!"

"Okay, Martha, one minute!", bawled this nurse, apparently Lizi.

The nurse continued our fatuous, but remarkable, dialogue:-

"Dr Charmliss is on holiday. He is over a hundred you know and still working!"

"Thank God I have evaded another of Nikolaus Terring's existential contradictions", I fantasized blasphemously and sarcastically.

How very different this bovine wench from my Darling Arnoldina, I thought.

"Lizi, have you met by any chance a woman called Arnoldina Feng or possibly Arnoldina Charmliss?", I asked.

"No I never met her, but I have heard a lot about her."

My heart jumped.

"Can you tell me where to find her?"

"I am afraid she cannot see you, Ducz. She died two years ago in this very room, tending her patients."

"How old was she?"

"We don't know. She was born in maybe Mongolia before the war. We would say about sixty."

"I want to leave some things on her grave."

"I am afraid she is buried in Westminster Abbey in Spalding next to Edith Cavell and it is restricted."

"What!?" I asked incredulously, "Westminster Abbey is in London. I used to see it from Tothill Street on my way to work every morning!"

"London does not exist, Ducz. Fifteen million people died in 400 milliseconds. It is very famous."

"She once spanked my bottom, you know", I remarked, I do not know why.

"I am not surprised!" Lizi exclaimed with the fake outraged surprise which nurses seem to reserve for senile old men, "You are a very naughty lad!"

"Now, Ducz before I go to coffee, would you like one yourself?"

"Yes, please. Black with no sugar."

"What is your religion, Ducz?"

"I am a Quaker. I am 104 years old."

"Yes, that's about right, Ducz"

"About right?", I thought, "I'm fucking telling you, woman"

"If you exhume Arnoldina you will find that her body is mostly metal, but she was my Wife and I loved her dearly", I remarked.

"Oh, Ducz, you are such a treasure. What lovely thoughts. We will miss you and I will cry", replied Lizi.

Lizi went away to the next room, brought the coffee, and bustled away again, with a professional smile and apparent good cheer.

I rested back with my coffee in an infants' sealed cup with a teat at the top. No: I did not have a teat at the top and I was not in a sealed cup. Again I mis-speak.

I thought, "I am now in one of the infinite number of cosmodimensional Chesters, and if I live until darkness there is a sporting chance I shall see Arnoldina's ghost patrol this ward, and if I am lucky or skillful I may even be able to commune with it."

A rather fat woman of maybe fifty-five or sixty entered and draw up a chair beside my bed. She bowed her head apparently in Prayer. She was wearing a tweed suit with a white blouse and four courses of pearls about her neck. This was exactly the outfit I preferred for Arnoldina. But this was not my slim and abstemious Arnoldina. This woman had permed, faux blonde hair.

At length she looked up but did not make eye contact and declaimed:-

"Life begins with horror and ends with hope."

She did not see fit to introduce herself or enquire after my health.

Then she took a red paperback from her bag and read:-

We give them back to you, dear God
Who gavest them to us.
Yet as Thou didst not lose them in giving,
So we have not lost them by their return.
For what is thine is ours always, if we are thine.
And life is eternal and love is immortal,
And death is only a horizon,
And a horizon is nothing more
Than the limit of our sight.

It was the Religious Society of Friend's Prayer for the Dead.

She replaced the book.

I said "I am not dead yet."

I was ignored and the woman left the ward.

The blinds went shrim, shrim, shrim and the ferule responded tap, tap, tap in their litany of consolational orison.

Then an old, drawn woman in nurse's uniform entered with a trolly on which was a kidney dish covered with a white face cloth.

I said to this woman:-

"Can you do me a favour?"

"Yes, what is it?"

"Can you get me a cold bottle of zero cola?"

"Yes, there is one in the machine in the waiting room. I will bring one."

She returned within five minutes and watched as I drank.

I rummaged under my pillow. I took out my Bible and the Wrortlemonger and Bierce 9mm pistol that Treagh had given me and which almost certainly saved my sorry life.

I offered these to the nurse and said:- "Here, throw these into my grave."

"I am sorry but you are going to be cremated. The furnacemen do not like mementoes in the oven."

"The Wrortlemonger would blow the fucking thing apart", I observed.

"Now, Ducz. You won't feel a thing. You will have a long sleep and when you wake up you will be with Jesus in Heaven."

"I don't care where I am as long as I am with Arnoldina"

www.ingramcontent.com/pod-product-compliance
Ingram Content Group UK Ltd.
Pitfield, Milton Keynes, MK11 3LW, UK
UKHW051606250225
455555UK00003B/21